TASH AW is the author of four novels and *The Face: Strangers on a Pier*, a portrait of a Chinese-Malaysian family. His work has won the Whitbread and Commonwealth Prizes, an O. Henry Award, twice been longlisted for the Man Booker Prize and he has been a finalist for the *LA Times* Book Prize. His fiction has also been translated into 23 languages. His writing regularly appears in the *New York Times*, the *Guardian* and the *London Review of Books*, among many other publications.

From the reviews of *Five Star Billionaire*:

'*Five Star Billionaire* opens with a bang, not a whimper … Aw is a master storyteller and *Five Star Billionaire* can be read as *The Way We Live Now* for our times'   AMINATTA FORNA, *Guardian*

'Few people can write about a place with both the astute observation of an outsider and the deep understanding of an insider. When the place is Shanghai, and when that writer is Tash Aw, we get a novel that is as multifaceted as the city itself, in which stories of the old and the new, the rich and the poor, the dreaming and the disillusioned, are woven together by a master storyteller. Tash Aw is an essential voice for the global world we live in today'   YIYUN LI

'Aw's style – terse but tender, lightly ironic without being snide – is fresh, bracing, and above all, compassionate. His characters, though shy and private people, form profound impressions on the reader. One simply cares deeply what happens to them, and this skilled writer never makes that an easy matter to predict'

HANNAH McGILL, *Scotland on Sunday*

'Tash Aw's brilliant new novel focuses on four Malaysian immigrants,   th fluctuating degrees of success   HN HARDING, *Daily Mail*

'It is a fascinating cast of characters, and Aw is at his best as he probes the mix of career ambition, familial duty and romantic longing at the heart of each of them ... Taken together, Aw's characters provide a finely detailed group portrait ... A panoramic, expertly detailed painting of contemporary Shanghai'

STEPHEN AMIDON, *Sunday Times*

'[Aw] is unmatched at evoking the smells and sounds of the land and cityscapes ... tales are told chapter by chapter, the characters slowly drawing closer together like flotsam in a vortex, before the stunning finale ... There is wit here, and plenty of acute observation and characterisation ... none of Aw's characters are two-dimensionally bad; they are just flawed men and women whose ultimate happiness is enthrallingly and sympathetically narrated'

SHOLTO BYRNES, *Independent on Sunday*

'Tash Aw's tale of five migrant workers carving out lives in a modernising Shanghai is the stuff of a hit TV miniseries ... the reading experience it offers is coolly engrossing'

ADAM MARS-JONES, *Observer*

'*Five Star Billionaire* conjures a wonderful picture of the city of Shanghai ... The storyline poignantly lays out the problems, dangers and the crippling loneliness of a modern megacity'

KRYS LEE, *Financial Times*

'A busy yet sophisticated portrait of life in one of the most populous cities on earth. Mr. Aw is a patient writer, and an elegant one. His supple yet unshowy prose can resemble Kazuo Ishiguro's'

DWIGHT GARNER, *New York Times*

'A new kind of immigrant novel. One that takes its place in our increasingly multipolar world and is, in some ways, a challenge to the old narrative.'

DAVID ANNAND, *Sunday Telegraph*

By the same author

The Harmony Silk Factory
Map of the Invisible World
We, The Survivors

For Aw Tee Min and Yap Chee Chun

Suppose one can live without outside pressure, suppose one can create one's own inner tension — then it is not true that there is nothing in man.

CZESŁAW MIŁOSZ, *The Captive Mind*

Foreword:
How to be a Billionaire

S ome time ago – I forget exactly when – I decided that I would one day be very rich. By this I mean not just comfortably well off but superabundantly, incalculably wealthy, the way only children imagine wealth to be. Indeed, nowadays, whenever I am pressed to pinpoint the time in my life when these notions of great fortune formed in my head, I always answer that it must have been sometime in my adolescence, when I was conscious of the price of life's treasures but not yet fully aware of their many limitations, for there has always been something inherently childlike in my pursuit of money – that much I admit.

When I was growing up in rural Malaysia, one of my favourite TV programmes was a drama series set in a legal practice somewhere in America. All the details – the actors, the plots, the setting – are lost to me now, blurred not just by the passage of time but by a haze of bad subtitles and interrupted transmissions (the power generator and the aerial took it in turns to malfunction with crushing predictability, though in those days it seemed perfectly normal). I am not certain I could tell you what happened in a single episode of that soap opera, and besides, I did not care for the artificial little conflicts that took place all the time, the emotional ups and downs, men and women crying because they were falling in love, or out of love; the arguing, making up, making love, etc. I had a sensation that they were wasting time, that their days and nights could have been spent more profitably; I think I probably felt some degree of frustration at this. But even these are fleeting impressions, and the only thing I really remember is the opening sequence, a sweeping panorama of metal-and-glass skyscrapers glinting in the sun, people in sharp suits carrying briefcases as they vanished into revolving doors, the endless rush of traffic on sunlit freeways. And every time I sat down in front of the TV I would think: One day, I will own a building like that, a whole tower block filled with industrious, clever people working to make their fantasies come true.

All I cared for were these introductory images; the show that followed was of secondary importance to me.

So much wasted time.

Now, when I look back at those childhood fantasies, I chuckle with embarrassment, for I realise that I was foolish: I should never have been so modest in my ambitions, nor waited so long to pursue them.

It is said that the legendary tycoon Cecil Lim Kee Huat – still *compos mentis* today at 101 – made his first profit at the age of eight, selling watermelons off a cart on the old coast road to Port Dickson. At thirteen he was running a coffee stand in Seremban, and at fifteen, salvaging and redistributing automobile spare parts on a semi-industrial scale, a recycling genius long before the concept was even invented. Small-town Malaya in the 1920s was not a place for dreams. He was eighteen and working as an occasional porter in the Colony Club when he had the good fortune to meet a young Assistant District Officer from Fife called MacKinnon, only recently arrived in the Malay States. History does not record the precise nature of their relationship (those ugly rumours of blackmail were never proved); and in any event, as we will see later, imagining the whys and wherefores of past events, the what-might-have-beens – all that is pointless. The only thing worth considering is what actually happens, and what happened in Lim's case was that he was left with enough money upon MacKinnon's untimely death (in a drowning accident) to start the first local insurance business in Singapore, a small enterprise that would eventually become the Overseas Chinese Assurance Company, for so long a bedrock of the Malaysian and Singaporean commercial landscape until its recent collapse. We can learn much from people like Lim, but his case study would involve a separate book altogether. For now, it is sufficient to ask: What were you doing when you were eight, thirteen, fifteen, and eighteen? The answer is, I suspect: Not very much.

In the business of life, every tiny episode is a test, every human encounter a lesson. Look and learn. One day you might achieve all that I have. But time is sprinting past you, faster than you think. You're already playing catch-up, even as you read this.

Fortunately, you do get a second chance. My advice to you is: Take it. A third rarely comes your way.

出去

Move to Where
the Money Is

There was a boy at the counter waiting for his coffee, nodding to the music. Phoebe had noticed him as soon as he walked through the door, his walk so confident, soft yet bouncy. He must have grown up walking on carpet. He ordered two lattes and a green tea muffin and paid with a silver ICBC card that he slipped out of a wallet covered in grey-and-black chessboard squares. He was only a couple of years younger than Phoebe, maybe twenty-two or twenty-three, but already he had a nice car, a silver-blue hatchback she had seen earlier when she was crossing the street and he nearly ran her over. It was strange how Phoebe noticed such things nowadays, as swift and easy as breathing. She wondered when she had picked up the habit. She had not always been like this.

Outside, the branches of the plane trees strained the bright mid-autumn sunlight, their shadows casting a pretty pattern on the pavement. There was a light wind, too, that made the leaves dance.

'You like this music, huh?' Phoebe asked as she reached across him for some sachets of sugar.

His coffees arrived. 'It's bossa nova,' he said, as if it was an explanation, only she didn't understand it.

'*Ei*, I also like Spanish music!'

'Huh?' he muttered as he balanced his tray. 'It's Brazilian.' He didn't even look at her, though she was glad he didn't, because if he had, it would have been a you-are-nothing look, the kind of quick glance she had become used to since arriving in Shanghai, people from high up looking down on her.

Brazil and Spain were nearly the same, anyway.

They were in a Western-style coffee bar just off Huaihai Lu; the streets were busy, it was a Saturday. But the week no longer divided neatly into weekend and weekday for Phoebe; it had ceased to do so ever since she arrived in Shanghai a few weeks prior to this. Every day tumbled into the next without meaning, as they had done for too long now. She didn't even know what she was doing in this part of town; she couldn't afford anything in the shops and her Italian coffee cost more than the shirt she was wearing. It was a big mistake to have come here. Her plan was so stupid; what did she think she would accomplish? Maybe she would have to reconsider everything.

Phoebe Chen Aiping, why are you so afraid all the time? Do not be afraid! Failure is not acceptable! You must raise yourself up and raise up your entire family.

She had started keeping a diary. Every day she would write down her darkest fears and craziest ambitions. It was a technique she'd learnt from a self-help master one day in Guangzhou as she waited in a noodle shop, killing time just after she had been to the Human Resources Market. A small TV had been set on top of the glass counter next to jars of White Rabbit sweets, but at first she did not pay attention, she thought it was just the news. Then she realised that it was a DVD of an inspirational life-teacher, a woman who talked about how she had turned her life around and now wanted to show the rest of us how we too could transform our lowly, invisible existence into a life of eternal happiness and success. Phoebe liked the way the woman looked straight at her, holding her gaze so steadily that Phoebe felt embarrassed, shamed by her own failure, the complete lack of even the tiniest achievement in her life. The woman had shimmering lacquered hair that was classy but not old-fashioned. She showed how a mature woman can look

6

beautiful and successful even when no longer in her first spring-time, as she put it herself, laughing. She had so many wise things to say, so many clever sayings and details on how to be successful. If only Phoebe had had a pen and paper she would have written down every single one, because now she cannot remember much except the feeling of courage the woman had given her, words about not being afraid of being on one's own, far from home. It was as if she had looked into Phoebe's head and listened to all the anxieties that were spinning around inside, as if she had been next to Phoebe as she lay awake at night wondering how she was going to face the next day. Phoebe felt a release, as if someone had lifted a great mountain of rocks from her shoulders, as if someone had said, You are not alone, I understand your troubles, I understand your loneliness, I am also like you. And Phoebe thought, The moment I have some money, the first thing I am going to buy is your book. I will not even buy an LV handbag or a new HTC smartphone, I am going to buy your words of wisdom and study them the way some people study the Bible.

The book was called *Secrets of a Five Star Billionaire*. This is something Phoebe would never forget.

One tip that did stick in her mind was the diary, which the woman did not call a diary but a Journal of Your Secret Self, in which you would write down all your black terrors, everything that made you fearful and weak, alongside everything you dream of. You must have more positive dreams than burdensome fears. Once you write something in this book it cannot harm you any more because the fears are conquered by the dreams on the opposite page. So when you are successful you can read this journal one last time before you discard it forever, and you will smile to see how afraid and underdeveloped you were, because you will have come so far. Then you will throw this book away into the Huangpu River and your past self will disappear, leaving only the glorious reborn product of your dreams.

She started the journal six months ago, but still her dreams had not cancelled out her fears. It would happen soon. It had to.

I must not let this city crush me down.

Phoebe looked around the café. The chairs were mustard-yellow and grey, the walls unpainted concrete, as if the work had not yet been finished, but she knew that it was meant to look like this, it was considered fashionable. On the terrace outside there were foreigners sitting with their faces tilted towards the sun – they did not mind their skin turning to leather. Someone got up to leave and suddenly there was a table free next to the Brazilian-music lover. He was with a girl. Maybe it was his sister and not a girlfriend.

Phoebe sat down next to them and turned her body away slightly to show she was not interested in what they were doing. But in the reflection in the window – the sun was shining brightly that day, it was almost Mid-Autumn Festival and the weather was crisp, golden, perfect for dreaming – she could see them quite clearly. The girl was bathed in crystal light as if on a stage, and the boy was cut in half by a slanting line of darkness. Every time he leant forward he came into the light. His skin was like candlewax.

As the girl bent over her magazine, Phoebe could see that she was definitely a girlfriend, not a sister. Her hair fell over her face, so Phoebe could not tell if she was pretty, but she sat the way a pretty person would. Her dress was a big black shirt with loads of words printed all over it like graffiti, meaningless sentences such as PEACE$$$€♥♥PARIS, and honestly it was horrible and made her body look formless as a ghost, but it was expensive, anyone could see that. The handbag on the floor was made of leather so soft it seemed to melt into the ground. It spread out at the girl's feet like an exotic pet, and Phoebe wanted to stroke its cross-hatch pattern to see what it felt like. The boy leant forward and in the mirrored reflection he caught Phoebe's eye. He said something to his girl-friend in Shanghainese which Phoebe couldn't understand, and the girl looked up at Phoebe with a sideways glance. It was something Shanghainese girls had perfected, this method of looking at you side-on without turning their faces to you. It meant that they could show off their fine cheekbones and appear uninterested at the same time, and it made you feel that you were not important at all to them, not worthy even of a proper stare.

Phoebe looked away at once. Her cheeks felt hot.

Do not let other people step on you.

Sometimes Shanghai weighed down on her with the weight of ten skyscrapers. The people were so haughty, their dialect so harsh to her ears. If someone talked to her in their language she would feel attacked just by the sound of it. She had come here full of hope, but on some nights, even after she had deposited all her loathing and terror into her secret journal, she still felt that she was tumbling down, down, and there was no way up. It had been a mistake to gamble as she did.

She was not from any part of China, but from a country thousands of miles to the south, and in that country she had grown up in a small town in the far north-east. It is a region that is poor and remote, so she is used to people thinking of her as inferior, even in her own country. In her small town the way of life had not changed very much for fifty years, and would probably never change. Visitors from the capital city used to call it charming, but they didn't have to live there. It was not a place for dreams and ambition, and so Phoebe did not dream. She did what all the other young boys and girls did when they left school at sixteen: they travelled across the mountain range that cut the country in two to find work on the west coast, moving slowly southward until they reached the capital city.

Here are some of the jobs her friends took in the year they left home. Trainee waiter. Assistant fake-watch stall-holder. Karaoke hostess. Assembly-line worker in a semiconductor factory. Bar girl. Shampoo girl. Water-cooler delivery man. Seafood-restaurant cleaner. (Phoebe's first job was among those listed above, but she would rather not say which one.) Five years in these kinds of jobs, they passed so slowly.

Then she had some luck. There had been a girl who'd disappeared. Everyone thought she was in trouble – she'd been hanging out with a gangster, the kind of big-city boy you couldn't tell your small-town parents about, and everyone thought it wouldn't be long before she was into drugs or prostitution; they were sure of it because she had turned up one day with a big jade bracelet and a black eye. But from nowhere Phoebe received an email from this girl. She wasn't in trouble, she was in China. She'd just decided that enough was enough, and left one morning without telling her boyfriend. She'd saved enough money to go to Hong Kong, where she'd been a karaoke hostess for a while – she was not ashamed to say it because everyone does it, but it was not for long – and now she was working in Shenzhen. She was a restaurant manager, a classy international place, not some dump, you know, and she was in charge of a staff of sixteen. She even had her own apartment (photo attached – small but bright and modern with a vase of plastic roses on a glass table). Thing is, she'd met a businessman from Beijing who was going to marry her and take her up north, and she wanted to make sure everything was OK at the restaurant before she left. They always needed good waiting staff at New World Restaurant. Just come! Don't worry about visas. We can fix that. There were two smiley faces and a winky one at the end of the email.

Those days were so exciting, when they emailed each other several times a day. What clothes shall I bring? What is the winter weather like? What kind of shoes do I need for my uniform? Each email that arrived from China made Phoebe feel that she was one step closer to lifting herself up in the world and becoming someone successful. It made the hair salon where she was working at the time seem so small – the clients were *small* people who did not realise how *small* they were. When they said to her, Hey, Phoebe, you are not concentrating, she just laughed inside because she knew that very soon she would be the one giving them orders and leaving them tips. She was going to experience adventures and see things that none of them could even dream about.

It took her a few weeks to get enough money together for the ticket to Hong Kong plus a bit extra to get her to Shenzhen, but from then on it would be plain sailing, because she had a job lined up and she would stay with her friend for the first couple of months until she found her own place. She didn't need all that much money, she would start making plenty once she got there, her friend assured her. From then on anything was possible. She could start her own business doing whatever she wanted – some former waitresses at the restaurant were already going around in chauffeur-driven cars just a year after they quit their jobs. New China was amazing, she would see for herself. No one asks too many questions, no one cares where you are from. All that counts is your ability. If you can do a job, you're hired.

People say that it is hard to leave their lives behind, and that when the time comes for you to do so you will feel reluctance and longing for your home. But these are people with nice lives to leave behind. For others it is different. Leaving is a relief.

The emails continued, full of !!! marks as usual, but they were less frequent, and finally, at the internet café near East Tsim Sha Tsui station, waiting for the train to Shenzhen, Phoebe logged on for the first time in four days to find not a single email from her friend. Not even a short message that said, *Hurry, too excited*, followed by lots of smileys. When at last she got to Shenzhen it took her some time to locate the restaurant. The sign was proud and shiny. *New World International Restaurant*, it read above twin pillars of twisted gold dragons – Phoebe recognised it from the photos her friend had sent her. The menu was in a glass case outside, a sure sign of a classy joint. But as she approached, Phoebe's heart began to experience a dark fluttering in her ribcage, the way she imagined bat wings would feel against her cheek. It was a sensation that would stay with her for the rest of her time in China. The glass doors were open, but the restaurant inside was dim even though it was the middle of the afternoon. When she stepped inside she saw an empty space without any chairs and tables. Part of the floor had been ripped up, and on the bare concrete she could see messy patches of glue where carpets had once been laid. There was a bar decorated with scenes of Chinese legends carved in bronze, cranes flying over mountains and lakes. Some workmen were shifting machinery and tools at the far end of the restaurant, and when Phoebe called out to them they seemed confused. The restaurant had closed down a few days ago, soon it would be a hotpot chain. The people who worked there? Probably just got jobs somewhere else. No one stays in a job for long in Shenzhen anyway.

She thought, This is not a good situation.

She tried calling her friend's mobile phone number, but it was dead. This number is out of use, the voice told her, over and over again. Each time she dialled it was the same. This number is out of use.

She checked how much money she had and began looking for a cheap guesthouse. The streets were clean but full of people. Everyone looked as though they were hurrying to an appointment, everyone had some place to go. Amid the mass of people that swarmed around her like a thick muddy river, she started to notice a certain kind of person, and soon they were the only people she really saw. Young single women. They were everywhere, rushing for the bus or marching steadfastly with a steely look on their faces, or going from shop to shop handing out their CVs, their entire lives on one sheet of paper. They were all restless, they were all moving, they were all looking for work, floating everywhere, casting out their lives to whoever would take them.

So this is how it happens. This is how I become like them, Phoebe thought. In the space of a few hours she had passed from one world to another. One moment she was almost an assistant manager in a classy international restaurant, next moment she was a migrant worker. Her new life had materialised out of thin air like a trick of fate. Unattached, searching, alone. Some people say that when you find other people who are just like you, who share your position in life, you feel happier, less alone, but Phoebe did not think this was true. Knowing that she was the same as millions of other girls made her feel lonelier than ever.

She went back to her lodgings. The door wouldn't lock, so she slept with her handbag tucked into her belly, curved into a tight C-shape.

Those first few months in Shenzhen passed very quickly. During this time Phoebe did a number of jobs that she would rather not talk about right now. Maybe some day, but not now.

You can only rely on yourself. There are no true friends in this world. If you place your trust in others you will open yourself to danger and hurtfulness.

She got a job at a place called Guangdong Bigfaith Quality Garment Company, a factory that made fashion clothes for Western brands – not the expensive labels that Phoebe had heard of but lesser ones that sold shiny, colourful clothes, though the other girls told her that these were trendy shops even though they were low-cost. Apparently in the West even rich people buy cheap clothes. Personally Phoebe did not want any of the skirts or jackets or blouses that were made at the factory; they looked unclassy even to her. Her job was to match up the orders to the delivery notes and make sure that everything tallied. It was not a difficult job, but still she cried every night. The hours were long and at night she had to endure being in a dorm with the other girls, so many other girls. She hated seeing their underwear strung up on washing lines in every room, even in the corridors, drying in the damp air. Everywhere you went in the dormitory block all you saw was lines of damp underwear, and the whole place smelled of detergent and sweat. All day and night there was arguing and crying. She hated this, especially the night-time sobbing. It was as if everyone thought that when it was dark no one could hear them cry. She had to get away from them, she was not like them. But for now she had no choice.

The other hard thing to deal with was the jealousy, the things that were said about her. (How did she get such a good job straight away? Why was she in admin and not on the production line when she had only just joined the company? I hear she hasn't even been out for long.) Well, Phoebe wanted to explain, first of all it was because she could speak English and Cantonese, the language of all the rich factory-owners down here in the south. And, quite simply, it was because she was better than the rest of them. But she knew to keep silent. She was afraid of the large groups of girls who came from the big provinces, especially the Hunanese girls who smuggled things out of the factory to sell outside and threatened to kill anyone who reported them. They liked to fight. Everyone had their own clan for protection: the Sichuan girls looked after each other, even the Anhui girls were numerous enough to have support. Only Phoebe was alone, but she would rise above them all because she was smarter. A line stuck in her head, advice given to her by the self-made millionaire. *Hide your brightness, remain in the shadows.* So she had to endure the jealousy and the detergent and the sweat and the crying. But for how long?

Do not let lesser people drag you down. You are a star that shines brightly.

She had a picture of a Taiwanese pop star by her bed. It was just a page torn from a magazine, an advertisement for cows' milk, but it was a nicer decoration than the strung-up panties that the other girls had. It was a struggle to keep the Sellotape attached to the glossy painted wall because of the humidity, and the top corner kept falling away. But she persisted in sticking the picture up so she could look at him and dream about a world where there was no sobbing. If she turned her body at an angle there was only him and her in the world. She liked his delicate smile and watery eyes, and found even the silly white milk-moustache on his lip endearing. When she looked at his face she felt hope swell in her chest. His gentleness made her forget about the harshness of life and made her believe that she could work hard and show the world her true inner beauty. Maybe she could even be his girlfriend one day. Oh, she knew that it was just a fantasy, but he was so dreamy, and reminded her of the boys she had grown up with, whom she would remember forever as teenagers, even though they had now all moved to the cities and were selling fake leather wallets and probably amphetamines on the side. They had been so happy before, and now they were all growing old so quickly, including Phoebe.

But you are so young, little sister. That was what the new manager of her division began saying to her one day. He was a man from Hong Kong, not fat not thin, not ugly not handsome, just a man from Hong Kong. Once a month he would visit the factory and spend four or five days there. Every time he came he would call her into his office and show her the gifts he had brought for her – a bag of the juiciest tangerines, small sugary pineapples from Taiwan, strawberries, some foreign chocolate that tasted bitter and floury – delicacies that people bought when they could afford to travel. The hamper of fruit lay on his desk wrapped in stiff crinkly plastic that made a loud noise when she touched it. She did not know how she was going to carry it all the way back to her dorm, across the huge courtyard and the basketball courts, did not know where she would keep it or how she would explain it to the other girls. The jealousy against her had not really gone away; the tide had just subsided for the time being, but was waiting to well up like a tsunami at any moment. She knew that the gift was wrong, that she had not really done anything to deserve it, but as she looked at the shiny ripe persimmons, she felt special. Someone had noticed her, someone had thought of her enough to buy her nice things. It had been a long time since anyone had done that, so she accepted the gift.

As she carried the basket down the corridor to her dorm, she could feel the other girls' hot stares burning her with their envy. She was sweating, and her heart was heavy with guilt, heavier than the basket she was carrying. But as she walked into the dorm she found herself talking freely, the words flowing easily from her mouth. *Ei*, everyone, look what I have! A cousin of mine in Hong Kong got married to a very rich man and they had their wedding. I couldn't afford to go so they sent me some tokens of their big celebration. Come, come, let's all share!

Hei, you did not tell us you are from Hong Kong.

Yes, Phoebe said. From just near the border, in the New Territories.

Oooh, the girls said as they reached for the fruit. So I guess it's natural that you speak Cantonese! We thought you just learnt it to curry favour with the boss!

This is how things happen in China, Phoebe thought as she sat watching her new friends sharing the basket of fruit. Things change so fast. From then on all the girls knew who she was, and they were nice to her. They took her clothes and washed them for her when she was on a long shift, and some of them began to talk to her about their private lives – where they were from, their boyfriend problems, their ambitions. One day she was talking to a girl, just someone she shared meal breaks with in the canteen sometimes, not really a friend. The girl's mobile phone rang, and she just looked at the screen without answering. Her face twisted into a pained expression and she handed the phone to Phoebe. It's the boy I was telling you about, the one who bullies me. Phoebe took the phone and did not even say hello. This is your ex-girlfriend's cousin, she said. This mobile phone belongs to me now. Your ex has a new boyfriend and he is rich and educated, not a stupid peasant like you, so just go away or else I will make trouble for you. I know who you are and which lousy place you work at.

Wah, you are amazing, Phoebe! Everyone was laughing and someone even reached out and put her arm around Phoebe's shoulder.

On her first day off that month she went with some other girls to the cinema. They stopped at a fast-food place and had bubble milk tea before buying a box of octopus balls which they ate while strolling through the night market, linking elbows as if they were still in middle school. They turned their noses up at the cheap clothes, far cheaper than the ones they made in the factory, stall after stall of thin spangled nylon. The music on the speakers was loud, thumping in their ribcages and drowning out their heartbeats. It made them feel so alive. The smell of fried food and charcoal grills felt familiar to Phoebe – she did not feel so very far from home after all. They saw posters advertising the latest concert of the Taiwanese singer she liked, and the ticket prices did not look too expensive.

Hei, we should all save up some money and go! someone said. Phoebe, you love Gary, don't you? Maybe we can share the cost of your ticket, because you are always cooking for us and sharing your food with us. I hear he's going to sing some Cantonese songs too, since it's here in Guangzhou, so you can teach us to sing along! She was happy that they offered, but she knew that these were empty promises and that no one would actually buy her a ticket.

She stopped to buy a shiny black top decorated with beads, but the other girls scolded her. Forty *kuai*! Too expensive. *Aiya*, new girls are always the same, always spending money on useless things instead of sending it home. Besides, you should be buying nicer clothes, something that suits your slim figure better, not some Old Mother style! But Phoebe bought it anyway, she didn't care. It had pretty embroidery, a red rose adorned with silver beads that fanned out from each petal.

But as swiftly as the bright cool days of autumn give way to the damp chill of winter, life also changes. Phoebe knew this by now. Nothing ever stood still in China, nothing was permanent. A person who is loved cannot expect that love to remain for long. There is no reason for them to keep this love; they do not have a right to be loved.

She shared her third basket of fruit and other delicacies with her dorm friends. This time there were bags of dried scallops and a tin of abalone, which none of them had ever tasted before, and they gathered to cook a meal together. It was too luxurious for lowly people like them, one girl remarked – this meal was all thanks to Phoebe.

Really, said another girl, lifting her rice bowl to her mouth. Boss Lin says this kind of thing is not so special in Hong Kong, everyone eats it over there.

How would you know? When do you ever talk to Boss Lin?

Hm, it's true. I rarely get a chance to speak to him. The only person he speaks to is Phoebe.

I wish he didn't, Phoebe joked. He is so boring. *Hai*, it's only because of my stupid job that I have to have contact with him.

It seems he takes a special interest in you. He even calls you into his private office.

Yes, but only to scold me for tasks I haven't done! Come, eat some more!

The next month, Mr Lin summoned Phoebe to see him as soon as he arrived. He shut the door; the blinds were already down as usual. There was no fruit basket this time, only a small box. He opened it and held out a brand-new mobile phone, the type with no buttons on the screen, just a smooth glass surface. It was something a tycoon's daughter would have, or a businesswoman. Phoebe didn't even know how to turn it on.

But I already have a phone.

It's OK, take it. Just tell your friends you won it in a competition.

She held it in her hands, turning it over and over again. She held it up to her face. It was like a mirror – she could see herself in it.

You like it? Mr Lin was standing next to her, though she had not heard him approach her. He put his hand on her buttock, the palm flat, burning through her jeans. Hours later, she would still feel the imprint of his hot hand on her, leaving its mark where it had stayed for less than half a minute, maybe not even that long.

In the dorm someone said, What's happened to your cousin in Hong Kong? No food hamper this month? I think the cousin must have suddenly died and turned into a ghost!

Next day, two Shaanxi girls from the next block were taken away by the police. When Phoebe asked why, one of her dorm mates said it was because they didn't have the right papers. They were illegal, and one of them was underage.

But I thought you said that kind of thing doesn't really matter, that the employer doesn't ask too many questions, where you're from and all that, Phoebe said.

Sure, that's right, her dorm mate replied, smiling. But rules are rules. You can dodge the regulations for so long, but if someone makes a formal report there's nothing anyone can do. Half the girls here are lying about something, and most of the time it's OK. Even if you don't have a proper *hukou* or your papers are fake, who cares? Only when you step out of line do others make trouble for you. Those girls were unpopular, they were arrogant and made enemies. They thought they were better than everyone else, so what could they expect? It was just a matter of time.

One morning Phoebe came back after a night shift and saw that the poster by her bed had been defaced. The pop singer's moon-bright complexion had been dotted with acne and now he wore round black glasses and there were thick cat whiskers sprouting from his cheeks.

Time was running out for Phoebe. From the first moment she set foot in China she had felt the days vanishing from her life, vanishing into failure. Like the clock she stared at every day at work, her life was counting down the minutes before she became a non-person whom no one would ever remember. As she sat during lunch break on the low brick wall next to the volleyball court, she knew that she had to act now or she would forever be stepped on everywhere she went. The grey concrete dormitory blocks rose up on all four sides of the yard and blocked out the light. There was Cantonese pop music playing from somewhere and through an open window she could see a TV playing reruns of the Olympics, Chinese athletes winning medals. She watched the high jump for a while. A lanky blonde girl failed twice, flopping down heavily on the bar. One more go and she was out. It didn't really matter, since she wasn't even going to win a medal. Then suddenly she did something that made Phoebe shiver with excitement. For her third and final jump she asked for the bar to be raised higher than anyone had jumped so far, higher than she had ever attained in her whole life. She had failed at lower heights but now she was gunning for something way beyond her capabilities. She was going to jump all the way to the stars, and even if she failed she could only come down as far as the lowly position she already occupied. She stood at the end of the runway flexing her fingers and shaking her wrists, and then she started running, in big bouncy strides. Phoebe got up and turned away. She didn't want to see what happened, it was not important to her. The only thing that mattered was that the blonde girl had gambled.

She took her expensive new phone to a Sichuan girl who traded things in the dorm, and sold it for a nice sum of cash. She washed her hair and tied it neatly before going to Boss Lin's office. She was wearing her tightest jeans that she usually reserved for her day off. They were so tight that she could not sit down comfortably without them cutting into the tops of her thighs.

Little Miss, it's highly irregular for us to hand out salaries before payday, he said, but he was already looking for the number of the accounts department.

Come on, it's almost the end of the month, only a week to go. Phoebe twirled her hair and inclined her head the way she noticed other girls doing when they talked to the handsome security guards. Anyway, she laughed, our relationship is a bit irregular, don't you think?

Foshan, Songxia, Dongguan, Wenzhou – she was going to bypass them all. Her bar was going to be raised all the way to the sky. There was only one city she could go to now, the biggest and brightest of them all.

The girl at the next table was still reading her magazine, her boyfriend sending messages on his iPhone. Sometimes he would read out a message and laugh, but the girl would not respond, she just continued to flick through her magazine. He looked up at Phoebe, just for a split second, and at first she thought he was scowling in that familiar look-down-on-you expression. But then she realised that he was squinting because of the light. He hadn't even noticed her.

The girl's mobile phone rang and she began to rummage in her handbag for it, emptying out its contents on the table. There were so many shiny pretty things, lipstick cases, keyrings, and also a leather diary, a pen, stray receipts, and scrunched-up pieces of tissue paper. She answered the phone, and as she did so, stood up and gathered her things, hastily replacing them in her bag. Her boyfriend was trying to help her, but she was frowning with impatience. A 5-*mao* coin fell to the floor and rolled to Phoebe's feet. She bent over and picked it up.

'Don't worry,' the boy said over his shoulder as he followed his girlfriend out. 'It's only 5 *mao*.'

They had just left when Phoebe noticed something on the table. Half hidden under a paper napkin was the girl's ID card. Phoebe looked up and saw that they were still on the pavement, waiting for a gap in the traffic to cross the road. She could have rushed out and called to them, done them a huge favour. But she waited, feeling her heart pound and the blood rush to her temples. She reached across and took the card. The photo was bland; you couldn't make out the cheekbones that in real life were so sharp you could have cut your hand on them. In the photo the girl's face was flat and pale. She could have been any other young woman in the café.

Outside, the boy was leading the girl by the hand as they crossed the road. She was still on the phone, her floppy bag trailing behind her like a small dog. The skies were clear that day, a touch of autumn coolness in the air.

With a paper napkin, Phoebe wiped the breadcrumbs off the card and tucked it safely into her purse.

2

初露锋芒

Choose the Right Moment to Launch Yourself

Every building has its own sparkle, its own identity. At night, their electric personalities flicker into life and they cast off their perfunctory daytime selves, reaching out to each other to form a new world of ever-changing colour. It is tempting to see them as a single mass of light, a collection of illuminated billboards and fancy fluorescent strips that twinkle in the same way. But this is not true; they are not the same. Each one insists itself upon you in a different way, leaving its imprint on your imagination. Each message, if you care to listen, is different.

From his window he could see the Pudong skyline, the skyscrapers of Lujiazui ranged like razor-sharp Alpine peaks against the night sky. In the daytime even the most famous buildings seemed irrelevant, obscured by the perpetual haze of pollution; but at night, when the yellow-grey fog thinned, he would sit at his window watching them display boastfully, each one trying to outdo the next: taller, louder, brighter. A crystal outcrop suspended high in the sky, shrouded by mist on rainy days; a giant goldfish wriggling across the face of a building; interlocking geometric shapes shattering into a million fragments before regrouping. He knew every one by heart.

Buildings were in his DNA, he sometimes thought. They had given him everything he had ever owned – his houses, his cars, his friends – and even shaped the way he thought and felt; they had been in his life right from the beginning. The years were rushing past, whatever he had left of his youth surrendering to middle age, yet bricks and mortar – real estate – remained a constant presence. When he revisited his earliest memories, trying to summon scenes of family life – his mother's protective embrace, perhaps, or praise from his father – the results were always blank. They were present in his memories, of course, his parents and grandmother, hovering spectrally. But, just like in real life, they were never animated. All he could see and smell was the buildings around them, the structures they inhabited: cold stone floors, mossy walls, flaking plaster, silence. It was a world from which there had been no escape. A path had been laid down for him, straight and unbending. He had long since given up hope of departing from this track, indeed could not even remember any other option – until he came to Shanghai.

The summer of '08 had been notable for its stillness, the unyielding humidity that lay trapped between the avenues of concrete and glass. He had arrived in Shanghai expecting a temperate climate, but summer had stretched far into September and the pavements were sticky with heat, the roads becoming rivers of exhaust and steam. Even in his gated compound in Pudong, with its American-tropic-style lawns and palm-filled gardens, the air felt lifeless.

He had known little about Shanghai, and assumed that it would consist solely of shopping malls and plastic reproductions of its history, its traditional life preserved in aspic as it was in Singapore, where he went to school, or inherently Third World, like Malaysia, where he grew up. It might be like Hong Kong, where he had begun his career and established his reputation as an unspectacular but canny businessman who would hold the reins steady as head of the family's property interests. Whatever the case, he had assumed he would find it familiar – he had spent his life in overcrowded, overbuilt Asian cities, and they were all the same to him: whenever he looked at a tower block he saw only a set of figures that represented income and expenditure. Ever since he was a teenager, his brain had been trained to work in this way, calculating numbers swiftly, threading together disparate considerations such as location, purpose and yield. Maybe there was, in spite of everything, a beauty in the incisiveness of his thinking back then.

But during those initial few weeks it was not easy for him to get any sense of Shanghai at all. His driver picked him up at his house and drove him to a series of meetings punctuated by business lunches, each day finishing with the soon familiar flourish of a banquet. He lived in a development called Lisson Valley, which was owned by his family. This, together with a more modest development in Hongqiao and a condominium block in Xintiandi, were all that they owned in the largest city in China, and they had decided that they needed to expand, which was why he had been sent here. They had spent a hundred years in Malaysia and Singapore, and now they needed to branch out in a serious way – like the great Jewish families of Europe in the nineteenth century, his father had explained, as if the decision needed to be justified. On the annual Forbes list of billionaires his family's business was described as '*Henry Lim and family – Diversified Holdings*' – it always made him wince, the term 'diversified': the lack of specificity carried with it an accusation, as if the source of the wealth they had amassed was uncertain and, most probably, unsavoury.

'You're too sensitive,' his father had chided him when he was young. 'You need to grow out of it and toughen up. What do you care what other people think?'

It was true: what other people thought was entirely irrelevant. The family insurance firm, established in Singapore since 1930, had not only survived but prospered during the war, and was one of the oldest continuous companies in South-East Asia. By any reckoning his family now counted as 'old money', one of those overseas Chinese families that had risen, in little over a century, from dockside coolies to established billionaires. Every generation built on the achievements of its predecessor, and now it was his turn: Justin CK Lim, eldest son of Henry Lim and heir to the proud, vibrant legacy of LKH Holdings, established by his grandfather.

Property clairvoyant. Groomed from a young age to take over the reins. Steady hands. Wisdom beyond his years.

These were some of the things the *Business Times* said of him just before he arrived here. His father had had the article cut out, mounted and framed, and had sent it to him gift-wrapped in paper decorated with gold stars. It arrived two days after his birthday, but he was not sure if it was a present. There had never been presents on his birthday.

From the start of his time in Shanghai he was invited to the best parties – the numerous openings of the flagship stores of Western luxury brands, or discreet private banquets hosted by young local entrepreneurs with excellent connections within the Party. He could always get a table at the famous Western restaurants on the Bund, and because people soon got to know and like him – he was easy, unshowy company – he was rarely on his own, and increasingly in the public eye. At one party to launch a new line of underwear, held in a warehouse in the northern outskirts of the city, he found himself unconsciously shrinking away from the bank of flashbulbs that greeted the guests, so that when the photographs appeared, his head was cocked at an angle, as if he had recently hurt his neck in an accident. There were a dozen hydraulic plat-forms suspended above the party, each one occupied by a model clad only in underwear, gyrating uncomfortably to the thumping music; every time he looked up at them they threw confetti down on him, which he then had to pick out of his hair. The event organiser later sent him copies of the photos – he was frowning in every one, stray bits of confetti clinging to his suit like birdshit. Shanghai *Tatler* magazine photographed him at a black-tie charity event a few weeks after he arrived, his hair slickly swept back in a nod to the 1930s, a small white flower in his buttonhole, and a young Western woman in a *qipao* at his side. The caption read, 'Justin CK Lim and companion'; he hadn't even known who the woman was. He bid for a guided tour of the city by Zhou X, a local starlet just beginning to make a name for herself in new-wave art-house films. It cost him 200,000 *yuan*, the money donated to orphans of the Sichuan earthquake. The men at the party nudged him and whispered slyly, 'Maybe you'll get to see the most secret sights of Shanghai, like she showed off in her latest movie.' (It was a film he'd heard of, set in a small village during the Cultural Revolution and already banned in China; the *New York Times* review of it called Zhou X 'the intellectual man's Orientalist fantasy'.)

If he felt a frisson of excitement it wasn't because of his glamorous tour guide, but because it was his first proper outing in Shanghai, his first sight of the daytime streets at close quarters, unencumbered by briefcases and folders. If anything he felt resentful at Zhou X's presence; she sat in the car idly sending messages on her BlackBerry, her only commentary being a recital of a list of projects her agent had sent her. 'Wim Wenders – is he famous?' she asked. 'I don't feel like working with him – he sounds boring.'

They stopped outside a tourist-class hotel on a busy thoroughfare lined with mid-range shopping brands in what seemed to be a fairly expensive part of town (low occupancy, medium yield: unrealised rental potential) – a strange place to start a tour of Shanghai, he thought, as they walked through a featureless archway into a narrow lane lined first with industrial dustbins and then, further on, with low brick houses. These were the famous *longtang* of Shanghai, she explained, the ones foreigners fell in love with – though personally she couldn't understand why anyone would want to live in a lane house. 'Look at them, they're so primitive and cramped and dark and … old.'

He peered through an open doorway. In the gloom, a staircase of dark hardwood; a tiled kitchen with a two-ring stove-top cooker. He stepped into the house – its quiet half-light seemed welcoming, irresistible.

'What are you doing?' Zhou X cried.

But he was already up the stairs, treading across the uneven floorboards, the deep graining of the wood inviting him to bend down and trail his fingers over the smooth, worn surface. There were signs of life — pots of scraggly herbs and marigolds, towels draped on banisters, lines of washing strung up across the small square rooms. And yet there was a stillness that settled heavily on the house, as if its inhabitants had recently abandoned it; as if the present was already giving way to the past. The small windows on the landings allowed little light in, but Justin could nonetheless see that there was dust on the surface of some cardboard boxes that lay stacked in a corner of the room, and also on the handrails of the staircase. He could not decide whether the house was decaying or living. He retreated and joined his companion outside. In spite of her huge black sunglasses she was squinting, shielding her face from the sun with her handbag.

'You're crazy,' she said. 'You can't just go poking your nose into other people's houses like that.'

Justin looked at her and smiled. 'I've paid for this, haven't I? I need to get my money's worth.'

At his insistence they drove from *longtang* to *longtang*, their SUV cruising through the narrow streets lined with plane trees, the balconies of the old French-style villas occasionally visible over the tops of stone walls. Some of the larger houses had shutters that were tightly closed, and in their gloom these mansions reminded him of the house in which he had grown up, full of silence and shadows and the steady ticking of grandfather clocks. He remembered the hallway and staircase of his family house, the ceiling rising so high that it created a cavelike gloom.

As the car crawled through the traffic he began to notice the number of people on foot: a group of middle-school kids, spiky-haired and bespectacled in tracksuits, rushing to beat each other to the head of the queue to buy freshly made *shengjian*, exclaiming gleefully as the cloud of steam billowed from the pan; an elderly couple crossing the road just in front of the car, walking arm in arm, their clothes made from matching brocade and velvet, worn but still elegant; and at an intersection, about fifty construction workers sitting on the pavement, smoking on their break, their faces tanned and leathery, foreign-looking – Justin could not place where they were from. He wondered why, in the many weeks since arriving, he had not noticed how densely populated the city was. All that time driving around in his limo, he thought, he must have been working on spreadsheets or reading reports.

'You're so easy to please,' Zhou X said, tapping away on her phone without looking at him. 'All I have to do is show you old houses.'

They stopped the car because he had seen a small lane of nondescript houses that seemed derelict at first glance. It was the property developer's instinct in him that spotted the lane, he thought, for it was barely distinguishable from the dozens of others they had seen, and in fact a great deal less attractive. Tucked behind a row of small fruit and vegetable shops, the low brick houses had not long ago been rendered in cheap cement and now looked, frankly, ugly: low residential value, ripe for development. Wires sagged along the façades of the buildings, competing for space with lines of washing hung up to dry; a small girl came out of a door-way carrying a basin of grey-hued water, which she splashed into the street. There was something about the way of life here – families living at close quarters, spilling into one another – that reminded him of the slums not far from where he used to live: hundreds of identical, flimsy houses, thousands of lives that seemed to blend into one. Sometimes they would catch fire and the entire area would be razed to the ground, only to be rebuilt a few months later. He had never known any of the people who lived in that world, and even before he became an adult, the shanties were cleared to make way for a shopping mall.

He'd remembered to bring his little digital camera, and began photographing the narrow, sunless alley and the shabby shops that surrounded it; as he did so, an old woman emerged from one of the houses, carrying a few plastic bags bulging with clothes. On the LCD screen of his camera she appeared smiling, gap-toothed, spontaneously lifting her bags to the camera as if displaying a trophy.

'Hey, people don't like you interfering with their lives,' Zhou X called from inside the car. 'Can you hurry up? I'm late for my next appointment.'

For days afterwards he looked at the picture of the old woman, even putting it on his laptop so that every time he turned it on she was there, smiling at him. There was something about her thin hair, dyed jet-black and set in tight curls, that reminded him of his grandmother – the attempts at vanity making her seem frailer, not younger. He remembered his grandmother's room: the chalky smell of thick white face powder and tiger balm interlaced with eau de cologne. He would sit on the bed and watch her undo the curlers from her hair; she liked having him around, liked talking to him, even though he could not yet understand all of what she said. He must have been no more than five or six and she was already in her eighties, already weak. And he was surprised by the glassy clarity of these memories, the way they settled insistently on his waking days like a thin, sticky film that he could not shake off. He had never even been close to his grandmother.

With the photo enlarged, he could make out the colour of some of the clothes through the translucent plastic bags the old woman was carrying: a jumble of cheap textiles proudly displayed to the beholder. Her cheeks were red and coarse, her remaining teeth badly tea-stained. He wanted to go back and try to find her, maybe take more photographs – and who knows, on further inspection (and without a nagging actress on his back) he might get a clearer view of those small houses and the neighbouring shops. A thought flashed across his mind: maybe he could restore them, save them from further degradation by thinking of some clever scheme whereby the residents could continue paying low rent and the shops could be run on a cooperative basis. The entire site would become a model for modern urban dwelling in Asia; young educated people would want to come and live cheek by jowl with old Shanghainese.

He jotted down a few rough figures, arranging them in neat columns: how much financing such a scheme might take to work

– nothing serious, just the vaguest estimate, and yet, as always, the moment he thought about money, the project began to feel real, crystallising into something solid and attainable. He kept the piece of paper on his desk at work so he would not forget it.

But the whole of the next week was taken up with meetings with bankers and contractors, dinners with Party officials, preparing a presentation to the Mayor's office; the following week he had to go to Tokyo, and then Hong Kong, then Malaysia. When he finally made it back to Shanghai it was turning cold and damp with the onset of winter, and he did not feel like venturing out much, did not have the energy to track down the old woman and her little lane, for he did not know where it was exactly – maybe somewhere between a highway and a big triangular glass building? He barely had any time to himself these days. Most evenings he was so tired it felt too much of an effort even to shower and clean his teeth before he went to bed; all he wanted to do was fall asleep. His limbs ached, his mouth was dry all the time, and his head felt cloudy, as if set in thick fog on a muggy day, a headache hovering on the horizon. He got the 'flu and was laid up in bed for over a week, and then bronchitis set in and he couldn't shake it. His bathroom scales showed he had lost nearly ten pounds, but he wasn't too worried – he was just overworked; it had happened to him before. Whenever he worked too much he got sick. But still he got up every morning, put on his suit, went to meetings, studied site plans and financial models.

After months of planning his family had decided on their masterwork, a project that was to announce their arrival on the Mainland and define their intentions for the coming decades. All his groundwork – the endless days and nights of negotiations and entertaining – had finally unearthed a potential site befitting his family's ambitions: a near-derelict warehouse built around the remains of a 1930s opium den, surrounded by low lane houses, between Nanjing Xi Lu and Huaihai Lu – an absolutely *chao-A* prime location. There had been other alternatives, such as a much bigger site in Pudong, large enough to accommodate a skyscraper

– a genuine, brash, half-kilometre-high Asian behemoth, but his father and uncles had preferred the old fashioned prestige of this address. 'It'll make more of a statement,' his father said, his voice measured and steady, but tinged with excitement nonetheless. In the coming year they would make a bid for the site and decide what they would do with it – something outstanding, of course, a future landmark. There was still the matter of greasing palms, identifying the officials who might need to be persuaded to allow the deal to go through, but he was not worried about that – it was something at which he had years of practice. It had become his speciality, people said, making things happen that way.

One cold, crisp morning, during a lull in negotiations – it was that dead time in January when the Westerners were still lethargic after their return from Christmas and the locals were beginning to prepare for the Spring Festival – he woke up to brilliant sunshine and a day off: the first of either that he could remember in a long time. His joints did not feel swollen as they usually did, and his lungs craved air. He called for a taxi and set off vaguely in the direction of the lane he had seen all those months ago, and when he felt he was in the general vicinity he alighted and continued on foot, strolling along the streets lined with low stone houses. The air was cold and sharp in his lungs, almost cleansing; the streets were busy with crisscrossing bicycles and electric scooters, merchants pulling carts of winter melons and oranges. The branches of the trees had been pruned heavily for the winter, and stood sentinel-like before the handsome old European-built houses. On foot he noticed the stone ornaments and moulded window frames that adorned the upper floors of these small buildings – it was impossible to see any of this from a car: all he usually saw was the ground floor, invariably occupied by a featureless shop selling down jackets or mobile phones. He stopped to buy a bag of oranges for the old woman, just in case he saw her again – he wasn't far now; he recognised a few shops, a familiar curve in the road.

He rounded the corner of where he thought the lane was, but all he saw was a wide, empty square of dirt dotted with pyramid-shaped piles of rubble. The shops had disappeared, and the lane with it. He paused and looked for things he remembered – an old barbershop, a strange Bavarian pebbledashed house on the corner: this was definitely the place. But all that was left of the houses was the faintest imprint of where their foundations had been – shallow, barely discernible. He had his camera in his back-pack and wanted to take a photo, but he had the big bag of oranges in his hand and didn't know what to do with it; all at once it seemed redundant. He looked around, hoping to give it to some-one. But for the first time he could remember since arriving in Shanghai, the streets were almost empty – no bored young woman leaning out of a shop entrance, no street vendor watching him suspiciously, not even a child on a tricycle. After a while an old man cycled past, his face creased and leathery – in the basket between his handlebars there was a small poodle wearing a pink quilted coat. It looked at Justin as it went past, its mouth drawn wide as if in a smile, but there were streaks running down from its eyes, like black tears. Justin stood in the brilliant winter sunshine, the bag of oranges cutting into his hand. He had forgotten to wear gloves, and his fingers were getting numb.

He left the oranges by a pile of rubble and walked into the middle of the cleared space. It wasn't very large, bounded on three sides by old houses. It would have made a lousy building site; he was glad he wasn't the one developing it. It had seemed larger when those few houses and shops were still on it, so full of life and potential. Maybe he wasn't a property genius after all. He looked around one last time, hoping to see the old woman he had photo-graphed – it was stupid, he knew, for she had gone.

Just before he left he took some photos of the empty plot of land. In the pale winter light the earth looked so dry it could have been in a desert. The only patch of colour was the electric blue of the plastic bag that had fallen open, revealing a few plump oranges. He walked around a little bit more, coming across more and more pieces of land that looked to him to have been recently cleared – some tiny and compact, some vast and unbounded, hollowed out by bulldozers. He took pictures of each one, and walked until it began to get dark. The winter air felt sharp and icy in his chest, as if he was inhaling tiny shards of glass.

The following week his cough seemed to get worse again; the long walk in the damp January air seemed to have weakened his lungs, and he found the mere act of breathing an effort. In a meeting with potential bankers he was unable to finish his sentences because of a tickling in his throat that rose as he spoke, swiftly triggering a rasping cough that left his chest and ribcage feeling hollow and achy. The doctor prescribed another course of antibiotics – his third since the new year – and ordered some X-rays, which came back clear. He just needed rest, the doctor said; he was run-down. But his days and nights did not get any shorter – the gruelling meetings lasted all day, bleeding into the evening's social round of banquets and bars. Once he got over the initial few days of feeling ill, the exhaustion became familiar, almost reassuring. It was always like this: whenever a big project was on the table he would slip easily into the grinding nature of this routine, finding comfort in the constancy of his fatigue. When he woke up each morning he could feel the puffiness of his eyes, knew that they would be bloodshot; his breathing would already be desperate, the air feeling thin in his lungs. His limbs would be heavy, but after a shower and a double espresso he would feel better, though he would never satisfactorily shake the mild headache that was already descending on his skull, already escalating into a migraine. He would work through it – it wasn't a problem.

Besides, he didn't have a choice. There was a problem with the deal. All the arrangements that had been slotting obediently into place just before Christmas were now looking shaky. Someone was refusing to take a bribe – an official in the municipal Urban Planning Department, a mid-ranking engineer who had found an irregularity in the paperwork, a discrepancy, it seemed, between the proposed project and the preliminary drawings. More buildings would have to be demolished than had been declared in the proposal, and this was a problem because many of those buildings were in the local vernacular. This engineer – a glorified technical clerk – was resisting the pressure placed on her by her superiors, most of whom were sympathetic to the Lim family venture. It was awkward when someone acted out of principle; it would take more than money to solve the impasse. And now the delay was leading to further complications: another party was interested in the piece of land, and there was talk of an imminent bid to rival theirs.

He pressed for emergency meetings with high-ranking officials for whom he had bought Cartier cigarette lighters and weekend trips to the Peninsula Hotel in Hong Kong. There was nothing they could do for the moment, they claimed: his project had to work its way through the system, there was a formal procedure which they couldn't alter, it would just take a bit of time. Each official he spoke to reassured him gently without committing himself; they were sure the other bid would come to nothing. They said this in a way to suggest that they would do something to prevent it, but now he was not so sure. He was not sure about anything in Shanghai any more.

In the meantime his secretaries began to speak of an internet campaign – a blog site entitled DEFENDERS OF OLD SHANGHAI. They showed him pages and pages of angry commentary under the discussion thread: *Save 969 Weihai Lu from destruction by foreign companies!!* It was full of accusations that wildly exaggerated the effect of the project on the existing buildings, so, using the pseudonym 'FairPreserver', he personally wrote replies to the most outlandish claims. It was not true that the Lim family company were uncaring capitalists wanting to take advantage of China, he said; he had heard from insiders that they cared greatly about history and would do everything in their power to preserve what they could. They had a long record of restoring heritage buildings and would never dream of destroying anything the city deemed to be important. They cared greatly about the lives of the common people and always sought to be considerate and fair when dealing with property belonging to people of modest means, never forcing anyone to move against their will and always providing compensation where necessary.

HAHAHAHA, came the first reply, within minutes of his post. *What a joke, are you paid by the Lim family to say these things???*

Everything he argued was met with contempt, but still he battled on. No, it was not true that the Lim family had made their money by kicking people off their land in Malaysia; no, they were not going to do the same here. He began to spend hours each day posting replies on the blog site, rushing back from meetings to check what had been said in response to his posts and to write something himself. But then, one day, all of his posts suddenly vanished – he could find no trace of any of them. Every single one had disappeared in the space of an hour, and he was forced to read from the sidelines, marginalised, silenced. He tried inventing a new pseudonym, but every time he posted something it would last less than a day before disappearing. He felt powerless, and was often almost overcome by the urge to scream as he read what was being said about him. He did not know who these people were, and had no way of getting in touch with them. He could only watch helplessly as the blog pages grew longer and more animated with each day; soon all this chatter about his property deals would be in the newspapers. Once it became public the project would be doomed – none of the officials who had been expensively recruited to help facilitate matters would be willing to support his bid openly.

Frustrated by the lack of news, his father rang him on his mobile one evening, catching him by surprise. He tried to explain that it was not his fault, that things in China moved so quickly that it was impossible to anticipate every development in advance. It wasn't like Indonesia or Singapore; China was at once lawless and unbending in its rules. He talked and talked, his speech cut to ribbons by his cough; he felt the dryness of his throat and mouth and realised he hadn't drunk anything for hours. His father listened patiently and then said, 'I see. But I know you will make a success of this deal.'

Soon he was spending all night monitoring the blog site. Sleep evaded him; it was superfluous to his current state. All that seemed relevant to his life now was this torrent of words written by unseen, unknown people. He felt he knew them now, felt he was somehow linked to them, and just before the first of the comments citing him by name appeared, he had a strange presentiment in his stomach, a sensation of exhilaration mixed with nausea, as if he knew what was to come. *Justin Lim has been trained by his family to be uncaring and ruthless. From a young age he was already displaying these tendencies. Justin Lim is a wolf in sheep's clothing, he smiles to your face but is ready to eat you up whole. Justin Lim is handsome but like all handsome men cannot be trusted one inch. Justin Lim is a man with absolutely no feelings whatsoever, he does not possess a beating heart. Justin Lim is not human. Justin Lim has committed some terrible acts in the past. Justin Lim will stop at nothing to fulfil his aims, he will crush you like he crushes insects.*

His father began to ring him more frequently – every other day, then every day, then several times a day. Each time the phone rang he could sense his father's anxiety in the ringtone, swelling with every beat. At first he made excuses – he was just going into a meeting, he couldn't speak. But then he stopped answering the calls altogether, letting the phone ring on to the voicemail; he never checked his messages. He stopped going to the office, for there was nothing left to do now except look at the things people said about him on the blog site. He never strayed far from his laptop, and even if he had to go to the toilet he hurried back as quickly as possible. Taking a shower made him anxious, made him fear that he was missing a new comment on the blog.

One night he managed two hours' sleep. It had made him groggy but strangely lucid, and his head filled for a moment or two with a painful awareness of the weakness of his body. He went into the bathroom and stepped onto the scales out of curiosity: he had lost even more weight. He splashed his face with water and looked in the mirror. His eyes were sunken and dark, glassy and staring, like a fish's at the market, his lips chapped and sore: a simulation of life. When dawn broke he packed a few things into a suitcase and checked into a hotel. From there he rang a friend of a friend of a friend who referred him to an estate agent who found him an apartment within three days. It was just off the Bund, on the edge of Suzhou Creek, in an Art Deco building that seemed semi-derelict. The rooms were large and sombre and quiet, the furniture sparse and nondescript; outside, the corridors were badly lit and deserted. He moved in late that afternoon, and when night fell he discovered that he had a view of the skyscrapers of Lujiazui, framed in the sweep of old windows that ran the length of the apartment. From this side of the river, the opposite to the one on which he had lived previously, the towers of Pudong seemed beautiful and untouchable. Before, they had been functional and dull, filled with ballrooms and boardrooms, each one indistinguishable from the others; now they trembled with life, intimate yet unknowable.

That night, his first in the apartment, he slept almost all the way through to the morning. His new bedroom was cavelike in its darkness, and he could hear nothing except the vague metallic creaking of pipes in the night, a comforting faraway echo. It was the first proper sleep he had had in over two months. When he woke up he looked at the mounting number of messages and emails on his BlackBerry. He turned it off without looking at any of them and went back to sleep.

In the days that followed he spent much of his time in bed. Often he would not be able to sleep, his mind completely empty, his body alternating between aching and numb. Sometimes he was afraid he was going mad. He had never been like this before, and the thought of madness panicked him. Yet he could do nothing about it. He lay in bed with the curtains drawn during the day, feeling the dampness of his sheets as he sheltered in his lightless room. At night he would open the curtains and watch the lights of the skyscrapers glinting until he began to recognise their rhythms, the exact hour they would come on or off, when they became brighter and how long it took for each sequence to repeat. When he had stared at these repeating patterns long enough they became abstract, divorced from the real world. Once or twice he felt strong enough to venture out for a stroll along the creek, and sometimes he was compelled to go out to buy drinking water from the convenience store down the road, but the slightest effort weakened him, filling him with a sickening anxiety. He longed for the safety of his bed, and decided not to leave the apartment again. He had his meals delivered to him once a day, deposited at the door. He would sometimes hear the doorbell at lunchtime but could not summon the energy to get up until the evening, when it was dark. The bag of food would still be on the doormat, cold and unappealing. Twice a week his *ayi* would come to clean the apartment, and from behind his closed bedroom door he would hear her gently moving the furniture and washing the dishes. He told her he was sick. She said, 'I guessed that.' One day he emerged from his bedroom to find that she had double-boiled a chicken with medicinal herbs to make soup for him. He sat before it at the kitchen counter, unable to eat it. He found himself crying – hot streams of tears flowed down his cheeks. He hated crying and didn't know why he was doing so. The strangest thing was that he felt nothing – no sadness or bitterness or loneliness. And yet he was unable to stem the tears.

He felt the walls of the apartment draw in on him, encircling him, making everything beyond their confines seem irrelevant, reducing the city to a mere idea, a vague memory.

Late one sleepless night, the hundreds of messages on his BlackBerry did not seem so terrifying, so he began to work his way through the emails and voicemails, deleting most before getting to the end of them. There were dozens of messages from his family – his uncles, father and brothers – whose title headings charted a growing sense of worry. It was fine, he thought: he was immune to their anxiety now. A few weeks ago he would have been panicked by their panic, but now none of it touched him. It no longer bothered him that he was uncontactable.

But among the more recent messages, one caught his attention: a voicemail from his mother, who rarely rang him. It began calmly, saying they missed him, and whatever wrongs they might have committed against him, would he please forgive them. They needed him now, he was the only one who could save them, his brother was not good at this sort of thing. His father had become very ill because of the situation, and there were creditors hovering like vultures. She sounded as if she was beginning to cry: she didn't understand this sort of thing very well, but she knew the situation was very grave.

The situation. What situation? He checked earlier emails from his father. His tone was, as always, dry, the messages dictated and typed out by his secretary. There was no unnecessary information, just the basics: the family insurance business had collapsed. It had not withstood the global crisis. The biggest, oldest insurance firm in South-East Asia, founded by his grandfather, was no longer. Now an investor was offering them $1 to buy the entire company that, just a year ago, was worth billions. It was humiliating. They were facing ruin. He was their only hope. Maybe the property market in China would save them. Whatever the case, he had to take over the running of the entire family business now.

One other message he checked said, simply, Where are you, my son?

He turned off his BlackBerry and stared at the skyscrapers. It was after midnight, and most of the lights were off now, but still the buildings glowed softly. He went to bed without drawing the curtains, gazing at the watery quality of the sky, the swell of the low rainclouds illuminated by the fading lights of the city. He tried to feel something – anything. In his head he replayed his mother's tearful voice, cracking, weak. *We're sorry for things we might have done.* He imagined his father, proud even in his humbled state.

But none of those images and sounds moved him. He felt nothing. As he closed his eyes he could just make out the very tip of a skyscraper, a sharp rod stretching into the sky. It seemed fixed not just in space but in time, its metallic glint impervious to the passing of the days, months, years.

And he thought, I am free now.

How to Achieve Greatness

Greatness is never measured purely in terms of money. You must always remember this. For history to judge a man as truly remarkable, that man has to leave a legacy more profound than a collection of Swiss bank accounts for his children. He has to enrich the world around him in a way that is permanent and *moving*.

Recently I have been thinking of ways to leave behind something meaningful to the world once I am gone. My various philanthropic efforts are well documented, but I nonetheless feel that I have not yet given enough to mankind. All my donations to charity are, I feel, ephemeral; the giving of cash to the needy is a mere Band-Aid on a gaping wound. If I were to die tomorrow I would be known primarily as a visionary entrepreneur and perhaps a brilliant motivator. Occasionally at public events someone will realise who I am and insist on bathing me in compliments, which embarrasses me, for I have always scrupulously avoided the public eye. Adulation is a funny thing. Most people seek it in vain, often unconsciously, from their spouses, children, professional colleagues, or – the ultimate dream – from the public at large. To be admired by people who don't know you would seem to be the summit of human achievement. Yet those of us who are in this position know that to be the centre of attraction in this way is not only distasteful, it is empty.

Once, and only once, I gave an interview. I was young and just beginning to make waves with a succession of audacious acquisitions. I was also, I admit, slightly prone to vanity in those days. My interviewer, a young woman from a respected local newspaper, peppered me with banal questions about my business strategy and then probed me with inappropriate questions about my private circumstances. Did I find it difficult to sustain relationships because of my punishing schedule? What did I look for in a partner? Was it true that I was so dedicated to my work that I had broken off not one but two engagements in the past? Had I even cut off contact with close family members? What about rumours that I'd changed my name to make myself appear more Westernised? She kept calling me 'Walter', in that familiar way that young people do these days, assuming it would be fine to address me by my first name rather than as 'Mr Chao'. I asked if it was truly necessary to obtain this information from me. She shrugged and said that her editor had asked her for a 'personal angle' to the story. So incensed was I by this intrusion that I ordered the feature article to be reduced to a mere footnote in the business pages. Then, as an afterthought, I asked for even that little vignette to be deleted altogether. (There is a postscript to this because, a few years ago, when the newspaper was ailing, I bought it and fired the editor who had commissioned the interview. He was in his sixties and ready for retirement anyway.)

I have never done anything for the sake of public acclaim. Even my books have been written under a pseudonym. I want to inspire people – *you* – not because I seek gratitude or glory but because I gain immense pleasure just from the knowledge that I might have been able to help them, to change their lives. Giving without receiving. That is what truly satisfies me. In all the years of working hard, of the accumulation of huge wealth, I admit that I sometimes lost sight of this sentiment of charity, which is why I sometimes felt exhausted and dispirited and negative – as I suspect you do on occasion after a long, fruitless day at work. Maybe your boss has not acknowledged your talent and dedication. Maybe your clients are late in paying you. Maybe the taxman is being uncooperative. Maybe a colleague you thought was a friend is now brown-nosing his way ahead of you. Maybe you've come home after a nightmarish day in the office and your partner hasn't done the washing up or made you dinner. Yes, it is dispiriting. But only if you are working only for yourself, if you are seeking *praise*. Let go of this neediness. Say to yourself: I am not working for glory, but for the joy of it. One day – soon – I will be dead, and who will remember my petty little promotion to Assistant Executive Managing Sub Director then?

Work to help others.

Elevate yourself from trivia.

That is the only way to true greatness.

All this brings me to the question of how best to leave my legacy without being thrust into the limelight. It is sad that even philanthropy these days is tied to celebrity, but I have to accept that this is the world we live in. Reluctantly, therefore, I might have to accept the accolades that will surely accompany my project. There are still many details to be ironed out before I can announce the nature of this venture, but for now I can reveal that it will be a sort of community centre for the twenty-first century that will benefit the young, the poor – all those who need nourishment, either for their stomachs or their minds or spirits.

The idea comes to me because, looking back at my own underprivileged childhood, I realise that the village school I attended between the ages of six and twelve carried an importance far beyond its modest proportions. Its three classrooms and tin roof were typical of primary schools in rural Malaysia at the time, but it was supported by wealthy benefactors, which meant that we had generators to power the ceiling fans and provide lighting during the monsoons when the storms were at their fiercest and the feeble electricity supply most vulnerable to power cuts. There was a paved lane leading to it from the main road that carved its way through the jungle, and at the confluence of the two there was a bus shelter so that we could remain dry from the rain while waiting for the bus that came by only three times a day. I was lucky, for my journey beyond where the bus deposited me was only twenty minutes long, on paths that rarely flooded. Others had over an hour to walk across muddy terrain with tracks that often got washed out by the rain.

None of us was ever earmarked for greatness. From birth, we were the also-rans in life's great race, kept afloat because we were human and someone – thank God – could not bear to let us wither away and die. So rich people paid for us to have the basics, salving their consciences, thinking that they were doing the bare minimum and nothing more. They never thought that their small acts of mercy would ever produce anything remarkable. They did not believe that amongst those they had written off as menial and pathetic and worthy only of pity, there would be one who would rise to glory.

Some might say that my beginnings are irrelevant, that wherever I came from, a man like me would still have been a success. Who I am today cannot be attributed to that little school. But that would be ungenerous, and I wish to acknowledge those early days, because when I look back at them I feel something. Not much, but a small debt of gratitude nonetheless.

Despite the charitable nature of its aims, my project will not be modest. It will not be a modern version of the old village school. Its reach will be wide and deep and long-lasting. A hundred years from now, its beneficial impact should still be felt. Every venture needs a physical space, its own village school, as it were. I think I know where mine will be situated – I've drawn up a shortlist of cities – and I am in the process of considering a suitable architect. At the moment I am veering towards Rem Koolhaas, or perhaps Zaha Hadid. Someone iconic, in any case, whose work, like mine, will last well into the future.

When planning any venture, always think of how it will be remembered by future generations.

Always think of how *you* will be remembered.

3

惊天动地

Bravely Set the World on Fire

Gary won a talent competition when he was two months short of his seventeenth birthday. It was a small provincial affair in the north of Malaysia, not very professional, but it enabled him to move down to the capital to take part in a bigger contest which was televised on all the main channels. The finale was watched by nearly four million people, and over two million voted by SMS. At the time, Gary was amazed by these figures. He came from a town of two hundred, and could not believe that so many people would ever listen to him sing. He performed three songs, one in Malay, one in Mandarin, and the final one in English – an arrangement of a Diana Ross song, the words of which he did not fully understand. He was the youngest contestant and was shining with the innocence of a boy recently arrived from the countryside. His hair was spiky and dyed with flame-coloured streaks, which he had done himself. Recently he saw a video of this performance on YouTube and could not believe how bad he looked.

After the first song the judges said he had the voice of an angel. But even before that, from the moment he opened his mouth to sing the very first note, he knew he was going to win. He heard the strange, pure sound of his voice amplified by the microphone in the vast auditorium, its echoes separated by a split second from the time he felt it in his throat. He recognised that the voice was his, but he felt distanced from it too. It sounded as if it no longer belonged to him. In the audience, young girls were waving multi-coloured fluorescent batons that glowed in the dark. When he sang the love ballad in Mandarin everyone screamed as he hit the high notes in the chorus. He felt the noise they made reverberating in his chest and ribcage, and he knew in that instant that his life was going to become confused and messy, full of privileges and sorrows he hadn't asked for.

He won by a landslide.

He did not have time to celebrate his victory because he was signed up by an artist-management company that arranged for him to go to Taiwan two weeks later. He stayed in a hotel with a bath-tub in which he had his very first bubble bath. The furniture was modern and new, with clean lines and leather upholstery. The room smelled of paint, but he thought it was extremely luxurious. Now he realises, of course, that it was only a modest and functional hotel used by sales companies wanting somewhere cheap to hold their training conferences. These days, Gary only stays in the most exclusive hotels in every city he visits.

In just under eight years in Taipei he released four albums, each of which sold more than three million copies across Asia. In the months following the release of his debut album, *Rainy Day in My Heart*, he narrowly missed out on winning the Best Newcomer category at the Golden Melody Awards, and starred in a film as an apprentice cop who ends up accidentally shooting the gangster girl he has fallen in love with. The film was a total failure at the box office, but everyone who saw it remarked that Gary's face was perfectly proportioned, beautiful to look at from every angle. Maybe you saw it too and came to the same conclusion. Teenage girls began to send him presents – designer clothes, jewellery, watches, home-made CDs, cards with photos stuck to them, and even highly personal items, such as the girls' own underwear or antiques that had belonged to their families. Every week his record company would receive enough of these gifts to fill a room. He would stare at this unwanted pile and feel guilty that so many fans wanted to give him such valuable things. He could not bear the thought that all these people, whom he did not know, were thinking of him. They were thinking of him so much that they would spend time and money sending him objects that represented parts of their lives – of themselves. And he felt bad because he was not strong or big or deep enough to accept their love. The record company arranged for it all to be donated to charity or simply destroyed, but still he could feel their desire for him lingering over him like a raincloud on a muggy day, refusing to budge.

Early last year, on the eve of a major concert at the Taipei Arena, Gary collapsed and was admitted to hospital. The diagnosis was not serious – he was anaemic, which explained not only his famously pale complexion but his frequent dizzy spells. He was also found to have low blood pressure and an elevated cholesterol level for someone so young. It was all the takeaway curries, the pizzas and other junk food he ate during late-night sessions in the recording studio. His punishing work schedule exacerbated these underlying conditions, and it was no surprise that he eventually succumbed to the pressure, the doctors said. They prescribed a fortnight's complete rest, some supplements, and a balanced diet. Before he left, one doctor asked him if he was *stressed*. When Gary appeared somewhat confused by the question, the doctor posed it again, this time asking whether he found it difficult to deal with the pressures he had placed upon himself and whether, for example, he worried about things beyond his control. Gary thought for a few seconds before truthfully answering no. Because when he stopped for that moment to consider his life, he realised that there was nothing in it that was within his control. Every minute of his day was organised by his management company, even the number of hours he should sleep. It had been like this for so long that he wondered if he had ever known a different way of living.

The press was full of hysterical reports. Some said he had fallen ill from toxins ingested while eating moray eel down on the coast, some said he had suffered an overdose, others said he had AIDS. He had not been seen in public or been photographed by the paparazzi for only five days when one tabloid newspaper began to surmise that he was dead. From his apartment he peered cautiously out between the metallic slats of the blinds and saw a group of teenage fans holding a vigil for him. At night they lit candles and huddled together to console each other. In daylight, he could see that some of them had been crying. He wished they would go away, and after two days he began to resent them. Their presence weighed down on him, and he couldn't sleep. He longed to be free of his apartment, which he hated even at the best of times. He had become used to having the blinds down all the time – from the moment he moved in, he had never seen the apartment in daylight, not even for one minute. It was always night in his home.

What most bothered him was the lack of activity. He wasn't used to having time on his hands. Now that he was rested and feeling better he could not stand the hours spent watching DVDs or Korean TV dramas. He tried strumming tunes on his guitar or tinkling on the piano, but the apartment was too dark and oppressive, and he could feel no enthusiasm for music. He began spending too much time on the internet, on websites he shouldn't have been looking at. In fact, it was during this period of imprisonment that he first discovered sexually explicit sites. At first he hated himself for trawling endlessly through them, but he was surprised at how his initial feelings of wariness and guilt soon gave way to an unthinking numbness, and he would spend hours sitting in the semi-dark staring at images that were initially shocking but quickly became dull. He would fall asleep at odd hours because he could not stop sifting through the pages for new images of graphic sexual acts, even though he felt nothing when he looked at them. He went to bed feeling empty and full of anger at his fans outside, for they were the ones who had forced him into this position.

Finally his management company called a press conference at which Gary appeared, happy and smiling, saying that he had taken some time off to return to Malaysia to spend time with friends and family following a 'sad occurrence' which he would rather not discuss in public. Relieved that he was alive and in good health, his fans did not press any further, assuming that his temporary disappearance was somehow linked to the fact that he was an orphan, raised by distant relatives with whom he had enjoyed no closeness. His troubled youth following the death of his mother was well documented – it was something that made him appear human and vulnerable to his fans. As his manager once told him, his childhood tragedies were a great selling point. But though he was grateful for his fans' loyalty and adoration, when he looked at the mass of jubilant teenage faces at his next concert, he found their joy so empty and unquestioning that it unnerved him, and he could not get rid of the feeling that had entered his soul during the ten days of confinement in his night-dark apartment. It was unmistakable. He had started to hate them.

That three-week period of internment and difficult public relations upset his tightly packed schedule and cost him in many ways. Not only was the cancelled concert an expensive write-off, but the negative publicity surrounding his sudden and mysterious disappearance caused several projects to be suspended, and one or two sponsors even doubted whether they should continue to support him. His calendar became compressed to the point where he could not fulfil his obligations, and his scheduled participation in the Beijing Olympics music video was cancelled, depriving him of a chance to be seen widely by the biggest audience of them all.

Now he had to work twice as hard to penetrate the Mainland market, his management team said. Everything they did over the coming year would be geared towards establishing him in China – every song he recorded, every TV show he appeared on, every commercial he shot, every hour he slept, every meal he ate. He had everything it took to be a superstar in China, but it would be hard. He had to be ready to sacrifice everything. Gary thought about all the things he had already sacrificed – friends, a social life, family commitments, love, relationships. And he was not at all frightened by what he was about to embark on, because he had none of the things that people normally hold dear. He had nothing to sacrifice.

The giant billboards that stood along the elevated highway bore the poster announcing Gary's ground-breaking concert in Shanghai. *Music Angel has arrived! The Angel of Music is here to save us* … His image was spread across each billboard, his newly gym-toned torso showing through a shirt that had been strategically slashed to display his abdominal muscles, the result of eight months' work with a personal trainer. His head was bowed to show off his thick black hair, that looked slick with sweat, and computer trickery had provided him with a giant pair of angel wings, giving the impression that he was landing gently on earth after a celestial journey. It was impossible to miss these posters. As his car drove him along the busy highway, he reckoned that they appeared every couple of miles, each time positioned in the middle of a cluster of three billboards. On one side of him there was a young woman dressed only in underwear, her index finger to her lips, which were pursed in a hushing shape; on the other side were washing machines and refrigerators.

He had just performed a sell-out concert in Wuhan which had been widely covered in the local press and gained enormous publicity for his principal sponsors, a soft-drink company. They had shot a TV commercial to coincide with his tour, a big-budget production involving sophisticated computer graphics, in which the Angel Gary flies over a devastated landscape defeating gruesome monsters by shining a light that emanates from his heart. As Gary flutters softly to earth, the desert around him turns lush and green. *The power to turn darkness to light*, he whispers, looking at the camera with his trademark sideways glance before taking a sip of soda.

It was remarked within the industry and by the public alike that Gary was looking great. After many months of limited public appearances, during which he was rarely photographed, he had unveiled his new image – muscular and with a streak of danger. He was still boyish and innocent-looking, but his presence now carried a faint physical threat, as if he had a dark side to him. His stylists and costume designers were showered with praise, as were the people at the record company who had devised the new marketing strategy.

'Thank goodness we invested so much in your gym work,' his agent said as they drove past the fifth billboard. 'Your physical condition is crucial. We can't afford to have a repeat of Taipei last year.'

Gary did not answer. As usual, the previous night's concert had left him both exhausted and unable to sleep. It was always like this. The adrenalin of the performance would rush through his veins, and he would feel the deep pounding of the bass notes reverberate in his chest and ribcage hours after the concert had ended, when he was lying in bed trying to sleep. Every tiny light in the room – the green numbers showing the time on the DVD player, the red dot on the TV set – seemed noon-bright and blinding even when his eyes were closed. Often he would just sit in front of the TV with the remote control in his hand, staring at the black screen. He could not even summon enough enthusiasm to turn it on. Sometimes he would eventually fall asleep at around three or four o'clock, but often he would just count the hours until dawn, which would come as a relief, because daylight brought with it activity, and he would not have to sit alone with only his thoughts for company.

In Wuhan the night before, he had tried to surf the internet for the porn sites he had become addicted to, but had failed. That was the problem with China – he could not access any of his usual sites. It had become a late-night ritual for him: turning on his laptop and idly searching for new, more dangerous sites each time. He did this after work or a concert, when he was alone in his apartment or hotel room and the night ahead seemed very long. He was not even excited by these sites any more; they had simply become something like a calming reassurance after a long day. Even the nastiest failed to provoke any response from him. The moment he arrived on the Mainland, however, he was deprived of this source of comfort. He had spent several frustrating hours after the concert searching for the kind of hard-core images he was used to, but the best he could find were women who, though immodestly dressed, wore more than the models he was now seeing on billboards in Shanghai. So he had opened the mini-bar and drunk all the vodka in it, and when he finished he rang to order some more.

Drinking was a recent thing. It helped him sleep, that was all.

He had now been on the road for sixteen days, and in that time he had played fourteen concerts.

'But, Little Brother,' his agent continued, 'you need to sleep. I don't know what you are doing at night – probably chasing girls, I suppose – but we need to do a lot of public appearances, and you can't wear your sunglasses all the time. The photoshoots, they're OK because we can always adjust the photos later, but in public – that's different. You know what these Shanghainese are like. They will scrutinise your appearance to the very last detail! Please remember what a huge investment we have made for this album – who else gets concerts like the one you've just had? Don't waste this opportunity.'

Gary adjusted his sunglasses. They were becoming his trademark – oversized black plastic shades that gave him a mysterious, futuristic appearance.

'We can't say no to the press conferences and guest appearances at malls. You have to look good, Little Brother. To be honest, at the moment even our make-up artists are saying it's hard to disguise the shadows under your eyes. If we send you out wearing too much make-up these Shanghainese will laugh out loud. They're haughty and not easily impressed like provincial Chinese, you know. Hey, Little Brother, are you paying attention? Shanghai is at your feet. You can be one of the biggest stars in China, you're almost there! We have two days to charm them before your concert.'

As his agent spoke Gary knew that sleep would be impossible that night. He tried to remember when he had last slept through the entire night and woken up feeling refreshed and free of worries. It did not seem as if there had ever been such a time. He could fall asleep easily on planes and in cars, and have uncomfortable fifteen-minute naps, but night-sleep was unattainable.

That evening, when he had finished the last round of press obligations, Gary went back to his hotel. He promised his agent that he would have a bath and a massage and go straight to bed, but of course he turned on his laptop instead and began to search idly for sites that did not load properly. He did not feel like drinking on his own while continuing a frustrating search for internet porn, so he took a cab to the Bund, where he knew the high-end Western bars were located. Going out in public, unaccompanied, just before a concert, was contrary to all the advice he had ever received, but he thought that if he went to a place frequented only by Westerners he might not be recognised. His guess proved to be correct. He found a place with a view of the wide sweep of the river and the skyscrapers of Pudong. Although the music was loud and the bar was evidently popular, it was large enough to have plenty of darkened nooks and comfortable chairs from which Gary could sit and watch the crowd of foreigners, some of whom were dancing in the spaces between the tables. They were heavy-footed and big-thighed, their buttocks clattering into chairs and occasionally upsetting the drinks of passers-by. He ordered several unfamiliar cocktails that turned out to be too sweet, and then changed to vodka. He kept his baseball hat on, having decided that the sunglasses would be too ostentatious. It was a relief for him to be away from his hotel room, to hear music that he did not have to perform to. For at least two hours he sat near a window, quietly sipping his drinks. He felt his cheeks flush with the alcohol and his temples begin to throb, but it did not matter – at least he was not alone in the oppressive silence of his hotel room.

His discomfort began when he noticed a few of the Chinese waiters huddling together and whispering. They were trying to hide their curiosity, but could not resist glancing at him. He did not want to leave the bar. It was not yet one o'clock and there were too many hours of darkness left ahead of him. And then the pleasant Australian couple sitting near him – who had just been holding hands and kissing – left, and their place was taken by a sweaty Western man who tried to engage Gary in conversation. The man was drunk, but Gary did not feel like moving from his spot. Soon the man would grow tired and leave him alone.

'What's the matter, cat got your tongue? Don't feel like speaking, eh? Jeez, you Chinese are so goddamn unfriendly. Hey, *look at me* when I talk to you.'

Gary looked around. The bar was full and there was nowhere to move to.

'Hey, I'm *talking* to you.'

Gary turned and said, 'Fuck off.'

The reports that began to appear the following morning were full of inaccuracies as usual, and there were conflicting accounts from bystanders as to who had started the ensuing altercation, what it had been about, who had taken the first swing. What was in no doubt was that Gary had swiftly lost control and knocked the other man off his feet, even though he was heftily built. The internet was full of photos taken with camera phones – grainy and badly lit, but clearly showing Gary standing over the man with his fist raised. The now-infamous video – again captured on a mobile phone and freely available on YouTube the next day – shows Gary swaying and unsteady on his feet, then bouncing up and down like a boxer ready for a fight before stumbling towards the man on the ground and aiming a casual kick to his midriff as if toe-poking a football. When the man shouts out an inarticulate insult, Gary attempts to pick up a bar stool, presumably to attack him with it. But the stool is fixed and doesn't budge, so Gary turns his attention to a signboard that says *WOW!* and rips it off the wall. When some of the waiters attempt to restrain him he fights them off and shouts, *Don't touch me. Do you know who I am? Do you know who I am?* The camera wobbles and cuts out, and when it begins to play again Gary is seen surrounded by a group of consoling strangers. The rest of the bar is emptying and the music has stopped. His head is in his hands and his shoulders are heaving up and down as he sobs. In the grey-pink half-light of the video, he is briefly seen in profile, silhouetted against what seems to be a curtain made from shimmering glass beads that look almost electric in the way they sparkle. Although it is dark and his face is not properly lit, his features are unmistakable – the perfect straight nose that ends in a delicate point, the soft angle of the jaw, the hair that falls over his brow. His head is bowed, his shoulders hunched and defeated. It is this image that graces the cover of all the tabloid newspapers the following evening.

4

往事如烟

Forget the Past,
Look Only to the Future

That morning's emails bore no shocks, only positive developments. These days there were no longer any brutish demands from creditors or feeble excuses from non-paying clients, and the daily ritual of replying to emails each morning had become a pleasurable affair for Yinghui, to be carried out at an almost leisurely pace over a cappuccino. There were, amongst other upbeat messages, an invitation to the opening of a new hotel on the river in Shiliupu and an interesting proposition from someone wanting to build a carbon-neutral cultural centre in the middle of town. New contacts and possibilities revealed themselves nowadays without her even having to seek them out. What a change, she thought, as she finished her coffee.

Business was going well for Yinghui. The two upmarket lingerie stores she'd established were flourishing, and in little more than a year she had broken even and was now watching the profits accumulate, week by week, the spreadsheets filling out with handsome-looking figures bursting with promise. Occasionally, when she glanced at the documents her breathless accountant showed her, she ceased to take note of the substantial numbers, for their trajectory was so steep that she had difficulty imagining where they would take her twelve months hence. And yet she was not a person with a modest imagination – quite the opposite.

Her ad campaigns had been striking and wildly successful. She had used only Chinese models, never mixed-race ones, and they never flaunted their bodies in an overtly sexual way. Although they did display a good deal of bare skin, the models were styled beautifully, and the overall aesthetic was classy rather than trashy. The catchy taglines were mysterious and playful, like the images themselves.

Elegant Outside, Passionate Inside
Secret Exciting
Amazing Beautiful You

Although she had originally thought that the shop would cater mainly to the wives of high-ranking party officials and low-profile billionaires who wanted a discreet custom service, Yinghui soon found a huge demand amongst ordinary professional women who were willing to spend upwards of four hundred *yuan* for the simplest bra. The low lighting and shadowy spaces of the stores, together with the women-only entry policy and touches of luxury such as the Venetian chandeliers created an ambience that proved incredibly popular, with many clients lingering on the plush sofas, and leafing through the glossy magazines and catalogues as they chatted and decided what else to purchase. Before long Yinghui had taken over the adjoining shops and added a coffee bar in one store and a wine bar in the other, extending the opening hours and turning both venues into destinations in their own right. The lingerie was all but removed from the store itself and transferred into specially designed semi-private 'modelling rooms', and the newly vacated space was now filled with stylish mannequins, artwork, and giant floral displays.

The income and publicity generated by the two stores made it possible for Yinghui to seek business partners for new ventures on a much larger scale, and her financial projections were such that banks were suddenly willing to listen to her requests for loans. Her plans for expansion included a chain of small shops in metro stations, which would sell the basic Amazing Beautiful You range; twelve shops selling clothes for teenage girls called FILGirl (Fly in Love Girl); an internet-based cosmetics brand called Shhh … aimed at women over the age of forty; and a luxury spa modelled on a northern Thai village, the construction of which was nearing completion.

These exciting ventures made people in the retail industry take notice of Yinghui, and the expatriate community was especially interested to learn that a foreigner was able to negotiate the complex world of Chinese retail. She began to give talks to the various foreign Chambers of Commerce, speaking to budding entrepreneurs about the pressures of being a foreigner and a woman in a male-dominated world. As she became more visible she did an interview with the *Shanghai Daily* – a brief article, nothing more – in which she was asked to reveal the key to her success at a time when many businesses were experiencing difficulties due to the global recession.

'I smile every day while coolly evaluating my business model,' she replied, smiling coolly. 'I remain 100 per cent optimistic even in a crisis while being decisive enough to act as required.'

Was she ruthless? the interviewer asked.

'Sure,' she said. 'You have to be tough to succeed.'

Even as she said it she regretted the way she sounded – matter-of-fact, unthinking, as if nothing bothered her. She tried immediately to laugh and find common ground with the interviewer, a young woman in her mid-twenties. But as Yinghui joked about things in the news – celebrity gossip, cute pop singers, the latest films – she could feel the journalist withdrawing behind the safety of a polite smile, the gulf between them widening. She felt old, her laugh sounded fake and robotic; the girl merely smiled and listened as Yinghui's jokes became more and more risqué.

That interview sealed her growing reputation in more ways than one. Her image hardened into this: a bold businesswoman, certainly; but also a super-efficient, humourless automaton who would coldly plunge a knife into you, but she wouldn't bother to do it in your back, she'd stick it in your chest. She saw this written in a 'joke' email circulating in her office, copied to her by mistake. Ultrawoman, Dragon Queen, Terminatress, Rambo – these were some of the nicknames she discovered as she scrolled down the email chain, which was full of comments on her boring suits and severe hairstyle – 'like a rural Party official dressed for an interview with Hu Jintao', someone joked. Some months later, at a cocktail party thrown by an American law firm, she heard one Western man say to another, 'Hey, look, there's that Chinese lesbian.'

She had got used to having her hair short – it had been her style for almost twenty years, ever since university days. There was a time when people found the look charming and gamine, like Jean Seberg in *À Bout de Souffle*, from which Yinghui first got the idea. She didn't think she'd changed much since then – she didn't look very different from the Yinghui she saw whenever she looked at her college photos – but she wondered if she was getting a bit old for the hairstyle now. No woman in Shanghai had short hair – they all seemed to have long glossy locks that fell to their shoulders or were gathered in a dramatic pile on their heads in the style of air hostesses. She began to grow her hair out, but was frustrated by how long it took. At first it became thin and shabby, like a scarecrow's, then thicker but still messy, like a schoolboy's. When, finally, it reached a decent length, her hairdresser said, 'Don't expect me to perform miracles.'

She began to dread the social functions that were becoming an increasing necessity in her professional life: a thrusting entrepreneur had to go out and be seen, but a single, always unaccompanied woman of thirty-seven was, in Shanghai, an invitation for people to comment. The locals had names for women like her, whom they considered sadly past their prime. *Shengnü, Baigujing* – that sort of thing. Sometimes she wondered if she really was that: a leftover woman, the dregs; or a shaggy monster waiting to be slain by the Monkey God.

'Style issues.' That was the phrase her friends used to describe what her new priorities should be. She needed to find a look that projected an image: someone effortlessly successful, who had accomplished all that she had while remaining gentle and feminine – a real Chinese woman. She wanted to ask what a real Chinese woman was, whether in some way she differed from a real Indian woman or a real American woman. And if she wasn't a real Chinese woman, what was she – a fake one?

These new concerns – *style issues* – were not a welcome addition to her list of considerations. She woke every morning at 6 a.m., had a glass of fruit juice, then went for a forty-five-minute run on the treadmill. After a breakfast of soy protein and mixed berry fruitshake she would head down to the office and begin to deal with phone calls and emails before the first meetings began to force their way into her day. In a city where lunch breaks began religiously at 11.30 a.m., she rarely had lunch unless she had arranged a business meeting at a restaurant. Most of the time she would work through midday and simply forget to eat. Afternoons were reserved for visiting her various businesses, spending time chatting to the staff in the stores, gauging their morale and energy levels – the little human touches that made her a good employer. The evenings were nowadays taken up with entertaining or being entertained, which she neither enjoyed nor disliked. She would get home at eleven and answer any outstanding emails on her BlackBerry while in bed, in the few moments other people might have spent reading glossy magazines to 'wind down'. At precisely midnight she would put the light out and swiftly fall asleep, rarely allowing the thoughts of her day to overspill into her slumber.

Three times a week she went for Power Yoga at a studio in Xintiandi, never speaking to the other women who had time to hang around and chat in the corridors. At the end of her session, when she lay briefly on her mat blinking at the pistachio-green ceiling, her mind would still be racing, energised by the thought of all the things ahead of her. Empty your mind and be still, her teachers would say, enjoy being in the present: *Let go of all that has happened in the past. Do not think about what lies ahead but stay in the stillness of this moment.* But this was not possible for her. There was too much for her to do, too many thoughts spinning and clashing in her mind. She needed to look ahead, map out her future, every minute of the day – like a constantly moving ocean creature that would drown if ever it stopped swimming, forward, forward.

She could never stand emptiness, and stillness was even worse.

She had a small group of friends, a mixture of local and expat women, with whom she tried to meet up for dinner once every other week – the last semblance of her dwindling social life. They usually met at a Hunan restaurant on the top floor of a Japanese department store on Nanjing Lu, not far from Yinghui's office. Recently, she had begun to notice during these get-togethers that the other women would casually mention male friends of theirs, all of whom seemed to be single or divorced and in their late thirties or early forties. Discussion of these men seemed innocent enough at first; Yinghui tried to shrug it off as merely catching up on gossip. But after a while she could no longer ignore the fact that her (securely married) friends were taking pity on her, particularly as the men in question were almost exclusively Western – for everyone knew that once a woman was past thirty-five, there was little point in even trying to hook up with a local guy: Westerners were so much more accepting of *age*.

'Are you trying to matchmake me?' she challenged them jokingly one day as the double-chilli fish head arrived. She expected them to be embarrassed by the exposure of their scheming ways, but instead they were upfront about it. 'Let's face it,' one of them said, beginning to pluck the meat from the fish cheeks with her chopsticks, 'you can't be happy in a place like Shanghai if you're single. We're all feminists, blah blah blah, but this is not London or New York, you know, this is China. Without a husband, you won't be successful in your work. You can't expect to work the hours you do and come back to an empty apartment. Besides, if you want children, you have to get moving. We know it sounds cruel, but … get real.'

Yinghui stared at the dull-eyed fish, its eyes opaque and porcelain-white. She reached for it with her chopsticks and prodded it slightly without great enthusiasm. 'I'm too busy for a relationship,' she said.

'Listen, where do you want to be in ten years' time? Still flogging panties to rich women?'

Yinghui could not hide her annoyance, but nonetheless she allowed herself to be persuaded to go on a couple of blind dates – friends of friends of friends. The first was in a Mexican restaurant near Tianzifang, the next in a Xinjiang restaurant at the far end of Hengshan Lu. On both occasions the men were polite, professionally successful, and bland. Towards the end of the second date, Yinghui decided that it would be her last. As she watched the man (Michael? Mark? A nice American lawyer) pull the leathery pieces of lamb off the skewer, she realised that she wasn't able to summon any energy to be witty or flirtatious, to behave as she knew she should on a first date with a perfectly OK man. It wasn't, as her friends claimed, that she was out of practice: she doubted she had ever known how to do so. The small talk left her feeling bewildered and exhausted, and she was constantly afraid that the conversation would turn towards more personal things, towards the past: how and why she had first come to Shanghai – the normal things foreigners asked each other. She tried to seize control of the conversation, filling it with lengthy explanations of how each dish was prepared, what bizarre Xinjiang ingredients they contained. The man listened politely and asked questions with the requisite level of cultural awareness, which made the transaction less painful for Yinghui. At one point, as she felt the evening slipping dangerously into 'Tell me about your family' territory, she changed the subject abruptly by turning to the waitress who had fortuitously arrived with more tea. She began to engage her in idle chat, hoping to glean insights on her exotic homeland, which she would then translate as conversation fillers, making it impossible for Michael/Mark to ask more personal questions. The waitress's name badge read 'Aliya' – such a beautiful Xinjiang name, Yinghui remarked; tell us about where you are from. The waitress giggled and shrugged

– she was actually from way down south, Fujian province; she wasn't an exotic Muslim at all. Mercifully, the lights suddenly dimmed for the entrance of the Uighur dancers. Yinghui was pleased that the music was loud and that the dancers yelped and shrieked all the way through their performance, for it meant that no further conversation was necessary. She smiled at Michael/ Mark, and he smiled back.

She really did not need a man to be successful.

One afternoon Yinghui left work early to get dressed for an evening function. It had not been a particularly stressful day, but she was fidgety and distracted. Hours before the event, she had begun to feel anxious; even thinking about what dress to wear and how to style her still-too-short hair made her nervous, which in turn filled her with self-loathing for having allowed such trivial concerns to enter her life.

She had been nominated for the Businesswoman of the Year awards, in the 'Breakthrough' category, in which she was the oldest person. The ceremony was held in the ballroom of a hotel in Jing'an, decorated with huge bouquets of pink flowers and banners bearing quotes from Sunzi's *Art of War*: 'Opportunities Multiply as They are Seized'; 'A Leader Leads by Example, Not Force'. The other nominees all looked the same to Yinghui – pretty, sylphlike, twenty-something local women, their hair effortlessly long, curling featherlike towards their collarbones. Yinghui wished she had been nominated for the 'Lifetime Achievement' award that was made up almost exclusively of older Western women; she might have looked more delicate and feminine lined up next to them when the group photographs were taken. Instead, surrounded by women at least ten years younger than herself, she looked square-cut and boxy. She did not win the award (which went to a girl of twenty-four who sold recycled toilet paper to Europe), but her work gained considerable publicity.

Among the guests were a few people she knew well, including one or two she considered friends, some business associates, and many others who were mere acquaintances. A man caught her eye but she couldn't figure out which category he belonged to. He had a familiar gait – stiff at the joints, the way a marionette might walk, like an arthritic soldier. He was about her age, well-groomed, impeccably dressed, deliberate in his movements: the way he shook hands, firmly, or held chairs back for women, or leant forward to kiss them on both cheeks in a courteous but professional manner – every gesture seemed elegant yet practised. He carried an air of privilege, but he was certainly not Shanghainese. He was well packaged, Yinghui thought, the right age too. The right age: she hated how she had come to assess men this way, the way they assessed her – it was a way of seeing people that had seeped into her thinking unconsciously, as if by osmosis. Right age. Good match. A real woman. Style issues. That was what happened when you lived in Shanghai. She couldn't escape it now.

She circled him from a distance, trying to work out whether she really knew him. He was wearing a light-grey suit made of a fabric with a faint herringbone pattern, a pale-blue shirt and a dark tie. His jawline was just turning from sleek to heavy. She eased her way through the throng, dodging precariously held champagne flutes, keeping him on the edge of her field of vision all the time. He was on his own now, reading a brochure, wandering away from the crowd, slowly circling the room. She moved closer, making sure he could not see her. Then, when the time was right, she turned and caught his eye. She felt a tightness in her throat, a quickening knot that threatened to turn swiftly into panic.

'Sorry – Chee Keong? Justin?'

'Yes. Leong Yinghui!' He made a movement towards her, his head leaning forwards; but then he corrected himself and extended his hand. 'Hi. My God, it's been years. I'd never have thought I'd meet you at a business event.'

'Justin Lim Chee Keong. What a surprise.' She shook his hand as firmly as she could, with a brisk up-and-down movement. She wondered if her voice sounded artificially confident, over-bright. 'How long has it been – ten years? More, perhaps.'

'I'd say at least fifteen years. Though at my age I try not to keep count. You haven't changed at all – I mean, not one bit.'

'You too,' Yinghui lied. Up close, she could see the lines drawing down on either side of his mouth, the dark circles that shadowed his slightly bloodshot eyes. His skin seemed dry and brittle. When he smiled she saw vestiges of the person she had known – a young, physical man with a full, open face. The same features were now touched with a certain hollowness, a glimpse of what he might look like as an old man. 'So what brings you to Shanghai – don't tell me, family business?'

'What else is there in my life?' His laugh was rehearsed, mechanical, and it made him seem tired, not happy. He looked at her with a neutral expression; she searched for traces of shock or surprise in his reddened eyes, but could discern nothing. 'It's a real surprise seeing you here. I was just looking at the list of nominees for the awards, and when I saw your name I thought, "No way, that can't be the same person I knew." A *businesswoman*? I never thought that was possible. Amazing.' Yinghui thought he was going to follow up with questions about her life – how she had arrived in Shanghai, the nature of her business – but he merely continued to stare at her in a blank, awkward manner, exactly the way she remembered from all those years ago.

'Stranger things happen in life,' she said, filling in the silence at last. 'It's not exactly the Virgin Birth, you know. Anyway, how is, um, how is your brother?' she asked. 'I read about CS's wedding about five, six years ago – it looked very luxurious. I knew the bride at school. She was in the year above me. And your parents, still glamorous as ever?'

'I believe all is well with them.'

'I read about your family's business in the papers – not that I was looking out for it or anything, I just read an article by chance. Things must be tough.'

He shrugged. 'It's a global crisis, isn't it? It's tough for everyone – though you seem to be doing pretty well.'

A young woman appeared at his side and slid her hand around his waist, inviting him to do the same; but she was looking away from him, towards something behind Yinghui's back. There was a sudden burst of camera flashes around them, two or three photographers taking pictures of the couple. Yinghui stepped back and watched them strike poses as they faced the cameras – he stiffly, his new companion sinuously and expertly. Yinghui recognised her from magazines she'd read in the hairdressers – a local actress on the verge of stardom. She certainly did not have *style issues*. From a distance they made a handsome couple, Yinghui thought, and she could already envisage the photos in the magazines: a perfect union of modern Chinese beauty and old overseas Chinese money. The lines of his drawn, tired face would not be visible, and the readers would only see his good cheekbones, his perfect bearing and casual elegance – the sort of thing that could only have been produced by generations of good breeding.

He turned to look at Yinghui, mouthing the word 'Sorry,' and she mouthed back, 'No problem.' She hung about for a while, wondering what to do. Should she slip away in a dignified manner without a proper goodbye, or continue waiting for him, the feeling of being superfluous mounting with every second? She had just about decided on the former when she was suddenly seized by a need to talk to him – to *tell* him things. She felt a rush of unaired grievances welling up in her chest, pushing up into her throat; the need to vocalise them took her by surprise, shocked her. She wanted to sit him down, face to face, and speak at him. She didn't need him to reply, she merely needed him to be physically present while she said her piece. He could listen passively, unabsorbingly, and she wouldn't care, but she needed to catch hold of him.

This was ridiculous, she thought, just ridiculous. It was over fifteen years ago – what did it matter now? She was an entirely different person now. The quick flash of irrational hatred that she felt for him began to subside. He was a few years older than she was, a man slipping surely into middle age; he had his own problems. She hadn't felt even the slightest bit of malicious pleasure when she had read in the financial press about his family's business going bust. She had felt almost indifferent, her emotional detachment tinged with pity – much as she was feeling now. Look at him, taking up with a trashy actress fifteen years younger than himself. It was sad. He was sad. Yinghui had barely known him in the first place.

Never let the past affect how you perform. Every day is a new day. That was something else she'd said in that defining interview, so she ought to practise what she preached. She gathered herself to leave, and as she did so she dipped into her clutch bag for her business card – she was a consummate professional, and this was a professional setting. She reached across and handed it to him with both hands.

'So sorry, but I have to rush off now. Good to see you again, a real surprise. Here's my card if ever you need to get in touch.'

He accepted it, also with both hands, and she realised that the formality between them was entirely appropriate: they were strangers to each other now. 'Wonderful,' he said, slipping the card into his pocket. 'Great. I will call you.'

But she knew, as one always does in these situations, that he would not call her.

As she sat in bed that night she allowed herself one minute to remember how Justin CK Lim and the rest of his family had looked fifteen years ago, how they had behaved.

Just one minute; and then she would put them out of her mind.

She checked her BlackBerry, scrolling through the emails that had come in that day – all the fascinating projects she was going to begin in the weeks, months and years ahead.

How to Manage Time

When I was thirteen, I was sent away to live with relatives in the far south of Malaysia, at the opposite end of the country from where I had been born. Do not be alarmed – this sort of displacement is quite normal amongst underprivileged rural families. My mother had died a few years previously and my father, unable to care for me properly, decided to ask my great-aunt to take me in. He himself had to move away from our village to seek work in Kota Bharu, where he lived in one room above a tyre repair shop. It made sense for him to be free of me.

My great-aunt lived and worked on a small pineapple farm about thirty miles north of Singapore. The peaty soil of the region was famous for producing the best pineapples in the country, but ours were an exception to the rule, being meagre in size and acidic in taste. Nothing I did seemed to improve them – not the addition of buffalo manure or even the chemical fertilisers I found on a lorry parked by the road one day (there was no one about, and far too much fertiliser for any one person to use, so I helped myself). Even at that age I found the lack of a satisfactory solution very frustrating. Why couldn't I make those pineapples big and sweet? I worked on the farm every day after school – it was my way of earning my keep and it kept me out of mischief, said my great-aunt. I do not have fond memories of this period, because it involved failure: the only failure I have encountered in my life thus far. To this day, even a brief encounter with hard, unripe pineapple (of the kind one routinely encounters on aeroplanes) is enough to send me into quite a rage.

Life in the south was not a thing of beauty. The landscape lacked the soul of the north, the wilderness, the poetry. It is surprising how one's childhood days can be troubled by the finer concerns of the spirit, filled as they are with the anxieties of youth. I was picked on at school, teased for my accent, which I was never fully able to lose – the unconscious warping of 'a's to 'e's or 'o's, the dropping of the ends of words, the addition of unfamiliar emphatic exclamations. My speech marked me out as foreign and, unsurprisingly, I became known as a quiet boy who said very little. I spent much time lurking in the background, so to speak, watching from the sidelines and never thrusting myself into the spotlight. By remaining in the shadows I learnt to observe the workings of the human psyche – what people want and how they get it. Everything that I was to achieve later in life can be traced back to this period, when I began my apprenticeship in the art of survival.

All that earnest study of the cut and thrust of life meant that I did not have time to miss home. I did not suffer from any longing for my homeland in the north, with its strange, warm dialect and its melancholy coastline scarred with brackish streams that ebbed and flowed with the tide. It is only now that I have the luxury of time and rich personal accomplishment that I can sit back and appreciate a certain sentiment for the village in which I grew up. This does not, however, mean that I am someone prone to nostalgia. I am certainly not encumbered by the past.

Like most people in our position, we lived an industrious but precarious existence. My great-aunt had worked part-time in a factory on the outskirts of Johor Baru that produced VHS players for export, but, being in her fifties, she was soon laid off and had no work other than to tend to our smallholding, and we were therefore forced to be inventive in the way we made our living. Nowadays I hear liberal, educated people refer sympathetically to such a way of life as 'hard', or even 'desperate', but I prefer to think of it as *creative*. I had just turned thirteen, and thought that if we had more money I would be able to return home.

I began selling pineapples on a disused wooden stand by the side of the road that led to the coast, hoping to ensnare day-trippers from Singapore on their way to Desaru. Knowing that our pineapples were sour, I sold them cheaply, and in the first few weeks I managed to make a little money. But even this began to dry up as people realised the low quality of my wares. So one day I bought a supersweet pineapple in the market and cut it up in pieces, offering it as proof of my own fruit's tenderness. A number of people fell for it, and only one couple complained on their way back from the coast. I feigned innocence – I couldn't guarantee that every pineapple would be sweet. They showed me a pineapple cut in half, and I recognised its dry, pale flesh as one of mine. They insisted I give them five pineapples for free, and when I refused, the woman called me names and her companion ended up hurling the pineapple at my head. I ducked but it caught me on my ear, making it swell like a mushroom. Soon afterwards I abandoned the stall and got a job waiting tables at a local coffee shop.

I did not see my father for nearly four years. I received news from him occasionally, when a letter would arrive via my great-aunt. He would write about the Kelantan river bursting its banks in the monsoon season, the kite-flying contests that year, the second-hand scooter he had bought, things he had eaten in the market – uninteresting news of daily life. Once he told me he had bought me a large spinning top which awaited my return, but when I finally went home there was no further mention of it.

There was never any news of jobs or money – the very reason we had to move away from home. There was no indication of how he was planning our future, no sense that he was aware of the passage of time. I had never been aware of this myself, but now, hundreds of miles from home, I could almost hear the seconds of an invisible clock ticking away in my head. I had gone to live with my great-aunt thinking that it was temporary, and that I would be back home as soon as my father 'got settled'. That was what he told me. After a year I realised that my residence in the dull flatlands of the south was not going to be as fleeting as I had hoped. One learns quickly at that age. Like all children, I had never before appreciated what *time* meant – the years stretched infinitely beyond me, waiting, impossibly, to be filled. But all of a sudden I began to feel the urgency of each day. I counted them down, saddened by how much I could have been doing with every sunrise and sunset, if only I had been at home.

I waited for my father to think of a plan that would reunite us in our village, but, incapable of understanding that time was not on his side, he left me waiting.

You must appreciate that time is always against you. It is never kind or encouraging. It gnaws away invisibly at all good things. Therefore, if you have any desire to accomplish anything, even the simplest task, do it swiftly and with great purpose, or time will drag it away from you.

Four years. They passed so quickly.

5

改头换面
Reinvent Yourself

T he first rule of success is, you must look beautiful. No one taught Phoebe this secret, but she could tell by simple observation that successful people always looked good. Just by looking at the women hurrying along Henan Lu, running for buses, or reading their magazines in the metro at rush hour, she could spot the few who were on life's upward curve. At first she did not really think about the connection between appearance and achievement; she could not even imagine such a link. But then she kept noticing more and more women who looked immaculate in their dress, and what's more, that they often carried bags that looked as though they contained serious life items instead of mere beauty accessories. Often, these impressive-looking women would take out papers or a book from their sleek bags and read them on the bus with an air of purpose, and even if they were reading mere novels, Phoebe could see that they were absorbing the words the way high-achieving people do. All the time working, working, in a way that was steely yet elegant. It reminded her of a girl at school who always came first in class, the way that girl read books with a determination no one else had. All the teachers said she would go on to great things, and sure enough, she got a job as a quantity surveyor in Kuantan. Gradually, Phoebe realised that the reason these women looked so beautiful was that they had good positions in life; she could not deny that the two things were inseparable. Which one came first, beauty or success, she did not know.

She started taking notes on the type of clothes they wore, how they styled their hair, even the way they walked. When she compared these to her own way of dressing and behaving, it became clear why she had not yet been able to find a decent job in Shanghai. No one would look at her and think, that woman is going to astound the world with her abilities, we should give her a job. No, she was not someone you would even look at twice on the bus, never mind give a job to.

She knew she was not a mediocre person, but she looked like one to the outside world. This was not her fault, she thought; it was also because of where she lived. Every day she was surrounded by mediocre people who dragged her down into their sea of mediocrity. She had found a room in an apartment block not far from the river, which she had thought would be beautiful and prestigious. A girl she had worked with in a mobile-phone keypad factory in Guangzhou had a childhood friend who had gone to work in Shanghai, and she had a good job working in an office. The girl's apartment was just one room, but it had a small washroom and a space to prepare simple meals. Her name was Yanyan, and in her text message she said that Phoebe could stay there for free until she got a job – surely it wouldn't be long before Phoebe found a good position. When Phoebe looked at the address she saw that it was close to the centre of town, a nice area near some famous attractions that foreign visitors loved, and by the bank of the river, about which people wrote love songs. The apartment was on the tenth floor, so she imagined magnificent views of this great metropolis that would inspire her with the spirit of high achievement. Every day she would wake up and breathe the intoxicating air of excellence.

But when she came out of the subway station she found herself in a low-class shopping centre full of small shops that sold everything in bulk – clothes, mushrooms, teapots, pink plastic hairclips, fake trainers. She stood for a minute trying to work out the right direction. In front of her was a row of shops with makeshift beds outside them – there were people stretched out on each one, getting tattoos. She walked past them, looking at the huge rose being tattooed on a man's arm, its petals reaching around his biceps; an eagle on the nape of someone else's neck; a manga kitten on a young woman's ankle. Outside, the pavement was black with grease from the dozens of stalls selling skewers of grilled meat and squid. It was hard to walk properly because of all the discarded skewer-sticks, which made her feel unstable in her heels.

In the entrance hall to the apartment block there was a cramped wooden booth where two watchmen sat, drinking tea from plastic flasks. They did not even look up when Phoebe walked in; they did not care who came into the building. The floor was pale, with a covering of dust and streaked with black marks that Phoebe could not identify, and on the walls were patches of cement where the crumbling brickwork had fallen away and been hastily filled in. The wooden noticeboards and the metal pigeon-hole letterboxes were old and had not been changed for at least fifty years – their green paint looked almost black. The place was dirtier than some of the factory hostels she had lived in. As she waited for the lift to take her up to her new life, she felt the heavy weight of dread descend upon her shoulders. There were hundreds and hundreds of apartments in the building, and only one lift, and as she waited a crowd began to gather around her, everyone pushing forward. These people were not the sort of neighbours she had imagined. She had envisaged herself surrounded by the kind of women she saw on TV, well-dressed modern Shanghainese, but instead she found a crowd of old-age pensioners dressed in revolutionary clothes, stern padded jackets and shapeless trousers that matched their expressionless faces, which seemed to have crumpled inwards. No light shone from their eyes, no feeling sprang from their gazes, and when Phoebe looked at them she felt a shiver of fear run down her neck. It was like looking at an abandoned house where everything had been kept as it was in the past, the clocks ticking, the furniture clean and shiny, the plants watered, only there was no one living there; they had long since gone away. Even the younger people seemed old and worn down by unknown cares, their clothes as uninspired as their faces.

They shuffled past Phoebe as the lift neared the ground floor, their shoulders and arms jostling her. She watched the numbers light up on the counter, and as she did so she felt as though her life was also descending: 4, 3, 2, 1. Soon it would be zero. As the lift doors opened she saw that it was tiny and filled with cigarette smoke, so she decided to take the stairs instead. She only had a small bag with her – she had learnt to travel light. Even so, she was soon out of breath because the stairs were steep and the windows that lined the stairwell were open and let in the dust and pollution from outside. There were pipes everywhere, and some of them were leaky. Where they dripped onto the floor there were crusted brown patches that looked like mushrooms sprouting from the concrete.

As she climbed the stairs she could see a giant construction site taking shape right next to the apartment block. Huge steel columns jutted out from the hole being dug for the foundations. Beyond it was a shopping centre, painted in coral pink and blue. In the daytime its neon signboard looked like scaffolding, and it was hard to read what it said: *Shanghai Liteful Fashion Shopping Market*. The signboards that covered its entire length advertised cheap clothing brands that Phoebe had never heard of, the colours gold and bright green and yellow. Nothing matched. The streets below were dark with a mass of people waiting for buses or emerging from the shopping centre – it must have been a wholesale market where you could buy anything from skirts to electronic goods to dried food very cheaply. Even from where she was she could hear the thumping of music and the cries of advertisements from loud-speakers. She paused and looked at the scene – at the thick, wriggling river of bodies so dense and colourless that it was hard to make out each individual human being. She could be anywhere in China, she thought. In fact, she could be in any no-value town in Asia. She had known so many of them, and they all looked like this.

But maybe the apartment would be nice. Maybe her view would not be of this no-place city she was now staring at; maybe she would look out at the river instead, and wake up every day to views of Shanghai.

She reached the top floor. The corridor was long, and stretched into the gloom – she could not see the end of it. There were dozens of doors, each one a separate apartment. She walked down the corridor, counting down the numbers until she found the right one.

Why are you always so doubtful? Phoebe Chen Aiping, do not allow yourself to be dragged down by your childish fears.

The door was protected by a metal grille, just like all the others. Phoebe reached between the bars and knocked on it, but there was no answer. She knocked again and waited. Perhaps Yanyan had unexpectedly been called out to an important meeting, even though she had said it was her day off. It was often like this with busy people who had important jobs; they had to respond to unpredictable events at short notice and be flexible – they were successful because they were able to deal with stressful situations using their skill and talent. The door opposite opened and an old woman peered out, glaring at Phoebe and surveying her from head to foot. Phoebe wondered how she appeared to the old woman, whether she looked acceptable, a decent upstanding person paying a visit to a friend, or whether she looked like someone with shady intentions, a potential criminal. She reached into her handbag for her phone and rang Yanyan's number. She heard a ringing on the other side of the door, and a few moments later she heard the locks being undone from the inside, three of them, heavily bolted.

'Why didn't you call out and say who you were?' Yanyan mumbled as she opened the door. 'I thought you were the man coming for the gas bill again.' She seemed sleepy, her hair was a mess, as if she had just woken up, and she was dressed in pyjamas even though it was nearly midday. She let Phoebe in and went to sit on her bed. Phoebe thought, maybe she was very tired from working hard at her important job. Yanyan was wearing fluffy slippers in the shape of smiling puppies, and her pyjamas were printed with sunny flower-faces that grinned at Phoebe. There was only one single bed in the room, and a small chair piled with clothes.

'I'm so tired,' Yanyan said, kicking off her slippers and leaning back against the wall with her knees drawn in to her body. It was true, she looked very haggard.

'You must be working very hard,' Phoebe said. She did not know what to do, whether to sit on the bed or not, so she just stood in the middle of the tiny room. Looking around, she saw a cooker on one side of the door and a washroom cubicle on the other, so small that she was not sure there was enough space to stand and have a shower between the toilet and the wall. There was almost nothing in the main room apart from a small TV balanced on some shelves that held cooking utensils and a jar of pumpkin seeds. On the wall hung one of those calendars that fast-food chains give away free of charge at the end of the year if you are lucky and are there at the right time. The pages were open at June, four months ago.

Yanyan shook her head and laughed. 'I got fired. That's why I need someone to share the rent.'

Phoebe looked out of the window and saw the same view she had seen from the stairs, the deep hole of the construction site, the broad avenue cut by concrete bridges, the multicoloured Liteful shopping centre, the masses of people dragging heavy black bags full of cheap goods – a nowhere, could-be-anywhere place.

'I know the room's a bit small,' Yanyan said, 'but we can shift that chair and the TV and roll out the mattress.' She reached underneath the bed and attempted to drag something out. Phoebe could see that it was a thin mattress rolled up and stuffed under the low bed.

'It's OK,' Phoebe said. 'We don't have to do it now.' She calculated that with the mattress rolled out, there would be about a handbag's width between it and the bed. She wondered how long ago Yanyan had lost her job, how long she had spent her days waking up at midday, how long she had let her hair get greasy and go unwashed, but it did not seem the right time to ask such questions.

Imagine your new splendid life and it will soon come true!

Phoebe thought, it would be so easy to walk out of this tiny room. She could make up an excuse and say, I'm late for an appointment, but thank you for showing me the room, I'll call you later once I've decided. But she remained standing in the middle of the room, still clutching her bag. She did not know where else to go.

'Hey, are you hungry? It must be lunchtime now,' Yanyan said, looking around at the walls as if hoping to find a clock, but there wasn't one.

Phoebe shook her head. 'Don't worry, please don't go to any trouble. I've just arrived, I don't want to inconvenience you.'

'I'm starving – let's have a simple lunch!' Yanyan insisted, and went to the cooking area. Phoebe wondered what kind of meal she would prepare. Just thinking about lunch made her realise she had not had breakfast, and suddenly she felt so hungry her stomach began to swell with an ache she had never experienced before. As she listened to the sounds of Yanyan busying herself by the stove – water from the tap drumming against the bottom of an empty kettle, the clang of steel against steel, the click-clack of chopsticks, Yanyan humming a little tune – Phoebe felt tired and in need of rest. She tried to think of the number of times someone had cooked a meal for her since she came to China, the number of times she had sat in someone's home eating a meal – but not a single instance came to mind. She sat down on the bed and found the mattress thin but firm. The window was open and she could hear the noise of the traffic, the non-stop beeping of scooters and the growl of buses. A cool wind was blowing, making the room feel airy. She looked across at Yanyan, whom she had not yet had a chance to scrutinise – a tall, thin girl, scrawny, most would say, who walked with a stoop, which was a shame because her height would have given her a striking appearance were she not rapidly turning into a young hunchback. She could be beautiful, but instead she was mediocre. Maybe she would watch Phoebe and learn how to stand upright and keep her hair neat and stylish. Phoebe looked at Yanyan's long, unwashed hair, which shrouded her cheeks messily, making her look like a child who had recently awoken from a bad dream.

'Come, come, eat,' Yanyan said, and sat down next to her. She handed Phoebe a plastic bowl of instant noodles, spicy seafood flavour. She had not torn off the wrapping properly, and when Phoebe brought the bowl to her mouth little bits of paper tickled her lips.

'Hey, look!' cried Yanyan. She held up a cheap plastic toy – a keyring with a small blue plastic cat attached to it. When she pulled at the chain the cat lifted a pair of chopsticks to its whiskery snout, greedily slurping some plastic noodles. 'It came free with the packet of noodles. Here, take it – it'll be your good-luck charm in Shanghai. It will help you get the best job in the world.'

Phoebe took the blue cat and put it in her handbag. She did not want it, but she did not want to hurt Yanyan. She stirred her noodles with her chopsticks, watching the little bits of freeze-dried vegetables slowly uncurling. They all looked the same – she couldn't tell what they were supposed to be. From the construction site below, heavy works were starting up, and the deep booming sound of piledrivers resonated in her chest.

She wrote in her journal: *Wind and rain are raging, I am shaking and swaying, but I must recover, I will rise up.*

She went to the fake-goods market at Zhongshan Science and Technology Park, even though she'd heard it was cheaper to buy counterfeit products on the internet. The thing about luxury high-style goods was, you had to see what they were like in real life before knowing whether they would suit you; even she knew this. She spent a long time going from shop to shop, expressing interest in certain items before walking away, knowing that the same things would be on sale a few shops away, and that the shopkeepers would be forced to come running out to the street after her to offer her lower prices than their competitors. First she selected a purse made from glossy red leather with a gold clasp buckle, which even came in a box with the logo printed in gold above the words 'Made in Italy'. When she was bargaining with the shopkeeper, she said to him, You are so unscrupulous, you dare to say this is made in Italy when everyone knows it's fake, and the shopkeeper said, Little Miss, it's the truth! Don't you know, Italy is full of factories owned by Chinese people, and those factories are full of Chinese workers producing large volumes of luxury goods! Phoebe did not fully believe this – she could not imagine entire towns and villages in Italy full of Chinese people stitching clothes and handbags and having nothing to do with the locals – but maybe it was true, maybe she now owned a genuine foreign-manufactured luxury item. Next, she hesitated over a scarf with distinctive checks and some large shawls made from pure 100 per cent pashmina, and since winter was just around the corner she thought about buying a fashionable down jacket too, something in a bright shiny colour that would make her look energetic and sporty, and even give the impression that she had just come back from a holiday in an expensive snowy place like Hokkaido.

Finally she chose the most important item, a handbag. This is how people would judge her. From afar they would notice what kind of bag she was carrying, and would decide if she was a person of class or not. She knew which kind of bag she wanted: it was the most desirable brand, but also the most illegal of all the counterfeit products. Some of the shopkeepers thought she was a spy for the trading office, and asked her many questions before admitting that they kept it in stock. The difficulty in purchasing this bag made her feel excited, as if she was buying something very rare and exclusive, even though it was a fake. Eventually one shopkeeper pushed aside a wall lined with shelves to reveal a smaller room hidden behind it, and behind this smaller room, which was filled with ordinary bags, there was another, even smaller room, and it was here that the bag she wanted was kept. There were two other women in that tiny room, examining the high-quality stylish bags with care. They were both executive-looking women wearing business clothes and carefully applied make-up, and being in that private space with them made Phoebe feel equally important. There was only one brand of bag in that room – the coveted LV brand – but in many styles and variations, the famous pattern and coloured monogram repeating all over the walls and surrounding her like the very air she breathed, making her feel slightly giddy. Phoebe took a long time before selecting the one she wanted, for even the fakes were expensive, and in the end she had to settle on the most inferior model and style. But it was still beautiful, she thought, as she walked out of the shop with it already on her shoulder. She had transferred some of the contents of her old bag into the new one, and discarded all the unwanted items in a bin just outside the shop. When she looked at some of the things she'd thrown away – the cheap dried-up lipstick, a cracked mirror, a worker's pass from one of her old jobs in Guangzhou – she wondered why she had carried those dead objects with her for so long.

She went to an internet bar and made herself new profiles on QQ and MSN so she could chat with people online – so she could chat with men. Searching her email attachments, she found a nice photo of herself. It had been taken in Yuexiu Park in Guangzhou, but in the background there were only trees and lakes, so no one would look at the picture and make the link: Guangzhou, factory worker, immigrant. She remembered that day well – she had just left one job and was about to start another, but she had two days off in between and also some money saved up. She had dressed in nice jeans and a colourful T-shirt and taken the subway to the park as if she was having a day out with friends, only she did not have any friends. She bought red-bean shaved ice and ate it while strolling around the artificial lakes, watching the artists painting watercolours of goldfish and hilly landscapes and oil portraits of Hollywood actors. There were couples and families everywhere, and although she was on her own she felt that she was one of them, that she was someone who had a past and a future – and that life was only going to get better, just as it would for everyone around her. Near the boating lake she found a spot to sit under some bamboo trees. She was on her own, but it was OK, she was happy. She took out her phone and held it at arm's length, holding it up slightly so that she could look at it with a raised chin – it was better that way, as it made her neck look thinner. She took a photo, but it wasn't so good, since she was squinting a bit because of the sun. She tried it again, but it didn't work this time either. One of the old men who sold tickets for the rowing boats called out to her, asked if she wanted him to help her take a photo. 'Don't worry,' he said, 'I won't ask you to marry me in return!'

He peered into the narrow screen, and Phoebe worried that he didn't know how to work the camera. But as he held it in front of her he said, 'This phone is so old. My grandson had one just like this three years ago when he was still in middle school.' It made her laugh, and in the photo she appears sunny-faced and natural, full of the promise of the bounteous years ahead of her.

As she looked at the photo on the computer screen she knew it was just the right kind to have on her profile – taken by someone else, a friend on an outing, maybe even a boyfriend. It made her appear desirable, unlike the kind of blurry self-shot images where the person was always looking up at the camera, which instantly told the viewer: I have no friends. She wrote a few lines about herself, a 'professional career-oriented young woman with experience of foreign work and travel'. She gave her true age and stated that she wanted to meet respectable, successful men.

Within minutes of posting her profile she began to get requests from men who wanted to get to know her better. She was overwhelmed; she never imagined she could be so popular. Suddenly the whole of Shanghai seemed full of friends and potential partners, thousands of them. She began typing replies to the men she deemed the most suitable, her fingers moving across the keyboard trying to keep up with several conversations at once, but it was difficult, she was not used to typing so much and she knew she was making mistakes. Sorry for the delay in my replies, she typed as some of the men began to get impatient. It was thrilling to chat to people she barely knew, and she began to imagine what some of them might be like – rich, handsome, successful.

But very soon she realised that many of them were just high-school and college kids who were having some online fun – they said so themselves. They had no intention of ever meeting up. She became angry that they were wasting her time, so she learnt how to block them from contacting her. Young boys were no use to her; she needed to meet successful adults, she was not interested in spotty adolescents. Some men seemed OK when they first started chatting, but gradually Phoebe would discover something wrong with them.

> To tell you the truth, I am married, so I am just looking for casual fun.
>
> Actually, my age is 61, not 29, but I am still very energetic and strong.
>
> Honestly, I really do drive a Ferrari and I live in a luxurious penthouse apartment, but you cannot visit me because my grandmother lives with me and she is disapproving of the girls I meet – you should not suspect me of being a factory worker!
>
> My internet business is going so well at the moment but I have cashflow problems, could you lend me 2,000 yuan and I will pay you back on our first date?
>
> I am not so interested in knowing what your favourite ice cream flavour is. Right now I am imagining lifting your skirt and touching your thighs higher and higher until …

Some men became angry when she didn't reply immediately. They were pushy and said impolite things to her. But she couldn't type very fast, and it was hard to keep so many chats going at once. She soon learnt to tell which men were educated, because they were the ones who typed their answers very quickly, but she also discovered that educated men often used the most obscene words. And then there were men who seemed nice at first, but soon it was clear that they were just out to trick her. Even though she did not know what they could possibly cheat her out of, she sensed that they were bad people who were up to no good. She heard stories all the time, tales of swindlers and liars – *bamboozlers*. She did not want to be one of those poor victims who got bamboozled.

One by one, Phoebe deleted her newly made friends, blocking them until her contact list showed only a couple of guys – guys who had just said hello, how are you, but had not yet had the chance to show how deceitful and black-spirited they were. She began to get random messages that didn't even start with a greeting, just shameless suggestions for physical relations, most probably high-school students, but who knows, maybe they were frustrated middle-aged husbands and fathers. She knew it was because she had a nice profile picture, and decided she should replace it with something fake or a neutral image, like a cartoon character. A superhuman character with great strength, maybe. That would deter anyone with unsavoury intentions. She would become like so many other people in cyberspace, hiding behind an image of something other than themselves. But as she looked at the photo of herself she hesitated. Her eyes were glowing with laughter and promise, and the vegetation behind her was so lush it reminded her of her home. She could not bring herself to delete this image from her profile. When the rest of Shanghai looked at her, she did not want them to see just a grey shadow of a nobody; she wanted them to see her, Phoebe Chen Aiping.

She looked at her brand-new fake Omega watch. It was 6.55 p.m. She had not realised how late it was – she had spent nearly four hours in the internet café. She double-checked the time on the computer, just in case the watch she had been sold was a dud. It was still 6.55. She looked at the photo of herself one last time, just as another message popped up on screen. *Little Miss, hello, I like your profile, would you like to chat? I think we might be compatible.* She closed the page and signed herself off the computer.

When she got home the apartment was dark and Yanyan was asleep on the bed, wrapped in a thin blanket. The window was open and there was a slight chill in the room. Phoebe stood at the window and looked down at the blinking red and pale-gold lights of the cars below. The street stalls had their lights on now, the plumes of smoke from the little charcoal grills rising into the evening air.

'Where have you been? You're very late,' Yanyan said quietly.

'Trying to find work. Why are you in bed so early? It's barely eight o'clock.'

'I haven't got out of bed all day.'

'Oh, Yanyan,' Phoebe sighed as she sat down on the bed next to her. 'Not again. What are we going to do?'

As night fell, the giant hole in the construction site below the window looked black and infinite, as if it was ready to swallow up the cranes and bulldozers around it. Maybe she and Yanyan and everyone in their building would disappear into the hole too, Phoebe thought.

'Come, I'll make some dinner,' she said.

Yanyan sat up and pulled her knees to her chest, shielding her eyes as Phoebe turned on the light. The single fluorescent strip bathed the room in a harsh white glow.

'Only instant noodles again. Sorry,' Phoebe said.

'It's better than eating a banquet on your own,' Yanyan replied.

Later, once Yanyan had settled back in bed, Phoebe opened the Journal of Her Secret Self. She had not written in it for some days. She paused, knowing that Yanyan was not yet asleep – her breathing was even and almost soundless. Phoebe needed solitude when she wrote in her journal; she had become used to being alone when confronting her fears. It was easier that way, for she could be as weak and fearful as she wanted, and there would be no one to witness it. She turned off the light and waited in the darkness. When she heard Yanyan's breaths turn heavy with dream sleep, she held her mobile phone next to her journal and began to scribble a few lines in the ghostly blue light.

Time is flying past you, Phoebe Chen Aiping, you know you are being defeated. You are a new person here in Shanghai, you must dare to do things the old you would not have done. Forget who you were, forget who you are. Become someone else.

6

胜任愉快

Perform All Obligations
and Duties with Joy

The weather turned colder and sharper as Spring Festival approached. Most days, Justin spent the morning staring at the ice that had formed overnight on the balcony, bizarre shapes hanging from the railings in jagged shards or clinging to the drainpipes like brilliant shiny fungus. The leaves of the potted plants were coated in ice – fat glassy bulbs that reminded him of Christmas decorations. On brighter days the sun would be strong enough to start shrinking the icicles, and he would stand at the window watching the water drip slowly onto the cement floor of the balcony. Most of the time, though, the ice would stay hard and unmoving, glinting ever so slightly despite the absence of light in the pale, snow-shrouded afternoon.

He had not left the apartment for five days, not even to walk to the convenience store at the end of the street to stock up on bottled water and instant noodles. The apartment felt too warm and cosseting to leave, and the weather outside too harsh. Realising he had stopped going out altogether, his *ayi* came every other day now, leaving him enough food and water to live on – more than enough, it turned out, for she worried about him – so he did not have to venture out, did not have to see or speak to anyone, which suited him. If he happened to be in the living room when he heard the *ayi* unlock the first of the heavy double doors, he would retreat to the dark safety of his bedroom, knowing that she would not enter his lair. He would lie in bed and chart her movements by the sounds she made: the breathy exclamation on entering the over-heated apartment; the running of the tap in the kitchen; the expressions of shock and even mild revulsion when she discovered and disposed of leftover food festering on the kitchen counter; the clink of porcelain; the scrape of chairs on the wooden floor; the gentle tread of her feet as she dusted the coffee table. And, finally, the moment of relief when she left the apartment, pulling once, twice, three times at the door that always snagged on the rug as she closed it. Then he would be alone again.

Occasionally she would leave a note asking if he needed anything else, and he would scribble a reply – *All still fine* – and leave it with some cash on the kitchen table. He was thankful she came, but he could not bear the thought of interacting with anyone, not even someone as unobtrusive as a bespectacled middle-aged *ayi*.

All around him he could hear the sounds of families preparing for Spring Festival – children's footsteps upstairs, the occasional burst of excited chatter, the rumble of wheeled bags heavy with treats being dragged along the corridor. He heard people singing along to their karaoke machines, sometimes a family singalong with croaky old voices mingling with cartoon-happy children's voices, other times a lone female voice, surprisingly pure and sad, falling flat from time to time. He hated this voice; it wriggled into his head and cut into his innards, forcing its way into his space as if it wanted to be close to him. It was not like the other noises, which were impersonal and distant; this voice was intimate, intrusive, and he was thankful that it never lasted very long. He did not know where any of these noises came from, for they echoed strangely, rebounding in the walls and pipes.

He thought about what his own family would be doing at that precise moment – their New Year celebrations were a well-rehearsed ritual, comforting in their predictability. In the family mansion they would be taking delivery of inhuman quantities of food, and the caterers would be setting up for the open-house party that would take place over the first few days of the festival following the family dinner on New Year's Eve. His mother would play at being stressed by the pressure of organising affairs, even though her distaste for physical work meant that she rarely performed any function more strenuous than making phone calls to the florist or the confectioners, leaving the servants to deal with the deliveries and the setting up of tables and chairs. In recent years the family had even taken to having the New Year's Eve dinner in a hotel – the servants were getting old, his mother had said, and they simply couldn't trust getting a young Filipina or Indonesian maid (she'd heard such horror stories: family heirlooms being stolen, phone bills full of calls to Manila, people being killed in their own homes). So they would book a private room in the Chinese restaurant of a fancy hotel, twelve of them sitting in near-silence around a big table laden with food that would remain half consumed at the end of the evening. 'How lucky we are to have a family like this,' his father would say at the conclusion of the meal. He'd said that every single year Justin could remember. But those extravagant banquets of bird's-nest and shark-fin soups, whole suckling pigs, the finest New Zealand abalone, and strange sea creatures he hadn't even recognised – perhaps they were all in the past, now that his family was ruined. He wondered if they were having more modest celebrations, or if they were celebrating at all. He imagined bitter recriminations: mother blaming father, brother blaming mother, grandmother blaming uncle – for the loss of their fortune, for the loss of their eldest son.

But he was deluding himself. They would not be blaming each other for their misfortune; they would be blaming him. He had disappeared, he had let them down, he would not answer their calls for help, he was selfish – that was why they were in this mess now. It was a line of reasoning he had heard many times before, so often that sometimes he too believed it. It was all his fault.

As he stood at the window and looked out at the strange frozen shapes of the city – the glass-ice trees, the streets scarred by snaking tracks of snow – he thought of the family holiday he had once had

88

in Sapporo, when he was about thirteen, old enough to understand that the vacation was happening under a cloud of discontent; that it was not a holiday but an escape of sorts. It had taken place over the New Year period, the decision to leave for Japan made late in the day, when preparations for the usual celebrations were already well advanced. There had been no explanation for this hasty change in plan, which triggered a frantic search for the children's woollen jumpers and down jackets in the store room, and the attendant anxiety as to whether or not they had outgrown them since their trip to Canada the previous year. His mother simply said, 'I've always wanted to spend New Year's in a snowy place.' In the coded language of their family, full of unaired grievances, her firm statement of intent spoke loud and clear to Justin. Something was not right, and this something was compelling enough for them to leave home over the holiday.

The snow that blanketed Sapporo felt permanent, comfortably settled on the long straight avenues and the mountainous land-scape around it. The freezing air raked the lining of his nostrils, burning its way down his throat and into his lungs; his lips and fingertips became sore and chapped, and his thin tropical blood felt powerless against the cold. And yet he was not unhappy; the omnipresent snow had a way of silencing the unspoken troubles that had arisen in his family, dampening them, making everyone calm. His younger brother did not take so well to the cold: he whimpered softly and became sullen and uncommunicative, refus-ing to venture out of the hotel room. Justin observed the way his mother and father avoided each other – she lavishing extra atten-tion on the younger of her two sons while her husband worked on his papers even at breakfast, concentrating on indecipherable sets of accounts as he ate his rice porridge, rarely looking up at the rest of the family.

'I'm going to take Mother out to dinner tonight,' his father said one morning, without looking up from his paperwork, and Justin recognised this statement to be a sort of apology, or at least as much of an apology as his father was capable of offering. There was a cry from his brother, aged six – the start of a tantrum over being forced to finish his eggs; then he began to scrape a piece of burnt toast noisily, the black powder scattering on the cream-coloured tablecloth. No, his mother replied, that would be too much hassle – the young one needed looking after. Justin listened for signs of regret or gratitude in her voice, but could discern nothing other than the turbulent silence that descended on his family in times of anger and dispute. Outside the sky was clear, the winter light glassy, pale. He thought how fortunate he was to be in a foreign place, for somehow the problems of his family seemed easier to bear when they were far from home, in an unfamiliar land shrouded in snow.

With his mother clinging more and more to her younger son and his father disappearing to work for long stretches, Justin was left to discover the wonders of Sapporo with Sixth Uncle, who had come on holiday with them as he often did, partly to help with the children but mainly to organise the logistics of travelling in a foreign country – booking tickets, sorting out the best rooms in hotels, moving the family swiftly through airports, finding good restaurants. He always seemed to know people everywhere they went – contacts he'd met through business, or friends of friends of friends who were willing to help show them round or lend a car and a driver. He was 'good with people' – affable, insistent, often daring in his humour, occasionally foul-mouthed but always unthreatening in his chubbiness. He would flirt with hotel receptionists and sweet-talk directors of airline companies; he always got what he wanted. The youngest of the uncles, he was only twelve years older than Justin – barely in his mid-twenties at the time, though already very much a man, someone Justin recognised as inhabiting his father's world, not his, in spite of the childish banter that passed between him and Sixth Uncle.

They visited the Snow Festival, just the two of them. It felt like an adventure, striding forth into the bitter cold, walking through the snow and feeling it seep through their boots, leaving behind the younger brother, who was too small and weak, and his parents, who were too old and slow. 'I'm going to have my ass kicked for leading you astray,' Sixth Uncle said, and laughed as they walked around the fantastic ice sculptures. 'Your mother is going to bite my head off when she sees her dear little son frozen to the bone. Hey, look at that – remember that?'

It was the Leaning Tower of Pisa, which they had seen during a previous holiday, but made entirely of snow. Elsewhere there was a life-size Pyramid and a faithful reproduction of the Kinkaku-ji in Kyoto; there were fearsome ogres and cuddly polar bears and a herd of long-necked dinosaurs; Mount Rushmore with different, unrecognisable heads; Eskimos and penguins; a tropical landscape of palm trees and a beach with sun loungers – all glowing with the pale white-blue of snow and ice. They threw snowballs at each other, as people who are not used to snow always do, and if they tripped and fell they just lay on the snow, feeling its strange powdery-crusty texture beneath them. Justin no longer noticed the cold; his fingers felt swollen and numb but impervious to the biting frost, and he felt a growing strength in his legs as he ran along the edge of a perfectly flat snow-canal that led to a Dutch windmill.

'Little bastard, you've got a lot of energy,' Sixth Uncle wheezed as he caught up. 'Your grandmother keeps telling me I need to lose weight, but thank God I'm a bit fat because it protects me from this damn cold.'

They found a restaurant, a dimly lit place hidden down a nondescript alley – a tip from a local acquaintance, Sixth Uncle said, guaranteed to be the best food in the area. Out of the cold, the warmth of the small room felt delicious, the air humid and wood-scented. They ordered too much food, as was the custom of their family, and Sixth Uncle had a bottle of sake that seemed too big for one person.

'What a great holiday this is,' Sixth Uncle said as he refilled the tiny cup; he misjudged the size of it, and the sake spilled onto the smooth lacquered surface of the table. 'Thank goodness you're around, though, otherwise it would just be your shit-boring parents.'

Justin smiled; Sixth Uncle was the only person he knew who spoke of his parents in this way – irreverently, whatever respect he had for Justin's father well hidden under layers of coarse humour.

'How on earth did such boring parents bring up a happy, strong boy like you? If you were just a couple of years older I'd let you drink some sake while no one's looking. Hey – maybe I could slip it into your teacup? No, no, that would be *too* bad of me. Not even I would do that to my favourite nephew – though you've always been very grown-up for your age, so I wouldn't give a shit about getting you drunk. Only thing I'd worry about is your dragon-tongued mother. Oh my God, speaking of getting drunk, I think I'm already pretty wasted.'

Justin toyed with a piece of lamb that was drying out on the helmet-shaped griddle in front of him, slowly sizzling to a crisp alongside a charred piece of corn. Sixth Uncle had told him that the dish was called 'Genghis Khan' because the grill was modelled on the exact form of an ancient Mongol armoured helmet, but Justin had not believed him – Sixth Uncle was full of amazing, unbelievable stories. Often Justin had thought that they were Sixth Uncle's way of livening the heavy atmosphere at the dinner table, for he was the only one who would ever say anything amusing (and Justin would be the only one to laugh); but recently Justin had begun to realise that Sixth Uncle's anecdotes were aimed at him. He had sensed a growing connivance, Sixth Uncle reaching out to him tentatively, for reasons he was not able to fathom. He was glad of the jovial company, but troubled by the lack of clarity; in spite of Sixth Uncle's almost comic façade, he too operated within the family's unspoken language, in which one was some-how expected to understand all that was not articulated.

'Do you know what I'm going to do when I retire?' Sixth Uncle continued. 'I'm going to buy a stinking huge farm in Tasmania and never come back. People tell me property is dirt cheap down there. I can get a massive ranch with sheep and cows and live happily ever after.'

'But Sixth Uncle, you don't know anything about sheep or cows.'

'How difficult can it be?' Sixth Uncle poured another over-filled cup of sake and looked at the clear beads of liquid on the table. 'Must be easier than dealing in property.'

There followed a silence that made Justin anxious: one of those moments just before someone said something important. In his family's unsaid-said ways, he understood that this was a preparation for an announcement of some kind, the delivery of news that would mark a turning point – perhaps something relatively minor, but a shift nonetheless.

'Do you know what people in the business call me? "The Fixer". Sometimes they call me "The Enforcer", but I don't really like to hear that. "The Fixer" sounds better. Even the family calls me that sometimes.'

Justin nodded. He had heard his father refer to Sixth Uncle's pragmatic, no-nonsense approach to problem-solving, the way he could always untangle a sticky situation.

'In every generation of our family there needs to be a Fixer. Before me there was my Third Uncle, who you never knew. Without him the family business would have gone bust several times over – your grandfather was a clever man, but he wasn't streetwise at all. The family needed someone to look after the more practical side of things so the glamorous stuff could happen. The minor details are important too, that's what Third Uncle told me. I learnt everything from him. And after me it'll be your turn.'

The small window next to their table offered a view of the narrow alley; above the doorways, lamps had come on. Justin could not see the sky, but he guessed that the snow had made the evening draw in. A flag sign fluttered above an entranceway; amidst the Japanese characters he recognised the Chinese name for Hokkaido: North Sea Island, a place marooned in the cold north.

'Your father says it's not normal for the eldest son to do the work I do. He wants you to sit in a fancy office the way he does, or look after the money in Singapore. What a shit-boring job that is!

But what choice do we have? Look at your brother – he's a sweet kid, but already you can see that he's too weak, spoilt rotten, he'll never have what it takes to deal with the harsher things in life. At his age you were already much more mature, you were different. Remember a few years ago? When you fractured your ankle or leg or whatever and for a few days you were hobbling around? Your father got mad because he thought you were pretending. And then you just forced yourself to walk normally, and no one knew anything for months, until the doctor said, My God, I think he's fractured his leg. I thought, wow, this kid is *tough*! No one said so, but everyone was so impressed by your bravery. And I guess it's because of – OK, let's just say it – your background.'

Justin nodded. He tried to read the signs above the doorways in the alleyway outside; some of them were written in traditional Chinese script, and it was fun trying to make out the names. White Birch Mountain Village. Brilliant Plum Teahouse.

'But you know, you've been raised as the eldest son, you've never been treated as anything other than the Number One Brother, so whose blood you are exactly is not important. We're not *so* old-fashioned that we care about these things. It's just – like I said, it explains why you are different from your brother. And better than him, frankly. Yes, we should just say it! He's going to become a lawyer or an accountant; maybe he'll look after some small part of the business, like the tea or rubber plantations. Or maybe he'll do what your dad does now – sit in the office and watch the money coming in and sometimes play with the accounts before going off to play golf. That's for pussies. You're different. You're stronger. That's why you'll have to carry more responsibility.'

That he was different was undeniable, as was the fact that he was the eldest son. At times he wondered how someone who was not born of the family could be treated to its privileges – and now its responsibilities – but his family did not question it, and neither, therefore, did he. They had been clear about the situation from the start, had not lied or sought to protect him from the truth: they had taken him in, the infant son of a distant relative, a poor girl from the provinces who had been abandoned by her husband and could not cope with a baby. She was so tenuously related that she might not even have been part of the extended clan, though in the old Chinese way she was referred to as 'cousin', and in today's terms, in a family more modern than his, the process by which he came to live in his new home would be called 'adoption' rather than just 'taking in'. His birth mother had emigrated to Canada, and had he wanted to, Justin could easily have asked about her, perhaps even asked to see her. But he felt no filial curiosity; his bloodline offered no lure. His family had raised him as their own, and not just as their own but as the highest of the male cousins – the Eldest Son of the Eldest Son – a position not usurped even when his younger brother came along. His place within the family had always been indisputable, despite his provenance. And for that he would always be grateful. He would always obey the family and fight for them and never fail them; he did not need Sixth Uncle to tell him to do so.

'You need to start hanging out with me, I'll teach you a thing or two. Your dad wants you to start learning the business soon. With property, you have to begin with the basics. See that chef over there, slicing the fish as if he's creating some fucking work of art? Well, he started life as a kitchen porter, collecting scraps of garbage and dumping them outside for the rats to eat. Our work is like that too. You want to build apartment blocks all over Vancouver and Melbourne? Want to reclaim a bit of Hong Kong harbour so you can build a new office tower? First you have to learn the shit that I have to deal with. All the goddamn shit.'

There was no one else in the restaurant, except for the chef-owner who was now cleaning his knives with a small white cloth folded into a little triangle; when he finished each one he would hold the tip level with his eyes and stare at it for a few seconds before putting it away.

Still seated, Sixth Uncle began to pull on his down jacket. His arms snagged in the sleeves and the collar twisted awkwardly against his neck. He sat at the table rubbing his eyes, the puffy jacket making him seem even more rotund than usual. 'God, my head hurts,' he said.

Outside, the afternoon had given way to a long northern twilight that tinged the snow-draped city a faint electric blue. They walked slowly back to the hotel along the long, windswept avenue. All around them, the branches of the cherry trees were clad in sleeves of frost studded with ice crystals. In a few months they would be covered in blossom again. They paused to look at a snow sculpture of a plump little cartoon cat with its paw raised in greeting. 'Looks like me,' Sixth Uncle said. When Justin glanced at his uncle he saw that his eyes were moist, and tears were streaming down his reddened cheeks.

'Are you OK, Sixth Uncle?' he asked, returning his gaze to the cat.

Sixth Uncle blinked and wiped his eyes with the palms of his hands. 'It's just the wind. I hate this damned cold.'

They continued walking and Sixth Uncle put his arm around Justin's shoulders. 'I swear to God, the moment you're old enough to take over this damn family's affairs, I'm going to buy that farm and piss off to Tasmania forever.'

How to be Gracious

I think we have already spoken of the value of education. Those of you who follow the cut and thrust of modern international entrepreneurship will be quick to point out that the majority of the world's billionaires are not in fact highly educated in the traditional sense: all those Chinese property tycoons and coal-mining emperors, those Indian steel magnates – they skipped the glitter of Harvard and slid straight into life's great river, thrashing about in the muddy waters until they learnt to swim smoothly. The more pedantic among you will say that they were educated too, only in a different way – all that nonsense about 'the university of life', &c, &c.

But that is not what I meant when I spoke of education, for to my mind, learning how to double-cross someone is not *education*. All those fancy things that men (yes, it is usually men, though increasingly women too) of high finance speak about, like takeovers, selling short, asset stripping – are these not rich people's terms for bullying, gambling and cheating? I risk the wrath of my fellow entrepreneurial giants by saying this, but most tycoons I know are, frankly, not very gracious. What can you expect? *Tycoon. Mogul. Magnate.* Even the words these people use to describe themselves would indicate a certain mentality, for they are not kindly words, but ones designed to impress in the crassest of ways. They seek to dominate in that old-fashioned feudalistic way, to conquer, to destroy. And it is these base tendencies that you must resist if ever you are to become a gracious, generous billionaire. The time for that kind of old-fashioned accumulation of wealth is over. Indeed, part of the purpose of this book is to announce the end of this financial smash-and-grab and urge you to look away from the excesses committed by those who consider themselves the elite.

I say 'they'. But maybe I should say 'we'. Most of you who are aware of my reputation will have assumed that I belong to this band of brutal overlords, and I do not blame you for doing so. On paper, my ruthless credentials are impeccable: the swift mergers and acquisitions of well-known companies that take the markets by surprise, the penthouse living, the intercontinental first-class flights – certain elements of my life will not endear themselves to the casual observer. Sometimes when I read an article about myself even I recoil at the seeming callousness of my financial manoeuvring. I look at the unflattering photo of myself sitting in front of a microphone at some hastily arranged press conference, my face largely expressionless. What a dreadful life this Walter Chao must have, I think. Imagine being *him*. Often I forget that *he* is in fact *me*.

But then I remember my tireless charitable and educational projects, such as the construction of modern fibreglass bus shelters in rural areas of South-East Asia, which provide schoolchildren with respite from the downpours of the monsoon season, or the recent community centre built entirely of recycled plastic bottles – the first of its kind anywhere in the world, I think. I read with dismay a few ungracious accusations in the press that made it seem that my bus shelters were a sneaky way of marketing in hard-to-reach villages, simply because they happen to carry advertisements for the brand of soft drinks that I acquired several years ago. Next they will be saying that my carbon-neutral, waste-utilising community centre is a mere publicity stunt because it is made from the same soft-drink bottles.

Fortunately I pay little attention to these sorts of comments, just as I ignore the sneering that accompanies my self-help books.

I write these not to make money, you understand, but to share the map of my success with ordinary people in need of inspiration. Nor are these books an outlet for vanity or a search for deeper recognition: most of them have been written under various pseudonyms, including the multi-million-bestselling *Secrets of a Five Star Billionaire*.

So those of you who think you know me – think again.

Shrugging off all ungracious thoughts, let us return to the concept of graciousness and education. Of giving and not expecting any return. I mentioned before that I am planning a long-lasting legacy to the world, and the ideas are accelerating as I write. My original proposal to build a fairly unassuming cultural centre has mushroomed somewhat since I began working on it. I was at dinner with one of the world's leading avant-garde architects and urban planners (whose identity must remain secret until approval for the project is granted), who became terribly excited at my plans. This architect virtually leapt out of his/her chair as soon as I explained what I intended to do, nearly embarrassing our host (the cold hors d'oeuvres had barely been served). He/she called me a visionary – a compliment indeed, coming from someone responsible for some of the most arresting buildings in the world. He/she has flung him/herself with great enthusiasm at this project – the first set of drawings is in development right now: part charitable foundation, part cultural centre, part dreamscape. No municipal council in the world will be able to resist a work of such ground-breaking importance.

Annoyingly, I have been somewhat distracted from this noble project by developments elsewhere in my portfolio of interests – what the ungracious would call my 'empire'. But as I am on the brink of a daring acquisition of one of the oldest, most famous companies in South-East Asia, I suppose it is hard to dispute accusations of bravado and entrepreneurial plundering. Yet I am only doing what others have done many times before me. It will hit the headlines in the next few days, so you will know all about it then – there's no need to elaborate here. I will be a happier, more contented man once the deal is done and I can return to the work that really matters to me – the gracious business of giving.

I forgot to say that I have identified a site for my cultural centre. I will be travelling there very shortly to push matters along. The city? I said before that it should be one capable of showing off my legacy in all its twenty-first-century glory. That doesn't leave many choices. So in a few weeks I shall move my base of operations to the chosen city: Shanghai.

7

履险如夷

Calmly Negotiate
Difficult Situations

It seems that Gary has a history of misconduct which is impressive for someone so young. Readers of tabloid newspapers will not fail to be astounded by the unexpectedly long catalogue that is beginning to emerge. How the record company has managed to keep these incidents hushed up for so long is anyone's guess – public relations people are so powerful these days.

Among the revelations on the front pages of the papers these days are:

The wrecked luxury suite at the Mandarin Oriental hotel in Singapore after his much-lauded concert there last year (no comment was made by the hotel, which prides itself on its discretion, but everyone supposes that it was paid off by Gary's record company).

A hotel chambermaid in Hangzhou who claims Gary exposed himself inappropriately to her last week. She says that he came out of the bathroom and let his towel fall to the ground before making an obscene suggestion to her. She did not report the incident because she felt no one would believe her.

An unpaid bill of US$12,000 in an upscale Kuala Lumpur restaurant, which included five bottles of Krug champagne.

And an altercation in a trendy drinking spot in the Soho area of Hong Kong, when Gary allegedly grabbed a barman by the throat and threatened to kill him.

Yes, it is clear that Gary has a drinking problem, no one can deny it. Like many young people, he certainly does not react well to alcohol. But is it right for a superstar with so many privileges to behave in this way in public, especially when his actions hurt other people? This is a tragic affair, and no matter how many innocent, ordinary people are harmed by his alcohol-fuelled madness, the ultimate victim is Gary himself: the Fallen Angel.

Let us not judge him too harshly – he is a young man who should be left to deal with his problems in private, one magazine said, quoting a line from an interview with Vivian Woo, another Malaysian-born Taiwanese starlet who dated Gary for a few months. 'His heart is made of gold, it's just that he has a bad temper and sometimes does not know how to control it,' she said. 'That's why people think he is a disgusting person.' When asked if he was ever violent with her, she replied, *No comment*. The picture they ran with the front-page interview was of Gary in the bar on the Bund in Shanghai, his beautiful profile revealing a man defeated by his weaknesses. How could such an innocent face be capable of such dark hatred? This is the question the papers ask time and time again – a question that fascinates the general public, even people who are not interested in pop music.

It did not take long for the gutter press to find its way to Gary's home town in the north of Malaysia. Low-cost flights are so abundant nowadays that it is easy to send a small army of reporters from Hong Kong or Shanghai all the way to rural Malaysia. Within a week there were numerous stories of Gary's troubled adolescence, of all the fights he got into when he was a teenager, before he won his first talent contest. Various newspapers bore 'testimonies' of local youths who supplied snippets of information that proved Gary's waywardness from an early age, his propensity for physical violence. 'One time ah, I call him a bad name. Just joking only, what! That time, we all about thirteen year old,' said one young man, a truck driver for a local cement company. 'Suddenly ah, he just take a brick and whack my face, ha, like that.' In the photo, the man points to his jawbone, his face creased in pain as if the act had just been committed yesterday. From the cheap streaky yellow highlights in his hair and the gold bracelet on his wrist, it is obvious to most people that he is a small-town gangster, like many of the others interviewed in connection with Gary's scandalous youth, but this is not relevant to the sensational story at hand. Readers do not want to know about those incidental lives: the truck driver drives his truck, the ice-cream seller sells ice cream. People are only interested in those lives which are ruined. For when something is ruined, you can use the rubble to reconstruct something completely different, something that never really existed – this is something that Gary is beginning to realise.

As he sits in his hotel room looking at the newspapers spread out across the floor, Gary reads about himself with the detached haziness of a dream: the reassembled fragments of his life add up to someone who is definitely him, but also not him – a half-imagined, half-genuine Gary whom he has problems recognising. It is exactly how he feels when he sees himself in his music videos. He remembers hitting the truck driver twelve, thirteen years ago, when they were both still boys. With a brick, it is true – though it was only a fragment of a brick, so small that he could hold it concealed in his fist. And while Gary did make contact with the other boy's face, he was able to dodge the full impact of Gary's swing and was therefore not seriously hurt. He had lain on the ground for a long time after Gary hit him, the shock of the attack wounding him far more than the actual blow. It was the first real fight that Gary had ever been in, and it emboldened him, made him feel strong. Gary remembers standing over his adversary, whose friends stood in a semicircle around their fallen comrade. Some of their faces appear in the newspapers; Gary recognises them – older, bonier, the harshness of their faces accentuated by age, talking about how Gary was always armed with dangerous weapons – an iron bar, a penknife. He can remember, too, their endless taunts – the bad words thirteen-year-olds call each other: *bapok, chibai, kaneenabu*; can remember crouching in a foetal ball as they kicked and punched him; can remember the moment he saw the piece of broken brick and picked it up, swinging his arm as fast as he could; can remember the gang leader's face, the confusion and shock; can remember the wild sensation of adrenalin pumping into his forehead, the soft crunch of the boy's jawbone, the crazy exhilaration as the boy dropped to the floor, the knowledge that he could – and would – do this many times again in his life, that with every punch or kick he threw he would feel this doped-up rush once more. Above all he can remember the sad emptiness later, as the excitement drained away from his veins, leaving him to realise that even his newfound source of ecstasy would never truly satisfy him, that after lifting him to great heights it would always let him plummet once more.

Of course the newspapers managed to track down his foster father – a wizened, leather-skinned man standing behind the metal grille door of a small, badly kept, single-storey link house in a bad part of Kota Bharu. The photographs show the tiny cement yard in front of the house, the rusting, disassembled handlebars of an old motorbike, a pile of deflated tyres, an empty cage that might once have contained a few chickens or a medium-sized dog, and a clay pot full of weeds. The stories describe how from behind the bars of the door he shouts obscenities in Hokkien at any visitor. He is not used to company, he does not welcome strangers. One reporter recounts being physically chased from the house by this old grandfather wielding a broomstick. Now we know where Gary gets his tendency for confrontation, the journalist mocks. It is a hilarious image, a frail pensioner, barely five feet tall, chasing a fashionable young journalist from his shabby home, little more than a shack, with a broom. It makes readers laugh – this whole affair is not very serious at all. That's what these provincial people are like: their lives are hard, but, at the same time (let's admit it), slightly comic – the harshness of their meagre existence makes them act in strange ways. You can't really blame Gary for behaving erratically, for he can never escape his roots. He may have become a superstar who drinks $1,000 bottles of champagne at the age of twenty-two, but at heart he is just a small-town ruffian, a miscreant who will never be able to change. His whole life from start to present has been ridiculous.

Gary tries to remember if this little old man ever used a broomstick to hit him: rattan cane, broken table leg, plastic bucket, worn canvas boot, strip of an old car tyre – and yes, a stump of a broomstick. He would use any object that happened to be in his field of vision at the time of one of his tempers, but he never used his hands or fists, as if he was afraid of making contact with Gary directly – even a sharp blow with the back of his hand that would involve a split-second touch of Gary's skin. Gary had just turned eleven when his mother died and he came to live with this man, the skinny hunchback cousin of hers, a man who could barely support himself, never mind a hungry, growing child. At the age of sixty-six, he was still working part-time in a scrapyard, so it was no surprise that he did not take well to the arrival of a child in need of looking after. It was no surprise, either, that he beat Gary regularly, for he was already an alcoholic long before Gary arrived. Living in a cramped house with no money and no future is a hard thing to bear, and when another person arrives to share this space, it's not a total shock if this sort of thing happens. And in deprived provincial communities, it's rather common.

But this is not a tale of misery, it is a tale of comedy. Because there is something amusing in the gradual unearthing of Gary's life, for sure there is. Everyone who reads these articles says, Oh how terrible, how sad, what a horrible boy he is, what a tragic story; but they laugh too. They snigger at the calendar of scantily clad girls that hangs on the porch of Gary's uncle's house, the kind of freebie that you get when buying petrol or beer, clearly several years out of date but still hanging there because its owner is a dirty old man – can you imagine, a grandpa his age looking at pictures of young girls like that? When there is an interview with one of Gary's childhood acquaintances on TV, viewers make fun of his accent, for it really is very unsophisticated. When rural Chinese people speak English, it sounds as if they are speaking Hokkien. *An den I got say him, ey, why you want lie me, I no money oso you like dat one ah? Many people ah, they don like him is because he no money ma, so he got steal people handphone, people money. One time I got say him, ey, why I don do anything oso you lai kacau wo? Just say like dat oso kena wallop one.* The viewers don't mean to be rude, but really, even when this guy speaks Mandarin it is so thick with Hokkien overtones and also mixed in with Malay words that it is really funny to listen to – you don't even know what language he is speaking!

Once you have seen and heard these comic snippets from his past, Gary's recent antics seem pretty hilarious too. Watch again the video of him beating up the man in the luxury bar in Shanghai – he is swaying and unsteady, raising his fists as drunk people do in films. When he lifts the wooden signboard over his head and brings it crashing down on the man's body, over and over again, he looks like the villain in an old slapstick movie or even a cartoon, where people fall from great heights or get crushed by falling weights and all you do is laugh at them. His body is tiny compared to that of the inert fallen victim's – a seagull pecking at the corpse of a walrus. The single word on the sign flashes before you. *WOW! … WOW! … WOW!*

Yes, there is something comic about this young life, even though we know it is sad. Gary himself feels like laughing. Surrounded by the newspapers strewn across the floor – his agent has every single paper and magazine delivered daily to his hotel room as punishment for the mess he has got the whole company into – he sees just how ridiculous this situation is. If he were not the subject of these stories he would be eager to read all of them, because there is a sense of unreality about this whole affair – no one could possibly be so idiotic. Every day he would want to get the cheap newspapers and the magazines with their colourful covers and ask himself, chuckling, How can someone so famous be so goddamn stupid? He would be fascinated, but frankly, he wouldn't take any of it seriously.

And when he zaps through the channels on TV and sees people he knew in past times, he begins to giggle. Here is one, a boy who extorted money from Gary for two years, between the ages of thirteen and fifteen. The money Gary had was not even worth the effort, but he did it anyway, he and his band of friends, until the day Gary pushed him into a monsoon drain. And now here he is, showing off his fat, fleshy nose, which he claims Gary broke in a fight. He is wearing the uniform of a fast-food restaurant – the first KFC to open in that provincial town. When he speaks to the journalist he tries to summon up long-suppressed pain, his eyes narrowed, his voice anguished, as if the event traumatised him; but he cannot help showing a flash of happiness that someone has come all the way from Taipei to ask him questions and put him on TV, and the camera picks up a hint of a smile even as he talks about how Gary always had a 'dark soul', and how everyone feared him. This guy who spends his days serving fried chicken and cole-slaw and his nights racing scooters with his Ah Beng friends around a small town in the north of Malaysia – he is so proud to have forty-five seconds on TV. He is ridiculous. He makes Gary want to laugh out loud. LOL LOL LOL.

Gary's uncle appears on TV again. Now that really was a comic arrangement, if ever there was one. Gary had barely ever had a conversation with him, yet now he is being described as Gary's *foster father*. The two of them spent their entire time together in that house avoiding each other, timing their respective arrivals to minimise the chances of an encounter. Gary remembers the huge relief he felt whenever he came home and found the place empty; and the dread when he heard the front grille creak open in the night. Often he would come home and find his foster father/uncle slumped in the lounger made of plastic string, his mouth open, trails of dried spittle tracing the line of his jaw down to his bony collarbone like sea salt on rocks. His head was rounded at the back, the feather-white hair rising up in a wispy tuft, his nose pointed like the beak of a turtle. He really did look like a comic-book animal – an Old-Age Mutant Ninja Turtle. The first time Gary got thrown out of school (the exact misdemeanour is forgotten now – probably for smoking on school grounds during morning break) he knew all too well what would happen when he came home early. His foster father hit him, said it was a waste of money sending him to school, he should just get a job serving tables at the coffee shop or carrying sacks of rice. As he raised the shoe to beat Gary, his jerky movements and bony arms made him look just like a make-believe animal. Old-Age Mutant Ninja Turtle, Old-Age Mutant Ninja Turtle. Alone in his hotel room sitting amidst a sea of comic-book memories from his childhood, Gary feels like laughing, laughing, laughing.

Laughing until he cries.

This endless pantomime tires him, but now, thank God, there is a break. The celebrity news on TV moves on to someone else – an older pop singer who fell to the floor at a meet 'n' greet session last night, and now there is speculation that she is pregnant. Gary knows her. To the public she seems like a stuck-up woman, but he feels a certain closeness to her, because she gave him generous advice when he first moved to Taipei. When he was struggling with voice coaching and trying to break into acting at the same time, she said, Don't worry, one way or another, you will be a big star – you have no other option in life but to be a big star.

Ha ha, he said. Maybe I don't want to be a star.

She said, There is no other possibility for you.

They share a love of spicy beef noodles, and when she played her concert in Malaysia she spent much time eating at local street stalls in order to experience the regional delicacies Gary had recommended to her. In an interview with the local press she referred to him as her 'surrogate son', and even though they are not that close, Gary knew what she meant because he too felt, in a small way, that she was like his mother. He knows that she is indeed pregnant and that the father is a rich married man who will not leave his wife, and that she is very unhappy. At the age of forty-six she believes she has lost her charm and has resorted to plastic surgery, which lends her beauty a harsh, tense quality. The cameras wait outside the hospital day and night, making her even more miserable. But here's the problem: her sadness brings relief to Gary. Every moment the news concentrates on her, he is able to take time out from the ridiculous spectacle of his own life. He hopes the media will remain focused on her misery, but he knows that, sooner or later, the loop will come back round to him. For the fact is that her fame has diminished, whereas he is still a huge star. Or at least he was until a few days ago.

He turns the TV off and stares at the blank screen. His hand twitches, resisting the urge to turn it on again. He cannot bear the sad ridicule of his life, but at the same time he is used to it now. He wants to see those people from his past, see what has become of them – laugh at them the way others are laughing at him. But he manages to resist the temptation, and instead logs on to the Facebook page his record company maintains for him. He is not allowed to respond personally to any messages – whenever he makes a statement to his fans on this page, it is in fact the PR department that writes the words: *I'm deeply sorry for all the embarrassment my behaviour has caused. Knowing you are all there to support me has touched me deeply and keeps me strong. My problems have brought me closer to you all. Thank you, thank you.*

The messages of support stream in from all over Asia. Girls of fifteen, sixteen, refusing to give up hope in Gary. I will always love you no matter what you do because you are a beautiful human being. I refuse to believe Gary has done any of these things – his enemies are liars liars LIARS. Gary is an innocent of love's dreams! Gary is a victim! I LOVE YOU GARY YOU ARE MY SPECIAL FOREVER.

He thought he would be reassured by these messages, but he is not. Instead they make him angry. He hates his fans. They refuse to see the truth, they are blind to how rotten his life has become. They still believe he is a pure innocent person who can make their pathetic lives happy and bring meaning to their paltry existences, when in fact the only sensation he is capable of provoking is disgust. He loathes them for needing him in this way, for needing him to supply them with dreams. He will never be able to give them dreams. He closes his eyes and feels their neediness weighing down on him like monsoon days, heavy and unmoving, ready to engulf him. Like everyone else, his fans think that the stories they read in the magazines and on the internet are a joke, a fabrication of events, not to be taken seriously; but they do not realise that even if they are exaggerations, distortions, made-up stories by pathetic people with no lives of their own, they are true in one respect: he has always been a disgusting person.

He kneels on the floor and looks at the patchwork carpet of papers and magazines strewn in front of him; all the words and images that sum up his entire life. The room around him is filthy – clothes cling to the silk upholstery like rotting vegetation, and there are dirty plates and cups everywhere. No one has come to clean the room in three days. Maybe his manager has forbidden anyone to come in. Maybe the cleaning staff are afraid of Gary, and fear that he will hit them or even sexually assault them. He is suddenly very tired, but crossing to the other side of the room and climbing into the bed seems too much of an effort. His limbs ache, and his face and neck feel clammy. He lies down on the floor, but the newspapers and magazines are so densely laid out that he ends up lying on top of them, curled on his side in a ball. They make a loud rustling noise every time he moves.

In some ways all the reports of Gary's troubled, mixed-up life today are just a simple continuation of his troubled, mixed-up life before. We would all love to believe in a fairytale story of a village boy made good, becoming a world-renowned figure while retaining his simplicity and integrity, but the nature of our modern world is that everything is corruptible from the beginning, and Gary is merely proof that purity and decay are entwined, that beauty is another form of depravity. Vanity has its price, and Gary is paying it right now. Every single one of his major remaining concerts, including the events in Shanghai and Beijing, has been cancelled, and even the smaller venues in Xian and Fuzhou have postponed indefinitely. Already one of his major sponsors has cancelled his endorsement contract, rumoured to be worth RMB 10 million, and the posters of him smiling and drinking a can of soda are coming down from billboards across Asia. Others are certain to follow – you can't advertise wholesome cows' milk drinks if you are an alcoholic. No one will employ him any more, and his young career appears to be over. His innocence, which was his Unique Selling Point – in fact, his Only Selling Point – is now lost, and there can surely be no comeback. Like a brilliant show of fireworks, he dazzled for a while but now leaves us contemplating the dark night sky. Last week millions of teenagers aspired to live his celebrity lifestyle; today he is a cautionary tale of the excesses of modern society. What will he do now? Might you turn up at your local real-estate office a couple of years from now and find that Gary is your agent? Quite possibly. But should we be sad? Clearly not. He wanted this life, so we should not pity him for being where he is now. Nor should we mourn the loss of his talent (though therein lies another debate: was he actually talented, or just pretty?). Others will soon come along to replace him, and others will fall just as he has. Soon no one will remember him. So let us now leave this unfortunate young man to survey his broken career in peace and privacy. He deserves that much.

8

卷土重来

Always Rebound
After Each Failure

The restaurant was not Yinghui's choice, but she was immediately struck by just how appropriate it was. Set on the top floor of a handsome 1930s red-brick building on Shaanxi Nan Lu, its décor was rich, modern, and just a touch masculine – white oak floors, French bergères, plum-coloured rugs, and large paintings of swirly, abstract shapes. It was the perfect setting for a first business meeting. Floor-to-ceiling windows all round the room offered a view of a maze of streets lined densely with plane trees, and office blocks whose windows sparkled in a jigsaw of lights in the night sky. She could see the trails of traffic snaking their way through narrow alleys full of cheap hotpot and noodle restaurants and convenience stores lit by neon lights, and here and there, patches of darkness where buildings had been cleared to create construction sites.

The table was tucked away in a corner, discreet but not screened off from the rest of the restaurant, unlike the private rooms most rich businessmen favoured. Its balance of intimacy and openness made her feel at ease. She thought, This man has class.

She had arrived early, as she always did for such meetings, in order to familiarise herself with her surroundings and make herself comfortable so she would appear relaxed when the other person arrived. It allowed her time to compose her thoughts, to think of a few opening lines that would make her seem funny yet assured

– to assume control of the situation. The more important the rendezvous, the earlier she arrived; this time she was nearly half an hour early.

She sipped the house cocktail she had ordered (Insensé, it was called) and looked in her handbag for her host's card. It had made a striking impression on her when she had received it, by courier, together with a handwritten note confirming the date and venue of their meeting. This had, of course, followed a concise email from his PA which proposed a business venture that he would like to discuss with Yinghui – this man had perfect protocol, unlike most of the boorish types she had grown accustomed to dealing with. The thick, buff-coloured card had his name printed on it in English and Chinese, in scarlet ink: *Walter Chao*. No titles, posts or qualifications, just a phone number and the email address of his PA. Its edges were slightly uneven, a subtle hint at its handmade provenance, and she could easily imagine it having been crafted by a skilled Florentine printer.

As she retrieved the card from her leather card case, another slipped out with it. *Justin CK Lim*, it read, listing his various positions in the family conglomerate he headed. She had not thought much about him since she'd run into him at the awards ceremony several weeks before; she had decided, consciously, to put him out of her mind for good. And yet she was at a loss to explain why she had not thrown out his card, why she had not been able to cut away the association with her past, why she was not being her usual ruthless self. She looked at the conventional card and considered its banality. Even the company logo was dull – his grandfather's initials, LKH, squashed into a square, as if designed by a middle-schooler in art class. Over the years she had read and heard of Justin CK Lim's entrepreneurial skills, but as a person he had always seemed somewhat pedestrian to her. He spoke infrequently, and what little he did say was leaden, weighed down by platitudes. She remembered a discussion amongst friends in KL a long time ago, about the Israeli-Palestinian conflict. It became quite heated; they were all young and idealistic. But every time they asked Justin CK Lim what his opinion was, he said, 'Well, I think every country has a right to a peaceful existence'; or, 'Both countries have valid arguments, don't they?' Or, when pushed, 'I don't really know much about that.'

That discussion, like so many others, had taken place at Angie's, which occupied a unit in a modest row of shop lots in Taman Tun Dr Ismail, surrounded by streets of pleasant, identical suburban houses. Yinghui had opened the café more than a decade before she moved to Shanghai: it was her very first business venture – though nowadays she realises that it could barely be called a 'business'. It was not far from where she had grown up and still lived at the time, a fifteen-minute drive through the grounds of the golf club that, in her childhood, used to be jungle. Justin CK Lim's family had sold the land a few years before the crash of '97, when the property boom was in full swing, and within a few years the golf course, designed by a famous American player, had been completed, its velvety undulating terrain and neo-Grecian clubhouse bounded by a private road manned by Nepalese security guards. It had been a shame to lose the vast patch of forest, but it did make the commute between the smart middle-class suburbs in that part of the city so much easier.

Every day as Yinghui drove to the café, she passed the small cemetery where Justin's grandmother was buried. The family burial ground had been excluded from the sale of the land to the golf club and now lay protected by a pair of ancient banyan trees whose thick vines lent a curtain of privacy, shrouding the elaborate tombs from open view. Often, she would slow down as she drove past, watching out for signs of recent visits, but there was never anyone there, not even an old retainer or gardener. Yet the tombs were clean and neat, the forest kept at bay. It was exactly the way that family worked: silently, mysteriously, efficiently – as if they had been and would be there forever. It used to make her laugh, this little reminder of her growing involvement with the Lim family – there was her steady relationship with Duncan CS Lim, of course, and now she was driving past and paying her respects to his ancestors every day, as though she was already part of their clan. She was not even formally engaged to Duncan CS Lim, yet her daily rituals anticipated a marriage in the not-too-distant future. They were a good match, everyone said so. Right kind of family, right kind of education, that sort of thing. But they themselves knew that it was something else that counted: the right kind of temperament.

The younger of the two boys, CS was, predictably, the polar opposite of Justin: willowy and almost fragile in appearance, but opinionated and temperamental. He lacked Justin's athleticism and conventional good looks, but his angular features, coupled with permanently dishevelled hair and an artfully messy way of dressing, made him a striking figure. Yinghui and he had started dating just before they had left Malaysia to attend university in London, he at UCL, she at LSE. He had studied philosophy, she sociology and politics – subjects that their parents only half jokingly called 'useless'. It was this uselessness that bound them to each other, Yinghui knew, together with the appreciation that they were the children of families that could afford to be indulgent, and that had assigned different roles to each of their children. They both knew that their role was to be beautifully useless.

And so they spent all their time proving that they were not just useless rich kids. In London, while their friends spent long evenings in the student bar, they would seek out talks by obscure Eastern European writers on such topics as 'Ideas of Beauty in Post-Communist Guilt', or attend lectures on Sanskrit texts at the Brunei Gallery. They once went to a reading by a Chinese novelist whose latest work contained no fewer than seven scenes of hetero-sexual anal sex and four instances of sado-masochism, which led to a furious audience debate on the nature of censorship and prudish-ness in Asia, which in turn provoked a late-night argument between Yinghui and CS, after which they themselves had sex – rather more timidly than the characters in the novel they'd just read, they laughingly agreed the following morning.

In their second year, they decided to take the same course in political thought at the LSE. They would sit in lectures holding hands under their desks while formulating opinions on Miłosz and Aron and Sartre, and afterwards they would always go for dry-fried noodles at a restaurant in Chinatown, where they would exchange views with a vehemence that matched the strength of their growing relationship. He always played the role of the cynic, arguing that man had succumbed irreversibly to the unquestioning nature of authority; she was the wide-eyed optimist, believing in man's capacity for redemption. And although their debates were genuine in their ferocity, there was also a comforting quality to them – a feeling of permanence, as if the passions they felt at the time would accompany them into old age.

During vacations they would often go InterRailing, their backpacks reassuringly heavy on their shoulders, a constant reminder of their independence and liberty. They had a preference for youth hostels and never stayed in anything fancier than a one-star hotel, though arriving late in Bordeaux one night after a missed connection, they were forced by a lack of options to check into a three-star hotel, which Yinghui secretly enjoyed, although she never admitted to it. Everywhere they went, they sought out interesting fringe theatre productions or alternative music venues, and they never bought anything except at local markets. Towards the end of their time at university, however, they began to spend more of their vacations back home in Kuala Lumpur, where CS worked with a charity for leprosy victims and set up a salon for 'writers and thinkers' that met once a week. Yinghui volunteered twice a week at a refuge for victims of domestic abuse, and the rest of the time helped out in the office of Friends of Old KL, a charity that sought to preserve historic buildings. Dressed simply in jeans or cargo shorts and matching Che Guevara T-shirts they'd bought at Camden Market, their hair styled in similar fashion – short, boyish, with a cheeky fringe that fell across the forehead – they looked like beautiful twins who were only fully comfortable in each other's company, and whose lives would always be entwined with one another's. That was certainly the way Yinghui felt.

The idea to set up Angie's came as a result of the growth of CS's thriving literary salon, as it was becoming difficult for him to find a suitable place to meet every week. There were now more than a dozen regulars, and often the group ran to twenty or so – a difficult size, because they were starting to read their work out aloud, and there were few places where they could do that apart from private homes – and there was nowhere they could just drop in at during the day and find someone to chat to. They tried a few places in Bangsar, but the atmosphere there was becoming too overtly bourgeois, and besides, the area was beginning to attract too many Westerners, the type who thought it was cool to hang out with the locals.

And so, the year Yinghui graduated, she set about finding somewhere to establish a small café. She had a clear idea of what she wanted: a cosy, unfussy place that served simple organic meals and pastries and fairtrade coffee, locally sourced; in the evenings she would host readings and poetry recitals, and maybe even song-writers wanting to try out new tunes before a discerning audience. She had no business plan, no financial model, no idea even of how she would make money; all she had was a generous loan from her parents, which she swore to repay at some point in the future, although she, like they, knew that even if she did not, nothing would be said, and the entire venture would go down as 'a lesson in life'.

It took her only a few days to find somewhere perfect, in a residential area which at the time was not at all fashionable. Flanked on one side by a lottery shop and on the other by an old Chinese grocery, the space had been empty for over a year and had last been used as a *nasi kandar* store, until its owner had lost interest in running a restaurant business after returning from the hajj. It was the nondescript nature of the area and the row of shops that thrilled Yinghui – the café would be so unexpected in such surroundings that most people would pass it by without ever noticing it. Only people who knew it was there would come in; it was better than she could have hoped for.

As soon as the main building work was completed she and CS spent every evening at the site, scrubbing and oiling the sustainably grown hardwood work surfaces, sealing the cement floors and cleaning the brick and cement dust from the walls. They agonised over the colour of the walls, but finally decided to leave them unplastered: the bare concrete looked starkly chic, the ideal backdrop to their carefully chosen furniture (they had planned an artful mélange of mismatched chairs and tables salvaged from sixties vintage shops, coupled with old Nyonya pieces CS had found in his family's numerous store rooms). They left the heavy metal shutters drawn tightly shut as they worked, and in the harsh glow cast by the naked lightbulbs (their Noguchi paper lampshades had not yet arrived) they argued over the placement of the library of books and the newspaper stand; they got takeaway *charkwayteow* from the shop around the corner and ate it cross-legged on the newly polished floor, their wooden chopsticks scraping noisily on the Styrofoam boxes; and when it got late and they felt they had quarrelled too much and worked too hard, they had sex – as she bent over the pristine new counter she worried, slightly, that the sweat on her hands and elbows would leave marks on the smoothly grained wood. Later, still high on exhaustion but calmer after their lovemaking, he would paraphrase a Slovenian philosopher whose lectures they had attended as students in London: 'You know,' he would say, kissing her dust-and-paint-covered hair, 'it's a sign of true love that we can insult each other.'

'In that case: you are a dirty piece of shit,' she would respond, laughing, smelling the turpentine on his fingers.

They had the phrase written on a signboard in plain letters, along with other quotes stolen from European thinkers they admired, which they then hung randomly on the walls:

All Great Novels are Bisexual
Q: Why are you crying? A: Because you're not
True Love = Insulting Each Other

They didn't care if anyone would *get* these quotes; in fact, they were sure that few, if any, would understand them or would know where they were from. They themselves found the signs amusing, and that was all that mattered. On a whim, they decided to call the café Angie's, after a movie they had seen that year, one of those so-bad-it's-good films that CS loved. They had lost interest midway through the film and had engaged in surreptitious light petting to while away the time, and afterwards promised that when they were finally living together, they would own a cat called Angie. Or a car. Or a café.

Right from the beginning, CS's friends loved Angie's. *Their* friends loved Angie's; for Yinghui realised that CS brought many people into her life – into their joint lives. She was not the only one drawn to his blend of nonchalance and intellect, his elegant skinniness, his don't-give-a-shit attitude summed up by the perma-nent dark rings under his eyes and his charmingly dishevelled hair. Standing at the counter, pretending to tally up the figures on the cash machine which she never fully mastered, she would watch him slouch on the battered fake Alvar Aalto sofa, his legs stretched out, surrounded by a coterie of eager disciples, predominantly young women. He would often be content to let others do the talking; sometimes he would just stare into space or close his eyes as if he was thinking of something else entirely, but then, in the midst of the fiercest debates, he would begin to speak, and every-one would fall silent and turn to him. His one-liners were pithy and original and always provocative; often there would be a ripple of embarrassed laughter at what he said. Each night, just after 9.30, she would pull the shutters halfway down and lock the doors before opening a bottle of Cabernet Sauvignon. She would then settle down with CS and a few of his close friends – *their* close friends – and chat until the early hours of the morning, sometimes until they heard the call for *Fajr* from the nearby mosque. Often she would stretch out on the sofa, lay her head on his lap, and doze off to the sound of his voice.

She felt that she could spend every evening like this, for years and years to come, and very possibly forever.

The business side of Angie's was more bothersome. Yinghui struggled with the accounts, the indecipherable debits and credits and the never-ending trail of invoices from suppliers, which she would often forget or even lose altogether, yet pride prevented her from hiring a book-keeper. She had set out to run this business herself, to prove that she was not useless. Once she enthusiastically offered to organise a party for the launch of one of CS's friend's latest poetry collection. The evening was a huge success, with readings interspersed with music by a soulful folk guitarist whose slang-rich lyrics spoke of urban migration and loneliness. The next morning Yinghui realised that she had not agreed on a fee for any of the food or drink she had provided; her business had paid for everything, and she was left with the enormous bill. The Indonesian cleaners were late; the whole place was filled with the sour reek of stale beer; there were cigarette butts all over the floor; and someone had accidentally dislodged the plug to the freezer, leaving Yinghui to contemplate a few hundred *ringgits'* worth of melted organic home-made coconut ice cream.

'Sweetheart, why are you so grumpy?' CS said, putting his arm around her. 'It's really not a big deal. Next time, if you don't want to do stuff for our friends, just don't do it. No one's forcing you.'

'It's not that,' she said, shrugging away from him. 'It's just, well, Angie's is a business too, you know, not just a place for your friends to hang out.'

'So it's "my friends" now, is it? Just don't do it, then. No one asked you to lay on a party for Ramli.' He put a Tom Waits tape into the cassette player, and the music started playing loudly through the expensive German speakers … *colder than a well-digger's ass, it's colder than a well-digger's ass* … 'Anyway, Jojo was there last night. She's Ramli's publisher, for God's sake; you could have just asked her for some money if you're that worried about it.'

'Money's not the issue,' she said, staring at a pile of dried-up prawn-sambal canapés that had fallen onto the sofa.

'I know this is about independence and proving your worth and all that crap,' he said, sweeping aside the bits of food from the sofa before stretching out on it. 'But frankly, if the going's tough, why don't you just ask your dad to help you out for a while? We've got to get real here. Your old man's rolling in it at the moment – everyone knows he's just got a share of that big oil concession up north in Terengganu.'

'*Fuck* you,' Yinghui said. She realised she was wiping the counter with a damp cloth even though it was already clean. It was the only part of the café that was not filthy, the only bit she was in control of. 'How fucking dare you bring that up? That's rich, coming from you. Anyway, I said it's not about money.'

'*Ya*, sure. So what is it about then?' His foot was tapping to the rhythm of the music.

She looked him in the eye and then, fearing she would start to cry, looked away again. 'No one even thanked me.'

He was silent for a while, waiting, she thought, for her to cry. But then he came and stood behind her, circling his arms round her waist and drawing her towards him. 'Hey, hey,' he whispered. 'Shhh, you silly thing. Everyone knows this place can't exist without you. Everyone loves you, it goes without saying, huh? We're all so grateful and happy. What would we do if you didn't keep this place running? Where else would we go? Oh my God, we'd be screwed. The reason this place is so cool is you. Everyone knows that. Especially me. *Especially* me.'

She nodded, feeling his warm breath on her ear, his face pressing close to hers. She knew, then, that as long as he was around and happy to be at Angie's, she would keep it going, no matter how much it cost. They stayed wrapped in their embrace, saying nothing, listening to the music filling the empty space … *Lucky that you found someone to make you feel secure* … Yinghui chuckled. 'You played that song on purpose, you bastard.'

'No I didn't. It's kind of a sad song.'

… *'cause we were all so young and foolish, now we are mature.*

'You know that thing that you mentioned, that … oil thing. You're wrong. It's in Kelantan, not Terengganu.'

'Same difference,' he said, leaning in to kiss her. 'Somewhere up north, anyway. It's all the same up there. Beautiful and backward.'

The following week, without telling Yinghui, CS paid off all of Angie's outstanding loans, invoices and credit notes, and deposited an additional sum in the account. When she thanked him he shrugged and said it was easy; he'd done it through one of the family companies. Well, actually, his brother Justin had arranged everything for him, he said, reclining in his customary position in the low grey sofa. Just don't ask how it was done, because he did *not* understand. It was no big deal; it was just money, after all.

She was moved not so much by the generosity of CS's actions, but by the solidity of his intentions. There was a permanence in the gesture, a suggestion of longevity: he intended that their futures be entwined. It was irrelevant that his family would not even have noticed a sum of money like that – because, let's face it, her parents could have helped her out too (though perhaps not with such ease). What mattered was CS's swiftness of commitment. He had done it with his customary nonchalance, but in keeping Angie's afloat, he meant to keep Yinghui afloat too.

It was just money, after all.

It wasn't his fault.

It was her father's fault, the mess he had got them all into.

It wasn't her father's fault; he was dead now.

Too many thoughts, spinning and clashing in her mind.

It was just money.

These were some of the excuses that she ran through her head, a thousand times each day, barely eighteen months later, when CS decided to stop seeing her. She tried to rationalise his decision, but the logic of it defied her. There were too many lines of reasoning that crisscrossed without ever joining up. He would not answer her calls, would not come to see her. She passed messages through his friends – now she realised they really were his friends, not theirs

– but none ever got through. People stopped coming to Angie's, and soon there was no one left who could act as a messenger. Even when Justin was dispatched to explain the reason behind the break-up, Yinghui could not understand it. He spoke with his usual clarity – so clear as to make no sense at all. It was nothing to do with her, she had to understand that. It was just that, as a family, they had to think of the future happiness of each of the children, and also that of the family. It was not an easy decision. But, well, it was getting difficult now because of her family's position and the sad business with her father.

'What do you mean, *sad business*?'

'I mean, all the bad publicity. The whole … scandal.'

He smiled after saying this, as if the word 'scandal' would make everything clear. As he left, he turned back to look at her, and she saw that he was still smiling. He smiled in the way someone smiles when they don't know what to say; when they don't know what to say because they don't feel anything, because they are thinking of more important things in their lives. When he had left she looked around her, surveying the sudden neatness of the café, the stillness of her world: the chairs and tables pushed alongside one wall, some stacked on top of each other; the vintage jukebox she and CS had bought on a whim, dark now, devoid of sparkle; the wires hanging from the ceiling, stripped of their designer lampshades, which she'd sold to pay the electricity bill; the empty freezer, with its door left open – at its base there was a water mark, a dry ring where the thawing ice had stained the polish she and CS had applied to the cement floor. The only things that remained in place were the sofa on which she sat, the low grey sofa that CS had stretched out on, night after night, for nearly two years; and, on the walls, the signs she had not bothered to take down. *True Love = Insulting Each Other.*

She thought of the word 'scandal', letting it echo in her head for a few moments. It sounded wrong, provided no answers.

She decided that it was all about money. CS Lim, Justin CK Lim – they had plenty, would always have plenty, but she had nothing now. It was just about money.

When people heard of Angie's closure, or when they drove past it, they would shrug as if it was no great surprise. KL was full of places like that nowadays, they would say, opened and closed in no time at all. But they would snigger and add, under their breaths: She didn't know how to do business, that girl. She was just an airhead rich kid who thought her father's money would last forever. But, *ah-there*, you see? *Some more kena dump by that Lim boy. Serve her right*. If you act big, that's what happens. She didn't know how to do business at all, that girl, she was really stupid.

It was ten minutes past the appointed hour – not a good sign. Up to that point, she had assumed only good things about her host, had imagined someone with perfect manners. Walter Chao. Even the name had a stylish elegance to it, a restrained old-world quality that suggested courtesy and understated flair in a city where such things seemed to have been swept away by the relentless advance of concrete and steel, bright lights and nightlife – the kind of fast living that she herself had become accustomed to. She looked at her BlackBerry: no message. Maybe she was being stood up – maybe she should start composing a message, tell him she was feeling unwell and had been forced to go home; leave him in the lurch before he did it to her. But then again, she might never know what he was going to propose, she might miss the opportunity of a lifetime. She wasn't here on a date, for goodness' sake, she was here to do business. But was that really worth the risk of humiliation? She was just beginning to form the opening sentence in her head – *So very sorry, but I must have eaten something bad at lunchtime* – when she noticed the maître d'hôtel hurrying over to the table.

'Mr Chao is just coming up in the lift now,' he said. 'He is sorry to be late. He rang and left a message for me about ten minutes ago, but I was away and I didn't see it. I'm so sorry – please will you … be understanding when you speak to him. It's so busy tonight, and I just didn't see the message.'

Yinghui nodded and looked at her watch. 8.11 p.m. 'Not a problem,' she said.

'Thank you, madame,' the maître d'hôtel said. His French accent was charmingly stereotypical; it amused her. She was going to have a good evening.

For the next minute or so she pretended to read the menu, but every so often she would shift her gaze subtly, taking in the people coming into the restaurant, trying to identify Walter Chao. A gaggle of smartly dressed businessmen gathered at the reception desk, handing over their camel-coloured coats to the girls dressed in black trouser suits. A Middle-Eastern-looking man and his Chinese girlfriend stood waiting patiently behind this group. Then, from behind the crowd of people she saw the maître d'hôtel holding out his hand politely but firmly in order to clear a space. Behind him, Yinghui caught a glimpse of a light-grey jacket and sky-blue shirt. The maître d'hôtel hurried towards her like a one-man police cavalcade; she looked back down at her menu, turning the page as if she was deep in concentration. When she looked up she saw the maître d' inclining his head in a half-bow; next to him was Walter Chao. She stood up and offered him her hand, which he grasped firmly without squeezing it, while looking her in the eye.

'I am so sorry to be late. Like everyone else, I blame the traffic. Will you please forgive me?'

'Traffic is a part of life in Shanghai. Anyway, compared to Beijing, it's nothing. Please don't worry. You're not really late at all.'

The maître d'hôtel eased his chair into place as he sat down. 'That's very understanding of you. I can't abide tardiness myself.' He opened the menu briefly and then closed it, pushing it to one side. He was not a tall man, Yinghui had noticed – about the same height as her, maybe five foot five or six – and yet, once seated, he had a way of dominating the space at the table in the subtlest way, his forearms resting on its edge, his head leaning just the tiniest bit towards her, as if anticipating greater intimacy.

A waiter appeared with an ice bucket on a stand. He briefly showed the label to Walter Chao, who nodded without really looking, without really taking his eyes off Yinghui. He could not be considered handsome in any conventional sense, yet Yinghui felt the same sense of embarrassment she had experienced when, as a schoolgirl, she had spoken to the cool, good-looking boys in her neighbourhood – a sense of timidity mixed with excitement. That feeling felt entirely foreign to her now, belonging as it did to another era in her life.

She averted her gaze and looked at the champagne – a bulbous bottle with an unfamiliar label, not a high-fashion name favoured by gangster rappers and trashy heiresses but something with understated chic.

'Pink champagne,' she said. 'I haven't had that in years.'

'I like the idea of starting each new project with a celebration,' he said, 'rather than waiting for the end. That way I can look forward to a successful enterprise. I don't understand people who only celebrate a venture at its conclusion. But, please, do say if you don't like it. We can always order something different. Or just orange juice if you're not up for champagne tonight.'

'Oh no,' Yinghui said, lifting her flute. 'I'm always up for champagne.'

'I'm glad to hear that,' he said, lifting his flute to match hers, 'because I have a feeling we're going to get on very well together. Ever since I heard about you and read those articles in the business news, I thought, now there's someone formidable. Cheers.'

The night sky was heavy with a dusky purple glow, the lights of the city blotting out the darkness. She was glad she had arrived early, that she had had a chance to settle in and stake out her position at the table. She felt him watching her, and even though he did so discreetly, she knew that she was being judged.

'What are you going to eat?' she said. 'The good thing about arriving early is that I was able to decide what to have before you got here.'

'Great,' he said. 'I always have the same thing here. But I'm not going to tell you what it is, because I don't want to influence your decision.'

He brushed an invisible speck of dust off his lapel, and she noticed the quality of the fabric of his jacket: smooth, matt, unblemished. As he inclined his head for an instant she saw that his nose was uneven, curving to one side just at its tip; for the rest of the evening she would notice this tiny imbalance from time to time and be struck by how it made his face look damaged, in spite of his perfect grooming.

'I have an idea,' he said. 'Why don't we talk business for just a few minutes before we order our food? That way we can get it out of the way and enjoy ourselves – chat about life, find out more about each other, all the things normal people do when they first meet. What do you think?'

'I think it's an excellent idea. But let's get it done quickly, because I'm starving. And curious, too.'

When he laughed, his face creased into deep lines, ageing him. She had thought of him as around her age, but now she could see that he was quite a few years older, his skin weathered by the sun (she could imagine him on holiday on the French Riviera or Pansea Beach in Phuket, a compact, dark man dressed in Bermuda shorts and an ironed short-sleeved shirt). 'I take it you've Googled me, so there's no need to go into my background.'

'Not really,' she lied (she had spent a frustrating and ultimately fruitless hour on the internet trying to piece together a picture of this man, and then rung contacts in various countries in South-East Asia to see if anyone knew him). 'But I have a rough idea of your work. Very impressive. Of course I'd known about you vaguely in the past – especially the projects in Malaysia. I just didn't make the connection, that's all – I mean, I didn't know you were the person who'd done all of them.' She sipped her champagne and looked him in the eye. 'But I was always aware of your name,' she lied again.

He shrugged. 'Reputation is not important to me. The past is the past – what's important is what one does next.'

'I quite agree.' She pushed a small bowl of olives towards him. 'So, what is one going to do next?'

'That depends on how the rest of this dinner goes.'

'I see.'

He unfolded his napkin and placed it in his lap. 'Let me ask you a question. When you're working on a project – late at night, at the end of another sixteen-hour day, when you're utterly exhausted and wondering why the hell you're doing it – what goes through your head? I mean, what drives you? What are you hoping to gain by working day in, day out, being nice to people you don't really like, poring over accounts, talking to boring bankers and account-ants. What is it you're searching for? Is it money?'

'No. Well, yes. No one ever works to become poor,' Yinghui answered. 'But obviously it's not just about money.'

'What is it about then?'

'I don't really know.'

'I'll tell you: it's about respect. Money is the conduit for respect. The richer you are, the more respect you gain.'

Yinghui shrugged. 'I don't know if it's that simple.'

He smiled. 'You know it is. So let me tell you how I am going to help you gain plenty of respect. Great, massive piles of it.'

How to Invest Wisely –
A Case Study in Property Management

As I've said on many an occasion, the best way to sharpen one's business acumen is to analyse real-life situations. Consider the following example, paying close attention to the triumphs and errors of human judgement:

In 1981, my father bought a near-derelict building in Kota Bharu for 30,000 *ringgit*. City dwellers would scoff at that price, and it was not a lot of money even in those days. But back then it represented all of my father's meagre savings, plus a considerable amount borrowed from well-intentioned friends and relatives who believed that my father was going to make good this time and repay their loans with interest. They thought they were making an investment rather than lending money; I was the only one who was not convinced. Even though this was some time before the gambling properly took hold of him, I could see that his reckless fantasies were already becoming an addiction, and that no good would come out of this venture. It would be a failure like everything else he ever did; there would be no glorious curtain call. My time away from him had enabled me to see this as clearly as sunshine after a night's rain.

I received a letter from him telling me to take the first bus north to join him at his new home – our new home. I had been living, if you recall, with my great-aunt in the far south of Johor, and I had recently got a place at a technical college where I was learning to be an electrician, much to the joy of my great-aunt. That was the extent of her ambitions for me (people of my background, I remind you, were not primed for greatness). My father's note was brief but breezy in tone. I looked at the address of the building that had become both his home and his new business venture, the enterprise that would reunite us at last and provide us with a solid income sufficient to last him through his final years and – who knows – to provide a legacy I could inherit. The name of the building looked at once bizarre and familiar, and it took me a while to place it.

Speculatively built in the late 1960s upon rumours of vast, soon-to-be-discovered offshore oilfields, the Tokyo Hotel had been constructed in anticipation of an influx of low-skilled workers that never quite materialised. It was not designed to be anything but functional: a three-storey concrete block with small windows and a flat roof on which rainwater collected, breeding mosquitoes and dripping down the leaky gutters to form rivulets of black moss that scarred the building's façade. When the rumours of the oilfields turned out to be unfounded, the hotel quickly fell into disrepair – and soon into disrepute too. It was mainly Chinese girls who hung around the Tokyo Hotel, and sometimes Thai girls who came across the border with their travelling salesman boyfriends. One of the tales often told about the hotel – perhaps apocryphal, but who knows? – was that the rooms were rented strictly by the hour, and that each had an alarm wired to a clock that started ticking the moment you entered, and sounded right on sixty minutes. It was said that the clocks were the only things that worked in the rooms – none of the sockets seemed to be wired, which made the kettle and the plastic table fan redundant. Sometimes the ceiling fans worked, but they spun so languidly that they raised no breeze at all. Your hour there would be stifling, sweaty.

These were details I picked up from older teenage boys, some of whom claimed to have visited the hotel. They said the partition walls were so thin they could hear everything from the next room – local radio dramas, Thai news from across the border, sports commentaries: always the radio, to drown out the moaning and the breathy cries. And there were noises you simply couldn't recognise – one that sounded like the sharp slapping of a hand on bare flesh, but delivered with metronomic, machinelike regularity; or a noise like a coconut grater, almost like a dentist's drill, applied to soft rubber; or people speaking in strange, harsh languages that sounded like nothing you'd ever heard on TV, that not even the villains in Hollywood films spoke. Someone said he'd heard the voices of extra-terrestrials; one boy even said he'd heard his own dad.

Sometime in the mid-seventies, the Tokyo Hotel began to be raided by the religious police – once, twice, then every month. They'd heard that there were Malay girls from out of town who'd been seen there; one or two had even become regulars. No one really cared when it became obvious the place was going to close. It didn't seem exotic or exciting any more, just run-down and filthy. Everyone hoped it would be torn down, but it wasn't. Without the oilfields that had been hoped for, there was no money in town even to demolish a lousy building like that.

Left abandoned, the Tokyo Hotel became a hang-out for local junkies, increasing in number with the easy availability of Burmese heroin filtering across the border from Hat Yai and Songkhla. Whereas prepubescent boys might once have cycled past in the hope of catching sight of a scantily clad girl, they now avoided the needles and broken bottles, and the general unsavouriness that hung over the area. The entire street leading to the hotel slowly began to look shabby too – never one of the more bustling streets in town, it became decrepit, the shutters on the few remaining shops permanently pulled down. All the business had moved to the other side of town, closer to the market, where there were now modern department stores and an open-air plaza for food stalls, cooled in the evening by balmy sea breezes, its perimeter decorated with hanging neon lights. The contrast was almost laughable: why would anyone want to go to the part of town where the air was fetid and stagnant, the land becoming swampy and mosquito-ridden as it stretched towards the riverbank? The roads in the area were ravaged by floods, and as newer routes into the centre of town were built, the lanes became overgrown with weeds, and small trees sprouted in the gaps between the buildings.

From both a commercial and a lifestyle point of view, a derelict hotel in a rapidly degenerating part of town did not seem to offer any possibilities at all – any prudent entrepreneur would have shied away from it, any business manual would have warned against it; but it was at precisely this point that my father took over the Tokyo Hotel.

9

见利忘义

Pursue Gains, Forget Righteousness

That day Phoebe felt her life was awash with good feelings. She was dressed according to the rules of fashion that she had picked up from observing Shanghai women: wear the biggest sunglasses you can find, carry the largest handbag possible. The new attitude she had been cultivating was filling her with a magnificent confidence.

Already she could tell that she was making a good impression on the man she had just met. His eyes were wandering up and down her tight-fitting dress – he was making no attempt to hide the fact that he found her sexually attractive.

Good, she thought.

Even though the weather was turning cold and the light was not as bright as before, it was important for her to look as glamorous as possible, as if she was going to a fancy evening function, because that was the way women of style carried themselves. Whether on the streets of Xintiandi or on billboards or in magazines, this was the standard of woman she aspired to be, and on this day, going to have coffee with a man she'd met on the internet, she felt certain that she had finally attained that level of sophistication. Her life would now surely change for the better.

For a few weeks now she had been planning a new approach to finding a man, which was the key to finding success in Shanghai. She had invested a lot of time and money in observing the different methods of accomplishing this. To begin with, she spent many evenings in bars where she knew men and women gathered to meet each other. In one place in Hongqiao, which she had heard was favoured by foreigners, she saw that the local women were dressed provocatively, in figure-hugging dresses that showed off a lot of flesh, the very opposite of how Chinese girls were supposed to dress, with modesty and respect. Phoebe had always thought that nice girls could attract men with their demure charm alone, but now she could see that she had been wrong. That was such an old-fashioned and outdated way of thinking; she had to change her whole attitude. The black satin dress she had worn specially for such evenings out now seemed dull and overly modest, with its long sleeves and strip of see-through lace over her collarbone. She had thought it alluring, but now it made her feel like a Muslim wife, covered up so no man would approach her.

She watched as a young woman flirted with a group of American men at the bar. The men were laughing and touching her arm, her bare shoulder. They were drinking beer from bottles, Budweiser, and every so often they would clink the bottles together with a loud noise after they had made a joke. The bar was lit with neon lights set under the glass counter, and the colours that reflected in the faces of the men and the woman seemed too bright, unreal, as if in an old movie. The woman's heels were so high that her calf muscles were stretched and tense, which made her legs look long and muscular, like an African warrior's. She distributed her card among the men, and Phoebe could tell they were impressed by it. After a few minutes the woman left the bar with one of the men, their arms linked like long-time lovers.

When the group had dispersed, Phoebe saw that one of the woman's cards had fallen to the floor. It had a name on it, and the nature of her business: *PRODUCTS FOR THE BED*. There was no address, just a QQ ID number for online chatting and a mobile-phone number. Maybe she was a prostitute, Phoebe thought; maybe she was what people called *kuaican* – like so many girls Phoebe had known in the past, she was just a cheap, quick snack. But tonight she had a man, and maybe by tomorrow she would have a boyfriend. And maybe in a few months' time she would be married, and maybe she would have security for the rest of her life – maybe this was the last evening she would ever have to spend in a bar. And all because she dared to wear a short skirt and a top that showed off her too-skinny body.

In her Journal of Her Secret Self, Phoebe wrote down the following resolutions:

I must improve my appearance, I must dare to dress like a slut.
I must exercise my body, to be fat is not acceptable.
Sleep – five hours a day is enough.
I must improve myself always, I must practise my English.

She bought a few self-help books, cheap pirated copies being sold on the pavement near the subway station in Tiantong Lu, such as *Sophistify Yourself.* The most useful one was called *Why Men Love Bitches.* As she read it, she scribbled down more notes:

Use men just as they would use you.
Lying to a man is OK, as long as you get what you want.
Do not only stick to one man.
Being nice is your mom's job – and look where it got her.
Do not grow old waiting.

She started to spend more time on the internet again, but this time she was more careful. It was her best bet, since there were so many men out there. She put new photos on her profile page, images that showed her in outfits carefully selected in the cramped market in Qipu Lu not far from where she lived. She didn't really like going there, because it was full of poor people who reminded her of her desperate situation, but she told herself it would not be like this for long. In many of these new photos she adopted poses she had seen on other girls' profiles – side on, lifting her shoulder to her chin, or pursing her lipsticked mouth at the camera with her eyes raised teasingly. They looked so much more tantalising than her old photo, taken in the park in Guangzhou. If she were a man she would surely want to go out with such a sexy girl. She was about to remove the old photo from her profile, but then, for a reason she could not understand, she let it remain, the last of the many pictures, where it would not be noticed.

In keeping with her new rules, she was very discerning. She only chatted with carefully selected men who met her criteria. She mastered the art of chatting with three, four, five men at once, using only short sentences or single words to disguise the fact that she could not type as fast as the educated men that she was pursuing. Really? Amazing. Cool! *Ha ha. Aiiii. En. En. En.* Single words were all it took to sustain a long conversation. *Men do not really want to listen, they much prefer to talk.* It made her job easier.

Every time she chatted with a man she imagined herself doing all the things she had decided she would do. Doing things to him. With him. The more she imagined these things, the less bad they seemed. Her fear began to subside. She could do it. She had to.

The moment she walked into the Coffee Bean and Tea Leaf café on Wujiang Lu, she sensed that her impressive personal styling was drawing attention. The teenage boys and young men looked up from their laptop computers and followed her with lustful gazes, while the women looked at her with envy. The full-length red coat with fake fur lapels she had chosen was certainly making an impression. Her date stood up at the far side of the room – he'd found a secluded table in the corner where they would be able to talk quietly. He was better-looking than she had imagined, and younger too. She had selected her target well.

This was the third date she had arranged with a man she'd met on the internet. The first turned out to be twenty years older than his internet photo, while the second walked with a bad limp, the result of a recent accident for which he was having expensive medical treatment, leaving him in financial difficulties. On both occasions Phoebe just made an excuse and left – said she had stomach problems. *It doesn't matter if men think you are a bitch.* So, before suggesting a meeting with her third target, she asked him many probing questions and requested numerous photos in order to get clues about his life. He'd sent her a photo taken from far away, which made it difficult to make out what he looked like or how tall he was; moreover he was wearing big black sunglasses. But what was important was that she could see a nice car in the photo, and also quality leather shoes in the English style, plus what looked like an iPhone. These were the important elements. Nonetheless, she had to admit it was a bonus that he'd turned out to be better-looking than his photo suggested.

'Hi, nice to meet you,' he said, introducing himself with a name that sounded fake. He hesitated a little as he said it, as if he had been practising but was still a little unsure. Phoebe was alert to such things now; no one could cheat her.

'Nice to meet you … what's your name again? I didn't quite catch it. Sorry, the music …'

'Sun Xiang,' he repeated. It sounded more convincing this time, and when he smiled he seemed very charming, with nice straight teeth that suggested good calcium intake at an early age. His bone structure was good too, and he must have stood at least five foot eleven.

Phoebe sat down, but did not take off her sunglasses. She had done this before on previous dates – it added an air of mystique. She placed her handbag on the table between them, not on the floor or tucked in beside her on the comfortable low armchair, but right in the middle of the table so he could see it. Sure, the hand-bag was a fake, but it was a very high-quality copy which had cost her a lot of money – *chao-A* grade counterfeit goods were expensive and difficult to obtain these days, what with the Europeans putting pressure on the Chinese government to ban such items. That was what the stallkeeper had told her in order to justify the cost of over 1,000 *kuai*. At the time she had been astonished by the price, nearly five times what she had paid for her existing bag, which she had purchased in a market in Guangzhou and which was exactly the same brand. But she was in Shanghai now, and everything was more luxurious and more expensive.

'Sun Xiang,' Phoebe said, 'are you local?' She'd detected a Shanghai accent in his voice – she could pick up little signs which made it difficult for people to lie to her.

'Yes,' he replied. 'I was born and grew up here. You?'

She took off her sunglasses, noticing that people in the café were still looking round at her. 'It's complicated. I moved around a lot – abroad, mostly. My parents are from Guangdong province, though.'

'Abroad? That sounds interesting.' He was staring at her, his eyes settling on her bare knees. 'I'm sorry, I'm just … so nervous,' he said.

'Why nervous?' she said, reaching forward to shift her handbag for no reason whatsoever. His gaze followed her hand and remained on the bag even when she had relinquished her grip. Surely he was admiring the remarkable quality of the leather handle.

'I'm nervous because I don't do this dating thing often. In fact, this is my first time. I've chatted with a lot of girls on the internet, but I've always been too afraid to meet anyone. But you just seemed so … interesting.'

'Really?'

'Yes. And … and also, you are so beautiful. I guess that's why I'm nervous. You are even better-looking in real life than your photos.'

When she laughed she was aware of a tinkling quality to the sound, like the notes of a piano in the lobby of an expensive hotel, hearing which makes you happy.

'And your fashion sense is really excellent,' he continued. He glanced around briefly before looking down at his hands and adding in a quieter voice, 'Your skirt is very short.'

Phoebe tugged weakly at the hem of her skirt, a false show of modesty. She didn't care at all that her skirt was short, she had planned it that way. 'Are you going to get me a coffee, or are you just going to say flattering lies to me all day?'

'I'm sorry, it's so rude of me. I'm not my usual self today. As I said, you make me really … nervous. *Hai*, so stupid of me. I'm normally very confident. And it's not lies! It's true!'

She laughed. 'Young men these days, so full of superfluous nonsense!'

'What would you like?'

'*Macchiato*,' she said. She liked showing off her English. She could tell he was impressed. 'What are you having? *Caffè latte*?'

'Just tea. *Longjing*, if they have it. I'm very boring and traditional. I'm not used to this modern coffee-drinking.'

He reached into the breast pocket of his jacket and took out a long wallet that looked thick with credit cards. Phoebe tried not to show that she was noticing it, noticing where he kept it, how much it contained. 'What did you want again?' he asked. 'I'm so useless – I can't even pronounce it!'

As she watched him standing at the counter, Phoebe began to form a fuller picture of him, one that had eluded her during her online chats with him. There he had seemed more confident and daring, making wisecracks and stating his opinion in a forthright manner on many subjects, such as the outrageous property prices in Shanghai, politics and internet censorship. She had imagined him as an entrepreneur whose boldness came from having made money, probably older than he said he was, maybe married too – someone who would want to feel her up and take advantage of her. She hadn't cared. She too had her plans, and he had appeared to fit them perfectly. If he was insensitive and slightly lascivious, he would not sense that she was meeting him only to get money, would not realise she was using him until it was too late, until he woke up in the morning to find his wallet missing. Or maybe she would insist on him giving her some money once he was in a state of full excitement. *Men will do anything when they are past a certain point of sexual arousal.* She might find his wife's number on his mobile phone and threaten to inform her of his sordid extramarital lusts if he did not give her some money.

But in fact she had found someone younger, well-mannered and timid, the kind of man she might once have liked to go on a date with – the very opposite of the high-flying tycoon she had been searching for. She looked at his nice jeans and his well-made leather shoes, which had little tassels on them. His glasses were rimless and made him look like a nervous university student, even though he must have been in his early thirties. Frankly, he did not have an exhilarating appearance or personality; he was a perfect example of a *shiyong nan* – not rich but comfortable, not handsome but acceptable. A man whose worth lay in his practical value, who could satisfy your material needs to a reasonable level and would be a solid person to be with. She had not expected to meet such a person while chatting on the internet.

He kept glancing back at her from the counter and smiling shyly, but when she smiled back he turned away. It was because he was intimidated by her level of sophistication, Phoebe thought. Maybe she should not have dressed in this high-glamour way. She began to feel guilty about planning to use him for financial gain; perhaps he did not deserve that. But he was a man, he liked her, she could sense her power over him – he was ideal. She should not let the opportunity slip. Maybe he could even become a boyfriend. Who knew?

He returned with a small coffee for her, a pot of *Longjing* for himself.

'Oh, sorry,' Phoebe said. 'Let me move my handbag.' She shifted it slightly to make space for the drinks, but did not move it off the table.

'That's a very stylish bag,' he said.

'What? Oh, hm.' Phoebe did not want to acknowledge his comment too much; she wanted to show that such a luxury bag was not a big deal to her. But she felt a sense of triumph that her ploy had worked – the 1,000-*kuai* investment, the careful selection of the brand, had all been worth it.

'LV is so popular in China these days,' he said, 'even though it's so expensive. You must have a very good job.'

'I could do better, but it's fine for now, it pays the bills. Everything in Shanghai costs so much,' she replied, sipping her coffee. 'Tell me, what do you think of the new fiscal measures introduced by the government to cool down the overheated property market? I've been looking to buy a new place, but apartment prices are just crazy right now.' She had paid special attention to the duller parts of the newspaper, committing to memory such expressions as 'fiscal measures' and 'overheated property market'.

'You sound knowledgeable about property – don't tell me you're one of those rich speculators!' As he spoke she could tell that he was impressed by her chic demeanour. He would look at her but would not dare to hold her gaze for long, averting his eyes from her direct stare. Although he was careful not to show it, she could tell that he was intimidated because he would occasionally look at her legs and the skin around her breastbone, which she had left exposed to the November chill. But above all, his nervy glances kept returning to her handbag, which was still sitting on the table between them – proud, like a rare artefact recently removed from a museum. She began to feel sorry for this man, that he was so easily browbeaten and beguiled, and for a moment she wondered if she should soften her approach, but then she thought, No, this is what it means to be a modern woman in Shanghai; all the strong women are like this, we must dominate men. He was a Functional Man: his purpose was to be dominated by women like her. *Honey, if you don't take advantage of men from time to time, you can bet your bottom dollar they'll take advantage of you.*

'Of course I'm not a property tycoon,' Phoebe said. 'My parents are quite generous, they allow me to live with them, but I would like more independence.'

'If I were you,' the Functional Man said, 'I wouldn't bother to buy a place now. You're still so young. In a few years, property prices will hit rock bottom. Why? Think about it. I am thirty-four years old. When my parents die, I am going to inherit their apartment. My wife … well, I'm not married yet, but when I do get married, my wife will also inherit an apartment from her parents. That means when we die, our child will inherit two apartments. If our child gets married, his wife will also inherit two apartments. So if the one-child policy continues, everyone is going to have four apartments … who's going to want all of those places? You'll be able to buy them for nothing!'

Phoebe was impressed by his logic – she herself would never have been able to think like that. He really was a man of practical value! She said, 'That's really interesting, what else do you think?'

They spoke about all sorts of things – the Functional Man really knew how to talk. She was pleased with the way the date was going, because she could tell that he was really enamoured of her (*When men talk a lot, it's a sign that they've let their guard down – you've got them!*). But she was careful to remain aloof, leaning back in her seat and giving him cool looks to demonstrate her superiority and desirability.

'I'm sorry, I think I'm boring you,' he said after a while.

'No, why do you say that?'

'No reason. You seem a bit fidgety, that's all. Do you need to go to the restroom?'

'No, I don't. But I would like another drink. Maybe some tea. Wait a second, I'll get them this time.'

'Out of the question. A man cannot let a beautiful young woman pay for anything.' He reached inside his jacket, and Phoebe could not help her eyes being drawn to the spot where he kept his wallet.

'Hey, Big Brother, this is the modern world, you know.' *Do little things for a man when he least expects it, and you will soon reap the rewards.* As she reached for her handbag, she felt the tinkling laugh rising in her throat again. She unzipped the bag and reached inside for her purse, made of glossy red leather with a gold buckle that was bound to attract his attention. She went to the counter to order their drinks, and waited patiently to collect them. In order to maintain her air of cool superiority, she did not turn around to look at him; she did not want him to think she was impatient to get back to him, or was interested in him. She wanted to remain unattainable, just as her self-help books said she should. Everything she had learnt from them so far was serving her well. She stood upright, as straight as she could given her high heels, and pulled her shoulderblades back so they squeezed together. He would be excited by the sight of that, for sure he would. Warm air from the heater blew softly on her bare shoulders and swept around her neck, and the tight dress she was wearing clung to her buttocks; when she reached up to collect the tray from the counter she could feel the fabric stretch around her hips, the seams pressing gently into her flesh.

As she turned to make her way back to him she was disoriented by a group of high-school kids pushing past her, and for a moment she could not locate their table. She looked for the Functional Man, for his functional body, but could not see him. Then she saw, clearly, the table at which they had been sitting, tucked in the corner next to the newspaper rack. The magazine she had been reading earlier lay on the brown armchair she had occupied, just as she had left it when she got up to buy the drinks, but there was no one at the table. As she walked over to it, she hoped she was making a mistake, that this was not in fact the table they had been at, that she would hear the Functional Man's voice calling out to her from another spot in the room, saying, '*Ei*, you silly girl, it's over here,' or, 'Little Miss, I've moved to a better spot.' But even as she thought these hopeful thoughts, she knew it was no use, she knew what had happened.

Her handbag was gone. She looked around, but she knew she would not see him. She had been wrong about him. He had not been functional after all.

As she sat pretending to drink her scalding-hot tea, she kept her eyes down, averted from the other people in the café. She was sure they were still looking at her, and she was humiliated by their stares. They were all thinking, That stupid girl, she is so foolish. Abandoned by a man, and robbed too.

Phoebe Chen Aiping, do not let this city crush you down.

She looked up, challenging all the people in the world to look at her – she wanted to confront them and scream at them. But no one was looking at her. A mother and her small daughter were sitting across from her, the child playing with a handheld video device. Some boys were laughing and showing each other photos they had taken on their mobile phones. A young white man with his hair in short twisty dreadlocks was reading a Chinese newspaper. A businessman was talking loudly to himself, both hands moving angrily, jerking as if he was about to throw something across the room. It took Phoebe a moment to realise that he was not mad, that he had a wire dangling from his ear and was talking to someone on the phone.

Phoebe walked out onto the street, thinking about the things in her handbag – the money she had hidden in the inner lining, the make-up she had bought at great expense, her mobile phone, full of the names and numbers of friends she had made since coming to China, people who could help her. They were all gone now, vanished into the encroaching Shanghai winter.

She wrapped her coat around her, feeling how cheap and thin it was. What did she expect? It was a low-quality fake, just like her. She had not noticed how lousy it was before because her body had been warmed by optimism, because her life was about to change. Now she thought, Maybe it never will. She wandered aimlessly through the streets, her shoulders hunched and tensed against the cold. The fallen leaves of the plane trees lay thickly on the ground and crackled sharply as she walked on them; whenever there was a gust of wind they would swirl around her ankles.

Opposite a plate-glass window, she stopped and stared at her reflection. She looked red-cheeked and sad, so sad. Her hair had fallen flat across her forehead, and there were tears in her eyes. It was because of the bitter wind, she thought, not because she was crying. No, it was not because she was crying. It had begun to rain, a fine misty drizzle that made the air look grey and the shapes of the buildings vague, as if seen through a veil. She could feel the moisture gathering on her hair, making it cling to her face – it felt so damp and sticky and cold.

As she shuffled closer to the window to take shelter from the rain she noticed that the building had a curious awning made of wood, and when she looked up she could see that it was in the shape of the roof of a village hut, something rustic from South-East Asia, like the roofs of the houses on the edge of the jungle similar to those from her childhood. The sign on the door was very small, very classy and discreet. It read, APSARA Thai Spa. Inside, she could see walls lined with smooth dark timber and floors of expensive black marble. There was a bamboo cabinet with glass bottles displayed like artwork next to a counter made from grey stone. It was not the sort of place for people like her, Phoebe thought, but all the same, she found herself walking through the door. She clutched at her purse, it was all that she had now. She thought about how much money she had in it, counting it out in her head. It was not very much: enough to pay her share of the rent for this month and buy food for her and Yanyan – not proper food, just instant noodles and maybe some skewers or *xiaolongbao* or noodles from the stalls around Qipu Lu. Just once in her life, she would like to enjoy what other people had, Phoebe thought. Just once, she would like to experience life as a person of comfort and wealth, a happy person. And then she would never wish for anything again, she would become a poor person forever, she would just accept it. After all, it was her destiny in life to be poor, just as it was other people's destiny to be rich. It had always been that way, she'd been foolish to think she could change her fate.

She sat on a bench covered in fine silk, worrying that her damp coat would soil the beautiful cloth. There was no one around, and the place was in semi-darkness. There were glass jars with unlit candles everywhere, and the air conditioning was so silent you could not hear it. She heard music, stringed instruments and flutes that seemed familiar to her ears. Flowing water. Sounds from her childhood. She opened her purse and counted the notes in it. What would Yanyan say if she saw Phoebe right now, about to spend all this money on a manicure, money they could use to buy food and warm clothes for the winter? The cold wind was sweeping through the windows of their little room now; they could feel winter descending on them. In the mornings when they woke up they would just remain in bed, their bodies stiff and painful after a freezing night. They'd said that they would save money to buy a small heater or some thick blankets so at least they wouldn't be cold at night, but they never seemed to have enough spare cash. Soon, Phoebe had promised, very soon.

Just once. She wanted just once to know what it felt like to be rich, just for one hour.

But she closed her purse, zipping it shut, and tucked it back into her coat pocket. Then she bowed her head and rested there for a few moments while she gathered enough strength to go back out into the cold.

10

心如死灰

Never Lapse into Despair or Apathy

Morning: the distant noises of construction work, the rhythmic pounding of piledrivers that seemed to travel up through the soil, into the fabric of the building, underpinning the growing hum of traffic, of scooters beeping and buses squealing to a halt. Afternoon: children's after-school laughter echoing in the hallways, in the stairwell, rising from the streets below. Dinnertime: the lively clang of steel on steel, the rushing fizz of hot oil, the scraping of plastic stools on bare floors, the ceramic clink of plates and bowls being laid out, the sound of happy families. Evening: off-key karaoke singing, the tangle of voices making it impossible to recognise the songs.

That was how he marked his day – by the sounds drifting through his open windows, carried on the tepid spring breeze; that was how he knew that day was turning unhurriedly to night, and he could emerge from his bedroom to sit in the living room and stare at the view of the skyscrapers that were just beginning to light up against a mouse-coloured sky. He would wait until it was properly dark before venturing out to the twenty-four-hour convenience stores at the end of the street to buy bottled water and instant noodles, for somehow the city felt safer at night – fewer people, fewer stares, no one to notice his sallow complexion and too-long hair.

There was more warmth in the air now, the sun flooding the living room all afternoon, so that by sunset the green velvet sofa would be warm to the touch, and the room would be feeling airless and stuffy. He had taken to leaving the windows open on certain days, when he felt suffocated in his bedroom. With this simple act came a sudden awareness of the proximity of the other people in his building, of hundreds of other lives. The harshness of winter had isolated him from his neighbours; he had barely realised they were there. But the warmth of spring had brought them flooding into his consciousness, an intrusion he had not been prepared for.

One noise in particular began to force itself upon him, working its way into the previously closed world of his apartment by simple repetition until he could no longer ignore it. Unlike most of the other noises in the building, which occurred at regular times of the day, this one might start up at any time of the day or night, often in mid-morning or mid-afternoon, or in short bursts late at night, when the rest of the building was still – always out of sync with the rhythm of the other noises. It was a lone female voice – a young one, Justin thought – singing to a karaoke set. The music dissolved strangely into the fabric of the building, leaving only the voice. By turn muffled and amplified by the layers of concrete, it would insinuate its way into Justin's daytime slumber, making it impossible to remain in bed. He would get up and close the windows, but by then it would be too late: like a dripping tap, the voice had already registered its presence in his head and would not go away. He could make out the flat, almost tuneless voice singing old-fashioned love songs which he could often recognise. Sometimes, at night, this voice would be joined by another slightly more melodious one, and together they would perform duets, taking turns singing verses before joining together in an ear-splitting chorus that spoiled the peace of Justin's solitary evenings. He had become used to being alone in the dark with nothing but the lights of the city before him, but now this solitude had been violated.

It was the daytime singing that most disturbed Justin, for that was when he slept. Late one morning, long after the children had left for school and the mothers of the building were away running errands, he was just drifting into a thin, sweat-coated sleep when he heard the voice again, singing 'Little Moonlight Song'. He got up and made sure all the windows were closed before going back to bed; he put in his earplugs and listened to his heartbeat, quick and anxious in his chest. But suspended in this noiseless cavity was that voice, faint but distinct. Soon the room began to feel stuffy with the windows closed. He got out of bed, found a pair of jeans and a sweatshirt, and went out of the apartment, keeping the voice in his head, like a tracker dog following a scent. He stood in the stairwell: it was impossible to tell where the music was coming from. He went down a floor but began to lose the trail; he walked up the dusty staircase until he was at the top floor, and at last he heard the cheap tinkling of notes played on an electric piano, the sickly-sweet melody of violins, and, most obtrusively of all, the horribly off-key voice. He walked quickly down the corridor until he found the door, then paused for a moment, listening to the last strains of the song, the voice fading away, the final notes coming to an end. He tried to reach between the bars of the door's grille to knock, but the gap was too small for his fist, so he slapped the metal bars awkwardly with the palm of his hand. The next song had just begun to play, but it suddenly stopped. Justin waited a few moments, listening: nothing. He leant in closer, trying to discern any movement within, but the piledrivers in the adjacent building site had started again, and the deep, rhythmic pounding obscured any noise from the room. He smacked his hand heavily on the grille again; and again; the metallic rattling echoed down the hallway.

As he turned to walk away, he wondered if he had imagined it all, if he had misjudged the source of the music. The corridor was much narrower and darker up here than on his floor, the apartments packed tightly together. Many of them had their doors open, and Justin could see that they were little more than a single room with a tiny kitchen in front. Each one seemed crammed with boxes, chairs, piles of clothes on the floor, electric fans, heaters.

Their inhabitants spilled into the corridor, squatting on the floor or perched on low stools as they performed everyday tasks. An old man in an indigo worker's hat sat on the threshold of his room mending a radio. A child with a bad cough copied out lines from a textbook onto a notepad; she wore fluffy slippers with a lamb's smiley face imprinted on them. A few old women gathered around a piece of newspaper spread out on the floor in the middle of the corridor, peeling string beans, topping and tailing them and dropping them into an enamel bowl. They could have been in a village, Justin thought, not in the middle of the biggest city in the world. No one looked at him; they simply carried on with their lives – the same lives that had surrounded him for the last three months, lives he had barely noticed.

Diagonally across the hallway from the barricaded door sat an old woman stirring a pot of soup; the grille to her room was shut but the inner door was open. A toddler sat on the floor not far from her, playing with an armless doll, shaking it in the air and pulling at its hair.

'Excuse me, Auntie,' Justin said, 'but do you know if there's anyone in that room over there?'

'You're wasting your time,' the woman said, smiling. 'She won't answer the door. She thinks you're here to collect the gas or electricity money, or something like that.'

'In that case maybe I should shout out that I'm not asking for money.'

'It won't help you,' the old woman said, standing and coming to the grille. 'She keeps herself to herself. Anyway, she's a bit strange.'

'Strange?'

The woman twirled her finger around her temple. 'You know, *strange*. She has mental problems.'

'I see.'

'Her friend is better, more talkative, but she's always out working – working at *what* I don't know. Young girls these days, you never know what they get up to. She comes home at all hours of the night – you should see the way she dresses – and sometimes I can hear her speaking on her mobile phone and it's obvious she has men. Foreign too, both of them – not sure where they're from. Guangdong or Fujian or somewhere like that. Shanghai's full of foreigners these days, it's not the same as before.' The woman's friendly expression suddenly changed and she looked at Justin with a frown, as if something had occurred to her. 'Anyway, what business do you have with those girls?'

'Nothing,' Justin said. 'I'm a neighbour from downstairs. I wanted to talk to them about the noise coming from their room, that's all. The singing. It disturbs me.'

'What noise?' the woman said. 'They might be strange girls, but they don't make much noise.'

Justin shrugged. The sounds of lunchtime were starting up around him – the cacophony of pots and pans, crying babies, irate mothers, an old couple arguing, their voices frail but angry. A small girl, maybe ten years old, paced up and down the corridor, occasionally glancing at the exercise book she was holding. On the cover she had written ENGLISH CONVERSATION. 'At eleven o'clock, we have science. At eleven o'clock, *we* have science. At quarter past eleven, we have music. *I* like music. I *like* music. I-like-music.'

Three floors down, Justin was insulated from these lives; he had thought he could hear them, but in fact he heard little. He walked down the back staircase, pausing to look at the view from that side of the building – a vast building site, a deep hole gouged in the coppery-black mud; beyond, a road lined with cheap shopping malls and food stalls, the crowds spilling onto the street. Even from this distance the road looked black with tar and cooking oil. He hurried back to his apartment; he needed the reassurance of the view he had from the front of the building, the unchanging contrast between Old and New Shanghai, the elegant stone buildings framed by the lavish skyscrapers beyond. Their presence calmed him; he felt he belonged in that orderly cityscape.

For the next few days he attempted to recreate the existence he had had until just recently: the long dank days in bed, windows shut and curtains drawn against the noise of the city; quiet evenings gazing at the skyline, his mind perfectly empty, his body inert. But it did not work. Sunlight eased its way into his bedroom, and even through the thick velvet curtains he could sense the gathering intensity of spring. Then there was the noise, which would not go away now, becoming louder with each day, with more and more sounds becoming discernible. The outside world had forced itself into his existence; the safety of his winter retreat was over. He would have to find somewhere else to live.

He began to search on the internet for apartments to rent, but there were thousands of boxy places that looked identical. In the past he would have asked his secretary to do it for him, but he no longer had one; he no longer had an office or a car or a network of friends he might have rung, people who knew people who knew people. It would have been so easy to find an apartment through these friends, but they no longer existed for him. Three months was all it had taken for them to disappear from his life. As he scrolled through the bare, featureless apartments, he felt a shallow wave of nostalgia for his former life, the ease with which small tasks such as this would have been accomplished. But remembering the interiors of the offices in which he had worked – a world of veneered wood and padded black leather and hearty men in suits – he felt stricken by a sense of panic. He remembered his father's voice, solemn, unyielding; remembered the sickening weight of responsibilities; and he was glad all that had vanished. Convenience and obligation. That was all his life had been.

He clicked on his inbox to look at his emails – the first time in weeks that he had done so. He waited calmly while they loaded, not panicking as he had done before, feeling strong enough to deal with whatever appeared. Even when he saw the number of unread emails – 3,281 – highlighted in bold as if to emphasise his negligence, he felt unruffled. He scanned them swiftly; he could sense three or four calling out to him, like ailing antelope in a herd of thousands whose weak bleating drew the attention of the predators. They were from his brother, imploring him to come home.

Justin read them slowly, appreciating CS's facility with the written word: one message was curt, hurt, accusing; the next was generous, understanding, forgiving; the next was matter-of-fact, news-like; the last one cajoling, vulnerable. They were exercises in style for his brother, who had wanted to be a writer, but now – in Justin's absence – was forced to run the family business. Every one of CS's emails was intended to carry the same message: their family was ruined; CS was hapless, did not know how to run a business; Justin had abdicated in the hour of greatest need and had to return to save them. One ended poetically with a single line: *I am drowning.*

Justin stared at this line and remembered his brother once saying, 'The thing about you is that you have no *fantasy*. You can't imagine being anything other than yourself.' It was true. He had not been able to conceive of life in any other way.

With a few deft clicks of the mouse he selected all 3,281 emails in his inbox and, without hesitating, deleted every one of them.

He had been sitting on the sofa, the laptop balanced on his knees. Now he leant back and sank into the plush velvet, feeling heavy and immobile. He did not have to try very hard to imagine what the atmosphere in his family home would be at the moment – it came to him at once, clear and true as daylight: silent corridors, the whisper of accusation hanging in the air; the wary tread of the servants' feet on marble floors; wordless dinners, the array of dishes smaller now because of Father's diabetes and Mother's growing worry about maintaining a pleasing shape. Or maybe they would be at the old house by the seaside at Port Dickson, where the breeze and the darkness would make the silence more tolerable, and the foamy hush of the waves would calm Mother's nerves. The bamboo blinds on the veranda would be frayed and brittle, await-ing their long-overdue replacement; the sea would wash plastic bags, beer bottles and other debris up onto the beach, leaving a dark, snaky trail along the sand; and on the hills overlooking the bay and behind the house there would be yet another of those newly constructed condominium blocks that had been springing up over the decades, white and featureless. Father would grumble about all these things, and Mother would say, 'It wasn't like this when the boys were small.'

Contained in their small anti-rituals – Mother's failure to prepare afternoon tea, Father's firm refusal to go for his usual evening swim, which he used to perform proudly in front of his wife and young children, splashing powerfully through the low waves – was an intricate dance of blame, in which each would take turn to play victim and accuser. In her unwillingness to participate in the rituals of domesticity, Mother was blaming Father for the position they were in now – they could no longer afford the staff, no longer had the power or influence to buy the adjacent land to save their precious view; while by remaining housebound and static, he blamed her for the loss of his vigour and pride. They had always found ways to avoid the inescapable fact that they had ground each other down over the years, but now they would be forced together, in a house that was falling quickly into disrepair, with a view that was ruined, with children who were ruined. They had had to sell the penthouse apartment in Hong Kong, the giant pied-à-terre on the Upper East Side, and the bolthole near Regent's Park. There was nowhere for them to escape each other now. He wondered for a moment where Sixth Uncle was right now, whether he had escaped to a farm in Tasmania as he was always threatening to do, or whether he was where he had always been – at his family's beck and call.

Justin closed his eyes, glad that his parents did not know where he was, glad that there was a huge distance between them.

He reached for his laptop again and typed the name of the building he had wanted to buy several months previously, on which they had pinned all their hopes. The first news item confirmed what he had assumed: ***969 Weihai Lu Sold to Anonymous Property Magnate***. *In a deal estimated to be worth more than nine hundred million RMB, the historic building located in the prestigious Nanjing Xi Lu area of downtown Shanghai will be transformed into a civic centre with a concert hall, open-access library facilities and restaurants. Officials from the Shanghai Municipal Department today*

confirmed that the preferred bidder had been selected only because of the
exemplary nature of his charitable proposals, which would not only preserve
one of the gems of Shanghai's architectural heritage but also contribute to
the community. The reputed size of the deal had nothing to do with it,
Wang C from the Municipal Department said. 'There had been a fierce
bidding war and in fact we received a higher bid from another overseas
developer for this important site. We were not swayed by money.'

After months of not looking at a computer, Justin's eyes were beginning to tire. He decided to go for a walk along the river. At the entrance to the building he saw someone sitting on the front steps, a girl in her twenties playing with what appeared to be a stray kitten. Dressed in candy-pink pyjamas, her hair tied in a ponytail by a single elastic band, she looked entirely ordinary, and Justin would have walked straight past her if not for the song she was humming – 'Little Moonlight Song', out of tune, just like the voice that had ruined his sleep so many times. No longer filtered through layers of concrete, it sounded purer and gentler than that persecutory voice, and he wondered if he was making a mistake – but no, it was definitely the same person.

'What are you staring at?' she said, looking up at him.

'Nothing. Is that your cat?'

'No, I don't know who it belongs to. It comes every night at the same time as I do. We keep each other company. Sometimes I feed it.'

Justin watched as the cat arched its spine and rubbed itself against her. 'You shouldn't touch stray cats like that. You never know, they might be dirty.'

The girl shrugged and encircled the cat in her arms, lowering her face to allow it to rub the top of its head against her chin. When it finally stepped off her lap it landed on a large exercise book that lay on the step next to the girl. She picked it up and held it to her chest protectively, though Justin wasn't sure if she was protecting the book or herself. Her eyes were red and puffy from oversleeping – something that Justin recognised at once – and her skin was dry and brittle.

'What are you studying?' Justin asked.

'Nothing,' the girl said before standing and walking into the building. She went to the lift door and pressed the call button. There was a lift waiting; its flickering fluorescent tube bathed her in harsh white light, making her seem very small, barely more than a child.

The next night Justin went downstairs at the same hour, hoping to see the girl again, but she wasn't there, nor the night after. Her karaoke singing had stopped too, but he did not feel relieved; instead he felt worried that something might have happened to her. He went up to her room and rattled the grille, but he knew there would be no answer. Each night now he would go for a walk, always leaving just before midnight, feeling the first hints of summer infuse the breeze coming off the river.

Then, one night, she was there again, sitting on the front steps, dressed in her pink pyjamas and reading the exercise book. She closed it when she saw him approaching.

'Where have you been?' he asked. The urgency and relief in his voice startled him. 'I thought you said you came here every day.'

'Sometimes I sleep. What's it to you?'

He sat down next to her on the step, and she did not move away.

'Why do you sit out here to study at midnight? Isn't that sort of a weird thing to do?'

'I'm not studying. Anyway, why do you go walking after midnight? Isn't that a weird thing to do too? Seriously, Shanghai is so full of weird people.'

A movement startled Justin – the cat, padding its way silently towards them, easing itself swiftly into the girl's lap. He drew away slightly. 'You really shouldn't touch stray cats that way,' he said.

The girl laughed. 'You're scared of cats! That's so funny.' She cradled the cat in both hands and thrust it towards Justin. 'You're weird. Even a sweet baby cat can spook you. *Wah*, you really have big problems, mister. Go on, try touching it.'

'No.'

'OK then, let it just touch you a bit – see how affectionate it is!'

'Please just take it away.'

The girl giggled as she returned the cat to her lap. A gust of wind caught the pages of her exercise book and blew it open. On the front page, in boxy handwriting, someone had written: *Journal of My Secret Self.*

'Is that your diary?' Justin asked.

'You are so rude and nosy,' the girl said, pulling the book away. 'It's not mine. It's my roommate's.'

'You're one to talk – why are you reading your roommate's secret diary?'

The girl shrugged. 'She has an exciting life. She goes out all the time. Now she even has a rich boyfriend. When I read her diary I feel excited too, as if that life is mine. I used to go out a lot, to the cinema, music concerts. But it's been so long, and now I'm scared. I don't dare go out any more. This is as far as I want to go.'

Justin noticed a cut on the cat's paw; where it had rubbed against the girl's pyjamas there were small dark streaks of blood.

'Hey,' the girl said, as if suddenly remembering something important. 'Do you have any ice cream? You live here, don't you? I don't know why, I really feel like some ice cream.'

Justin shook his head. He did not want to admit that he had nothing in his fridge but a lump of rancid Australian butter. 'But I could get some for tomorrow. If you're going to be here again, that is.'

'Really? Promise?' When she smiled her face seemed to change entirely, an effect that disconcerted Justin; it transformed her from a young woman into a child, not even a pubescent teenager but a shiny-faced, unquestioning child. And suddenly it felt important to keep the promise he had just made. He did not know why he was providing a solemn undertaking to buy ice cream, why he was taking the trouble to ask what kind she liked, why he was pretending to share her love of red-bean flavour when he didn't even like ice cream; or why he cared about what was written in that diary, afraid that her roommate's life was heading for disaster. Why he was concerned about a hapless girl from the provinces who thought some rich man was going to leave his wife and marry her. These girls knew nothing. They had not seen the world. They were so young that they thought it was made of pop concerts and ice cream and baby cats and pink pyjamas, but now they were beginning to taste the bitterness that life offered. He did not want that to happen, but he could not prevent it.

'OK then, I'll get red-bean ice cream,' he said.

The next evening they sat eating ice cream at the same spot on the front steps of the building. She told him her name – Yanyan – and when he said his, she repeated it several times, delighting in the novelty of the English sounds. Just-*ying* was how he pronounced it, the two syllables infused with the rise and fall of Chinese, transforming them into something unfamiliar and wonderful. He had never thought of his name as anything but serviceable, had never imagined anyone would find it amusing.

She told him about herself, patiently going through the details of her life. He was a good listener – people had always said so, and he had always known it meant someone dull who had nothing much to offer, someone who absorbed rather than illuminated. Often he had found himself deep in conversation, enjoying what was being said, when suddenly the other person would stop and say, 'You know what? You're such a good listener.' He had always taken it as a euphemism for being boring, yet now it did not seem to matter. Yanyan needed to talk, she needed him to listen, she did not require him to participate.

And so on this and many subsequent nights, sitting on the front steps of the building, he learnt that she was from a village in Fujian province, and that she had worked in the office of a company producing health-food supplements until she had lost her job a year ago. It wasn't her fault, she hadn't done anything wrong, but the company had started exporting to the United States, and the authorities there had found some contamination in their products and the whole company had to shut down. She had taken it badly – 'broken confidence' was how she put it. She had always been delicate, even as a child; she was too much of a dreamer. She'd read an article about alien abductions in Hunan province, and for a while she was convinced that it had happened to her in her child-hood – it was the only way she could explain the white light that came to her in her sleep sometimes, or the feeling that she had left part of her body in another place far, far away. Now she could hardly face leaving her room; some days she didn't even get out of bed. The outside world scared her; just sitting on the front steps of the building like this was a big deal for her. Life had become much better since her roommate arrived – she paid the rent and bought nice food. But.

'But what?'

'But she has secrets,' Yanyan said. 'She shares a lot of intimate secrets with me, but not the most important ones.'

'Why?'

Yanyan sighed and then laughed, as if explaining a simple idea to a child. 'Because she wants to leave, but she doesn't want to upset me. That's why I have to read her journal – to know what's going through her mind. So I'll be prepared for the day she moves on.'

'Has she written in the journal that she'll be moving?'

'No' – Yanyan shrugged – 'but everyone does eventually. You can't stay in a city like Shanghai forever. You'll leave too, and so will I.'

It was true, Justin thought; he had left his details with estate agents who were now ringing back with messages about swanky places in Luwan and Xuhui, where all the foreigners lived. All he had to do was return their calls, and in a few days he would have a new apartment. He hadn't mentioned this to Yanyan; but then again, she hadn't asked.

'So, tell me something about yourself,' Yanyan said. 'You don't talk much.'

'There's nothing to tell,' Justin said. 'My life is very boring.'

'I think you have a lot of secrets.'

Justin laughed and stood up. 'If I had a secret journal like your roommate's, it would be empty.'

11

寻根究底

Inquire Deeply into Every Problem

What the newspapers cannot find are the missing pieces of the puzzle: what was Gary's life like before he moved into his uncle's dismal house on the outskirts of Kota Bharu? Who was Gary's mother, and what did she do? Was he already a miscreant at the age of nine or ten? Was he abused at a very young age? The trail has run cold, and it seems there are no more answers to be found in that rather depressed part of northern Malaysia. The out-of-town journalists who have been there for a couple of weeks are beginning to tire of the second-rate hotels, where the AC breaks down twice a day and the combination of Islamic laws and lack of development means there are no cool bars, no cinemas, no dancing, little alcohol, and certainly no girls. Besides, the TV channels have moved on from Gary-gate, as someone has predictably called this little episode; they are no longer interested in him.

Maybe if they could track Gary down and get an exhaustive interview with him, in which he recounted every detail of his life and then broke down in tears while apologising for his misdeeds – maybe then the story would be complete and his life could be restored. But Gary is not available for interviews. His record company says he is undergoing a period of self-reflection. According to most bloggers, this probably means he has taken an overdose, but by now even the cheapest tabloid newspapers do not have the enthusiasm to speculate on Gary's fate.

For once in his brief, previously glittering career, however, the press release is true. Gary is indeed thinking about himself. Not because he wants to, but because he is barricaded in his hotel room, immobile, for the first time in years. No meetings to attend, no chat shows, no dance rehearsals with girls dressed as sexy extra-terrestrials, no recording sessions that last into the early hours of the morning. Trapped in his room, he looks out at the Shanghai skyline, at the ribbons of elevated highways unfurling into the distance, twisting and curling into one another; at the brilliant gilding of Jing'an Temple amidst the blue-glass and chrome façades of the office blocks, at the crowds of people hurrying along the streets, distant but still close enough for him to pick out individual details in their clothing: a scarlet raincoat, a Burberry scarf, a yellow satchel. Everyone hurrying to or from somewhere, every life full of something about to happen, everyone looking forward to the next heartbeat of their existence.

But not him.

He keeps the TV on the Discovery Channel, for he finds it soothing to have a backdrop of constant motion, of constant savagery. Killer whales devouring seals, snakes swallowing pigs. He watches a lizard eating another lizard that looks identical, only a bit smaller. But the bigger lizard can't quite manage it – the smaller one keeps wriggling out of its jaws, its hind legs jerking as if electrocuted. Gary does not know why, but he starts laughing. Many of the things he watches on TV seem comical to him nowadays.

In front of him, little windows announce themselves on the screen of his laptop, popping into existence like beautiful, short-lived night-time flowers. These are the numerous online chat rooms he is on – about half a dozen at once. Most of the time he doesn't even bother to look at the messages, which are greetings from total strangers who don't even know who they are contacting. They don't care – they are all lonely and in need of someone to chat to. Everyone uses a false name, hiding who they truly are, just as he does. The only thing on display is their solitude.

A small window with a girl's face on it pops up with a bright *bling*. Gary has seen her before. It is rare to see a photo of a real face on these sites. The last time Gary saw it he decided that it must be a fake – no one would put a picture of themselves on the internet that showed them smiling straight into the camera. The photo was taken in a public park, not in a studio, and the girl was not even dressed up or prettified in any way. He thought it must have been a stolen image – someone playing a joke – so he took no notice. Her message this time is the same as the last time: sassy and challenging. *Hellooooo, anyone out there? Any human being, alien, even a talking monkey would be OK!*

Yes, it must be a fake, Gary thinks as he clicks on the window to close it. Besides, he is bored with these chat rooms now, bored with inventing stories about who he is, bored with lying about his age, job, home town – bored with the flattery and flirtation, the banality of the chat that is always the same and never goes anywhere.

Around him: an orchid in a stone-grey bowl, beige-and-black furniture: the same room for over two weeks now. Near the door are two trays piled high with dirty dishes and glasses, unfinished food clinging to the white porcelain. He does not call for anyone to take them away because he is ashamed of being seen by even the humblest cleaning girl. He does not want to know that she is sneering at him, sniggering with her friends down in the kitchen below. Every few days he waits until 3 a.m., when even the lifts are silent, and pushes the trays out into the corridor. He collects his food this way too, emerging swiftly to draw the tray into the room when he feels there is no risk of being seen, like a rat darting back into its burrow. So for several days the remnants of his meals sit in a pile, reminding him, just as his agent does every so often, that unless he gets some work soon, there will be no more money to pay the bills.

This is the reality of his life now: dirty, unchanging, helpless. There is nothing new or interesting for him to contemplate in his minimalist, sullied cell; he has exhausted all the possibilities of his life, cannot even look to the future as those people down on the streets can. The only thing that can occupy his thoughts is the past; not because he wants to think about it, but because he has run out of options. If the newspapers could see his past, maybe they would look more kindly upon him. But maybe not. Maybe they would see his childhood as a source of shame and ridicule, something else to make fun of.

He lived with his mother in a rural town called Temangan. If a place as small as Temangan could be said to have outskirts, the newspapers would probably write that he lived in them, where the low rows of shop-houses and cheaply-built houses bled into the countryside, fading into the sparse jungle that stretched for miles until the next town. There was something ridiculous about country folk like them and their neighbours trying to become modern city dwellers, saving up their money for a scooter, then a car, and dreaming of a job in the capital down south. Now that he has travelled so far in life, he can see just how futile that dream was, how justified those sophisticated cosmopolitan people were in laughing at their aspirations, because it was clear that they could never change their lives.

His father had walked out on them not long after Gary was born. 'Don't go looking for him,' his mother had once said. 'It's not worth it.' It was a superfluous thing to say, because Gary never had any curiosity about his father. When, recently, some of the newspapers cited the lack of a male authority figure as the cause of his delinquency, he had laughed. He was timid but self-contained as a child. Those who are born into a life of solitude learn to enjoy the space around them, he thought. They learn not to question the lack of love in their lives.

His mother never learnt to embrace this loneliness; she had been married, she had had a husband, she had known love, and – above all – she had grown accustomed to having someone around her. Now she resented life, not because of her circumstances – 'Look at me, I'm just a washerwoman,' she would sometimes joke, half bitterly, half blithely – but because of her solitude. The failure of her potential was reflected not by what she did for a living, but by her aloneness. Life had taken away her companion, and even as she encouraged her son to forget his father, she herself could not let go of him. She was the kind of person who needed someone to share her life, someone to be involved in the tiny dramas of her everyday existence.

Even as a small boy, Gary sensed the nature of her character, the way she absorbed him into the ups and downs of her life, enlisting him in the role of her companion. The tasks he carried out went beyond those expected of a young child in his position – helping her hang out the washing and deliver laundered clothes, or accompanying her when she needed help cleaning someone's house, or running into town to buy a forgotten bottle of bleach; in fact, every sentence she uttered was intended to be shared with her son, everything she did was for his benefit. 'This is what I have to do now,' she would say, sighing, as if it were a joke, as if she had accepted her fate. 'I just clean other people's houses.' Comments like that enveloped her son in a shared intimacy and involved him in her struggles; she worked as a washerwoman to support him, and everything she did that was demeaning, she did for his benefit. Even at a young age he could not escape the knowledge of his responsibility for this.

He knew that she had been a musician – a lost life that further flavoured the sacrifices she made for her young son. She had been a pianist, good enough to study with a famous teacher in Singapore. Her parents, who had been schoolteachers in Kota Bharu, had sold their car and the few bits of jade jewellery they'd owned, and used all their savings to pay for her tuition fees. In spite of the generosity of Singaporean cousins, who gave her a room for free, it was always a struggle – even in the seventies, Singapore was already an expensive place to live. Her parents were optimistic but realistic in their hopes for her; unlike other people from modest backgrounds, they did not allow themselves the luxury of imagination, and so did not heap the pressure of expectation on their daughter. Partly, this was because they did not really know what a pianist's life might involve, and therefore could not envisage all the possibilities open to her. Perhaps if they had been more worldly, they would have been more demanding. Humble, hard-working people like them did not hope for very much. They had seen what had happened in the sixties, not just in their country but in all the neighbouring countries too – the violence, the turmoil – and they knew that the lives of ordinary people could be changed in an instant. Acceptance was the key to survival; ambition would lead only to heartbreak.

All they hoped was that she would have enough of an education to be able to teach music when she was older. Teachers themselves, they knew it was a decent profession. They could imagine that sort of life.

The weight of expectation came from Gary's mother herself. A diligent, technically able student who was widely admired without being outstanding, she allowed herself to dream of playing in concert halls in Europe. She was aware of her limitations, but that did not quell her fantasies. As she practised her cadenzas, pushing herself towards greater virtuosity and expressiveness, she felt the growing tension between imagination and reality: she wanted to perform with more brilliance, but her fingers would not obey her brain; she wanted to express more profound sentiments, but she had nothing to say. Even as she pushed herself, she felt her talent shrinking within her.

Worst of all, she allowed herself to fall in love with her music teacher. He was twenty years her senior, with a failed marriage behind him, but she didn't care. He was kind, handsome and attentive, and had led the kind of life she dreamt of. He had been a student in London and had given small recitals in Paris and Vienna. She never questioned why he had returned home, never wondered about the reasons for his failure. Most importantly, like her he had grown up in rural Malaysia, in small-town Pahang. She thought he understood her.

If you read this in the Sunday newspapers, you might assume that it was the beginning of a love story reflecting the spirit of the time, the fortunes of a country – the change, the optimism, young people on an upward curve. And indeed, it could have been.

When she announced, a few years later, that she was going to marry this man, her parents objected not only to his age and to the fact that he had already been married. It was something else that troubled them – an untrustworthiness they saw in his face. He was too ready with his smile, and his hair was always neatly combed with a precise side parting. He knew the right thing to say, and was too quick to say it, as if he had prepared his responses, had rehearsed them in a similar setting. He was a handsome man, there was no doubt about that – but his eyes were set a fraction too close to each other, and his nose was thin, which lent him an effete air. Not feminine, just unreliable. These physical attributes, passed to his son through the filter of a generation, would produce a beauty considered rare, strange and delicate; but unlike the son, the father lived in an earlier, harsher time, when a man who looked as he did was judged to be not desirable but suspicious. What was his *use* in life, other than to be charming?

They married, drifted away from her parents, moved to KL, got a small link-house in Cheras. He found another woman. Gary's mother was four months pregnant when he left. Her life was beginning to feel full of choices she was free to make – but at the same time, not at all free. She wanted to pursue her husband and reclaim him, or else make him suffer, but her pride stifled such vengeful intentions; she wanted to go back to her parents and seek refuge in their care, but her shame made that impossible; she wanted to abort the baby, but the possibilities of love made her keep it. She realised that so many things in her life had given her the illusion that she was in control of her destiny, but she was in fact not really in control at all.

Her husband did come back, two or three times; but these visits lasted only a couple of weeks before he vanished again. Each time he appeared carrying his clothes in a small vinyl bag with blue-and-red checks, and with stories of new people he'd met, new things he was doing. He'd given up teaching, turned his back on music altogether. It wasn't lucrative enough, and there were so many other things he could do to make money. He was getting involved in door-to-door selling – a friend of his told him he could make a thousand *ringgit* a month selling the *Encyclopaedia Britannica*, and even Tupperware sales could bring in a bit of cash. He had many projects in the pipeline: he was also dabbling in small-time politics, canvassing on behalf of a businessman from KL who was standing in a local by-election. He wanted to get into journalism too, because he wanted to expose all the injustice, all the rotten things happening in the country – the politicians on the make, robbing and cheating their own people, letting down the ones who needed them most.

He seemed to have taken on the sadness of an entire country, seemed not to notice his wife's laboured movements or how heavy she had grown with the pregnancy. He rambled incoherently at times, and she remembered what her parents had said about him: 'an artistic temperament ... unreliable'. When he talked about politicians failing in their duties, she did not have the heart to say, *Talk about letting down the people who need you the most.* She could not explain why, during his brief stays, she continued to cook for him and lie down next to him at night, listening to his quick shallow breathing, as if he was the one who needed looking after. Even when he left for good, she continued to worry that he was not eating properly, that he might not have somewhere safe to sleep at night, that he had lost his direction in life.

Not long after her baby was born she heard that her husband had ended up in prison for organising a political rally somewhere up north. He was in and out of jail for a while, and then she heard no more news of him.

For a while she gave music lessons to middle-class kids whose parents wanted them to become *rounded individuals*. As she watched them resentfully going through their scales at the start of each lesson, she wondered why their parents were forcing them to learn something they hated; she wondered what being a 'rounded individual' really meant. 'If you want to go to Harvard,' one mother explained to her as they sat watching a six-year-old boy play 'Chopsticks', 'you need to be a rounded individual. That means you have to play the piano, doesn't it?' It was not what she'd imagined for her life, but it was OK – at least she was a teacher of music, even if she was teaching pupils who had no love of it; and when she closed her eyes during yet another mangled rendition of *Für Elise*, she could still pretend that she was doing something fine and admirable.

But this did not last very long – eight months, a year maybe. Taking the bus to Bangsar and Damansara – all those smart suburbs, so far away – and then walking, always walking, along the wide lanes lined with split-level houses and decorative trees in the gardens became too much for her to cope with. She would travel for four hours for a lesson that lasted one hour, and all that time her small baby was at home. Sometimes she left Gary with a neighbour, sometimes she hired an Indonesian maid with glassy red eyes and a vacant smile, but this left her with very little money to spare at the end of each week. And then there was the worry; always the worry. So many things could happen to her and her baby in the city. The way men looked at her on the bus made her feel nervous and uncomfortable. She couldn't afford to take taxis. She stopped working after dark. If anything happened to her, what would become of her baby? She knew she could not go on like this for much longer.

It was a relief of sorts when her parents died – first her father, then, a few months afterwards, her mother. She had to move back up north to Kelantan to sort out their affairs, which involved moving into their little house in Temangan, barely more than a village. It was not far from where she had grown up, and she appreciated the air and the landscape, the feeling of civilisation melting away into the wilderness – the feeling of isolation. Ten years previously she had found it stifling, but now it seemed comforting. Her parents' death gave her a reason to escape her life in KL. Everyone would understand why she had to give up all that she had had in the big city; her ambitions had reached a legitimate end; she could even pretend it was a hardship to return to a rural existence.

By the time Gary was old enough to put a name to simple human emotions – fear, loneliness, joy – his mother's life was already in retreat, its boundaries shrinking. In order to escape the feeling of being trapped by the confines of rural life, she surrendered to it. Her world was now defined by the rhythms of the market laid out along the dusty street every morning. She chatted with the old *makcik* who came in from the surrounding villages to sell vegetables and food – she knew each one by name, and sometimes even shared tea with the *dodol* woman. It was how she had grown up; she knew how to live like this. She tried to imagine that the roads leading out of town all headed north, to Kota Bharu and the other small towns in the no-man's land on the Thai border, or to the coast, where the long stretches of empty white-sand beaches were interrupted only by fishing villages; she wanted to imagine that she could no longer go south to KL or Singapore, or west across the mountains to Penang, where there were cities and music and foreigners and ambition.

At that age – six, seven? – Gary would notice her watching him as he played in the dirt yard in front of the house, and on a number of occasions he found her sitting by his bed when he woke up in the morning. But she would never hold him or pick him up to cradle him in her arms, or rush over to help him to his feet if he fell over. The look in her eyes was empty, hollowed out by fatigue: the mere act of reaching out to him was too great an effort for her. She wanted to love him, he knew, but she had no strength to do so. The divide between them always remained, and before long he became aware that he no longer needed her touch.

She worked every day, including Fridays, when many of the shops were closed for prayers. By now she was washing clothes and cleaning houses for a living. In those days there weren't any Indonesian maids, so it was still easy for a Chinese woman like her to find work. Occasionally she would mention the possibility of giving music lessons – often enough to make Gary remember that she had once been someone whose life had been full of potential; that she had been someone. But they both knew it was ridiculous

– there was no one in a small town like theirs who would want or could afford piano lessons. It was not like down south, where Gary knew there were concert venues that played host to foreign musicians. His mother had told him stories about recitals and concerts, but he knew that such things never happened where they lived.

Once a month his mother would take the bus into Kota Bharu. 'I have some friends – it's our music evening. They sing, and sometimes I play the piano. Traditional songs like the ones I sing for you sometimes. You know,' she said, breaking into song, 'like "Sweet Little Rose".' It was her one link with the musical world she'd inhabited in the past, he thought, even if it was not a very strong one. Nonetheless, he liked the idea of his mother playing the piano, and wished he could see her perform. For a few days after her music evenings she would often smoke cigarettes, usually Winstons out of a crushed pack. Gary never asked her about this, even though she didn't normally smoke; maybe a friend had given them to her. One day he noticed the book of matches she'd used to light her cigarettes; when she had used it up she'd thrown it into the waste bin, where it grew damp from the vegetable peelings before he had a chance to salvage it. Every month she came back with an identical matchbook, with a pair of bright red lips printed on a black background. By now he was old enough to read the words on it: Ichiban Karaoke.

It made him sad to think of his mother, who might have played in concert halls in Europe, in such a place as Ichiban Karaoke in Kota Bharu. He was just a child; it would be years before he would visit a karaoke bar himself, but already he knew that Ichiban Karaoke was not good enough for his mother, that she did not belong in a place like that.

People always say that their mothers are beautiful, that they are the most amazing woman in the world. Now that Gary has seen many pretty women all over Asia, he knows that his mother's looks could never be considered exceptional. To be honest, she was on the plain side. All the same, when he remembers the way she looked back then, with red, pinched eyes and the faint lines of age already beginning to show around her temples and her mouth as she sat on the front step of the house singing old Chinese songs, he thinks: she should not have gone to Ichiban Karaoke bar.

Every year, as he grew older, the dirt yard in front of his house seemed to become wider. Trees were felled and the scrubby under-growth was cleared, bringing the town nearer to them. This was a good thing, his mother explained, for it made it easier for her to get work. There were more houses that needed cleaning, more people who needed their clothes washed and ironed, and now they lived close by. Had she lived for another few years, their house would have been – almost – among them. Maybe things might have turned out differently for them both. Maybe the buses would have been more reliable, not so old and broken down. Maybe the roads would have been improved, with fewer potholes after the rainy season and the floods in November and December that always washed the tarmac away. Maybe she would not have had to catch a lift from a stranger on a two-stroke scooter when she was coming back from Ichiban Karaoke late that night. Maybe there would have been fewer goats and chickens straying onto the road and into the traffic. Maybe she would still be alive today, and Gary would be a bus driver, not a pop star. Maybe he would not be sitting here, flicking through the TV channels once again. Maybe he wouldn't be on the internet waiting for someone interesting to log on to MSN. But maybe it would not have changed a thing. She might have lived to become a fat, happy old woman, and he might have been a failed pop star anyway.

He changes the channel – he's tired of watching lions savage zebras – and finds the pop channels. Before long he sees the latest of his music videos, which includes arty black-and-white footage of his last concert, which had been hailed as a huge success. Even as he is being lowered onto stage in a messianic pose, surrounded by a huge dance troupe dressed as half-naked aliens, or when he is in the middle of a complex dance routine, he cannot fail to notice the vacant expression on his face, the absence of any enthusiasm. And he remembers how difficult it was for him to feel present on stage. His body and voice did what they were trained to do, but he imagined himself elsewhere. It is so obvious, now that he sees images of himself. Perhaps it is something he inherited from his mother, this absence of expression – her sole legacy to him.

This is why, when he sings love ballads – rather, when he sang love ballads (he must get used to speaking of his career in the past tense) – he often closed his eyes. Fans used to say it was because he felt so much pain, so much love, that it hurt him too much. But the truth is that he felt nothing. Which is why he had to close his eyes: so they would not betray him.

As he contemplates this emptiness once more, a text bleeps on his phone. It is his agent: *Hv to leave hotel tmrw. Hv fixed rental apt 4u. Taxi at 11am. Some work is coming thru. Will call u soon.*

Where r u

Taipei

Shd I come back

Better stay in Shanghai. Many journalists here. No work.

He looks around his room. Most people would panic at the thought of having to leave at such short notice, and would start packing their things immediately. But he has hardly anything to pack, so he goes back to the chat rooms on the internet. The girl he saw earlier is still online, still searching for someone. Her messages are not so bright and courageous any more: *Looking for any nice friend. I am alone tonight.*

Gary draws his laptop to his knees and begins to type a reply. *Hi … so am I.*

12

水乳交融

Work with a Soulmate, Someone Who Understands You

Thank you for your interest in working with me, but I am afraid I am otherwise engaged and will be unable to commit to any new business venture for at least 6–12 months. I am grateful for your enquiry and wish you great luck and success. Leong Yinghui.

She did not pause long to consider the tone of the message before sending it out as a standard response to the many proposals she was receiving. Ever since the awards ceremony, the number of people interested in developing a business with her, or hiring her in some capacity or other, had been growing every day. At first she responded fully and personally to each request, carefully considering its pros and cons before dictating an email to her PA. Although many of the projects seemed vague and flimsy or just downright ridiculous, there were more than a few that struck her as being potentially interesting, such as the proposal from a young woman who wanted to start a chain of tiny shops called Great Sunrise selling socks and undergarments in the dead spaces in metro stations all across the city. But as the number of requests multiplied, her patience began to diminish, until eventually she found it easiest simply to refuse them all.

She knew that amongst the rubbish she was probably also throwing away fascinating, potentially life-changing opportunities. Not so long ago she would have pursued every faint trail to its end, but now things were different. Since meeting Walter Chao, she no longer had to worry about finding that single, perfect project that would change everything. Besides, there were only so many times that one could revolutionise one's life. Sooner or later there comes a time when the frantic somersaults of fortune have to end, when the restlessness of desire fades. It was time – so all her friends said – for her to settle down. Such a strange expression, she thought: *settling down*, as if she was silt in a warm river, sinking slowly to the muddy bed. Still, it was an inevitable process, and mysterious too. Yinghui had never known how it would happen, until now.

'It's like love,' one of her girlfriends said at dinner at their usual Hunanese restaurant one evening (Yinghui's presence had become increasingly rare due to her massively increased workload, it was remarked).

'What do you mean?' Yinghui asked, nibbling on a cumin-grilled lamb chop.

'The moment you're in a relationship, guys start flocking to you. When you're single, you search and search and wait and wait, but no one wants you. I guess business is just the same. It must be some law of the universe that makes people behave like that.'

Yinghui smiled. There was something poetic about the way recent weeks had developed – so dramatic that it seemed almost comical, as if life was toying with her. After years of struggling to mould her fortunes, fortune itself had taken hold of her life and sorted it out in one swift manoeuvre. When she received the documents from Walter (a slim leather folder containing not more than half a dozen sheets of paper), she had sat in bed reading and rereading them late into the night. It was as if he had managed to access the farthest reaches of her memory, all her long-forgotten yearnings, and condensed his findings into a few pages of concise, matter-of-fact prose. At first she had thought it was a joke; or maybe she had been working too hard and, on the verge of an exhaustion-related breakdown, had begun to imagine things. But no: it was not a joke. He was not a mind-reader; it was just chance, pure and simple. All her messy ambitions had resurfaced, repackaged in sophisticated, adult form: the hyper-businesslike version of her vague ramblings of fifteen years ago.

> ... *in summary the project would, therefore, involve not just the preservation of the fabric of this historic building but the creation of a wholly contemporary, indeed revolutionary, state-of-the-art centre for the performing arts as well as a cultural resource centre supported by a combination of public and private financing.*

She turned back to the first sheet in the folder, which was marked 'STRICTLY PRIVATE AND CONFIDENTIAL'. It read like something she might have written herself fifteen years ago, when her interests extended beyond how to extract the most favourable terms of credit from textile suppliers:

> *First built as an opulent opium den in the early 1900s (the exact date is unclear but is believed to be sometime between 1905 and 1908, not long after the end of the Sino-Japanese war), the building now known as 969 Weihai Lu was later bought by a tobacco magnate who remodelled the rooms and added two wings to the structure, together with ornate decorative touches such as scrolled classical plasterwork on the external pillars and marble fireplaces, some of which survive today. In its heyday in the 1920s and early 1930s, 969 Weihai Lu witnessed extravagant gatherings that reflected Shanghai's position as one of the world's most cosmopolitan and hedonistic cities. Singers such as Yao Lee and other great artists often performed at private parties here, interpreting such sultry classics as 'The Cocktail Song' and 'Can't Get Your Love' (often called 'The Prostitute's Song', the first song to be banned by the communist regime).*
>
> *With the Japanese occupation of Shanghai, the building was abandoned, and it was later used for light industrial purposes. The generous proportions of its rooms lent them to housing a printing press, a tannery, and a match factory. Internal walls were demolished and the entire west wing was torn down in the*

1950s as industrial premises were built up around the original mansion, completely enveloping and dwarfing it by the end of the 1960s. The labyrinth of narrow, green-painted corridors dates from this period, as do the glass-and-lead ceilings in the north range of the site. Although this communist-era architecture might not appeal to modern tastes, it is a prime example of the starkly striking aesthetic that marked the Cultural Revolution, illustrating the peasant and industrial roots of that period of Chinese history.

We strongly reject the idea that the easiest architectural solution to 969 Weihai Lu is to tear it down. While reorganising its space and re-establishing a use for it will be a major undertaking, we believe that every effort must be made to preserve not only the fabric of the original mansion, but the seemingly ramshackle industrial additions that now form the bulk of the building.

Reading the documents in the folder, she felt the same passion she had experienced in her twenties, when, recently graduated from university, her view of the world had been clumsy in its naïveté, when she had seen possibility in everything – and, in particular, in herself. Now these sentiments were allied to a harsher, more solid appreciation of reality, which intensified that rush of optimism. These were no longer the empty dreams of youth: she *could* change the world; she could make it a better place for everyone, principally herself.

She took a few moments to consider how far she had come over the years, her gradual transformation from a girl who could barely distinguish between the debit and credit columns in the accounts of a tiny, cash-only café to the capable, successful businesswoman she was today. She had never really understood the financial pages in the newspapers, had always resented their existence even more than that of the sports pages, yet nowadays she read them diligently, paying particular attention to activity in the real-estate and retail sectors. It had been a slow, painful metamorphosis, she thought: a third of her life spent changing who she was. It was amazing what grief and pride could do to a person. But she did not wish to dwell on this just now; she merely allowed herself a brief self-congratulatory smile before continuing with the papers before her.

She looked at the financial provisions – an upfront lump sum plus a percentage of the total earnings of the centre on its completion. The projected profits (so many shop units, right in the middle of town, so many high-class tenants, so much advertising space) were astronomical, yet they were attainable. She triple-checked the figures, calculating and recalculating them in RMB and US dollars. They appeared, in many ways, almost too good to be true.

But this was China, she told herself. The unfeasible had a habit of coming true; she had to believe the unbelievable.

All she had to do was invest a not inconsiderable sum of money – in fact, most of the capital she possessed, augmented by a large bank loan. That certainly added a dose of reality, but it was only to be expected: a sign of her dedication to the project, a symbol of trust and cooperation. She liked the groundedness of the figure, the six zeros looking reassuringly weighty, anchoring her thoughts in the seriousness of the deal. This was business, after all, not a charity. Risks, yes, they existed, but she had taken far greater ones in her career so far.

Although it took her a few days to get back to Walter – she wanted to give him the impression that she was thinking long and hard about it, considering every minute detail – it had in fact taken her less than a minute to decide: she would do it.

'Great,' he said calmly when she rang him, as if her decision had been entirely expected. 'What are you doing this weekend?'

'Not much. Catching up on paperwork. Why?'

'How about going to Hangzhou for the weekend, to discuss our proposal in detail. Shanghai is too distracting for this kind of negotiation. I mean, we're talking about ideas, not just money. Why don't we escape for a bit, free our minds? One of the reasons I wanted you on board was that I need someone with imagination, not just some boring businesswoman. Let's just go and chat. I think it'll be very beneficial for our … transaction.'

Yinghui smiled. She liked the way he spoke, his curious mixture of easy and awkward, as if in searching for the words to express how he felt, he knew he was going to find the wrong turn of phrase. *Beneficial for our transaction*. What did he mean? Was it a pick-up line, an invitation to a romantic weekend? Or did he intend to spend two days in a conference room, standing in front of a whiteboard and PowerPoint presentations, expecting her to contribute with earnest financial calculations?

'That sounds appealing,' Yinghui said. 'It seems ages since I've had some time away from work. As for ideas, well, I don't know if I have any these days.'

He laughed. 'Of course you do. You're bursting with beautiful thoughts. Shall I pick you up on Friday, say, early afternoon?'

When she put the phone down, Yinghui found she was smiling. Maybe it was the thought of a weekend off work, her first in years; or the idea of spending time with a man she barely knew; or perhaps it was simply the way he had delivered that line – *bursting with beautiful thoughts* – a pretty, but frankly strange, way to describe a new business associate. Maybe it was because she wanted to believe it was true: that she was still full of beautiful thoughts.

They arrived at their hotel a few miles north of West Lake late in the afternoon, the driveway up to the main reception building rising and falling gently as it traced the undulations of the tea plantations that covered the hills in that area. They had talked little on the drive from Shanghai, other than to comment on the amount of traffic, the mass of cars that did not thin out no matter how far they travelled from the city. There was one point on the journey when, although they were both silent, Yinghui knew that Walter was thinking the same thing as she was: whether they would ever escape Shanghai, for its boundaries seemed never to end, stretching virtually all the way to Hangzhou. Perhaps their weekend would not be one of escape after all; perhaps, mired in a glorified suburb of Shanghai, they would simply speak of business and nothing else, all those beautiful thoughts remaining unexpressed.

But then, quite suddenly, out of the unremarkable urban mess of downtown Hangzhou, they found themselves beside the banks of West Lake, the surface of the water flat and cold and grey, tinged with mist so that the hills on the far shore looked dreamy and indistinct. Pagodas rose from the perfect flatness of the water, arching bridges traversed little creeks that fed into the lake – like a perfect *mise en scène* of a play that Walter was directing. Within minutes they were driving through tea plantations, the rows of velvety bushes stretching towards pine-covered hills in the distance. Every so often they would pass handsomely restored traditional villages, dotted with osmanthus trees; there were tourist buses along the route, big parties of old men and women following their flag-waving leaders like children on a school outing.

They were greeted at the hotel by the Swiss manager, who showed them to their rooms. Yinghui wandered around her suite – an entire village house gutted to create a bedroom and living room almost as large as her apartment in Shanghai, with a bathroom nearly as big as the bedroom, and an outdoor terrace of smooth cedar planks with a small pool set along its far edge.

'Just to avoid any awkwardness,' Walter had said in the car, 'my company is going to pick up the tab for this weekend, so please don't worry about anything.' He had said it as if issuing instructions, giving the impression that he did not want to discuss the matter – indeed, that he was not used to talking about such trivial questions as bill-paying.

As Yinghui admired the grey silk furnishings, she thought about how Walter had organised everything thus far, leaving her with nothing to do except turn up. Even though he had not said anything about dinner that evening, she knew it would already have been taken care of, as would everything else for the whole weekend. She tried to remember if anyone had ever done this for her – anticipated her every need and provided every conceivable comfort – but she was certain that no one ever had. It felt strange not to have to make arrangements for herself; she had grown so accustomed to handling every tiny detail that she did not know quite how to feel now that someone was taking charge of her this way. It felt odd, certainly – but not disagreeable.

They had dinner in the hotel restaurant, at a table in an alcove that afforded a view of the other diners on one side and the undulating tea slopes on the other, which spread across the verdant landscape like a fine rug. There were not many people in the restaurant – a group of Taiwanese men in golfing clothes and two or three Western couples, weekend refugees from Shanghai. The room had the minimalist aesthetic of a Buddhist temple, sparsely decorated with dark lacquered pillars and giant bronze pots sitting in pools of carefully trained light. Walter poured the wine after they had taken their seats, both of them delicately evading the matter of their impending business transaction, each waiting for the other to make the first move, neither wanting to seem vulgar or over-anxious.

After her first glass of wine, Yinghui found that she was talking more than her companion. As she progressed from telling him about her current life in Shanghai to her past in Malaysia, she wondered how it was that she had begun to open up to him; she had hardly talked about her pre-Shanghai life to anyone since the day she set foot in Mainland China. She had left all that behind – for good, she had thought. But somehow it seemed easy to talk to Walter; or maybe it was just that he was skilled at obtaining information. He mentioned having recently been in London, and asked if she knew it; and before long she was recounting humorous events from her university days. He was good at keeping her talking, interjecting with brief questions that betrayed (she thought) a real interest in her life. Most of what she was telling him was completely irrelevant to their work – he did not need to know that she had named her first-ever business venture after a second-rate American film, or that she had a liking for Siamese cats – yet she blithely spilled out such information. He appeared to appreciate this trivia, encouraging her with appreciative laughter here, a well-timed 'Oh my God' there. His questions were earnest, prob-ing, but never over-familiar. At one point, just as dessert arrived, she found herself beginning to tell him about the fiancé she had once had, all the disappointment she had endured. She stopped herself.

Walter said nothing, allowing the silence to settle on the table. Their desserts lay before them – fragile, multicoloured, architectur-ally precise confections arranged delicately on large white plates. Eventually he smiled and said softly, 'It's funny how life changes along the way – so full of disappointment, but also surprises.'

It was a nothing comment, thought Yinghui, a platitude; but somehow, in its timing and delivery, it was perfect, as if he could sense what was going through her head, and was trying to make her feel better without being intrusive.

She caught sight of her candle-lit reflection in the window next to the table, her face slightly flushed from the wine, eyes shin-ing, eager. She looked – it was so long since she'd been able to say this – like herself. 'True,' she said. 'You never know what's waiting round the next corner.'

When she returned to her suite, she left the blinds and curtains open, so that in the morning she would wake up to the summer light. For the first time in years, she did not set the alarm clock. Lying in bed, she could make out the dragon's-back undulations of the surrounding hills in the distance, their outlines fading into the warm summer night, leaving only hints of their shape; the paths that lined the river valley were lit here and there by isolated lamps, like fireflies lost in a field. As she thought about what the next day would bring she felt a warm sensation of unforced optimism, the way a child would. She drew the fine cotton sheets around her and appreciated the silence of the air conditioning, aware that she was smiling.

The next morning, despite the sunlight flooding the room, she slept until almost nine, an indecent hour by her standards. She showered and dressed hurriedly, but even before she walked into the breakfast room she already knew that Walter was still going to be there. His breakfast had been cleared away, and he was reading a book; there was a cup of coffee on the table in front of him, and a place set for Yinghui.

'What are you reading?' she asked as she sat down.

'Nothing special, just something silly I've been reading for ages and not really enjoying.' She caught a glimpse of the cover as he slipped the book into his briefcase: *The Poetics of Space*, she thought it said, but she couldn't be sure. It was a book she had read at university, nearly twenty years ago, when such non-commercial issues as the poetics of space still mattered to her. She would never have thought that a man like Walter Chao would read a book like that; but now that she was beginning to discover what he was really like, nothing surprised her any more.

'I was just thinking about the project,' he said. 'About what it is we're trying to do with the building. Are we trying to re-imagine an entirely new space – I mean, create a completely new identity – or is it just a re-interpretation of an existing idea? You know, using what's there as a template for a modern version of its predecessor?'

Yinghui hesitated for a second. 'Is there a difference? I mean, from a practical point of view. You want it to be a cultural resource centre with a theatre and a cinema, so that's what it's going to be, right?'

'My God, you really are very practical in your thinking! The end product might be the same, but imaginatively there is a difference: *how* you reach the final result is really important. All the building work – every screw and nail, every coat of paint – has to be underpinned by a certain philosophy. Without it, the building has no soul.' He stopped and smiled sheepishly, looking into his cup and finding only remnants of the foamy coffee. 'Sorry, I get carried away sometimes.'

'No, please don't apologise. What you're saying makes complete sense. It's just – well, I'm not used to business people in Shanghai talking in such terms. Usually they only want to know how much, how fast.'

He signalled to the waiter for another coffee. 'I agree. People nowadays are only concerned with the bottom line – nothing else matters. What would you like for breakfast, by the way? I had noodles in soup and some *guotie* – really good. I saw the pancakes go past, and they looked nice too. But maybe you prefer fruit and yoghurt. With a figure like yours I suspect you eat very healthily.'

Yinghui blushed. 'Well, I try, but I don't always succeed.' She had woken up starving and had been hoping for bacon and eggs, but now she felt she couldn't have them. Wanting to make a good impression, she ordered a Continental breakfast.

As they chatted about the project they were embarking upon, Yinghui felt parts of her brain, for so long dormant, begin to reignite. It was strange, hearing words and expressions that she had not used for over a decade trip so easily off her tongue: *imaginative space*; *mimetic desire*; *empirical needs of architecture*. But soon they drifted onto other topics: cities they had visited, past holidays, tiny incidents that remained etched in their memories. They discovered a shared liking for all that was eccentric – places, people, books and music that others considered bizarre; they admired simplicity, and spurned the flamboyant; they prized the unexpected, anything that was unannounced and discreet, and couldn't care less for the kinds of things other people thought of as majestic. She laughed out loud in agreement when he expressed a hatred for Gaudí's Sagrada Familia – too obvious, too obviously weird; he couldn't stand it that people who liked Gaudí thought of themselves as 'offbeat'.

'I totally, *totally* agree!' She laughed. 'You know, I never thought I'd meet anyone else who hated it as much as I do.'

They went for a walk along the banks of West Lake, tracing its shoreline without bothering to plan an itinerary. It seemed imma-terial where they might end up. They continued to talk about shared experiences and, as they progressed, shared desires: places they'd like to visit, things they'd like to achieve. None of these was related to money or career advancement.

'Hey,' she said, giggling as they stood at the centre of an arcing stone bridge, 'shouldn't we be talking about work?'

It had begun to drizzle – the faintest of droplets filling the air, barely more than a mist. Along the water's edge, the branches of the willow trees drooped and touched the surface of the lake.

'This is work,' he said. 'Sort of.'

She looked at him as he leant with his elbows on the stone parapet. He was smiling, but a faint frown had settled on his brow, and his gaze was distant. She wondered if something she had said had made him recall a past event – a moving or maybe even troubling chapter in his life. They had spoken so much about themselves, so unguardedly, not filtering anything they said. She felt guilty at having interrupted their conversation by mentioning something as crass as *work*. What had she become? At a beautiful spot in one of the most scenic places in eastern China, with a man who might be interested in her, all she could think of was work.

A group of tourists walked past, chattering noisily in a southern dialect Yinghui could not understand; they carried yellow umbrellas emblazoned in red letters with the name of a travel agency. The violent splash of colour cut through the muted grey-green hues of the lakeside landscape, and even when the group had crossed another bridge and reached the far bank, Yinghui could still spot them in the mist-shrouded distance.

'It's good that we've had this opportunity to talk, find out about each other,' Walter said as they began walking vaguely in the direction of the hotel. 'You're going to be a key person in this deal, the one coordinating day-to-day matters. It's such a sensitive job that I think it's important that we get to know each other well, especially since we'll be working so closely together.'

Yinghui nodded. 'Absolutely. But there's one thing I need to discuss with you before we go any further.'

'Oh dear, this sounds ominous. Are you going to pull out?'

Yinghui did not look at him as they continued walking along a snaking path that led them under some elm trees. 'The capital that I'd have to put into the joint venture company – well, you know that I don't have such funds readily available. I'd need a bank loan. Several bank loans, in fact. Several very big ones.'

'I thought that might be the case,' Walter said calmly, his voice carrying just a hint of a question, as if he was mildly surprised by her statement.

'And I don't know if I'll be able to get those loans. I'll be totally honest with you: I just don't have enough capital otherwise. Even if I sold everything I owned, it wouldn't be enough to cover the amount I'd need to put in. So you see, getting those loans is sort of, well, essential if I'm to go ahead.'

They stood sheltered from the drizzle for a few moments by the canopy of leaves. The paths that wound their way through the park by the lakeside were empty now; people were in the tea houses and restaurants, sheltering from the rain.

'You've been worrying about this, haven't you?' Walter said, turning to face her. 'You shouldn't. You'll get those loans easily, I'd say. Look at your track record – you're someone who's clearly on the way up. That's why I picked you out of all the people I could have chosen in Shanghai. You're special. Banks will be falling over themselves to lend you money. This is China. They know that people like you can make things happen.'

Yinghui nodded.

'You're so daring and original in your thinking that I'm almost tempted to say, You know what? Forget the capital, you don't need to put in any money, just come and work with me. But I don't think you'd feel right about that – I don't think it would be right for you to be a mere employee drawing a salary. I want this to be your project too. You need to feel as if you *own* it, right from the outset. I want you to be my partner. People like you are rare. Trust me, I know.'

'So you think there'll be no problem about getting the loans?'

He smiled and touched her forearm. 'Remember what we spoke about at our first dinner? Business is about respect. And bank loans are just the modern world's way of showing how much it values you. They're like credit notes in that respect. You *deserve* respect – it's yours. You'll get everything you want.'

'And if I don't?'

'If you don't, we'll both shrug our shoulders and walk away from each other. Before long I'll find another person to replace you. Maybe that new relationship will turn out to be as smooth as ours seems to be, maybe it won't. You'll move on too, and find success and respect elsewhere.' He paused and looked at her briefly. 'That's the life of business people like us. I'll regret never having really known you, but that's just how it is: you miss opportunities, you have to live with regret.'

The drizzle was turning to rain, falling heavily on the leaves overhead. Yinghui thought for a second that Walter might kiss her, but he did not. He merely looked up at the trees, his palms turned upwards to gauge the rain. They walked to the road and hailed a taxi back to their hotel.

Once she was back in her room she ran a very hot bath and lay in the vast cedarwood tub, looking out of the window across the rainwashed landscape, thinking about what Walter had said about regret. She did not want to live with regret; she would never do that. An image of Walter sitting at a table discussing business plans with another woman – someone sleek and well-groomed, who didn't suffer from *style issues* – flashed into her mind, making her feel anxious and slightly panicked. She could be replaced in an instant.

She closed her eyes and thought: she had to get those loans. All the respect that was due to her, accumulating over the years – she was going to cash it in, very shortly now.

How to Structure a Property Deal (for Total Beginners) – Case Study, Continued

My father had a friend in the land registry office, someone he'd known in primary school. He'd been to see this friend, who at the time was just a lowly clerk, but his humble post gave him valuable information: he knew which parcels of land were being sold on the cheap, which areas were going to be redeveloped, which houses were soon to be auctioned. (As an aside, I noticed this man's name in the newspapers just after the financial crisis in 1997: he'd been sentenced to a long time in prison after having embezzled twenty million *ringgit* from state funds. The poor idiot – he'd allowed himself to get caught. For this reason I will change his name, and call him 'Nik K'.)

If my father's ever-growing fantasies of quick riches were turning into an addiction, Nik K was his dealer. He told my father about the Tokyo Hotel and the small piece of land behind it: nothing to look at now, he said, overgrown and marshy as it was, but all my father had to do was cut down the trees, drain the soil – a simple procedure – and lay a mixture of concrete and hardcore on top of it, and it would be ready to be finished with tarmac, which would create a fine car park. The hotel itself was, frankly, in a bad state, but just imagine what might be achieved with a bit of investment: a solid three-storey building with a car park was virtually impossible to find at this price these days, and what's more, Nik K had heard from friends of his in other government departments that more offshore oilfields had been discovered, and would be operational in just a few years' time. When that happened, just think of the number of people coming to work in the support industries, all the seasonal workers from KL and beyond. Nik K himself had bought a few run-down buildings in the area for next to nothing – including the Tokyo Hotel, which he would let my father have for the same price he had paid.

We had to think big and think ahead, said Nik K; that was the future of this small town.

My father had virtually no money, but, fired by the prospect of turning a handsome profit in next to no time, he set about scraping together a lump sum with which to pay Nik K. He wrote to his distant relatives in Machang and Kuala Krai, and to cousins of cousins in Gua Musang and Kuantan – people he had never met but had heard of through the intricate spiderweb network of rural Chinese families. The note he sent was a cross between a begging letter and a financial prospectus, appealing to both their sense of pity and their greed. He got on his scooter and made long trips south to visit them in their villages and explain that the only way out of his predicament was for him to make a fortune; the only way he could be saved from ruin was to turn everyone into rich men. Double or quits; the only way was up.

Before long he had enough money to pay Nik K for the Tokyo Hotel, and the deeds were transferred to his name. But immediately there was a problem: he needed money for the renovation works. He drew up a list of essential jobs: repairing a section of the roof; securing the windows; replacing the wiring; restoring the water and electricity supplies; clearing the tangled mess of shrubs and trees from the small plot of land at the back. The amount of money needed for these works was nearly double what he had paid for the building. His despair did not last long, for Nik K again came to the rescue: he had contacts in the property world, people who owed him favours because he'd given them valuable tips on where to buy and sell land. He could arrange a loan for my father, he said, no questions asked – the sum my father needed was peanuts to these people. And so my father entered into a speedy, seamless arrangement with a Chinese merchant at 17 per cent interest. I remember the figure well, because it seemed a strange number, stranded between fifteen and twenty, as if someone had made an unconsidered compromise. To my father, the figure would have meant very little. His lender could have asked him for 0.1 per cent or 98 per cent, and he would have cheerily agreed. When he was in one of these moods, riding a high of optimism and desire, he would have said yes to anything. The number was also memorable to me because, as it happened, I was about to turn seventeen – an event of which my father was blissfully ignorant.

He started work on the Tokyo Hotel not long before my return from Johor, but even by the time I arrived, it was already clear that the renovation had run into problems. He had begun to clear the scrubby forest from the quarter-acre plot of land behind the hotel, but alone and equipped only with a *parang* and an axe, he was easily defeated by the dense vegetation. At the end of a long day, the huge pile of branches and tree trunks he had cut down seemed to make little difference to the immensity of unyielding foliage that remained. Without a bulldozer or a team of men with chainsaws, he could not overcome the jungle. So he turned his attention to restoring the electricity and fixing the plumbing in the hotel. He'd always been good at this sort of thing, having worked as a handyman at various building sites in the past (he said). He dug channels in the floors for new wires and pipes, knocked down some walls and scraped the plasterwork off others – better to make a mess at the start, he said in a letter to me, just before I abandoned my technical studies to go and join him. Although I had only completed one year of my electrician's course, I had already learnt enough to know that he had no clue what to do.

Fortunately, his shoddy wiring was never allowed to progress to the point at which it might have endangered his life and that of others. Alerted by news of building work at the Tokyo Hotel, two officials from the town council paid a visit to find out what was going on. They found my father stripped to the waist, surrounded by piles of broken masonry and half-mixed mortar and coils of electric cable. 'I'm going to start running a hotel,' he blithely informed them. 'Just as soon as I get the works finished.'

There were rules and regulations, they told him: he couldn't just fix up a building and start running a hotel. It was the eighties now; there was a modern system of doing things, and anyway this wasn't some *kampung* where anyone could do what he wished. He had to apply for planning permission for the renovation work; all the electrics and plumbing had to be carried out by someone with proper qualifications, and would need to be inspected; and he would need a licence to run a hotel, and a certificate to show he had done a course in safety and hygiene. All that would take time – and money.

In the meantime, the leaks in the roof were turning the plaster-work on the upper floors to mud, while a flash flood lifted up the floor tiles my father had proudly laid on the ground floor a few weeks previously, redistributing them in a kaleidoscope of cheap colour. Not one to be easily defeated, my father channelled his optimism (and his remaining money) into painting the façade of the building, on the grounds that a cheery exterior would give the hotel the beginnings of a new life, and would lead – somehow – to a turn in his fortunes. Although he did not say as much in his letters, I knew that he was waiting for me to return to help him – to save him.

I arrived to find the building clad in bamboo scaffolding, its top half mottled with patches of whitewash that accentuated the dirty grey background. My father had retreated to a small room at the rear of the ground floor, where he had installed a canvas camp bed and a two-ring tabletop cooker attached to a gas canister. There were streaks of mud snaking faintly across the floor – traces of the flash flood he had mentioned – but otherwise the room seemed dry and sound and cool, and a faint breeze came in through the single glassless window.

The rest of the building was a disaster. As I walked up the stair-case that had long since lost its banisters, it was virtually impossible to imagine what the interior had been like when it was first built (which must have been around the time of my birth – not all that long ago). Partition walls made of thin board had been half dismantled, uneven pyramids of bricks were piled in the middle of empty rooms, dried-up pools of not-quite-mixed cement crept across some floors, and gaps in the roof afforded me a glimpse of the grey rainclouds that hung low in the sky. I could not bring myself to ask my father whether it was he who had created this mess, or if the building had already been like this when he bought it. Nor could I bear to tell him there was nothing I could do to help him. It was hopeless, just as I had feared it would be.

Nonetheless, I spent two weeks there, explaining to him how fuses and junction boxes worked, how to create circuits with breakers and multiple switches. I drew designs on pieces of paper which he admired and pinned to the wall of his room as if they were works of art. He learnt quickly, and praised my knowledge as if I were offering him great revelations. He spoke of how he would have a fridge in every room, and eventually air conditioning too; how the hotel would be so popular that people would have to ring long in advance to book rooms. I agreed and enthused. It was the best thing I could do for him: to make him believe that his dreams could come true. After a fortnight of playing around with lengths of wire and patching up holes in walls with flimsy plasterwork that didn't quite stick, I made excuses about why I had to go back to Johor: my course would teach me more skills which I could use to help him; maybe I could also learn masonry and plumbing, which would come in handy when the hotel was up and running.

My father could not have been more delighted. Good idea, he said; those skills would be very useful, particularly since one day I would be the sole owner of the hotel, which I could take over as soon as I wanted. He spoke of a fully functioning hotel as if it already existed, as if it were not just a pile of damp rubble. I wondered whether he really believed what he told me, or whether he was merely playing along, as I was, in the charade that had become his life.

13

喜从天降

Luxuriate in
Serendipitous Events

As she stood to put her coat on, Phoebe took one last look around the luxurious place she had wandered into. She had never been in an upmarket beauty spa like this, which looked just like something out of a magazine, with low lighting and white orchids standing against dark stone. Even the air was perfumed; it smelled of lemongrass and spicy herbs that cleansed the smoky scent of the pollution that lingered in her nostrils every minute of every day. Sometimes at night when she woke from a nightmare, she would taste this bitter ash in her mouth. She wished she could stay here longer, absorb the smells and the glorious atmosphere of peacefulness and wealth, but this was not her place, she knew that now. She should not pretend any more; she should go back to Yanyan.

She began to walk slowly to the door, but then she heard footsteps behind her, a hurried clack-clack of heels on the hard floor. When she turned around there was a woman standing in front of her, wrapped up in a thick sand-coloured coat and a soft blue scarf. Although Phoebe could see that the clothes were expensive, she thought the woman looked very unstylish, like a farm worker who had been given a new outfit without a thought of whether or not it suited her. Her short hair was dull and a bit greasy; she had probably not even washed it that morning. She was holding a slim black briefcase and an umbrella, and her face was crumpled in a frown.

She looked Phoebe up and down, then glanced at the clock on the wall.

'You're very late,' she said. 'I was just going out. Next time, if you want to reschedule a meeting you have to give my PA more than forty-eight hours' notice.'

Phoebe tried to think if she knew this woman, but was sure she did not. She tried to think of a response, but all she could manage was, 'Sorry.'

'Sorry, sorry. That's what everyone says these days as an excuse for their lack of professionalism. If you keep changing appointment times, if you are so unreliable, how are you going to make a good receptionist?'

Phoebe looked down at the floor, and again she said, 'Sorry.' She didn't know why she was apologising to someone she had never met before.

The woman looked at her watch. 'I suppose you still want an interview now? It'll have to be quick, because I have another appointment over in Pudong. And I'm never late for my appointments, unlike many people.'

'An interview?' Phoebe repeated blankly.

The woman sighed. 'Yes, but it'll have to be quick. I can give you fifteen minutes maximum, but to be honest, for a receptionist's job, there's not much I need to know about you. Besides, I already have an idea of your approach to punctuality.' She turned and walked behind the counter, opening a door that led into a series of small rooms lit by stark fluorescent lighting – a bare sitting room with cheap armchairs, a microwave oven and a drinking-water dispenser; a store room full of towels and plastic bottles; and finally, an office that smelled of fresh varnish and paint.

'The building work isn't quite finished, but we need to open for business this week. Our first bookings are for this weekend, so I need someone who can begin work immediately,' the woman said, sitting down in a large black leather chair and gesturing to Phoebe to sit in the chair on the other side of the desk. Phoebe took her coat off, but as the woman did not do so, she left her scarf on.

'So frustrating when people cancel at the last minute. I had a receptionist lined up, contract signed, everything settled – then she just rings up and says she's found a job at a new hotel that's opened opposite Jing'an Temple. Just like that. Now I need to find a replacement in just four days. People say that Shanghai is a place of limitless opportunity because you can find people willing to work at anything – what nonsense! People here are so picky. Pay's not right, they're off the next day. Work environment's not comfortable, they're off too. New boyfriend, they disappear. Ask them to work extra hours, they go to your competitor. Sometimes they don't turn up for work because they've argued with their husbands the night before. I don't know ... I think people here are becoming like Westerners.'

'I agree,' Phoebe said. 'Shanghai people are really quite arrogant. I don't think they're unreliable, but maybe they're too proud of themselves. They're not lazy like Westerners, they're *rich* like Westerners. That's why they can be picky – because they can afford to be. If they don't work hard, it's because they have options, they are always thinking of things outside of work. People only work well when they are desperate, I think. When they have no other option for happiness. Well, I mean, that's just my opinion.'

The woman looked at Phoebe for a moment before reaching for a ringbound file on the desk. Phoebe noticed that the skin on her hands was dry and scaly, and her nails were cut short – she had not even used nail polish to disguise how cracked and unattractive they were. 'That's an interesting point of view,' the woman said. 'You're not a Shanghai local, obviously.'

'*Of course not*,' Phoebe said in the Shanghai dialect. She had learnt a few phrases since arriving here, but it was such a harsh and difficult language that she could not master even its most basic sounds. 'No, I'm from the far south. Guangdong province. But I've lived here for some time. That's why my accent is strange.'

'I see. I don't really care where people are from. What's important is whether they can do the job,' the woman said, flipping through her file. 'Remind me what your name is, please? I can't remember which candidate you are – we got so many, and I don't think my PA printed off all the résumés for me.'

'Xu Chunyan,' Phoebe said. The name from the ID card she'd stolen two months previously came easily to her. She had repeated it and repeated it, preparing for a time like this, when she would need to say it as if she had been born with it.

The woman ran her finger down a list. 'Xu Chunyan, Xu Chunyan … no, I can't find you. No matter – you seem quite bright, even if you're not very punctual. Why don't you just tell me what experience you have? I can always find your résumé later.'

Phoebe found she could lie easily – the list of imaginary jobs she had done came so naturally to her that she did not hesitate for a second. Even as she described one talent she had supposedly acquired, a new one came into her head, and she found herself recounting skills she never knew she had. Book-keeping, PowerPoint, Excel – things she had heard of but had no experience of.

'It sounds as if you've had some quite important positions,' the woman said. 'Are you sure you want to be a receptionist in a spa?'

'To be totally honest with you, I would like a change of direction. I would like to work somewhere more sophisticated than a big office. Besides, like you, I'm sort of, well, really fed up with these arrogant Shanghai people.' She said the last sentence in a hushed voice.

The woman laughed. 'I know what you mean. It's a great city, but life here is not easy.'

'I was just joking, but I knew you would know what I meant. You're not local either, are you?'

'No, I'm from Malaysia – although if you're from Guangdong, you're just as much a foreigner in Shanghai as I am.'

'True,' Phoebe said. 'Malaysia, huh? I knew your accent sounded familiar.'

'Familiar?'

'What I mean is, I've known many Malaysians in my previous workplaces. Well, to tell the truth, I once had a Malaysian boyfriend, not for long, though. It must be nice over there. I would like to go some day.'

The woman closed her file and scribbled on a notepad. 'Can you speak English?'

'*Of course*,' Phoebe said. '*No problem*. And I'm learning French too.'

'*Ah bon, tu parles français?*'

'Actually I haven't started yet, I've only just bought the book.'

The woman wrote something on the notepad, and finished by drawing a double line firmly under what she had just written. Phoebe tried to peer over to read it, but could not quite make it out. 'I like your attitude,' the woman said. 'I like people who try to improve themselves. Why don't we start you as a receptionist, then if you prove yourself capable, we can move you on to other duties, maybe administration or a managerial role, given your background. But let's see how you get on with answering the phone and dealing with clients – it doesn't sound like much, but it's actually very important.'

'Yes. Knowing how to deal with different people and situations is the key to all successful business,' Phoebe said, remembering a line from one of the books she had read.

'Hm,' the woman said, smiling as she fastened the buckle on her briefcase. 'You're obviously a person who takes her work seriously. That's good. When would you be able to start?'

'I can start any time. I believe in responding swiftly and positively to all work demands.'

'Excellent, Miss … Xu.'

'My friends call me by my Western name, Phoebe.'

'That's a nice name – we're anticipating a number of foreign clients, so it'll be easier for them to pronounce, too. Hopefully you'll build up relationships with them and encourage them to return. One more thing, Phoebe. Can I take a few copies of your ID for our files, please? Sorry to be troublesome, it's just that I like everything to be in order. Besides, I can't afford to risk breaching any regulations. We were going to hire a Filipina girl, very charming, excellent English and decent Mandarin, had lived here for over three years, so I assumed her situation had been, well, normalised. Turned out she was illegal.'

'Oh, sure,' Phoebe shrugged, opening her purse and producing the stolen ID card. She handed it over without even glancing at it, as if it were the most boring object in the world. 'As you can see, I'm much more attractive in real life.'

The woman laughed and said, 'Everyone is much more attractive in real life.' She took the card, and walked out to the photocopying machine in the corridor. It took her a while to figure out which buttons to press, and while the copies were being printed out she looked up at a calendar pinned to the wall in front of her. It had a photo of a snowy valley, the hills covered in frosted pine trees. 'In fact, everything is better in real life. Reality is beautiful, imagination is dangerous – it'll let you down if you're not careful.'

Phoebe did not answer as she watched the sheets of paper sliding out of the photocopier. Xu Chunyan, twenty-two years of age, slim-jawed, dreamy, full of hope. The machine fell silent, and the woman inspected one of the copies of the ID card. 'Yes, you do look better in real life!'

They walked back out into the warm, black-marbled reception, and paused in front of the exit. The music was still playing in the empty space, in anticipation of the many customers who would soon be walking through the door. But for now they were the only two people there.

'Can you come tomorrow morning? My PA will be here to give you some basic training. I like my people to work to certain uniform standards throughout my companies. She'll also sort out your paperwork and finances. We haven't got the accounts 100 per cent ready, so she'll give you your first month's salary in cash. Is that OK? She'll work everything out with you. Hey, we haven't even discussed your salary. But let me assure you, we pay more than most of our competitors.'

'For me, financial remuneration is not as important as job satisfaction,' Phoebe said. She was amazed by how much of her books she had absorbed.

'Great. I have to rush now. I don't know how often I'll be able to come here, but I'll get reports on your progress from my PA.' She reached into her bag and handed Phoebe her card. Her name was written in Chinese on one side and in English on the other. She did not have an elegant, Western-sounding name like Landy or Wena or Apple or Bambi, just a transliteration of her Chinese name. *LEONG YINGHUI.* It was boring, but it inspired confidence, Phoebe thought. Knowing the woman's name made her feel safe, though she could not explain why. It was an unremarkable name, but it suited the woman so well: she wasn't trying to be anyone else. Phoebe wanted to work for this woman; she would try hard and do her best. She felt a seed of unease as she thought of the face of the girl on the ID card, the face that was hers now, but quickly suppressed her anxiety. *You must overturn all your old beliefs in order to succeed in life.* All she had to do was concentrate on the glorious future ahead of her, and none of her lies would ever matter.

'Phoebe Xu Chunyan, see you again. Good luck. I think you will be a success with us. I hope so.' She held the door open for Phoebe, then locked it behind them. A car pulled up alongside the pavement, a large silver Toyota. As Leong Yinghui got into it she was already checking her BlackBerry. She did not look up as the car pulled away, leaving Phoebe standing alone.

The rain had dampened everything, turning the fallen leaves into a thick, slippery carpet that made the ground beneath Phoebe's feet feel uncertain. When she had been working in Guangdong, drifting from one temporary job to another, like millions of other migrant workers, people used to call her kind of existence *a floating life.* For so long that was how she had lived, in a floating world in which everyone longed for something more stable, in which every minute of her day was spent waiting for real life to happen, a life that would make it possible to have a home and a family. She had spent so long in that situation that even now she found it hard to lose a feeling of transience, a sense that nothing would last. But she knew, finally, that she was leaving that floating world, and that from now on her life would become firm and rooted in the concrete foundations of this city.

Her feet soon became damp from walking through the wet leaves. The moisture had seeped into the toes of her shoes, staining them a dark red, almost black, like blood. That's what happens when you buy cheap things, Phoebe thought. Fake leather looks great until you use it in a demanding situation, and then it shows its true colours, it lets you down. This was the last pair of fake leather shoes she would ever buy, because from now on she would have the salary of a working person in Shanghai. She would be able to buy clothes from the big Japanese chain stores, and eat in restaurants in the new shopping malls all over the city, where the floors were clean and there were no bad smells from the open drains.

The rain was falling heavily now, the drops splashing noisily on the hood of her coat. The air smelled of moss and smoke, or maybe she was just imagining it. She stopped walking and turned around. A taxi was approaching, and as she raised her hand it stopped alongside her. She opened the door and got in, and the driver waited to be told where to go, just as he would with any other passenger. He did not look at her shoes or criticise her dress; he just glanced at her briefly in the rear-view mirror, repeated the destination she told him, and nodded his head. He did not know that this was the first time she had ever taken a taxi in Shanghai; he simply assumed she was just like everyone else.

She did not ask the driver to take her home, but to People's Square. There she joined the queue for a famous *xiaolongbao* store that she had heard of, the long line of people trailing halfway down Zhenghe Lu. She stood patiently in the rain, the hood of her coat pulled loosely over her head, surveying the world she now lived in. When it was her turn she bought the best crabmeat dumplings, then took another taxi home.

'Waaaa*aaahhh*,' Yanyan cried when Phoebe showed her the dumplings. '*Toooo* good!' Phoebe ate two and gave the rest to Yanyan. They were delicious, the best food she had ever tasted in her whole life, so rich in flavour that they made her realise just how colourless her life had become, how empty of perfume and complexity. Just two mouthfuls, two morsels of food, made her whole body yearn for more. But she didn't mind leaving the rest for Yanyan, because now she could afford to eat them whenever she wanted. She would have more. And more and more.

In the weeks that followed, Phoebe made sure she seized every opportunity to present her most outstanding qualities, such as her willingness to learn and absorb new ideas, and her capacity for hard work over long hours. Even when she felt herself coming down with the winter 'flu that was afflicting everyone in the city, she pretended nothing was wrong, as she did not want to risk taking even one day off work. She feared being replaced, even temporarily. She needed to grasp each chance that came her way, and to treat every day as a new challenge. To that end she would have to make her body obey the ambitions of her spirit.

She took bookings by phone, speaking with the utmost courtesy, even subservience, to the female clients, and allowing just the smallest amount of flirtatiousness to enter her voice whenever she spoke to a man. She did this automatically nowadays, occasionally catching herself if she went too far. She was nice to men not because she had to be, but because she wanted to. She was glad she no longer had to tell them lies or flatter them outrageously. If she laughed with them or cajoled them into taking the most expensive massages, it was because she genuinely wanted them to enjoy the best experience possible. *Give yourself entirely to your work, and in return, your work will treat you with respect.* She remembered everything she had read from her books, and now it was paying off.

After two weeks Boss Leong's PA, who was also acting as the manager of the spa, apologised for not yet having hired a second receptionist to relieve Phoebe's workload, and Boss Leong herself even rang to explain that they were having difficulty finding a suitable person, and that she understood it must be hard for her. 'No, no, not at all,' Phoebe replied brightly. 'It's no hardship at all, I can manage everything. Please take your time. Even if you don't want to hire anyone, it's fine with me. Actually, I think one receptionist is sufficient.'

'We don't want to be exploitative,' Boss Leong said. 'While we look for someone, we'll pay you double overtime in recognition of your hard work.'

On three separate occasions, young women came in off the street seeking work as a receptionist or administrator. Phoebe recognised the look they wore – hungry, hard-eyed, desperate. They had decent qualifications, and could easily have done the work Phoebe was doing. Each time she apologised, and told them there were no jobs for them. 'But if you let me have your résumé I'll contact you if there's a vacancy. Could you, um, please leave now? Sorry, but our exclusive clients don't like seeing random people like you wandering in here.'

Twelve hours a day, seven days a week, Phoebe answered the telephone, greeted people at the door, organised the rota, served lemongrass tea to waiting clients, and made sure that the masseuses and beauticians maintained a harmonious environment. She gave the masseuses a daily lecture on the importance of professionalism and propriety, especially when dealing with male clients, and even more so with Japanese and Western customers who might have misconceptions about the services on offer. Once she saw an American client discreetly giving his phone number to his masseuse as he paid the bill. The next morning, at the daily staff gathering, she took great pleasure in announcing that the girl would be fired for being in breach of basic rules, and that this should serve as an example to all the others. Everyone said, 'Phoebe is so professional, she is just like the manager here. Surely she will soon be on a manager's salary.'

Her new workplace also made it possible for her own impeccable personal grooming to shine brightly and combine with her impressive work ethic. She wore a uniform that suited her, a slim black tunic made of raw silk, cut in the South-East Asian manner, fitting snugly around her waist and flaring out over her hips. On the advice of Boss Leong's PA, Phoebe changed her hairstyle, piling it up in a big bun in imitation of Singapore air hostesses. Sometimes she would catch sight of herself in the mirrored wall that lined one side of the reception area and be amazed that the person in the reflection was Phoebe Chen Aiping. Lit by soft spotlights and candles, she looked as if she had been born into this elegant world; she did not seem the tiniest bit out of place.

When the PA arranged for a photographer to take some pictures of the spa and its personnel, Phoebe persuaded him to take a few of her dressed in her uniform. His professional equipment and eye for composition produced results which overjoyed Phoebe. She placed the portraits on her profile page on the various dating websites she had signed up to, replacing some Yanyan had recently taken of her standing on the bank of Suzhou Creek, which now looked amateurish – her smile was too forced, her outfit too provocative for the humble public setting. The images that represented her now were classy and romantic; surely it was just a matter of time before she found the right kind of man.

But with the long hours she was spending at work, Phoebe was no longer able to spend much time on the internet. And besides, as Boss Leong had said, everything was better in real life. But the problem with real life was that it did not offer opportunities to meet real-life men. Every day there would be men in the spa, and often they were rich and good-looking. But Phoebe demanded professionalism from all her staff, and she knew that the best way to achieve the desired results was to lead by example (on the bus to work every day she read her books, which gave her many instructive tips: for example, that she should perform duties way above her position, in order to gain promotion more quickly: *Behave as if you are the boss, and soon you will be the boss*). She forbade herself any close involvement with the clients, even though, after less than two months, there were already regulars who came back time after time because they were drawn to Phoebe's charming manner and the excellent personal service she provided. For example, there was one man who came to collect his wife after her weekly massage, who always made sure to arrive a few minutes early so he could sit and watch Phoebe. Although he pretended to read a magazine, she knew he was appreciating her elegant movements and petite figure, which were accentuated by her slim-fitting black dress. She only granted him a small, courteous smile as she brought him a cup of tea. She did not wish to encourage him further.

Then there was the Taiwanese man who came twice a week, once for a Balinese seaweed wrap massage, once for a Shanghainese pedicure. When he filled in his form Phoebe had seen that he was only twenty-six, yet he dressed in immaculate designer clothes and always engaged her in lively, amusing chats, often making daring jokes. He had a smooth, clear complexion, and Phoebe had to admit that the moment he walked in the door she had thought, This man would make a wonderful husband. One day he came in with another man who looked just like him, a local boy who laughed and joked in Shanghainese with the manicurist who had just treated his friend. As he did so he traced his fingers over the Taiwanese man's hands, which were smooth and waxy and glowing after his manicure. Phoebe looked away as she handed them the credit card machine; she did not want to see them touching each other. 'Phoebe fancies a gay guy,' the other girls teased later. 'His boyfriend is more feminine than you!'

In a city of twenty million people, it was just impossible to meet men – all the girls at the spa agreed. They had come here from all over China to make money and find a partner, but they were beginning to think it was hopeless. All they could do was concentrate on their work and send money home so their parents could build a nice house in their village that would attract a nice boy; then they would go home and marry him, the slow-witted son of a farmer who had never ventured outside their province, maybe had never even gone to the provincial capital. They would give up their dream of getting married to a successful doctor or banker. Their adventure would last a few years and then, when they had got too old, they would just go home. *Going out* – that was something that belonged to their youth, a scary, thrilling ride that began in their late teens and lasted into their twenties, but they did not want to be thirty-five and unmarried, alone, childless. They saw all these well-educated women in Shanghai who dressed well and had good jobs, but were still single, unwanted – *remaindered*. What use was that? They had made a bit of money, their parents had a fridge and a colour TV, and there was enough left over for them to build an extension to the house, and even to hire help during the harvest season. Soon the girls would go home, to Anhui or Hunan or Sichuan or the frozen north-east.

Phoebe listened to their stories and thought, I am not going to go home. She could not go home, not yet, maybe never. She did not even know where she would go back to. She thought of her mother, living alone in that small town in the north of Malaysia, a town that was shrinking, becoming less and less alive as each year passed. It was the opposite of the Chinese villages that these girls spoke of, that grew and grew with the money they earned in the big cities on the coast, the fields of rice and wheat shrinking and eventually turning into industrial parks and high-tech factories, the villages becoming towns, the towns cities, because the girls who left would one day go back and get married, as certain as the seasons passed. No, the town where Phoebe had grown up was smaller now than it had ever been, and soon it would be dead. Her mother had never moved, and soon she too would be gone. Phoebe had left, but she could not go back.

She stayed late at the spa, past midnight, after everyone else had left, and used the fast new computers to upload the best photos of herself on her internet profiles. She joined every dating site she could find, concentrating on upmarket ones that charged a fee for joining. She changed her age from twenty-four to twenty-two, and made sure she only responded to men of quality who seemed to offer excellent long-term prospects. Some nights she only slept four or five hours because she chatted late into the small hours. It didn't matter: she was young, and didn't need sleep.

In the Journal of Her Secret Self, she wrote: *Phoebe Chen Aiping, every second of the day offers a beautiful opportunity to achieve success. Therefore you have 86,400 chances to change your life every day.*

14

明日黄花

Even Beautiful Things Will Fade

He had expected the office to be dark when he arrived, sunk in an atmosphere of mourning, or at least mild depression. But instead Justin found it quietly busy, filled with the sounds of clacking keyboards and the soft rhythmic *ke-chunk* of the photocopier. Even his own office was lit – as soon as he stepped out of the lift, he could see the conical Alessi lampshades glowing softly against the mahogany-lined walls.

The office manager was sitting in Justin's chair when Justin walked in; he was on the phone, using one of Justin's fountain pens to scribble a note on a pad in front of him. He signed off quickly when he saw Justin. 'Hello, boss,' he said, putting the phone down quickly; he did not stand up. 'What are you doing here? Your family said you were … ill.'

'I'm all right now.'

'Yes. You look … just the same.'

Justin glanced around the room and noticed that all his files had been rearranged, the leather-bound directories and coffee-table books of chic hotels had been cleared away, as had the framed photographs of himself and his family, replaced by brightly coloured plastic trays bearing stacks of paper that were too large for the custom-made hardwood shelves. There were piles of cardboard boxes in one corner of the room, as if excess stock from a small warehouse had spilled over into his office, and everywhere he looked he saw plastic jars filled with tea, the broad olive-coloured leaves sitting at the bottom. There was nothing of Justin's left on the desk except the penholder, which had been emptied of its contents, and a paperweight he had been given at the launch of an Italian fashion label on his arrival in Shanghai. His desk diary was gone, as was the miniature sandstone carving of a dancing Hindu god his brother had bought for him at the Met museum shop some years before.

'The thing is,' the office manager said, 'we didn't think you were going to come back. Your brother said you were no longer in charge of affairs, and we were to await further instructions, but then he never gave us any. We waited and waited. Meanwhile, people here were getting restless, and the landlord wanted to re-negotiate the lease and increase the rent. I read on the internet about your family's troubles in Singapore – you know, about the collapse of the stock market. So I had no choice.'

A young woman came into the office. She was dressed in acid-washed jeans that came down to her shins and a silvery T-shirt that said SMILE in English. 'Boss Wu, the bottled-water distributor is here for your meeting.'

'Who's that girl?' Justin asked once she'd left the room. 'And why are we selling bottled water? We're a property investment firm.'

'She's a new girl I hired. Jenny left because we were slow paying her salary. Anyway, she was too expensive. Shanghainese expect so much money nowadays. That girl is from Hubei – she's a friend of my sister's from back home. You won't believe how much I save on her salary! As I said, I thought your business was finished, so I let the landlord terminate the lease. But we still had three months here before we got kicked out, so I thought I'd change the direction of the business to try and make some money.'

'Change the direction,' Justin repeated blankly. He noticed that the cartons in the corner of his office were marked *All Natural Baby Food*.

'Yes, I'm now trading in domestic consumables – business is great! Excuse me, but I have a meeting now. Is there anything I can do for you?' He stood up and gathered a few pieces of paper and a card-covered book that resembled an old-fashioned ledger.

Justin shook his head. Outside the window, the skyscrapers of Pudong, clad in cobalt-blue glass, were reflecting the sky, warping the shape of the clouds so they looked like streaks of oil on tarmac, brilliant and purple; when they shifted in the wind the sun would burst through, dazzling Justin for an instant.

'Your personal items are in that box over there, I think. No, that one over there. The girls cleared everything away before they left. OK, I've got to go now. Goodbye.'

A translucent blue plastic crate sat on the leather sofa, surrounded by samples of health-food supplements with bizarre names that Justin had never heard of – Cat's Claw, Dong Quai, Fo Ti, Horny Goat Weed. He lifted the lid on the crate and looked at its contents – his desk diary and three silver-framed photographs lay inside, together with his personal organiser and the two mobile phones he used when he was in Malaysia and Hong Kong: the sum total of his working life, barely able to fill a single packing crate. Another person might have had a painting or two, or colourful crayon drawings by his children, he thought; or postcards sent by friends from sunny places, maybe a flag from his home town or souvenirs of foreign trips; or a snapshot of himself with his wife, taken on their latest anniversary, looking joyfully up at the camera he was holding himself. He looked at his possessions: hard-edged, cold, functional; black and silver, plastic and metal. Even the photographs of his family were posed studio images. He pondered them for a while, wondering if he should take them. Eventually he slipped them into his briefcase, leaving everything else behind.

Back at his apartment he flicked through his Rolodex, briefly considering each name – how well he knew the person, whether he could ring them after so long, how awkward it would be. He felt a sense of urgency as he scanned each card, a feeling he could almost describe as strength, which he had not felt for many months. But gradually this sense of fortitude began to turn to panic, and he realised that it was not in fact strength, but desperation, that drove his actions. Each time his eyes alighted on a name that seemed hopeful, there was always a reason not to ring that person – an unbridgeable distance. The truth was, he now knew, he had no friends.

He found one business contact, someone who had never been a proper friend but whom he had known since school days, a fellow Malaysian who owned a series of factories in Wenzhou that made those tiny clips on bra straps – 60 per cent of the world's supply of bra strap clips, he had once claimed; local businessmen admiringly called him 'Bra Button King'. Justin had lent him 1,000 *ringgit* when they were nineteen years old, and he was starting his first business buying and selling used office furniture.

'*Justin*. Hey, man. I didn't know you were still in Shanghai. I thought, all that stuff going on back home, surely you'd be back in KL. Must be tough back there, huh? *Ei*, sorry, man, I'm quite busy at the moment. Can I call you back? Still the same number, right? Let's have lunch soon, *ya*? Of course, I promise. Call you soon.'

He rang two or three other people, but it was the same each time: they'd heard the news, were sorry about his family, and yes, of course they'd love to meet up, but things were so busy in China these days, you know what it's like, just non-stop. They promised to call back, but their voices were full of a fake cheeriness that signalled to him that they would not. He had done the same thing so many times in the past; he never thought he'd be on the receiving end of it.

This was what life was like in China, he thought: stand still for a moment and the river rushes past you. He had spent three months confined to his apartment, and in that time Shanghai seemed to have changed completely, the points of reference in his world rearranged and repositioned in ways he could not recognise. Just as he had lost his car and driver, he was also having to navigate his way through life without a map – as if the GPS in his brain had been disconnected, leaving him floundering. Everyone in this city was living life at a hundred miles an hour, speeding ever forward; he had fallen behind, out of step with the rest of Shanghai.

He arrived at the end of the Rolodex, the cards flipping over hopelessly towards the X, Y, Zs without a sign of anyone who might help him. He was speeding through the Ys when he stopped, and reached for a card printed with a feminine, scrolling typeface: Leong Yinghui. It was not filed under her surname, but he knew that had not been an error, that he had done it by pure instinct, for he could not think of her in any other way than simply as *Yinghui*. It was familiarity and habit that had misplaced the card, not carelessness.

He had thought he had lost the card, and maybe a part of him had even wanted to do so, uncertain and possibly afraid of what a reunion with her would involve. Throughout his winter solitude, when his thoughts had been blank and his body numb, he had sometimes wondered what he had done with it. Images of her came to his mind, but the prospect of getting in touch with her again was not enough to get him out of bed to search for the card. All the yearning and regret that might once have stirred him into action were now absent. That was when he had known that he was really ill, that it was not just a passing cold-weather virus but something darker, something he would not be able to shake off easily.

He had met her again in what he now recognised was the first stages of his breakdown, when he was already in a state of permanent distraction, his mind cloudy, his vision and thoughts unfocused. He had been dragged to the event by Zhou X, the actress he had met at the charity auction at the start of his time in Shanghai. 'I need someone to accompany me to an awards ceremony tomorrow evening,' she had said brightly on the phone. 'Some female business award thing. No one wants to go with me, everyone says it's too boring! I don't want to go either, but my agent says it'll make me appear serious and hard-working. *Please* come.'

On the way to the event, Zhou X spoke constantly; she had recently returned from Europe, where she had been filming in Berlin and Paris and sound editing in London. She had opinions on everything – European food is awful: meat, meat, meat, always in huge lumps, often not even cooked. She went to a Chinese restaurant in Paris – the rice was like little plastic pellets. German people are fat. Dutch people are tall. French people are elegant but rude. English people dress very messily. London is dirty but it has nice parks. The hotels are old. People are lazy and always on strike. But she bought a nice handbag in Paris – limited edition, not available in China. Europe is good for luxury items, not so good for life.

As soon as they arrived at the five-star hotel she drifted away from him, shepherded by her manager towards the crowd of photographers hovering by the entrance to the ballroom. She beckoned Justin over for a few photographs, hanging on to his arm while she posed for the cameras. He stood rigidly, trying not to blink before the brilliance of the flashbulbs. He felt like a tourist monument – a statue beside which she was striking amusing poses, the photos soon to be posted on her Facebook page or emailed to friends and family. Before long, thankfully, she moved off, seeking brighter, more useful people than Justin.

Left alone, Justin wandered amongst the tables looking at the decorations and place names. The chatter in the ballroom, the glittering smiles, the crowds milling aimlessly, the camera flashes, the banners, the music – all this made him feel anxious and claustrophobic, and he withdrew towards the edge of the room. Memories of teenage awkwardness came back to him with startling clarity – endless parties at which he had spoken to no one and merely lurked in the shadows on his own, much as he was doing now.

He found a brochure on a table and pretended to read it so his isolation would appear less noticeable. It was about foreign companies in Shanghai, and was full of phrases such as 'deepening ties' and 'bridge-building'. He walked around the room as he read the brochure, looking at the pictures of the nominees for the evening's awards – young women with battle-hardened faces, their eyes already bearing signs of disillusionment and disappointment. They were only in their thirties, some of them even younger, but already they had a world-weariness that he recognised only too well, a hardened edge that seemed to announce that life could no longer surprise them, that the only route to happiness lay in the accumulation of more – of more and more and more.

Then a face looked up at him from the pages of the brochure; he stopped and stared at it, allowing his brain time to process the image, affixing it to his consciousness: the close-set eyes that seemed to focus intensely on whatever they were looking at, the small mouth that could seem either delicate or ready for an argument, depending on her mood. At first he assumed he had made a mistake – the small studio portrait was overlit, making the woman's features look blander than he remembered. Her hair was different too – longer, but strangely more severe than the short gamine style that had once been her trademark (if it was indeed her). Her cheekbones seemed more angular now, her eyes expressionless. He really wasn't feeling well, he thought; maybe he was genuinely going mad – she was someone who had dismissed business as an immature game played by boys who refused to grow up. But here she was, nominated for an award, her name printed in capital letters under the photo, the distinctly non-Mainland spelling announcing her foreignness: *Leong Yinghui*. He examined her face again. It was definitely her. He looked around the room but could not see her; surely she must be here somewhere. Suddenly he became aware of his every movement – the way he placed one foot in front of the other, the way he smiled at passers-by, the way he breathed. And then, when he turned around, she was there, as if waiting for him.

'Chee Keong? Justin?'

'Yes. Leong Yinghui! Hi. My God, it's been years.'

Her tightly held mouth had relaxed into a smile, but she did not seem surprised or happy at this chance meeting; she seemed annoyed, as if he were an unexpected inconvenience.

They chatted for a few moments with all the awkwardness of former friends who have not seen each other for many years, each hoping (he thought) to recapture their past intimacy; but then he remembered that they had never really been friends, despite his longing that they should. He answered her polite questions mono-syllabically, which frustrated him, because he had always wanted to be witty and expressive with her, but was never able to be. He had once thought it was a matter of youthful shyness on his part, and that when he was older and successful he would chat with her with greater ease, but things had not changed.

Zhou X suddenly appeared at his side again, and clutched his arm. More cameras, more smiles; people crowding in on him. Amidst the bank of camera flashes he looked for Yinghui, fearing that she had walked off. But she reached towards him, holding her business card, and then, as he was blinking from the glare of the lights, she escaped. He posed for a few more photographs, but all at once he felt exhausted, his limbs weighing heavily, his joints aching, his head cloudy and his mouth dry. Music was playing through the loudspeakers now, signalling the start of the prize-giving, but he made his way to the door, crossed the hotel lobby and headed straight to the cab rank, from where he took a taxi home.

Now he sat before the Rolodex with her card staring at him – a link to all that he had once wanted but now feared. Too much had passed between them; and the passage of time had not made things better. He hesitated for a while before flipping the card over and looking through the surnames beginning with Z. He had left the windows open all day; the apartment smelled of cooking fat from the kitchen above.

He simply couldn't call Yinghui; she would have nothing but contempt for him.

15

气吞山河

A Strong Fighting Spirit Swallows Mountains and Rivers

As Gary steps onto the stage he is struck, first of all, by how small it is. It is years since he performed on a stage this size. In a second the backing dancers are going to appear, and he has no idea how they are all going to fit on a platform measuring only twenty by fifteen feet, covered in a green Astroturf-like material with pots of plastic flowers at each of the front corners – the only decoration there is. It feels flimsy under his feet, little more than a big hollow box made of plywood, ready to collapse at any moment. The papers are always full of stories of freak accidents in public places, roofs falling down on cinemas, whole ice rinks being swallowed up by the ground. Maybe this will be one of those sad, bizarre stories.

The music is already playing loudly in the atrium of the shopping mall – a bright, breezy tune with uplifting guitars over a simple melody and a heavy drumbeat, the kind of music that makes teenagers want to get on their feet and sing along while bouncing up and down on their heels. He hasn't sung this tune in years – it is from an earlier time in his career, when he was so young and malleable that he would sing anything he was told to. The shopping mall is decorated with huge plastic banana trees in plastic pots, and there are banners streaming down from the upper floors announcing, *Opening Celebration, Big Discount*. Now he understands why his agent had said, 'It's the perfect song for the setting.'

A cry goes up from the small crowd – about a hundred people – as he walks to the middle of the stage. It feels strange to be in front of an audience again. Even though he still cannot fully understand why he has bothered to come all the way out here, and he has not rehearsed at all for this gig, he begins to sway in time with the music. He is a professional; his body knows what to do even if his spirit is absent. In a few moments he will lift the microphone to his mouth and his voice will emerge, bright and clear, without him even commanding it to do so. Just like driving a car, he thinks, although he doesn't know how to drive.

It has now been more than four months since news of Gary's various misdemeanours was splashed over the cheap newspapers and colourful magazines and internet gossip sites. In the intervening time he has spent long periods in a rented apartment in Zhabei, which has two bedrooms, a modest sitting room, and a small kitchen that looks out onto the five other tower blocks that make up the condominium complex. In the middle of these thirty-storey towers is a bright-blue swimming pool shaped like a gourd, two circles joined together, one larger than the other. From the twenty-eighth floor, where Gary lives, the pool looks fake, one-dimensional, fringed with palm trees; and because it is shielded from the sun by the high buildings around it, the water is always cold and there is never anyone in it, even now that spring is turning to summer. This is the only view he has, apart from into the apartments in the adjacent blocks.

During his first few days there, Gary hated it and felt homesick for his apartment in Taipei, but then he realised that for the first time in years he was able to spend whole days and nights without having to close his curtains. There were no paparazzi trying to take photos of him with lenses the size of rocket launchers, no one rummaging through his rubbish bins, no one dressed as a gas inspector pretending to have come to read the meter. With the curtains wide open, he was the one doing the looking. He could see right into other people's apartments, and watch them eating dinner under harsh fluorescent lights. Later, the children would settle down to do their homework while their parents sat in front of the TV – dozens and dozens of families doing exactly the same thing at exactly the same time. He could see what programmes they were watching, and even the coloured circles of the PowerPoint presentations they were preparing on their computers, and sometimes he would sing along to the music from their karaoke sets. It made him smile when they sang one of his own hits that had become karaoke classics, such as 'Sunshine After Rain' or 'Y-O-U', or his rendition of Leslie Cheung's 'Bygone Love', with his own arrangement for strings and piano.

No doubt they too can look into his apartment, and he is sure that they cast casual glances across from time to time, but all they would see is yet another bored single man, of whom there are plenty in Shanghai, strumming his guitar or playing on an electric keyboard or idly zapping through the channels on his forty-two-inch TV while chatting on the internet. He is just like hundreds of other young people in this apartment complex, and because there are so many residents living so close to each other, no one ever looks into the next person's life very closely. Everyone is busy preparing for tomorrow; no one has time for him, no one cares about his life.

He likes it here.

Gary begins each day full of hope, optimistic that his agent will ring with news of a new record deal or a small concert somewhere, maybe in Thailand or Indonesia, where he is still quite popular, because not many people have access to the constant barrage of negative publicity in the Chinese-language press. But his agent has not rung much, barely once a week, if that. At first Gary called her often, chasing up possible leads; he had begun to realise how much he missed singing, how keenly he felt the loss of his stage personality, the rush of adrenalin he experienced when performing. Soon, however, he stopped calling, because it was embarrassing to chase after her, awkward to keep reaching her answering machine and leaving messages in which he did not really know what to say. It was, to be truthful, humiliating to know that not so long ago, if ever he rang anyone in the record company his call would be answered immediately, with great enthusiasm. He knew the way the business worked. If you are a success you wish that you were not, you wish that everyone would leave you alone; and when you are no longer a success, you lose the right to wish for anything.

For his part, Gary has been concentrating on his music. He has been writing a few songs and rearranging some traditional melodies in a more modern style. (He imagines that in interviews later in his life, when journalists ask him where he got the inspiration to write and reinterpret these songs, he will say, 'It all goes back to that dark period in my life, when I was all alone, listening to these songs on other people's karaoke sets in the apartment block.') He has been trying to remember why he loves music, trying to forget about performing. It is not easy. He is happy because he is writing music after a long break from it, but he is sad because he knows that he might never perform before a big audience again.

He is also spending a lot of time online, but not looking at the sordid porn sites he used to frequent, which are banned in China and difficult to access anyway. No, it is because he has found himself in a sort of online relationship.

Is she a 'girlfriend'? Or a 'soulmate'? Is he in love with her, or are they just close friends who understand each other deeply? Of course he does not love her, but he finds that he does have feelings towards her. It's just that he cannot put a name to these feelings. It is a weird, exciting position to be in. He knows that she feels the same, that she does not consider him to be a boyfriend, but that she too is happy whenever she receives a message from him. He keeps his laptop on all the time, waiting for her to log in. Even when he is practising the piano he has it on a little table next to him, just in case the familiar box with her smiling face pops up with a note saying: *Little Cat is here!*

They chat every day, sometimes three or four times a day. In the evenings they will talk for two or three hours, way past midnight, and the following morning he will receive a message saying, 'So so so so tired but … so so so happy. Going to work now. Think of me and wish me success at work today!'

It is the first time in his life that he has been so close to another person. He has never had a conversation lasting more than five minutes, unless it concerns music or his career. He has never had the opportunity to chat about simple, silly things like what kind of food he likes, what his favourite animals are, what he thinks of the plight of migrant workers, the fate of children orphaned in the Sichuan earthquake. She asks him questions such as, 'Who causes more misery to the opposite sex, men or women?' before offering opinions such as: 'Women seek to change men, men seek to educate women, and they end up making each other unhappy.' When he first started chatting with her, he realised that he had no opinions on anything. He could barely be considered a normal human being. Or rather, he did have feelings and opinions on many subjects, but he had never had the chance to articulate them. He has never been in a position to examine his thoughts about important issues in his life. Until now, no one has ever asked him, 'How are you feeling this morning?' No one has ever said, 'Is everything all right with you today? You seem a little sad.' This girl has the ability to discern sentiments in him that he himself is incapable of noticing. But the moment she mentions something – 'You seem a little depressed today'; 'You seem optimistic this evening' – he realises that it is exactly how he feels. *Depressed. Optimistic. Brooding. Assured.* She has a way of understanding what is going on in his head when even he does not.

And yet he has never met her in person, or even heard her voice. On one or two occasions she has suggested swapping phone numbers so she can text him while she is at work, but each time he has changed the subject rapidly. He still cannot get rid of his manager's first piece of advice to him, permanently imprinted on his memory: the first rule of self-protection is never to give your mobile number to anyone.

In fact he divulges very little information about himself. He does not say what he does for a living, how it is that he comes to be in Shanghai, or which district he lives in. When she asked him where he was from, he said, simply, 'Taiwan,' to which she replied, 'Yes, I know.'

'How?'

'Because when I asked you what your favourite fruit was, you said *fengli* instead of *bolo*, and only a Taiwanese would say that.'

For now she seems content with this lack of information. She says she does not want to pry – if he is married or holds an important public position, she understands and will not seek to know any more. All she knows is that he is nice to her, and that is what matters. 'If you are obese or deformed, I don't care. I don't care who you are in real life. I like you because … you are like me.'

She is open, trusting. She sends him photos of herself in a variety of settings – in People's Park, at the top of the WFC, looking down at the crystal spire of Jinmao, at the Star Ferry pier in Hong Kong. Most of them are taken by herself, always from the same angle, the camera held at arm's length, slightly above her face, from which Gary deduces that she does not have many friends.

What else does he know about her? Quite a lot, actually, because she loves to talk about herself, recounting every aspect of her life in detail, describing not just her own emotional state but those of the people around her. Sometimes Gary feels that he knows these people personally, and that he is part of her life. Her name is Phoebe Chen, and she hopes that she will soon be promoted to manager of the upmarket spa where she works in Jing'an – she told him its name and address, but he's forgotten them now (though he had figured out that if he were a normal person who wanted to visit her, there was a direct metro line that would get him to her workplace in just over twenty minutes). She has always worked in the hospitality industry, in the luxury sector, such as five-star hotels and casinos, which is why she has lived in several countries across South-East Asia. Her current workplace is not as high-profile or glamorous as some of the previous ones, but it offers her numerous challenges and advantages. She works with a team of fifteen full-time and part-time therapists and beauticians. Many of them are uneducated girls from the countryside – you wouldn't believe how difficult it is to manage them! Always in crises, always having problems. The other day, would you believe it, Little S didn't come in to work because she thought she was pregnant, and when Phoebe asked her why she thought she was pregnant, she replied, Because the fortune-teller told me I would get pregnant on this date if I ate a herbal soup double-boiled with bird's nest. How stupid. She pays so much money to someone who will tell her anything she wants to hear. This is the sort of thing Phoebe has to put up with all the time these days.

Phoebe is not from Shanghai, but Gary isn't clear where exactly her roots lie – 'Somewhere in the south. It's complicated,' she said. If he listens carefully he imagines he can make out a Cantonese accent. She is very bright, but she has not had a great deal of formal education. He can tell, because educated girls type very quickly and use words that his lyricist and other clever songwriters use. On the few other occasions that he engaged in chats with girls, he was not able to keep up with the speed of the conversation. No sooner had he pressed the 'send' button than a reply would come through. And they would type complicated sentences that took a long time to read and digest, until they would become impatient and say, 'Why are you not responding? Are you chatting with someone else?' Also, professional women tended to ask him questions he could not answer: How much is your salary? How much are your car instalments each month? Do you have promotion ambitions?

With Phoebe, it is different. He can tell by the simple words she uses that she is just like him, unlikely to have stayed at school beyond the age of fifteen or sixteen. The fact that she has succeeded in such important positions at such a young age means she must be sophisticated and intelligent in ways traditional education cannot measure. He likes her occasional awkwardness, which makes him feel less embarrassed about his own shortcomings, his lack of articulate responses. If he ever asks her a difficult question, or one she does not want to answer, or if they speak about something emotional, she sometimes responds by simply saying, '*En*.' And he understands what she means by this. Just that brief, barely uttered word is enough for them – they do not need fancy words and complicated sentences.

The questions she asks are so simple, but they make him think about parts of his life that he had thought were so dull they were beyond analysis, so ephemeral that they would not be fixed in memory.

What can you remember about your mother?

Not much. She loved music.

En.

Don't forget, I was only ten when she died.

En.

She used to sing when I couldn't sleep.

What kind of songs?

Love songs. In *Minnan hua*, which was her dialect. *Qian wo de shou*, that sort of thing. I understood the words but I didn't know what love was.

But now you know?

Hello? Handsome brother, you still there?

Yes. I was just thinking …

What?

Maybe one day I will sing those songs for you.

Ha ha!

I'm serious.

En.

There were other questions too, more difficult to answer:

What kind of girl do you like?

Don't know. Nice ones. Difficult to say.

Ha? You are kidding. Are you … gay?? I don't mind if you are. It's just …

He had stared at the screen for some time before answering. The questions did not shock him. In fact, he had asked himself the same things several times. What kind of girls do I like? Am I gay?

There was a time when the press was full of rumours about his sexuality. The fact that he had never had a proper girlfriend was often cited as proof that he was gay. He had once had to endure a press conference laid on specifically to counter rumours that he had become the catamite of the (male) CEO of a well-known pharmaceuticals company. Shortly afterwards, the gutter press was full of pictures of a lookalike actor taken from a Japanese gay porn film, and once again Gary had to appear in public to assure his fans that it was not him. It was so demeaning. Really, the newspapers have no shame.

Teenagers had filled the blog sites with evidence supposedly for or against his homosexuality. At the time he thought, 'Don't these people have anything better to do with their time?' He felt disgusted by how much interest strangers took in his private life. But above all, he wished he could have simply said for certain, 'Yes, I am gay,' or 'No, I am not gay.' Because the truth was, he did not know the answer himself.

He tried, on a couple of occasions, to put his sexuality to the test. Never having wanted a girlfriend, he thought maybe he should experiment with boys. Because of who he is, it has never been difficult for him to find willing participants for such tests. The first took place when he was about twenty, and beginning to be aware that he was the only person he knew who had never experienced any form of physical intimacy, not even holding hands, cuddling or kissing. An older producer – a man of about forty, who had always joked about getting Gary into bed – finally manoeuvred him into the studio late at night. They were in the closing stages of putting an album together, those frantic days and nights when everyone is rushing to make the final changes to each song, when paranoia reigns and long evenings in the studio are the norm. Gary and the producer were fine-tuning a love song, listening to it on their headphones: a song of great quiet and stillness,

Gary's voice low and breathy over a simple piano arrangement. He knew the man was going to touch him – the situation lent itself perfectly to the act – and he thought, 'This time, I'll let it happen. I want to see how it feels.' He could feel the heat of the man's body on the bare skin of his arm as the man moved closer; then he felt a hand on his thigh. He closed his eyes. He felt fingers on his neck; the hand on his thigh moved further up, towards his groin. He waited to feel a frisson, a thrill of danger – but nothing came. His mind and body felt blank, empty. He could hear the man's breathing, quick and shallow, and smelled the sourness of his mouth, as if he had just eaten *kimchi*. In his ears he heard his own voice soaring to great heights, rich with sadness. He tried to concentrate on the music, but could not fight a rising sense of revulsion: the closeness of the man's breath, the heat of his body, the insistent poking of his fingers. Gary stood up and reached for the volume control, pulling away as he did so. When he sat down the man had moved away, and they both understood that nothing like that would ever happen between them again.

The second occasion, a couple of years ago, occurred in his suite at the Peninsula Hotel in Hong Kong, after the last of his sell-out concerts there. There had been a big, drunken party afterwards, which lasted into the early hours of the morning. When Gary woke at dawn, everyone had left, apart from a young dancer from the backing troupe who was stretched out on the sofa. A popular, engaging, outrageous, slightly effeminate character, this boy was known to be promiscuous, and he was always boasting of his exploits in G-bars across East Asia, always picking up strangers in the cities they performed in. He spoke in strange, provocative slang that no one could understand: he had spent the night with a *bear* and a *little monkey*, and had a great time even though he didn't consider himself a *baboon*, but maybe that's because he is neither *gonggong* nor *gongshou* – that sort of thing. He often flirted harmlessly with Gary, saying how beautiful he was. Now he lay asleep on the sofa, his fashionable ripped T-shirt exposing half his chest, revealing his fine, taut muscles and flawless skin. Gary sat down next to him, sinking into the plush cushions, and ran his fingertips along the dancer's collarbone; his flesh was like cool stone. Gary looked out across the harbour, motionless at that hour. The first rays of the sun were colouring the skyscrapers across the water, making them glint. He lifted the boy's T-shirt and looked at his stomach, the smooth incised shapes of the abdominal muscles rising and falling gently. He laid his head on the exposed skin, hoping to feel some jolt of excitement, the warmth of intimacy. He waited; but nothing came. The boy opened his eyes; they were bloodshot but narrowed with pleasure. He stretched his body, raising his arms above his head and spreading his legs – it was clear even to Gary that this was an invitation for him to go further. Gary looked at him for a moment; then, still feeling not the slightest charge of passion, he stood up, went to the bedroom and shut the door before falling asleep again.

Now, when his newfound friend Phoebe asks him, 'Are you gay?' he tells her about these encounters, changing the scenarios to more banal settings in order to disguise his identity (the first one, for example, he says took place 'in an office where I worked'; the second 'in a hotel with a colleague').

'I think you are closed to the world,' she replies. 'You cannot let yourself be close to anyone. Therefore gay or straight is an irrelevant question. In order to fall in love, first you have to love yourself.'

'*En.*'

He thinks about Phoebe all the time – not the romantic thoughts he imagines other men have about women, but something more meaningful. He has so many things to tell her about himself, and though for the moment he keeps his life hidden from her, he realises that the reason he is so excited about his relationship with her is that it offers him a chance to do the most exciting thing of all: to reveal his true identity to her. He keeps thinking about how and when he will do this – how he will tell her absolutely everything about himself, from childhood to the present, and because she understands him so well, she will be moved by his honesty and love him even more. When he thinks about this a huge rush of pleasure courses through him and makes him feel strong.

There is rarely a moment when he does not think about how wonderful it will be to tell her about himself; even now, on the makeshift stage in this suburban shopping mall, he is imagining the sheer relief of sharing his life with someone, imagining the liberation and clarity and warmth.

Hello everyone, he shouts when his opening song comes to an end. *Are you happy? I am so happy to see you.* His words are swallowed up in a mangled squeal of screeching feedback from the speakers, which makes everyone cover their ears. Some of the teenagers are smiling and swaying to the music, but he can tell that something is not right: they do not recognise him. In the past, as soon as he appeared in public, even if he was just walking swiftly through a restaurant to a private dining room, he could feel the quick flush of excitement rippling through the crowd as they spotted him; but this thrill is absent now. One or two people turn to each other, and he can tell that they are wondering whether he is the real Gary, or just an impersonator. As he begins his next song, he notices a group of schoolgirls huddled in discussion. One of them laughs, shakes her head, then they all walk away. There are so many copycats these days, bad singers who make a living by touring cheap bars pretending to be a celebrity. Everyone knows they are imitators, but no one cares, for they can sing along to the songs and appreciate the kitsch appeal of someone who looks like Aaron Kwok or Jacky Cheung or Selina from S.H.E.

China is the land of copycat power, people say. There are even Mao Zedong copycats everywhere, so a Gary copycat is nothing special.

He got the call from his agent three days prior to this appearance – a quick, breathless voice message left at 2.31 a.m. when she was obviously standing outside a nightclub, the heavy thumping of the bass notes tapping out a rhythm in the background. 'Found you a job – just a small thing, but better than nothing. You need to start rebuilding your brand, get close to the ordinary people again. You need … sympathy. Don't fix your hair or wear any special outfits, just dress in jeans, a T-shirt and some clean trainers. Simplicity and innocence, OK? Just like before, when you were starting out. I'll arrange the music and dancers. You just turn up and do your thing.'

Dressed in his simplest clothes, his hair washed but unstyled, he had been driven along expressways between ranks of perfectly symmetrical apartment blocks, colourless in the haze of pollution. The road out of town was lined with boxy hotels for businessmen and low, squat office blocks with windows of blue mirrored glass. He could tell by the names of the factories that they were moving further away from Shanghai – Nanxiang Apollo Everbright Electrical Co. Jiading Apollo Cement Factory. Lontang No 1 Friendly Light Industrial Machinery. At last they reached their destination, the newly opened Taicang Greenleaf Commercial Centre, the inauguration of which was being marked by 'a special performance by a mystery guest'.

'Is this still Shanghai?' he asked the driver.

'Actually, we are in Jiangsu province.'

As Gary walked into the mall, he had to dodge the construction workers who were putting the final touches to the not-quite-finished building. The drilling and hammering and sanding drowned out the music inside. He tried not to remember that only last year he had played to 15,000 people at the Taipei Arena.

As the first verse rises in a crescendo, Gary knows the dancers will appear at any moment, as they always do at this point in the song. He worries again that they will not fit onto the stage – in Wuhan, during his last concert, he had a troupe of twenty-four; even half that number could not squeeze on this flimsy platform. He closes his eyes and lets his voice soar for the first notes of the chorus, and as he does so he feels the footsteps of the dancers behind him. He smiles and turns around to applaud them. There are just two of them – two girls dressed in matching outfits of spangly red blouses over black trousers, with what look like feathers attached to their arms – twirling awkwardly in the narrow space behind him.

He turns to face the audience once more. The air is rich with the smells of varnish, paint-thinner and glue, and above the thumping of the bass line Gary can hear electric saws slicing into plywood, stop-start drilling and the rhythmic tap-tap-tap of hammers. Across the atrium he sees a vast restaurant. *RED ROOSTER HOTPOT Spicy … Do you dare???* Its emblem, printed on posters everywhere he looks, is a rooster straddling three red chillies. In the forecourt of the restaurant is a children's play area with a bouncy castle and plastic seesaws. Some of the restaurant staff have come out to watch the show. Their uniforms are red and black – the same as those of his backing dancers. He turns around once more, sweeping his arms together in exaggerated applause for his dancers. Behind them is a big sign that says:

Red Rooster welcomes you to Taicang Greenleaf Centre.

He doesn't know how he didn't notice it before.

He has another chorus to go, and then two more songs. That was the deal – it is not so bad, he can do it, he is a true professional. A few people in the audience are swaying to the music; a mother is holding her child by both hands and dancing in little jerky steps. Gary closes his eyes and allows his voice to do its work as usual, but his mind begins to drift, imagining all the things he is going to tell Phoebe on the internet later this evening. He wishes he could tell her about this awkward, even humiliating experience, but he can't. He will simply say that he had a difficult day at work, that he lost face. But don't worry, he will say brightly. I want to change jobs. I'm going to change the direction of my life. I want to be more like you, to have a quiet life doing something I enjoy; a glittering career and burning ambition will not make me happy. I want to follow your example. You are so good for me.

The audience applauds, a thin smattering of claps that cannot compete with the building noise around them. He waits for the next song to start, to bring the end of his misery closer, but there is a problem with the music system. He can hear the technician behind the stage cursing as he tries to fix the problem; someone groans and says, 'I hate this cheap equipment.' The dancers hold the pose with which they ended their last routine – down on one knee, their arms spread wide to reveal their chicken-feathered costumes, super-bright smiles etched on their faces.

As Gary stands in the middle of the stage, the audience begins to drift slowly away. The waiters from the Red Rooster stay at the front of the restaurant for a while, but eventually they go back inside. He waits, and waits some more: experience tells him that the sound system is broken; there will be no more music. But he is a professional, he will finish his job here. He lifts the microphone to his lips and begins to sing unaccompanied, his voice frail amidst the sounds of the building work ringing out around him.

16

天有不测风云

Beware of Storms
Arising from Clear Skies

Yinghui thought about what Walter had said about bank loans amounting to respect. It had seemed an odd concept at first, but gradually she began to see how true it was – that a person's standing in society could be measured by how much bankers trusted and respected them. What she actually contributed to the world was irrelevant. Maybe her father had been right all along – she would never understand the way money worked.

As she prepared her dossier for the meetings she had arranged with the banks, she thought about how her father had spent his whole life working to amass respect. Money was – it was clear to her now – a secondary consideration for him, despite what the newspapers had said in the aftermath of the tangled mess that followed his death. Yinghui had not been able to bear all that was said about him during that time; after the funeral she had fled, first to Singapore, which wasn't far enough away, then to Hong Kong, which had been lonely, and finally to Shanghai, where she ran little risk of running into anyone from home.

In common with most people who craved respect from others, her father had led a life based on caution. It was a value he had sought to inculcate in his daughter, who as it turned out showed little signs of prudence even at an early age. Like other poor people who had become middle class, he was always careful; and like other people who were born middle class, she wanted to be anything but. But in the main, Yinghui was (more or less) dutiful and respectful, and she did well at school. She helped her mother prepare meals and do the shopping at the market, where her mother tried her best to teach Yinghui the value of thrift – another attribute much prized by the new middle class. Even after her father had reached the ministerial position in which he was to end his life, her family continued to make a virtue of their frugality, as if to emphasise their disadvantaged rural origins in the face of their growing urban wealth.

Dinners were the primary showcase for their carefulness with money – elaborate spreads consisting of five or six dishes when it was just the three of them on a weekday evening, double that number when they had a couple of guests on a Sunday. Always, there would be discreet (and sometimes not-so-discreet) mention of how inexpensively those delicious meals had been prepared – comments on how cheap spinach was that month; how they would usually have used *choy sum* but didn't because the floods had made it expensive; how the *kembong* fish was very cheap but underrated; how the judicious addition of Chinese black mushrooms could make nondescript vegetables seem luxurious; how the free-range village chicken they were serving that evening was a rare treat, seldom seen in their household. Her mother assumed a gentle air of martyrdom as she smilingly produced these meals from the large but sparsely equipped kitchen; of course they did not have anyone to help, not even an Indonesian maid as most people in the neighbourhood seemed to have in those days.

Looking back on it now, it was clear to Yinghui that this was not a charade to deflect the attention of their friends and neighbours from their new Mercedes (and driver), or their extended bathroom suite and generally upwardly mobile status: her parents truly believed that, by clinging to a way of life that was no longer truly theirs, they could protect themselves from the unknown dangers of newfound wealth, even as they revelled in it.

By and large, Yinghui was comfortable with their *modus vivendi*; having grown up with it, she did not find it unusual, and came to admire their financial prudence and their general distrust of ostentatiousness. Indeed, in her later teenage years she began to affect a certain down-at-heelness, a disregard for material possessions that, she now realises, only well-off people are able to enjoy. The resulting over-casual nature of her dress style – consisting largely of cheap, loose-fitting T-shirts she bought from the night market, worn with bleached jeans – attracted only mild rebuke from her parents, who were evidently pleased with their daughter's sartorial miserliness. 'People will think you're a washerwoman,' her mother once said, but in this seeming criticism there was a clear message: that it was safer for strangers to think of you as a servant than as the daughter of a government minister.

It was only when Yinghui started going out with boys that she began to discover that her parents' natural prudence extended way beyond money, affecting every aspect of life. She realised how little of it she had absorbed into her own philosophy of life and, most of all, how much she hated it. 'Be careful, don't take buses. Be careful, don't take taxis on your own. Be careful, don't go to Brickfields. Be careful, don't eat *laksa* there. Be careful, Singapore is so expensive these days.' She could accept these, albeit with a growing annoyance common to all teenagers, but she had a harder time dealing with the warnings about boys, which were more forceful and therefore harder to shrug off. 'Don't go out late, otherwise people will talk. Don't have too many boyfriends, otherwise people will think you are loose.'

She dated two boys, both briefly, knowing the relationships would amount to nothing. And then, not long after turning eighteen, she met CS Lim. It was at this time that she found out just how much her parents had based their lives on caution and respect.

Don't hang out with that Lim boy. We hear the younger one is bad news.

Don't let people know you are seeing him. Second Auntie saw you the other day.

Don't get so close to him.

Don't let his parents look down on you.

Don't go out to those flashy Western places with him, his friends are too flashy.

Yet four years later, when she and CS had returned from university abroad and were still happily a couple, her parents managed to overcome their former disapproval of CS and his tendency for flamboyance. Yinghui and he had lasted more than three years, which must mean they were serious. They could not quite understand the nature of the relationship, which involved dressing like hippies long after the end of hippiedom, going on trips to India and hanging out with people who seemed never to work but spent their lives arguing about politics and philosophy; but they could understand that three years signalled a certain intention, and it was this that they supported.

Her father gave her a generous loan to start her café – she was so bad with money that she forgot how much it was for even as the cheque was being written. It was clear that he did not expect the money to be repaid; it was more, even, than a gift: it was a symbol of her parents' trust in her relationship with CS Lim, of whom they had once disapproved. Of course they never quite *got* the concept of the café, and whenever they visited it Yinghui was treated to such comments as 'I didn't even know they grew coffee in Australia,' or, 'Tofu … in a bun? *Ei*, is it the same tofu that we use, *ah*?' Yet they laughed when she came home and told them tales of her gross mismanagement: how she had placed a bulk order for coconut milk without specifying that it should be tinned rather than fresh, and was now facing hundreds of *ringgits*' worth of fermenting *santan* in the store room; or how some of her friends were running up credit accounts worth a thousand *ringgits* just for espresso and cake (her parents couldn't believe that coffee could *ever* amount to that much). All her father offered by way of chastisement was a benign comment now and then: 'You have so much to learn about money,' or, sighing, 'I don't think you'll ever understand money.'

They were being indulgent, they knew; but they also knew that Yinghui was happy living her life differently from theirs. In their own way, they too must have sensed that the world was changing, and they were happy with this change.

Maybe their more relaxed approach to Yinghui and CS's lifestyle (which they might not long ago have deemed too ostentatious) had something to do with her father's growing ease with being in the public eye. He had been in his post for over seven years by the time Yinghui and CS returned from university – long enough to become accustomed to being in the press and on TV on a regular basis. As Deputy Minister for Housing and Local Government, he was not one of the more high-profile members of the administration, and his natural awkwardness in front of the camera did not make him an obvious candidate for media appearances. Nonetheless, a certain degree of exposure to the press and the public alike was required of a man in his position, and he gradually became used to the idea that his life was no longer, and could never again be, entirely private.

The house in which they lived began to reflect this change in attitude; this was clear to Yinghui even at the time. They continued to live at the same address, but the building's structure had grown enormously, nearly doubling in size following renovation work of various kinds – two new guest bathrooms, an entirely new kitchen, an air-conditioned breakfast room that led to a shaded terrace cooled by ceiling fans and capable of being turned into a banqueting space that seated fifty quite easily. Everything was done to accommodate the increased entertaining they needed to carry out at home: messy, private spaces were converted into coolly impersonal public ones. The shabby pieces of mismatching furniture were either thrown away or banished upstairs to bedrooms, replaced downstairs by carefully coordinated, bland, modern furniture. 'Good taste,' Yinghui joked, 'is the curse of the nouveaux riches.' Sometimes, when she came to visit, she would be struck by how the once-expansive garden had been reduced to a few slivers of grass here and there, bordered by palm trees; the rest had been swallowed up by the immensity of the house. Stealthily, and without them even realising it, her parents' own lives had become the very thing they most feared: flashy.

Yet still they clung to the token displays of frugality at their family dinners, which were now confined to Sunday evenings, when Yinghui's café was shut and her father was freed from ministerial duties. The dishes they ate were markedly different now, vegetables augmented by abalone as well as mushrooms, the meat often taking the form of whole suckling pig; and they would have Western desserts too, plus chocolate – previously unthinkable symbols of decadence. But the appearance of these items was easily explained: they were gifts from a colleague of her father's, or from Sr Franchetti, a visiting Argentinian dignitary, and so on. Left to their own devices, they could never – would never – afford such extravagant treats.

This was the pretence that Yinghui found harder to stomach with each passing Sunday: that somehow their new wealth was an accident, a burden that had happened to befall them but which they shouldered admirably by pretending it didn't exist. Even as the driver sat outside in the black Mercedes, waiting to take her father to a late-night meeting, her mother would be complaining about the price of vegetables now that everything was being exported to Hong Kong and Singapore.

Perhaps the fixation with the minutiae of food economics was a way of avoiding talking about other things – like her father's new job, which was still referred to as a recent occurrence, even after eight or nine years. Yinghui had little idea of what he actually did on a day-to-day basis, and she did not try to find out. Like most of her friends whose parents were well-off and successful, she had drifted naturally and easily into an anti-establishment circle, surrounding herself with other overseas-educated young people who adopted an anti-government point of view as a matter of course. For reasons of street cred and unproblematic conversation, their parents' jobs were conveniently ignored. It was almost an unwritten rule that the sources of the money that allowed these bright young things to spend so much time discussing how to improve the world were better left unexplored. Ignorance was by far the best way to advance social change.

Nonetheless, there were many things that made the indiscretions of the older generation impossible to overlook – cases of fraud or embezzlement, or abuses of power that were just too excessive even in a country already becoming inured to excess. There was a geeky boy who liked jazz and who had been at St John's Institution with CS Lim; his father was a lawyer who had got rich handling the corporate affairs of government companies – a shadowy area if ever there was one. Even though everyone had their doubts, nothing was ever said apart from good-natured teasing whenever this boy appeared with a new pair of shoes, or a new laptop: 'Looks like the government's doing good business in hi-tech shares!' But when the scandal broke in the press that his father had in fact been channelling parts of the proceeds of share deals into a private bank account, humour was no longer possible. All the jokes Yinghui and her circle had been making now carried a dreadful truth. Likewise, when the father of another member of their circle, a state minister, was found stealing from public funds, all the banter that the group had previously shared became out of bounds. Although the subsequent inquiries cleared both men of any wrongdoing, as they always did, there was only one option left to their children – they had to slip away quietly, detaching themselves from their circle of friends, who would in turn refrain from ever speaking about them.

There were important nuances, however. If someone's parents were exposed as shady characters because they had fallen out of favour with the government, *that* was acceptable, and would in fact increase their children's street cred among the cool kids: their family was being *persecuted* by the establishment, even though they had been enriching themselves within it for years. That is what happened to a scholarly, Godard-loving girl called Nurul: it wasn't her parents' fault that they'd backed the wrong horse, a minister who had been ousted from power and whose entourage was now paying the price. Their predicament earned her the right to deliver lengthy, impassioned analyses of the ills of the country to a sympathetic audience every night at Angie's, where Yinghui made sure she never had to pay for her cappuccinos. Her presence added to the café's edgy, on-the-fringes appeal, until finally she fled to Australia to do a PhD in Asian politics in Canberra.

Yinghui's father's accession to the highest reaches of government placed her in a tricky position. On the one hand, the very fact that he was a member of the cabinet meant that he was part of the malaise facing the country. On the other, his relatively uncontroversial position meant that the potential for abuse was limited – deciding on the routing of interstate highways around housing developments seemed to be as serious as his job got. Besides, his reputation was as a modest, somewhat unimaginative workhorse, someone so dull he was above corruption. He was from the far northern reaches of Kelantan; his fluency in the local Malay dialect and his continued loyalty to the region had proved an asset to the government, which needed someone with strong grassroots appeal. He was a rarity, a minister who not only identified with voters in the poor, anti-government north-east, but who had genuine multiracial credentials, being firmly Chinese yet speaking the Kelantanese dialect as his first language.

These were the attributes that Yinghui liked to drop casually into conversation, often disguised as a complaint. 'Oh God, my dad's English is so bad. He didn't even learn to speak it until he was, like, thirteen or fourteen. His Malay is crap too. Kelantanese is basically his first language.' She would boast about his rural origins, just as he had done when she was a child – it was as if, by emphasising his backwardness, she could reduce the possibility of scandal; as if she already sensed what was going to happen.

The first of the rumours began to circulate not long after the completion of another extension of the north–south highway. It began as an environmental issue, with ecologists claiming that yet more jungle had been needlessly felled to make way for a highway that no one needed. That was easy enough to answer: there were new oilfields on the east coast that needed supporting infrastructure, her father told the press. But then more and more allegations began to surface, evidence of road-building contracts worth billions of dollars, when the real cost of construction was found to be a fraction of the stated price; huge roads that led to nowhere; and, worst of all, vast tracts of forest cleared for sprawling housing estates that swiftly came to resemble ghost towns. In every case, it was Yinghui's father who had approved the projects.

He must have enemies in the government, Yinghui protested to CS; he must have done something to upset someone powerful, who was now organising this whispering campaign. Everyone – *everyone* – knew that if the government didn't want the public to know about something, it would be kept under wraps, it would never come out in the newspapers, would it?

'But is it true?' CS said in his customary detached way. The more heated the topic, the higher the stakes, the more languid he became. 'That's the important question. Not whether it's a campaign against him.'

'Of course it's not true,' Yinghui said. 'Otherwise, why would the newspapers be making such a fuss about it? Since when did you start believing what you read in the papers?'

CS opened his book and leafed through it until he found his page marker. It was something he liked to do when he got into an argument – pretend to read a book. 'Listen, sweetheart, I don't really care what your old man does. If it's proved he's a cheating crook, who cares? He's not the only one. And I'll still love you. But if he is indeed a bastard, you have to admit it. What your dad does is nothing to me, but what *you* do is important. I don't want to get married to a fantasist who can't admit the truth.'

Yinghui was arranging the wheat-free brownies in the chiller cabinet. 'He's *not* a cheat like the rest of them. Why do you keep saying he is?'

'I'm not saying he is, I'm just asking if he is. You know, making enquiries.'

'Based on what?'

'Based on what people are saying. And also, look at how rich he's become in the last few years.'

'I don't believe I'm hearing this from you. Look who's talking about being rich.'

CS looked up at Yinghui from his favourite spot on the low grey sofa. 'Money isn't necessarily dirty. Money is money, dirty money is dirty money. People don't understand the difference these days.'

'"People?" Which *people* do you mean, exactly, when you use that tone of voice?'

He shrugged, raising his arm in an airy wave in the direction of the entrance. 'You know, the nouveaux riches who seem to be springing up everywhere, with their vulgar cars and handbags. God only knows how they got their money. They can't see the difference between money and *money*.'

'"Money is not the same as money." Only really loaded rich dicks like you can say something like that. What the hell is the difference?'

'Respect. Some money you respect, other money you don't. Clean money versus dirty money. It's how you earn it, how you spend it. It's whether people respect you.'

Yinghui wanted to protest, but it was no use; he had begun to read, holding his book up as he stretched out on the sofa, signalling the end of the discussion.

The simplest solution, she knew, was to ask her father a direct question. Were the allegations true? Did he take bribes in return for granting contracts? When he'd taken Mum to Tokyo last month and bought her that pearl necklace, was it really because he'd had official duties to carry out and would have been lonely without her – or was the trip funded by a company hoping to gain favours from him? When she saw him at home for their weekly dinner that Sunday, she waited for a suitable moment, a chance for her to steer the conversation in the right direction before asking him in a measured, non-confrontational manner about what was being said in the press.

But their dinners were set pieces specifically designed to avoid uncomfortable exchanges; that had never been clearer to her than it was now. All that talk about how expensive vegetables and fish were these days eliminated the possibility of anything controversial or troubling being raised. It was a performance her parents had honed to perfection over the years, just in case they would need it one day. Now that day had come, and the actors were each playing their role, including Yinghui. She was complicit in the charade, she realised now. She could so easily have ruptured the falseness of their happy-family image with a direct question; even if it upset the dinner, it would at least make them talk. But no; every time she felt the urge to blurt out her question – *Is it true?* – an equally strong sensation arose in her, a feeling of guilt and responsibility which negated the impulse to seek the truth. She looked at her father, his face bent over his bowl, lips trembling slightly as he sipped his soup. There were dark spots on his hands, and his skin was cracked and wrinkly. She had not appreciated how much he had aged in recent years; his movements seemed fragile now, uncertain. 'It's the pressure of his job,' her mother had whispered to her recently. But it was more than just the job, Yinghui thought: it was as if being rich had taken its toll on his body.

Yinghui watched him as he nodded in agreement with her mother's tales of vegetable woe. He had the air of a defeated man – an old, broken man. Her mother's unrelenting assessment of food prices suddenly felt reassuring. It never changed; it had provided solidity to their Sunday evenings all these years, and now, more than ever, they needed it. Yinghui realised that she did not want to change that.

The court case started over a year after the first allegations against him surfaced. At long last, some people said, a government minister was being tried for his misdemeanours. Poor fellow, others felt: someone must have had it in for him. He was the fall guy, taking the flak for something that had happened higher up; either that or he had been too greedy and stepped onto someone else's patch, someone more powerful. But most people – especially the kind who hung out at Angie's, the kind who had once been Yinghui's friends – did not express great interest in the trial. It was a joke, they said. Everyone knows he'll get off without any punishment. He won't even have to resign from his post.

They were both right and wrong. He was eventually acquitted after a messy trial that dragged on for several months, including two adjournments. He was found innocent of all charges except for the most minor one – accepting a free weekend at a hotel in Singapore owned by a property development company whose owner and CEO was a personal friend. It was the sort of thing most people didn't even think of as a crime. During the proceedings many embarrassing allegations were made, most of them completely unfounded: for example, that he had visited a famous (and famously shady) karaoke bar in Kota Bharu. His connections to various companies were also exposed, and though there was no evidence of impropriety, it was enough to make people raise a knowing eyebrow. His relationship with Lim Kee Huat Holdings, for example, surprised no one – after all, his daughter was the girl-friend of the younger Lim grandson. As some of their ex-friends said, shit sticks.

The weight of lingering suspicion began to affect his health, and he suffered a small stroke one night. Although his condition improved enough for him to return to work, he resigned a few months later, his reputation ruined. If people remembered him at all, it was not as a hard-working man from humble roots, but as yet another politician whose major preoccupation was to amass as much money as possible before he was exposed. But in this regard he was hardly unusual, and after a few years no one would remember him at all. No one remembers you if they don't respect you, and he had lost all the respect he had worked so hard to gain.

When he died, several months after resigning, the scandal reignited briefly before fading away again. The manner of his death was fitting for a corrupt politician, violent and sudden, and even – to be honest – unsurprising. That was what most people thought in private, Yinghui knew. For her, the end was not the end, it was merely the postscript: his life had finished the moment he had lost the respect he so craved.

She left Malaysia two months after his funeral, heading for Singapore, but it was too familiar, too much like home. It was not until she reached Shanghai that she felt she was sufficiently far away from all she had lost. She began to change the way she lived, consciously hardening herself against the world around her, taking an interest in things she had barely noticed before. All the things she had once loved – art, music, literature – now seemed less solid, more dangerous in their fluidity than business and finance: she found reassurance in the methodical workings of money. Every time she found herself struggling to comprehend something in the financial press, she remembered her father saying that she would never understand how money worked; and she would begin to cry, though she was not sure if it was out of frustration or grief. She pressed on, forcing herself to be at ease with company reports and meetings with bankers. She would become a great businesswoman, she promised herself. Her parents had been wrong about her, as they had been about so many things. Every time she thought about them she felt a huge swell of sadness, an inarticulate yet crushing sense of injustice: her parents had been victims, yet there had been no persecutor, no target for her anger. She had messed around with a boy who hadn't loved her, devoted years of her life to him – the memory of her fecklessness, too, made her teary and unstable, and even ashamed. Her businesses comforted her, made her feel that she was on solid ground; they helped her forget the aimless young girl she had once been.

Time and distance allowed her to look forward, ever forward, and as the years passed the momentum she built up on her journey enabled her to breathe, to settle, until she became who she was now, gazing, still, into the future.

As she walked into the offices of the bank in the new IFC Tower, the sweet-toxic smell of varnish hanging richly in the air, an image briefly came to Yinghui's mind: her mother crying at her father's funeral. No, not crying, but wailing, the loud sobs turning to shrieks, all her poise lost as she muttered gibberish about the injustices her husband had suffered, about the cruelty life had inflicted upon him, sprinkled with profanities against his numerous and unnamed killers.

It was so undignified, a total loss of self-respect.

After just an instant Yinghui snuffed the memory out. Like a candle flame pinched between the fingers, it hurt for half a second before being extinguished.

After announcing herself to the receptionist she sat down to wait and to take one last look at her papers. She had spent most of the previous evening rehearsing what she had to say, and how she would say it: a winning combination of forcefulness and seduction. Walter had rung her from his car at midnight, just as she was finalising her presentation, to see how she was doing. He had just finished a long, tedious evening with some business associates, and wanted to ring her before it got too late. He was brief but warm and encouraging. And that morning, the first message on her BlackBerry was from him: *They will BEG to give you a loan. Hugs W.*

She checked her appearance in the compact mirror she kept in her handbag, then stood and smoothed her trouser suit, glancing discreetly at the mirror that ran along the wall of the reception. She breathed steadily, calmly.

She would never allow herself to be like her mother, not even for one second.

How to be Inventive – Property Management Case Study, Continued

Nearly two months passed with no communication from my father, and then, suddenly, a letter brimming with his customary positive thinking arrived. He had had a bad cough, he said, and had spent several feverish days confined to his little room. Lying on the camp bed, he noticed small, quick birds flitting in and out of the airy rooms on the ground floor. When he finally summoned the strength to go upstairs, he saw more of them darting about in the darkness like bats, even though he had boarded up the windows to protect the building from the elements. They were squeezing through the gaps in the plywood, wheeling around in the gloom. He had mentioned his discovery casually in the coffee shop one day, and was surprised to learn that everyone seemed to know about these birds: they were swiftlets, the very kind whose nests were prized as a delicacy by the Chinese, who boiled them in soups and served them at banquets. Yes, the famous bird's-nest soup that cured everything from bad skin to rheumatism to lethargy to sluggish digestion – it came from these little birds. And Kota Bharu was becoming a bit of a bird town. The swiftlets fed on the clouds of tiny winged insects along the banks of the great muddy river, and colonies of them were beginning to establish themselves in the abandoned buildings in this part of town. No one knew why they went into some buildings and not others, but if they were nesting in your house, it was as good as having a jewellery shop. Did I know what those birds' nests sold for in Hong Kong? US$100 per hundred grams, or just three nests. As soon as you harvested one nest, the birds would simply make another, which you could then go on harvesting – it was as easy as that!

So began a frenzy of building work of a bizarre nature, which added to the hotel's air of decrepitude. Every single window except the one in my father's room was boarded up and sealed with cement rendering. Water was allowed to seep through the leaky pipes, making the floors and walls damp with constant humidity ('Lucky thing I could not afford to replace the old pipes with good new ones!' he exulted in one letter). The aim, he explained, was to recreate the atmosphere of a dank, gloomy cave – the natural habitat of the birds. Spurred on by acquaintances and other birdhouse owners who offered helpful tips, he bought a portable stereo and played a hissy cassette recording of the birds' sonar clicking that echoed in the darkness of the Tokyo Hotel. Hearing the noises of a nesting colony would not only encourage birds to enter the building, but once they were inside it would make them feel at home and believe that there were many other birds already breeding there. He had to use all these modern scientific techniques, you see.

I began to receive excited letters detailing his progress with increased frequency. He had never been a literary type, and most of the time he provided only the bare outline of what he was doing, but it was easy to chart the upward curve of his ambitions, initially at least:

Birds nesting on floor number 3! Number of nests: 4. Must increase humidity level. Just finished closing up windows on floor number 2 – very dark up there now!

Birds on floor number 2 now too. Number of nests: 9 already! They are stuck to the ceiling like big cobwebs.

Birds on floors 2 and 3, but not descending to floor 1. Number of nests: 16.

Still no birds on floor number 1. Don't know what I am doing wrong.

Number of nests: 28! Have bought heavy locks for the front and back doors. Uncle Yong told me that people will break in and steal the nests if I am not careful.

Number of nests today 41! I read a book my friend Lee gave me, which says I can start harvesting the nests soon.

Some nests have disappeared. Maybe I miscounted before. Today only 34.

Number of nests 21. I have not yet harvested any. I found 3 fallen on the floor. Maybe someone is stealing the rest. Yes, I think so.

Number of nests: 11. My friends say don't worry, I am doing all the right things.

Number of nests: 6. I am sure they will build more soon.

I did not receive any further word from him for nearly two months. I was working as an apprentice electrician at that time, earning a lowly wage which I am now too embarrassed to reveal. (When I think of the sum nowadays it seems hardly possible that a human being could survive on so little, but indeed I did.) Fearing for my father's safety, I took the bus up to Kelantan again, and when I arrived I found the hotel almost resplendent in its dereliction. With its windows sealed up and its front door shut against the elements it looked like a sculpture: had it been transported in time and place to a modern-day metropolis like Beijing or London, it could easily have passed for an art installation, its ghostly isolation making it seem almost beautiful. But it was not in one of the world's great cities: it was on the shabby side of a shabby town, bordering marshy scrubland that served as a breeding ground for dengue fever, so it looked only sad. I went round to the back, where I found my father sitting in the shade of the porch, piercing an old rubber hose with a large needle, over and over again.

He looked up and said, 'It's my new humidifier system.' He spoke to me as if I had just popped out to the shops for a packet of cigarettes and had come back after an absence of ten minutes, not four months. 'I think it's because it's too dry in the house. Birds like moisture, otherwise they get mites in their feathers. Don't know why, but Lee's house just down the road has got many, many birds. Last week he harvested over eighty nests. Sold them to a dealer from Hong Kong. Know how much he got? Thousand-plus *ringgit*. People in Hong Kong going crazy for birds' nests. Don't know why my house got no birds.'

'*Ba*,' I said, 'what if the birds never establish themselves here?'

'They will! I know they will. I just need a bit of luck. They are everywhere. Look!' He pointed to the sky, and in the fading light of that warm, still afternoon, just before the skies turned purple with dusk, I could see tiny birds wheeling and swooping in the air.

'I just need a bit of luck,' he said again.

In the days to come I tried, gently, to persuade him to give up on his venture. He might be able to sell the hotel and cut his losses. He had debts to repay, I reminded him: if we sold the building he'd be able to pay everyone back and maybe have enough left over to buy a small place somewhere, and he could get a job, nothing special, maybe help out at a garage or a shop or a rice merchant or something, and now that I was old enough to work too we would be OK, we could live a simple life, just like before.

He laughed away my suggestions, smiling benignly as if I, not he, was the fantasist. On more than a couple of occasions over the next few days he simply walked away from me as if I had not even been addressing him – as if I were mad. He could not abandon his project, he said, as if explaining a simple fact to a small child: his friends and relatives had lent him money, and it was his duty to see that their investment bore fruit. They had placed more than just money in his hands: they had invested trust in him. Profits take time to accrue, my son, he said. And trust – trust takes a lifetime to repay.

He never mentioned the words 'saving face', but I knew that for him the birds' nests had become an exercise in avoiding shame.

None of the people who had lent him money were rich; they were village folk, just like him, scraping by with little to spare. There was no turning back for him.

17

突梯滑稽

Cultivate an Urbane, Humorous Personality

The week began well for Phoebe, just as the astrologer had said it would. It had cost her 400 *yuan* to have a full assessment of her prospects, including detailed advice on how to maximise the chances of meeting a suitable partner and gaining promotion at work. At the time, Phoebe had thought it was scandalous to have to pay so much money, but now she could see it had been worth every *mao*.

On Monday morning she received an SMS from Boss Leong informing her that, in recognition of her excellent level of performance, she was being promoted to the position of manager of the spa. Boss Leong was opening another two branches in the city and needed someone reliable to look after the original establishment. Phoebe was the first person who came to mind. Her salary would increase nearly threefold, and she would be required to wear a smart suit, or at least a jacket, replacing the Chinese silk dress she had worn as a receptionist.

Two days later, while she was still floating on a wave of happiness, she received an email from a man on a dating site she had signed up to, who proposed a dinner date with no obligations to take things further if they did not like each other. This was a proper matchmaking website for professional people, expensive to join, so she was naturally more optimistic when men sent her messages on this site. Of course, she had long since learnt that appearances could be deceptive, and she treated all approaches from men with the same caution she would adopt when shopping for counterfeit luxury goods. China was full of copycat products and people. She was now experienced enough to be able to tell from just one message whether a man was serious or not, whether he was just looking for sex, whether he was married and in search of a mistress, or was indeed looking for a future wife. She could tell if a man was lying about his identity, his job and income, where he was from. She could tell if he was from Beijing or if he was a Pakistani pretending to be from Beijing. All those scam marriage proposals from Indian, Nigerian and Arab men – she was aware of them, and made sure she stayed clear of them even though she did not know what they wanted from her. She had become an expert in the courtship rituals of the internet; no one could cheat her with flowery words or insincere promises. To Phoebe, internet dating had become like a book written in a language that she had mastered, just as she had conquered the rocky path to employment in Shanghai.

She had struck up a few online relationships with men – two in Shanghai and one in Beijing – but she knew that none of them would lead to anything serious. All of them were hiding something; she could sense that they were not telling the full truth. She laughed and shared some of the details of her life with them, sometimes even opening up her troubled heart and allowing her frustrations to spill out onto the computer screen, but she held back her deepest thoughts, disguising her true identity just as she disguised herself at work. These men would only see what she wanted them to see, they would never know the real Phoebe Chen Aiping. She could see that they were not serious, and so, in keeping with the wise advice gained from her books, she kept her distance. (*Being open and honest with a man is like asking him to drive over you with a bulldozer!*)

From the moment this new message came through, however, she sensed that there was something interesting about this man. He did not make any comments about her appearance, but said simply that she struck him as someone who could make him laugh, with whom he could share long conversations on many subjects. The photo of her that he liked the most was the one she had forgotten to delete, taken in the park in Guangzhou. He made no mention of the sophisticated fashion-style images shot by the professional photographer in the spa. As usual, she suggested chatting on QQ or MSN, but he declined, saying he would prefer to meet in real life. He also refused to send a photo of himself, saying he did not want her to judge him by how he looked, but that she would have every right to leave the moment she saw him if she didn't like him. He gave her a phone number and a list of dates on which they could meet, all in the following week. 'I am just looking for a companion who can understand me,' he said. 'Someone I can have sweet, peaceful times with.'

At first, the serious tone of his messages made Phoebe doubtful of his sincerity. No man had been so earnest and straightforward with her since she came to China. He must be a sexual pervert, she thought. But as she reread the messages her fears subsided. She checked the piece of paper on which the astrologer had written about her romantic prospects: the dates the man had suggested coincided perfectly with those in the box marked 'Time of Perfect Meeting with Lifelong Soulmate'.

She emailed back, accepting a date the following Sunday evening.

Yanyan helped her choose her outfit. Together, they laid out the various combinations of clothing on the bed and contemplated them while sipping tea. It was just like looking at the sea, Yanyan said.

'The sea?' Phoebe asked.

'Yes. When I was small my parents took me to the coast on holiday. I thought we were going to play and have fun, but all we did was look at the sea. It was so boring at first, but then I found it very beautiful. Nothing ever changed with the sea. There were waves, it moved, but it didn't change. I liked it.'

Phoebe looked at Yanyan. They had been sharing the tiny room for months now, but still Yanyan would sometimes say things that

Phoebe did not understand, things that made her think she would never understand the life Yanyan had lived before they met. She simply smiled and nodded.

They consulted several of Phoebe's books for advice on how to approach such a date, paying special attention to a chapter entitled 'Dress for Sex-Cess', which recommended showing off as much of her feminine attributes as possible. *Men only care about one thing, and we all know what that is* … In the end, they decided that Phoebe should wear a long-sleeved shirt buttoned up to her neck for a demure look, balanced by a short skirt to discreetly suggest sexual availability. 'Anyway,' said Yanyan, reading from another book, '"Your beauty comes from your inner confidence, it does not matter what you wear."'

As the first warm winds of spring swept through Shanghai, and the sun shone brighter, chasing away the grey of winter, the memory of snow began to melt away. People hurried through the streets, busy but calm, the excitement of Spring Festival forgotten. The red lanterns that hung in the trees had finally been removed, replaced by colourful globes of blue and green and white, and now the branches were full of buds too, green flecks already bursting into leaf here and there. Phoebe got off the subway one stop early. She liked this part of town, the wide, clean streets lined with modern buildings and expensive shops whose windows glowed jewel-like at night. On the street corner a man with a cart was selling home-made CDs of romantic songs. Spanish-sounding music was playing through the single loudspeaker mounted on the back of his motorbike, the singer's voice filling the air with a sound that was soft and melancholic and sensual. The rhythms of the song were delicious, Phoebe thought; they made her feel beautiful and elegant, even though she could tell it was a sad song. She felt strong; she enjoyed being able to recognise sadness without being crushed by it.

As she entered the sudden darkness of Jing'an Park, excitement began to creep into her heart. Her neck felt warm, although her hands were cool. She allowed herself a moment of doubt, a few seconds to wonder whether she was making a big mistake. Maybe the man would be so ugly that she would not even be able to look at him. Maybe he had a physical deformity, and that was why he did not want to send a photo of himself. But then she thought, she had wasted so much time with men in Shanghai already, one more meeting would not matter. She would press on until she found someone who would make her life easier. This had long ago ceased to be about love; it was about usefulness.

Trapped between a stretch of elevated highway and the shiny high-rise buildings, the small park offered a respite from the city's light and noise. In the darkness Phoebe could not see the faces of the couples walking arm in arm until they were close to her. She followed the snaking paths that led to a pond fringed by tall reeds, its surface glinting here and there with the reflections of oil lamps that lit a large wooden deck on its far side. A small bridge led from the deck to a timber building that rose to two levels, the eaves of its roof decorated with wooden carvings. Phoebe could feel her breath quicken. She blinked, and smiled. She could hardly believe she was in Shanghai. It was a scene that was familiar to her from her childhood. As she made her way to the restaurant she could see waitresses dressed in batik sarongs and tunics of dark-coloured lace. She was greeted at the door by a woman with a frangipani flower behind her ear, who led her out to the wooden deck, where a man was sitting at the farthest table. His head was turned away from her, towards the pond. He did not look happy to be waiting for a beautiful date – to tell the truth, he looked as if he was thinking about something else altogether. Phoebe thought, This man has more important things in his life than spending an evening with me. The fortune-teller must have been wrong. This guy doesn't look like my soulmate.

'Hi,' said Phoebe as she settled into her chair.

'Oh, hi. Sorry,' said the man, 'I was just daydreaming.'

'But it's night-time,' Phoebe said. By habit, she placed her handbag on the table before realising that she no longer had her super A-grade fake bag, just a cheap one she'd had for a long time.

She didn't dare carry an expensive-looking bag now, after what had happened.

The man laughed. 'True. In that case I was night-dreaming, with my eyes open.'

He was not young, but nor was he old. Phoebe guessed he was about twenty years older than her, but his face was not easy to read – his features were boyish, almost babyish, with ears that stuck out like bat wings, but his skin was tanned and leathery, with lines around his eyes and mouth and a deep groove between his eyes. From some angles he appeared young, from others ancient. She studied him carefully without letting him see that she was doing so; she was very skilled at this, no one could get the better of her. His clothes were expensive and quite stylish, even though they were a little plain – blue shirt, light-grey jacket, nothing flashy. His mobile phone lay on the table – it was an expensive model with a slide-out keyboard as well as other functions that she knew were frequently used by businessmen. There were car keys too, but Phoebe did not recognise the insignia – it wasn't BMW or Mercedes, she had seen those before.

She thought, no, her soulmate was still just round the corner, this was not him. This guy was just someone she could use.

'So, Mr Chao, what do you do in Shanghai?'

He laughed. 'Wow, straight to the point. Do you want to know how much I earn, too?'

'Only if you want to tell me, but most guys lie about their salaries.'

'First of all, could you call me Walter? And I'll call you Phoebe. This isn't a business meeting, is it?'

'OK, Walter,' Phoebe said, pouring herself some San Pellegrino water. 'So, what do you do in Shanghai? You seem a little evasive.'

He opened the menu and looked down at it. 'I'm one of those people known to the rest of society as "an entrepreneur". Whenever anyone says it, it seems like a dirty word. No one's really sure what entrepreneurs do, except make money. Have you had a chance to look at the menu? I don't know if you like this kind of food. It's supposed to be Balinese, but it's not really – just generic Indonesian and Malaysian. There's good curry, but Chinese people don't usually like curry. I should have asked you. But I thought, the setting is so nice that even if we don't eat anything, we can enjoy the lake, the plants, the sound of frogs in the middle of the city. It's quite romantic, I think. Don't you?'

Phoebe looked at the pond. The surface of the water was calm and still, the flames of the oil lamps reflected like the uncertain glimmer of stars in the night sky. She thought of the lake on the outskirts of the small town in the heart of the countryside where she had grown up, thousands of miles from here. It was deep and dark, and in the rainy season its waters rose and flooded the fields and scrubland around it. The half-submerged bushes looked as if they were floating in the water, and as Phoebe and her friends walked to school through the fields that bounded the overflowing shores of the lake they would let the floodwaters wash through their rubber slippers, warm and silty between their toes, stained with the colour of red earth.

'If you are an entrepreneur, that means you are rich,' Phoebe said, laughing in the way she had often rehearsed: teasingly, flirtatiously, charmingly feminine, but not sexual – not yet. She knew men liked that.

'Everyone is rich compared to somebody.'

'Are you married?'

'No.'

'Fiancée? Girlfriend?'

'I'm single. I told you in my message – I just want … a companion.' He lowered his menu briefly to look at her, then raised it again, so Phoebe could not see the expression on his face.

She laughed again. 'I'm just teasing, having some fun.'

'What are you going to have? The curried river prawns are very good. Or the grilled lobster, if you like lobster.'

'I don't know anything about Malaysian or Indonesian food – it's all just curry, curry, curry,' she said, repeating what she heard

Mainlanders say all the time. She was pleased with herself – it sounded natural, as if she really believed it.

He closed the menu and smiled. 'Fine, I'll order for us both.' He raised his hand to beckon the waitress over. She was Indonesian, dark-skinned, pretty. She began to speak in Chinese, her accent heavy, the words stumbling off her tongue. But then Walter Chao spoke to her in her own language, and her face became open, smiling. They shared a joke, the sound of their southern tongue filling the air with warmth.

'I'll tell the chef to make sure the food is not too spicy, just in case the lady doesn't like chilli,' the waitress said in Malay, looking at Walter.

'It's OK,' Phoebe said. 'I like spicy food.'

Walter raised his eyebrows. 'You understand what we're saying?'

'Oh no, I was just guessing. I had a Malaysian boyfriend once, you see. When I was much younger.'

Phoebe liked the fact that Walter studied the wine list with attention. Everyone knew that if a man knew about wine it was a sign not just of wealth, but of education – and a foreign education.

'So, Walter, I take it you're Malaysian. Tell me how a Malaysian guy like you ended up working in Shanghai.'

'The same way a girl from Guangdong like you did. Tell me about yourself. Is business going well? Owning a whole chain of beauty spas must be tough work. How do you find time to socialise? You studied economics at university, right? There are so many questions I want to ask you.'

When men ask you questions, it is just a seduction technique, Phoebe remembered from one of her books. *They are not really interested in your answers*.

Phoebe shrugged. 'My life isn't so special, you know.' But still, she began to talk. About the harshness of life in the city, about the aloofness of the Shanghainese, about the loneliness, about being far from home. She had told him her usual story about herself when they had exchanged emails, about coming from Guangdong province, about being a university graduate and the manager of a chain of luxury health spas in which she also owned shares. She had even said it was partly her business, and that she had set it up with a rich friend. She was so well rehearsed in this history that she did not even have to pretend any more; it felt as if it truly belonged to her. But now, sitting by the edge of a lake under the eaves of a teak building, she found herself speaking of how hard it was to make friends in this city, how hard it was to find someone special, someone to love. She could so easily have said, I am lonely because I am just like you, I am a foreigner. But unlike you, I cannot go home, I must stay here. I am an illegal worker. She could have told him where she was really from, could have told him that only recently she had been sitting in bars waiting to pick up men like him who might give her money for sex, that until three days ago the high point in her career had been working as a receptionist in a beauty salon.

But she did not say any of this. Instead, she said, 'Life in Shanghai is so tiring. I think I'll go to Hainan Island next weekend, just to get away from it all.'

When she finished speaking she noticed that Walter's gaze was fixed on her; he had been listening attentively to every word she had said. He seemed to be smiling, but the corners of his eyes were pinched, and she could not tell if he was happy or was just squinting in the dark. 'I know how you feel,' he said. 'Shanghai is a beautiful place, but it is also a harsh place. Life here is not really life, it is a competition.'

Phoebe nodded, trying to keep her poise by maintaining perfectly straight shoulders, which she knew he would admire. But all of a sudden she felt really tired, as if speaking about being fatigued had actually made it happen. Walter had shifted his position in his chair slightly, and was sitting low with his elbows hanging over the edge of the armrests, the way he might have done when relaxing at home.

'Yes, I think I'll go away at the weekend,' Phoebe repeated, imagining the white-sand beaches and marble-floored hotels she knew she would never be able to afford. 'Just to enjoy some sunshine and a nice hotel down there. It's very luxurious in Hainan these days – I take holidays there all the time.'

Walter laughed. 'You're funny.'

'What's so funny?'

'Nothing,' he shrugged, still looking at her. He was definitely smiling this time. 'I'm just laughing because you are a total stranger, yet you make me feel very comfortable. I usually don't trust people much.'

'Weirdo,' Phoebe said, adjusting the top button of her blouse; the collar was a bit tight, making her feel hot and uncomfortable and adding to her sense of weariness.

'If you need someone to go to Hainan with you, let me know,' he said. He looked away, out across the darkness of the pond once more, as if suddenly embarrassed to meet her gaze. 'I've been feeling a bit lonely recently, so I could do with some company.'

The food arrived. The waitress found that the table was too small, and asked politely if Phoebe could move her handbag. Walter stood up and hung it on the back of Phoebe's chair. He looked at it briefly and said, 'Might be time for you to get a new bag. The zip's broken on this one.'

It was true. The zip had broken months ago, and Phoebe had stuck a safety pin through it so she could open and close the bag.

'I've just been too busy to replace it,' she said. As she spoke she thought she sounded sad and depressed, which was not at all the impression she wanted to give. She'd intended to be bright and seductive – she did not know how she had let herself fall into this mood, sullen and crushed by life.

'You work too hard,' Walter said, placing his napkin on his lap. 'Let's just enjoy our dinner and not think about anything else for a couple of hours.'

Phoebe nodded. The smell of the food made her feel hungry in the way she remembered from childhood, her hunger boundless, as if it could never be sated. She lowered her head and began to eat. She did not care that she had lost all her elegant bearing; she was too tired to remember the tips she had read in the chapter 'Seduction at the Dinner Table'. Her head and shoulders slumped, her hair fell forward and shrouded her face. I must look a real mess, she thought. But all she wanted to do was eat.

'Don't eat so quickly,' Walter said in a soft voice. 'You're guzzling your food just like the poor village girls where I grew up. You don't have to rush, we have all evening.'

Out of the corner of her eye, she could see the reflection of the oil lamps dancing on the surface of the black, black water.

It didn't take long for all the girls at work to know that Phoebe had a new boyfriend, and what's more, that he was rich.

'You really have the look of a settled-down woman. When is he going to marry you? This guy has *serious* money. *Wah*, a purse too? It matches your new LV bag! He must really be considerate.'

They asked all sorts of questions – how much did he earn, what car did he drive, was he, um, had they, um, what was he like when performing intimate relations? Phoebe did not know how to answer. She accepted all Walter's gifts, enjoyed going out to dinner with him, but she did not know how much she liked him. He was definitely not the soulmate the fortune-teller had said she would meet. That must have been a mistake – the fortune-teller had clearly said, Your soulmate will be a sensitive and romantic soul. She'd even written it down, so Phoebe had proof of what she'd said. Phoebe considered ringing the fortune-teller and asking for her money back.

When the other girls forced her into showing them a photo of Walter she let them see one she'd taken on her mobile phone, which showed him dressed in a light-grey jacket and open-necked shirt, an outfit that made him appear rich. He was standing in front of his car, and although you could only see part of it, you could clearly make out that it was a large black 4x4 with smoky windows. She chose that photo because she knew it would impress the other girls, that they would only notice the clothes and the car and not his average looks, and that would be enough to make them say, *Wah, handsome brother!* They would not notice the lines around his mouth and his narrowed eyes as he tried to smile. He was the only person Phoebe had ever met who looked in pain when he attempted to express joy. Sometimes when they were in the car, driving in silence – they always drove in silence, because it seemed he had very little to say to her, and she was fed up with trying to start a conversation – she would look at him and wonder if he had ever experienced joy. And she decided that most probably he had not, because he did not make her feel joyous.

What was more, they hadn't even *done it* yet. After four weeks, all they had done was hold hands, and on two occasions he had put his arm around her shoulders – once not long after their very first date, when they were standing on the Bund looking across at the skyscrapers in Pudong. It was after dinner, and there was a cool breeze coming off the river, making the smaller boats rock from side to side. Maybe he was cold, and needed her body for warmth. He rested his arm heavily on her shoulders without moving it for a very long time, and frankly it felt uncomfortable after a few seconds. The other time was when they were on top of the Financial Tower one night, looking at the city spreading out below them until it disappeared from view in the distance, the roads fanning out in every direction. He had put his arm around her and drawn her towards him. She thought he was going to kiss her, on the cheek at least, or whisper something suggestive in her ear, but all he said was, 'It didn't look like this where I grew up.'

He never sought more physical intimacy, never accidentally placed his hand too high on her thigh or on her bare knee when she wore a short skirt, never even attempted a good-night kiss. He must have sexual problems, she decided. Anyway, it was better that he didn't push for closer bodily contact, because she did not find him physically desirable. For the time being, it was nice to play the role of the morally correct, educated girl. After all, it was what he was expecting from her.

She must have been convincing in this role, because once he said, 'It's strange, but I really feel at ease with you. There's something about you I can't quite place – you're just so different from the other women in Shanghai. I don't really understand you yet.'

Her books had been right: men only wanted what they couldn't get.

She made a decision, and it was an easy one: she would use Walter for as long as she could. She had to be ruthless. She would accept his gifts of luxury handbags and Italian shoes and British raincoats and jewels from Hong Kong. She would not only enjoy the fine dinners, but use the opportunity to learn about the Western countries he had visited. She would listen carefully to his stories about getting lost in Rome and his description of the view from the Eiffel Tower, and would store them away for use one day, when she was with someone else, her true soulmate. She would accept all his offers of evenings at the opera and the ballet. She would use him to make herself better. *Make use of men as they would make use of you.*

One evening, as he was driving her to dinner in his leather-seated car, she wondered where in this never-ending city her true soulmate lived. Perhaps some element of fate had failed to fall into place, like a fine piece of thread that comes loose from a tapestry. Maybe that had been enough for her to miss her connection, and now her true soulmate was driving around in a car with someone else he too *sort of* liked, but not *really*.

Nonetheless, having a steady male companion of any kind was an achievement in Shanghai, even if he was not a soulmate. What the girls at the spa said was true: Phoebe herself could see a change in her behaviour. She was nicer to the other girls; the silly things they did no longer put her into such a bad mood. Now, if their performance was lacking she did not get a headache, but gave them advice, calmly but authoritatively. She had also started leaving work earlier, taking evenings off without worrying that something would go wrong in her absence.

One Sunday morning she and Walter saw some people dancing in a small park, right next to a busy highway. When they stopped at the traffic lights Phoebe could hear the same kind of Spanish-sounding music she had heard on the night she had met Walter for the first time, but quicker and more exciting. The people were spinning and shaking their shoulders and hips – it looked thrilling. Phoebe felt her body wanting to move to the rhythm. The lights turned green, and as they drove off Walter said, 'That's salsa dancing. Let's try it sometime.' Secretly, Phoebe signed up for evening classes at a dance studio in Zhabei. She wanted to be well prepared by the time Walter took her on their first salsa date – she did not want to make a fool of herself.

She also started learning French on her journey into work and during lunch breaks. She'd bought a book and accompanying CDs from a stall on the pavement near Tiantong Lu, where she often bought useful, life-improving books. The book had a colourful cover, with a picture of a smiling Chinese woman wearing a beret and a striped shirt. It was called *C'EST FOU! CRAZY MÉTHODE: Speak French in Three Weeks.*

Phoebe did not understand any French at all, but the book said this did not matter one bit. All she had to do was to master the beautiful sounds of the language, and the rest would quickly follow. So she put her headphones on and patiently repeated after the elegant-sounding voice:

Qu'est-ce que c'est? C'est un arbre?
Non, c'est un camion.
Non, c'est un camion.

She could feel her life changing. She could feel herself becoming the person she'd always wanted to be.

She insisted that Walter take her to Western restaurants. They were so much more sophisticated than Chinese restaurants, which she now found too noisy and crowded for her taste. Even when you made a booking you were not sure of getting your table; often they would give it away if you arrived ten minutes late. Walter would sometimes say, 'I've heard of this great little *ramen* place in Xuhui, near the indoor stadium. Maybe we should try and find it on Sunday, just hang out together for the afternoon, chat a bit?' She would flatly refuse. It was so annoying of him to suggest travelling long distances just to eat in the kind of low-class place she had been frequenting all her life.

Soon he understood that she much preferred the upscale European restaurants around Huaihai Lu, or on the Bund, or on the top floors of hotels in Pudong, with views of the city, the kind of places with subtle lighting and well-dressed waiters. Before their first few outings Phoebe consulted her books and made lists of things to remember – how to use the cutlery, what to do with the little baskets of bread that arrived before the meal, how to deal with olives – but she quickly mastered these problems, and soon she did not need to look in her handbag for the piece of paper on which she had written: 1 Soup (+ bread). 2 Fish (flat knife). 3 Meat. 4 Cheese. 5 Dessert. 6 Coffee. She even understood, without having read it in any of her books, that the tiny glasses filled with a semi-liquid puree that resembled baby food were a variation on the nibbles served before the meal. (These were a sure sign of a superior, stylish restaurant.)

During these meals, Walter would often ask about her life.

'What kind of food did you eat when you were growing up in Guangdong?'

'Guangdong food.'

'What is your favourite food nowadays?'

'Hamburger.'

'Did your mother cook a lot?'

'No.'

'Did you spend much time with her when you were small, or did she have to work? Didn't you say that she was a single mother?'

'Can you stop asking me so many stupid questions, please? I can't enjoy my food with you talking so much.'

'Sorry. It's just that I want to know everything about you, get to understand you properly. I just … I just need to feel closer to you.'

Phoebe found his questions annoying. It was hard enough remembering that she should not hold her knife like a pencil, and to dab her mouth with the corner of her napkin frequently but discreetly. Of course, she knew from her books that dinner in a restaurant was a perfect opportunity for intimate conversation, but she did not want to talk about the things he asked her, she did not want to be reminded of all that.

Walter would also talk about himself over dinner – incidents from his work, how he had been feeling that day – often quite emotional matters that Phoebe tried to blank out because they made her feel uncomfortable. For example, he told her that when his father had died he had not even known, because he was too busy with work, and that recently his father had begun to appear in his dreams, haunting him. Once he mentioned that he had never known his mother, and that he dreamt of being held tightly by someone who would look after him. Phoebe did not understand why he was telling her such intimate feelings, did not know how she was supposed to respond. None of her books had advised her about how to deal with men's emotional neediness, they just told her that men were simple and straightforward, and that she could easily manipulate them.

Thankfully Walter's moments of solemnity never lasted long, and his mood would swiftly become jovial again. 'I love talking to you,' he would say. 'I really feel you understand me.' Then he would go back to telling her about his trips to exotic European countries, about the restaurants and museums and shops to be found there. She preferred hearing about such things – she could learn from them, they made her feel uplifted.

After dinner, they would often go to karaoke. Her favourite was in Wulumuqi Lu – she liked the places with a wide selection of Western songs, and that did not have too many cheap-looking girls hanging around. She had nothing against the girls themselves, even though they wore too much Lycra and exposed too much flesh, but she did not want to be reminded that she herself had been one of them once, not so long ago, hanging around waiting for Friday and Saturday night when there would be more customers, singing songs for them and bringing them drinks. Anyway, she did not have to see them now, because Walter always booked the most expensive private room, just for the two of them.

The first time they went she found herself sitting next to him on the sofa. It was made of real leather; she could smell its rich, luxurious scent and feel its smooth grainy texture under her fingers. The room was so well soundproofed that she could hear only the faintest noise from the other rooms, unlike the KTV places she was used to, where you could hear the off-key singing from next door. Walter sat looking at her. The blue light from the blank screen made his eyes look watery, but in the dark she could not see the lines around his eyes and mouth clearly, so for once his smile seemed happy instead of happy-sad. She thought, This is the moment he is finally going to kiss me. But he did not, he just looked at her without saying anything, until she became fed up and said, 'Who's going to sing first? Or shall we sing a duet?'

'Let's try and find something nice,' he said, scrolling through the list of songs. 'Why don't you sing something first? One of these, maybe. You mentioned that you used to sing songs like this with your mother when you were small. I love hearing them.'

Phoebe looked at the song titles – 'Just Like Your Tenderness', 'Moonlight Serenade', 'Neverending Love', 'I Have Known a Love' – they were all traditional, old-fashioned melodies.

'You must be joking. No way.'

'Why not?' Walter asked. He was still pointing the remote control at the screen, the cursor hovering over 'Green Island Night Song'.

'Tooo boring! Let's try a Western song. Hey, how about a French one?'

'You speak French?'

'*Bien sûr.*' She had not told him about her self-taught lessons – she wanted to surprise and impress him. She also did not tell him that since it was karaoke, she did not have to understand any French, she just had to follow the words on the screen. The music started, a famous tune that conjured up visions of elegant women strolling along tree-lined boulevards a long time ago, when life was gentler, when things were not vulgar and flashy. Phoebe sat up straight. As she began singing, the words felt like sweet drops of honey on her tongue. Even though she did not understand a single word of the song, she understood the feeling – the sad beauty of a sensitive soul. She caught a glimpse of Walter, and knew that he was moved and impressed. He would not know that she was just following the words on the screen.

Gon-di le pun le hua

deh mo de doo leh yoo-ha

i-le en un-t-eh

dang mon g-he

seh hua bu-he mu-a

tu me la-di

labeh-hesu-a

u-ne ba-he

don ye gon-mal

seh-tua mu-a

la yu-heh

labeh-hesu-a

mon ge-he gi baaaaaaa

He smiled and clapped when she had finished. 'Thank you, Edith Piaf,' he said. 'Life really is *en rose* when you sing. It makes me happy.'

She did not fully understand what he meant, but she knew that she had been beautiful and impressive.

That night, in the Journal of Her Secret Self she wrote: *I will become a woman of infinite class. I must not be afraid of using him. Maybe he is a nice guy. But even nice people can be used.*

Yanyan said, 'Are you writing secret things about your new love?'

'I don't love him.'

'But he looks really great. And he's so rich! We don't have to worry about paying the rent any more. And look at the nice things he buys you. He even gave you tickets for the Sichuan earthquake charity concert next week – do you know, those were hot-selling six months ago? How many men would be so generous? Look at the list of performers. Oldies like Tsai Chin together with cool guys like Chang Chen-Yue.'

'You can go – I have no enthusiasm for such things any more.'

'Really? But you love music. Surely you should suggest to Walter that you and he go together.'

'What do you know? You've never even met him. He's nice, but I have no feelings for him.'

'Then why are you in such a good mood all the time these days?'

Phoebe turned out the light. Yanyan's questions had put her in a bad mood. As she lay on her mattress on the floor, she wondered why she still stayed in this tiny room with Yanyan when she could afford to rent a place of her own, in a proper modern apartment block with fast lifts that were not littered with cigarette butts and corridors that were not dark and smelling of dogshit. She could be in a place with wardrobes to hang her clothes in and a bathroom with a powerful shower and a Japanese WC with a heated seat and automatic wash and blow-dry; she would never have to step over a sleeping, jobless roommate on her way to work, or take turns to use the mattress on the floor.

She listened to Yanyan humming a Chang Chen-Yue song; it was out of tune, and kept her awake. But Yanyan sounded so happy, like a small child singing before she had enough words to sing properly. Yanyan only knew one line in the whole song, which she repeated over and over again. *Love me don't go* … It really gave Phoebe a headache.

Lying on the floor and gazing up at the window, she could see the night sky, hazy and purple with the lights of the city, as if it was forever dawn. She closed her eyes and tried not to think of anything. In her head she could still hear the words of the elegant French song she had sung at the KTV place. *Seh tu-a pu mu-ah dang la wi, tu me la di la du-reh ne la wi ... mon ge-he gi baaaa.*

18

粉身碎骨

Be Prepared to
Sacrifice Everything

The first time Justin ever spoke to Yinghui was at Subang airport, just before she went through into the departure lounge to board the plane to London. She was pointing at the swifts swooping and darting in the heights of the cavernous, tent-shaped ceiling, laughing as if she had just spotted something surreal.

'I wonder if they shit,' she said. 'And if so, why we don't feel it. There are loads of them up there.'

'I don't know,' Justin replied. 'Guess it evaporates on the way down.'

All around them were Malay families sending relatives off on the hajj; a small child was crying inconsolably as her mother went through the gate. Yinghui was wearing sky-blue jeans that were too baggy and short, with hems that ended at her ankles. She had tied a coarse, coffee-coloured jumper around her waist, and fiddled with it as she waited for CS to check his bags. When he had finally finished, they touched hands briefly; they had been boyfriend-girlfriend for only a couple of months, and were not yet sure how much affection they could display in public.

'Hey, thanks for the lift,' CS said, slapping Justin on the back. 'Seeya soon.'

'Least I can do for my little brother.' But CS and Yinghui were already walking through the gate, towards their new life. It was

1990; a Sheila Majid song was playing on a radio somewhere, and the air smelled faintly of *kretek* and curry leaves.

Justin had seen Yinghui once before, several weeks earlier, at a party thrown by a friend of his brother, a casual get-together for their contemporaries who had just finished school and were soon to go abroad to continue their studies – to America, Britain and Australia. There had been a certain amount of one-upmanship, of course, the Oxbridge- and Ivy League-bound kids sorting themselves out in a subtle hierarchy, but in general the party had been marked by an atmosphere of camaraderie, everyone present united by their knowledge that they were members of an elite. They were all leaving, and they knew that in Malaysia, to leave meant to be privileged.

But Justin was not leaving. He was not going to college abroad, or indeed anywhere; already he was as rooted in local life as his parents were. He was five or six years older than anyone else at the party, sent as a chauffeur and discreet chaperone to keep an eye on his brother, who was already showing a tendency towards excess – Marlboro reds, experiments with alcohol, a fondness for the wrong sort of nightclub. An artistic temperament – that was how his parents explained CS's behaviour, with a smile and a shake of the head. They were not concerned about his foibles; it was as if they thought his misdemeanours were counterbalanced by Justin's steadiness and reliability, one brother cancelling out the other. Things would always be OK if Justin was around.

That was why he found himself at this party full of kids high on tequila and the anticipation of ivy-clad colleges; that was why, as usual, he was sitting on the edge of the room trying not to be noticed – the dull older brother of the mercurial CS, the one who'd finished his education at eighteen, after barely scraping through his final year of school. He knew all the people at the party: he had grown up with them. He watched as two boys pushed each other into the swimming pool; noticed a boy and a girl creeping into a shadowy recess of the garden, framed by a pair of spreading palm trees; caught sight of another couple sneaking upstairs separately, boy following girl after a gap of thirty seconds, hoping their assignation would not be noticed. But nothing escaped Justin; it was his job to take in the little details of human weakness; it was his job to put things right.

When Yinghui arrived it was already late. The initial excitement of the party had petered out, and people were beginning to settle down in little cliques. Justin saw her making her way up the snaking Balinese-style stepping-stone pathway, her taut calves illuminated by the garden lights housed in low stone pagodas. She wore Bermuda shorts and walked with a slouchy gait, her body held loosely, as if she was bored and did not really want to be there. Her hair was cut on the short side, messily finished, making her head look square; dangling from a strap over her shoulder was a small cloth bag, a Himalayan-type pouch decorated with colourful beads.

'She's going to London, right?' Justin heard a girl say to her friend as they saw Yinghui arrive.

'Yes. She'll be able to buy lots of lesbian clothes there.'

Yinghui stood in the middle of a small square of lawn next to the swimming pool, scanning the thinning crowd. Her eyes caught Justin's for a half-second before she turned, made her way over to a small group of people and eased her way next to CS. He exclaimed theatrically in a high-pitched, look-at-me voice, fuelled by over-sweet rum punch, then leant over to kiss her on both cheeks. Justin did not know where or when his brother had learnt this affectation; he'd never seen anyone else do it in real life.

Over the next three years, whenever Yinghui and CS came home during the vacations, they seemed more splendid in their coupled isolation than the previous time, as if every term abroad had brought them closer to each other, and made them more divorced from the rest of the world. Justin would come back from work to find them slouched on the sofas reading the papers, occasionally commenting on a news item in a bored, mildly disaffected manner. Once he had just sat down with a can of Coke and turned on the TV when Yinghui let the papers fall to the floor with a sigh, lay back, gazed at the ceiling, and said, 'It's all just so shit.'

'What is?' Justin asked.

CS was stretched out on the same sofa as Yinghui, his ankles entwined with hers. He did not look up from the book he was reading. 'You know that's what it's like in this country, sweetie. You're never going to change it.'

'Look,' Yinghui said, staring at the news on the TV. Justin had been about to change the channel, but now he paused. 'Watching the news is like reading a novel – it's just pure fiction. Look at him, that fat-ass minister behaving as if he really cares about the floods. That cheque he's handing over is to buy votes, not to pay for a new bridge.' She glanced briefly at Justin, as if he was somehow implicated in it all. Floods, corruption, suffering: it was his fault. He changed the channel and found the football.

'Don't know why you stress about these things, babe,' said CS. 'It's not as if any of this is new, is it? You grew up in this shit. You of all people can't say you're surprised by it.' The book he was reading had the words *Western Aesthetics* on the cover, but Justin could not make out the whole title.

Yinghui sighed again and turned on her side, scrunching up a cushion to make a pillow under her head as she gazed idly at the TV screen. 'Yeah, I guess. It just seems worse now, that's all. People don't give a damn any more. All they do is make money, hang out and watch sport.'

They spoke as if Justin wasn't there; they barely looked at him.

They travelled widely, in Europe as well as in Asia, each time coming back with a fund of stories, the dizzying wealth of which they would hint at by keeping silent. When asked what the newly reunified Berlin was like, they would simply say, 'Just ... amazing,' without elaborating any further, leaving the listener taut with anticipation. Rome? 'Has issues.' St Petersburg? 'Beautiful but ... complicated.' Occasionally they would write articles about their travels – Yinghui had a piece published in the *New Straits Times* which detailed her views (mainly negative) on the architecture of Gaudí and her dislike of Barcelona generally; CS contributed an essay to the *Star* titled 'Schopenhauer in a Bangkok Brothel', which all their friends read but did not understand.

Their visits to India swelled their already considerable air of mystique even further. They came back wearing clothes made from colourful printed cotton that they had bought in a village in Rajasthan and had transformed into fantastic flowing kurtas in Delhi. CS carried a goatskin satchel given to him by a man they had helped with a punctured tyre on the road to Jaipur; Yinghui had an amulet given to her by a local soothsayer. Everything had a story, nothing was ever just bought in a shop. Even their ailments seemed exotic, with names no one had heard of before – once, when they both came back twenty pounds lighter after a bad bout of food poisoning, they shrugged and said, 'Oh, just a little *Campylobacter jejuni*.' On more than one occasion Justin heard people ask them what India was like, whether it was poor and dirty or exotic and colourful, to which they merely sighed and shook their heads without deigning to reply. They started doing yoga, and sometimes made references to 'when we meditate'. Every time Justin saw them, their faces glowed with the satisfaction of being perfectly and utterly together.

When he was in Yinghui's presence he felt nervous and unintelligent, which frustrated him, because in the rest of his life, he was neither – he knew that much about himself. Conversation with her was difficult; his views and observations on life seemed trite, not worth mentioning. If she asked him a question, she would fall silent and fix him with a firm stare, holding his gaze as she awaited his response. Any thoughts that might have formulated in his head would seem inadequate, and he would hesitate; but she would not fill in the silence the way other, more sociable people did, would not alleviate his awkwardness. Instead, she would merely wait until he managed to stammer out some banality. She had little in the way of small talk – everything she said was aimed at acquiring information.

'What do you think of this latest scandal involving the port authorities? All that land being sold to government cronies at cut-price rates.'

'Um, it's really bad, I guess.'

'*Bad*. Hm. I see.'

He got used to being a witness to the intellectual intimacy she and CS shared, a closeness so intense that it cut them off from the rest of the world, as if only they knew the words to some elaborate song they were singing; and even if Justin managed to learn them, they would always be ahead of him.

'Corruption is quite comforting, really,' CS once said as they were driving down to the coast. 'I mean, it suits us, suits the Asian temperament. Westerners aren't comfortable with it, not just because they have stricter rules in place, but because something in their nature prevents them from appreciating it. They're more, hm, how shall I say … rigid. Less malleable. Do you know what I mean? It's got nothing to do with being more principled or honourable. It's a question of, like, *supplesse* – blowing with the wind. I'm not saying it's right, and I definitely don't agree with it, but let's face it, it's part of our nature.'

'Yeah, I guess I would go with that,' said Yinghui, reaching across and idly stroking CS's hair. Justin, who was driving, could see them in the rear-view mirror, their heads thrown back to catch the breeze fluttering through the half-open windows. 'It's like the Chinese and gambling. We can't get rid of that character flaw. There's a certain beauty in living that way – quite poetic, I think, to live with something that you despise, and to know that it will destroy you, but at the same time recognising that it'll always be part of you. Don't you think, Justin? Hello? Anyone there?'

He nodded. 'Um, ya,' he said. Sitting in the driver's seat with no one beside him, he felt like a chauffeur; he had not even demurred when they climbed into the back seat together, leaving him alone in the front. Their coupledness was unshakeable; there was no point in resisting it. As he looked at them in the mirror, their eyes shaded by jet-black sunglasses, heads tilting towards each other, Justin felt old. He was only six years older than CS and Yinghui, but he had a job and an office, his life was already so firmly fixed in a mould that he would never be able to change it. They still occupied that wonderful terrain on the other side of the fence between youth and adulthood, Justin thought; and he envied them because their lives would always be colourful and full of change, even when they were no longer young.

Only once did he succeed in making Yinghui laugh, and even then it wasn't intentional. He had just returned to the capital after a long drive up the east coast, all the way to Kota Bharu, where he had been inspecting one of the family's latest concerns, a vast housing development in the countryside for members of the new middle class who wanted to leave their flimsy timber-and-cement dwellings to live in neat, clean streets of low brick houses bounded by chain-link fences. It had been a tiring trip, and not particularly productive, but vital nonetheless. Palms needed to be greased – one or two officials who had the potential to be uncooperative – and cordial relations maintained. Justin had travelled up there with Sixth Uncle to host a dinner or two, discreetly handing out expensive gifts before the all-day drive back down to KL. When he got home, he found Yinghui sitting on the steps of the porch, a large sheet of paper spread out in front of her on which she was making some rough drawings.

'Plans for my café,' she said. 'Not sure if it'll ever happen, but it would be fun, I think. CS needs somewhere to host his literary gatherings, and I could bake the cakes. Can you imagine – me, baking cakes? That would surprise everyone. But I kind of like the idea.'

'What about the business side?' he asked. She did not seem to Justin to have a clue about finances or the simple mechanics of making money, and he couldn't imagine her running a business. Her world was entirely cerebral: she inhabited the books she read, and had no concept of providing service in return for money. She would lose everything.

'That'll just sort itself out, won't it?' she said. 'CS says that if I want to do it, I should just go ahead. He says business is fundamentally simple when you strip it down to its basics. Once it's deconstructed, you can see that it's philosophically unchallenging. That's why no businessman is ever a great genius.'

'I see.'

'Anyway, how was Kelantan? Beautiful?'

He nodded. 'Yes.' She held his gaze steadily in her wide-eyed fashion, waiting for further details; waiting. 'Beautiful,' he said. He searched his brain for thoughts that had occurred to him during his trip, but all he had seen was a huge residential project of cheap, boxy houses, and the only people he had spoken to were local officials with whom he had made small talk about food and fishing. 'Backward,' he said, suddenly. He did not know where the word came from, or if he actually thought Kelantan was backward, but he was glad nonetheless that he'd come up with an observation.

Her face opened up into a smile, and she laughed. 'Beautiful and backward. I like that! What a great description. The poetic gene must run in the family.'

From then on, every time Yinghui described a place she'd visited, she would say, 'Beautiful and backward,' and nod knowingly to Justin. Sometimes she would even say, 'As Justin says, "Beautiful and backward."' She and CS began to describe people they met as 'beautiful and backward' – the glamorous trophy wives of rich men in KL ('There goes another B&B'). For a while, Justin felt as if Yinghui had finally taken him into her life. He knew he only hovered on the periphery of her world, but it did not matter, it was enough for him.

Around this time he was charged with looking after the dealings concerned with the New Cathay Movie Theatre, the first and most famous of the dozen or so cinemas to have been built in KL during the 1920s and thirties. Most of them had been torn down during the boom years that had begun in the eighties, but the New Cathay still stood. Small fig trees sprouted from cracks in the masonry on its roof, the ornate plasterwork of scrolling leaves that adorned the façade was cracking in many places, and its handsome columns were streaked with black moss where moisture leaked from the drainpipes. Whereas once it had always seemed splendidly bathed in sunlight, it now lay permanently in the shadows, crowded on all sides by the high-rise office blocks that had sprung up around it.

Yet in spite of its dereliction, the New Cathay continued to screen films every day of the week, as if refusing to acknowledge the changes taking place around it. Audiences had dwindled, of course, and when Justin stopped by early one Friday evening to see for himself how dire the situation was, he found only one other person in the auditorium, an old Indian man who had fallen asleep despite the pounding music of the Bollywood film that was showing. Justin stayed for fifteen minutes, watching the colourful images dance across the screen, before wandering back out into the street. Office workers dressed in smart grey slacks and white shirts were hurrying to dinner, high-spirited in anticipation of the weekend; teenagers in school uniform were rushing to catch their buses home after an afternoon hanging around the shopping malls. No one showed any interest in the New Cathay.

It had not always been like this. Justin could still remember when, once a month, his parents would take him and CS to the New Cathay to see a film on a Sunday afternoon – that rarest of treats: a family outing. Even as recently as the late seventies, the New Cathay would show the newest films, despite the establishment of big, modern cinemas elsewhere in town. Justin recalled seeing the remake of *King Kong* and – could this be right? – *Star Wars* at the New Cathay, as well as numerous Chinese classics in the great tradition of the Shaw Brothers studios. But the films were immaterial – what he had loved was sitting in the best seats, in the middle of the front row, a newspaper cone of steamed groundnuts in one hand, a bottle of Fanta in the other, his parents staring silently at the screen, as if they were young lovers. A sense of togetherness, away from their everyday disputes. The old Indian *jaga* who would give him bags of rambutans from his garden after the movie. An almost normal life. That was what those evenings represented – an illusion of stability, of ordinariness. It was not long, of course, before Justin was old enough to see these outings for what they were, a temporary relief from the unvoiced unhappiness that lay underneath his family life, but still he would go along with the pretence, gratefully accepting the bag of rambutans even though he didn't especially like them, for they were part of this small ritual of normality.

The family had acquired the cinema in the late 1940s, when post-war fatigue had not yet been replaced by pre-Independence fervour; when nerves were still raw and money scarce. The owner had fled to Thailand during the war and had not come back, and almost the only person who had the money to buy the place was Justin's grandfather, one of the few Chinese to have come out of the war with his fortune intact, if not – this was always said in hushed tones – actually increased. Once bought, the cinema was smartened up, its fine masonry restored and repainted, its sagging old seats replaced with vinyl-covered ones from America; and for a decade, from the mid-fifties until just after Justin's birth, it enjoyed a second heyday, with audiences streaming in nightly to watch Technicolor films in modern comfort. But by the time Justin was old enough to be taken on those family outings it was past its prime, and by the eighties and nineties the huge multi-screen cinemas in the giant shopping malls ensured the demise of the New Cathay.

'We can't hang on to it just for sentimental reasons,' his father said one day at a family meeting convened to discuss it.

'Yeah, I agree,' said Sixth Uncle. 'It hasn't made a single *sen* since 1971. Not kidding, not one bloody *sen*. We've been subsidising it for too long. For what?'

'For the sake of heritage,' Justin said. 'For tradition. It goes back a long way in our family.'

'Tradition my foot,' Sixth Uncle said. 'Who gives a damn about history in this town anyway?'

'All right, all right,' Justin's father said. 'Son, you are right, it is valuable in that regard. But we have to face the facts – it's right in the middle of town. If you were to look at a map of KL and mark its exact centre, it would be directly where the New Cathay is. It's the most valuable piece of real estate in the country.'

'So what? Do we need the money that badly? Who's going to buy it anyway?'

His father exchanged glances with Sixth Uncle, and their tiny interaction did not escape Justin. He knew something significant would soon follow.

'Consider this, son,' his father continued calmly. 'No one might be interested in buying the cinema itself – there are modern cinemas everywhere now. But the land value is tremendous. The cinema can always be torn down.'

'But as I've said, do we need the money that badly?'

'It's the last bit of land in the centre of town that doesn't have a premium development on it. Sooner or later, it will happen. What if, say, the government makes a compulsory purchase order? They did that with our Pudu land just last month, remember? And we didn't get the right price for it. It's much better to act while we can still control the situation.'

'But Father, this is one of the last heritage buildings in the city. Surely the government can't destroy it for another office block.'

Sixth Uncle snorted.

'And what about the people who have worked there for forty years?' continued Justin. 'The old Indian *jaga* was still there the other day. It's, like, his home.'

'For goodness' sake,' Sixth Uncle said, 'we're not a damn charity.'

'But,' Justin began to say; and then he stopped, for he knew the decision had already been made.

'We thought you should be in charge of the site. We have a couple of people interested in buying it, but we're thinking of developing it ourselves too. You need to … explore the options.'

Sixth Uncle looked at Justin, who remained slumped in his chair. 'The boy isn't up to it,' he said. 'He doesn't want to do it. Guess it's too big a job for a kid.'

Justin's father said, 'He isn't a child any more, he's twenty-six years old. It's high time he assumed responsibility for important matters.'

Justin thought it was strange that people spoke about him in the third person, as if he did not really exist.

What made the situation worse for him – what made him feel physically sick – was the thought of how he would explain his family's plans to Yinghui. She had started working part-time for a charity, Friends of Old KL, which campaigned to preserve the few remaining historic buildings in the city – the once-grand colonial mansions and the handsome Chinese shop-houses that were being bulldozed to make way for the tower blocks she described as 'pathetic phalluses'. Justin had been present on several occasions when she and her conservation-minded friends had discussed their work. They'd called people of their parents' generation 'mindless vandals' who were depriving future generations of their rightful heritage: prison would be an appropriate punishment for such crimes. He had felt guilty by implication, as if he belonged to that older generation – part of an unfeeling establishment that kicked aside anything that stood in its way.

'But there's a question of practicality,' he had once ventured. 'Old buildings aren't practical. You can't live in them easily, they're hard to maintain.'

Yinghui had simply rolled her eyes and said, 'You just don't get it.'

But he *had* got it; he understood perfectly what the position was. For a week or two after the meeting with his father and Sixth Uncle he avoided Yinghui, feeling as if she would see the guilt imprinted on his face, all those crimes against culture brewing within him. When he came home after work and saw her lounging on the sofa with CS, he did not stop as he usually did to share a Coke and a quick chat with them, but headed straight upstairs instead. He decided he would not tell her; she would not know anything until it was too late, until after the bulldozers had done their work. He would then vaguely lay the blame on his father, his family, the government – whomever. He would be no more to blame than the rest of the whole damned country.

He saw her and CS by chance one day at the *nasi kandar* place in Taman Tun. They had been to look at a small, vacant shop in the area with a view to starting a business of some kind (she was actually going ahead with it, he thought, feeling slightly alarmed); he had just finished a round of golf with some prospective business partners at the nearby club.

'Very busy these days?' Yinghui asked as she sipped a cold rose syrup.

'Yes, kind of.'

'*Wah*, I'd like to have a job where playing golf counts as working.'

Justin shrugged.

'Or maybe you were paying homage at the family cemetery?' she continued. 'Tell me, how difficult was it to keep hold of that when you sold the land to be developed into a golf course?'

'I don't know. I was just a teenager then. I wasn't involved in any of that.'

'Must be hard, selling off all that family land to big government companies. But I'm sure you guys didn't do too badly out of it.'

Their food arrived. Justin had been hungry, but now he felt too hot and sweaty to eat; he'd ordered too much, and he didn't really feel like *nasi kandar* now.

'Explain to me how it works – how you deal with it, emotionally I mean, when you sell off something that's been in the family for generations. Is there, like, any sentimentality involved? Or do the billions you get from the sale compensate for the loss? When you go past a shopping mall with a KFC and a McDonald's and all that, do you ever think, Wow, that used to be where my granddad started his first business? Or do you just think, I'd like a Big Mac?'

CS looked away, searching for a waiter. 'Anyone want another soya-bean drink?'

Justin shook his head. 'I don't know. I don't run that side of the business.'

'Liar,' Yinghui said. Her face suddenly flushed; it was a very hot day, and she was sweating. 'You are such a fucking two-faced snake. Sitting here in front of us and saying you don't know anything about it. Hanging out with my friends and saying, Yeah, isn't it terrible, all this mindless development going on around us, we don't need it, it's just to show the West that we're a rich, modern country, we should preserve our soul. And then you turn around and raze everything to the ground. You know what? Fuck you.'

'I have no idea why you're getting so worked up. Why are you attacking me? Just calm down.'

'"I have no idea why you're getting so worked up,"' Yinghui mimicked. 'So you have no idea what's going to happen to the New Cathay cinema? No plans to tear it down and sell the land to the highest bidder? Beautiful piece of land – prime location, isn't it? Shame it happens to have the first Art Deco building in KL on it. Oh well, too bad, just destroy it. You are such a ruthless bastard.'

'No one's supposed to know about that,' Justin said quietly, looking around to see if anyone was listening. 'How did you find out?'

'Luckily not every member of your family is as heartless as you.' As she said this she reached across and took CS's forearm; her hand rested on his skin, her grip light but firm. CS continued to eat, looking intently at his food without meeting Justin's eye. 'Justin,' Yinghui continued, 'you can't let this happen. Don't you have any sense of responsibility at all? To your friends? To your history? To … us?'

'But my father … my family – that's what they want. You know it's my duty. They need me.'

Yinghui paused for a moment. She looked up to the ceiling, as if contemplating the infinite replies floating in the ether, then said calmly, 'When will you ever be your own man, with your own life? When will you be free?'

She and CS left the restaurant, their food unfinished, neither of them looking at Justin. He stared down at his nearly untouched plate of food. Two flies had landed on the piece of *sambal* chicken that lay next to the pile of rice, clinging to the meat like bits of charred skin. Yinghui's words remained in his head: *When will you ever be your own man, with your own life? When will you be free?* He asked for the food to be packed up in a takeaway bag, but as he walked back to his car he thought of the curry seeping into the rice, making it mushy and unpleasant. It would quickly turn rancid in the heat. He flung it into the monsoon drain before driving away.

Case Study:
Human Relations

This takes place outside the Bottega Veneta store at the Golden Eagle shopping mall on Shanxi Bei Lu. I shall describe the situation and leave it up to you to decide how best to resolve it – a small test to see how much you have learnt and observed thus far:

Two people, a man and a woman, have just met up for the evening and are idly wandering around the shops killing time before going to dinner. From a distance, they look typical of the sort of couple you frequently see in certain moneyed venues in Shanghai. He is older than she, possibly a foreigner, and obviously wealthy, dressed in a golf shirt, comfortable slacks and leather loafers with tassels; she is in her twenties, slender, giggly. Sometimes she appears to act much younger than her age, almost like a teenager; at other times she seems harsh. Her eyes can look either watery and soft or firm and cold, like an old auntie who has been through a lot.

They pause in front of a shop window, looking at the women's bags on display – a patchwork of colourful leather. He does not know what to do with his hands; at one point it seems as though he is about to reach out to her, but he does not. Instead, he clasps his hands behind his back, then puts them in his pockets. He is a touch nervous, it would seem. Maybe they are not yet actually a couple. There is something not quite right about this pair. What exactly is the nature of their relationship?

The air conditioning is very strong; it feels cool against the skin, and gives her goosepimples on her bare arms. She draws a fine shawl around her shoulders. It is a deep red colour that matches her shoes and goes well with her complexion. She makes a joke and laughs coquettishly, looking at him and touching him lightly on the shoulder. Is this an invitation for more intimate contact? Still his hands remain tucked in his pockets. She laughs once more; it is a sweet, earthy laugh, richer than her delicate looks suggest, even a touch coarse. He nods and now, at last, puts his hand lightly on her back, resting it on the shawl. She holds the shawl tight, protectively, as if it is very cold. From a distance it might even look as if she were afraid of something. The shawl she is wearing – look carefully. It glistens in the harsh lighting, it is artificially shiny. Perhaps she is afraid he will guess it is made not from pure pashmina but from a mixture of nylon and other synthetic textiles – the kind of thing you can buy for 20 *kuai* on the steps leading down to most subway stations.

She points at a handbag in the window. It is scarlet in colour and has been placed next to other bags of a similar hue and design. Red is obviously her favourite colour. She looks at her companion; he smiles and shakes his head, as if she has just told him something amusing.

Should she:

(a) Drape herself against him, whisper tender words and pout in a seductively adolescent manner – *fa dia*, as Shanghai lovers would say – before leading him into the store so he can buy her the handbag? (Everything in China these days involves straightforward bartering, including personal relations, so he should be used to it.)

(b) Wait for him to suggest that he buy her something from the store, treat her to something luxurious – but then refuse to accept his generosity on the grounds that she is a principled, successful woman and does not need to be spoilt with gifts as if she were just one of those pretty young concubines in search of a rich man to support her?

(c) Walk away from the store and out into the street where, even in this part of town, there are provincial street merchants, men from Xinjiang and other remote parts of China selling cherries spread out on pushcarts, hoping that the change of scenery will encourage him to show her a little affection, as she is beginning to yearn for some physical comfort?

Should he:

(a) Continue to stare impassively at the window display, glad that its dazzle and artistry provides a talking point and a distraction from his reticence, all the time wondering, What does she want from me? Does she genuinely like me?

(b) Be warm but maintain a distance from her, confining his physical contact to the occasional friendly pat on the shoulder or hand gesture that may be interpreted as platonic – until such time as he can be sure she is not just with him for the luxury lifestyle he can offer her?

(c) Accept that she is a high-maintenance woman who needs to be entertained in a particular way, and just go along with her wishes, even if he suspects he is being taken for a ride, for she is strangely charming and amusing, while he is a man who has lost his youth and has been lonely for a very long time? Yes, he has been on his own for too long. After all, everyone says women in Shanghai are complicated and difficult to please. Everyone knows they are *zuo*.

19

箭在弦上
There Can Be
No Turning Back

*W*ooohoooo, Gary shouts into the microphone. *You are so great today, thank you for comiiiing.* This kind of high-voltage showmanship comes so easily to him, he can turn it on whenever he wishes; it is almost as it was in the old days.

The old days. He calls a period of his life just seven months ago 'the old days', as if it were such a long time ago; but in a life such as his, time passes quickly, and China has a way of accelerating time for him, speeding up the ageing process. Whenever he looks at himself in the mirror these days he notices how much he has aged in the last few months. It is not simply the harsh Shanghai pollution or the late-night chats on the internet or the diet of instant noodles that make him look haggard, it is that he is actually growing old very quickly. After years of being indifferent to the passage of time, he now finds he has so much to do in life, and so little time in which to accomplish it. Every second he spends on stage is wasted time, he thinks.

A new week, a new shopping mall: the stages on which he performs nowadays are all tiny, set up to mark the opening of shopping precincts which are springing up everywhere on the outskirts of Shanghai. When he grumbled about this to his agent recently, she pointed out, rightly, that at least he had work these days, and that, slowly, his career might be rebuilt. All he had to do was carry on singing, do what he was good at, and things would fall back into place.

The problem is, he knows that this will not happen – his career will never again be as it was back in the old days. He senses that his time is over. When he says, *Come on, sing along with me, I know you know the words*, no one joins in. In former times, all he had to do was hold the microphone out, pointing it at the audience, and they would break into song. Whenever he said, *Raise your hands and clap*, thirty thousand hands would move in unison; it was as if he was a puppet master, capable of doing anything he wished. Now, no one is interested, not even the tabloid newspapers, which can't muster the energy even to gloat over his being reduced to performing in shopping malls. They were only interested in his fall, not his mediocrity. Only the sensational has a right to exist in the pages of modern life; there is no space for the ordinary.

But it doesn't matter. He has decided that this life of his is over, he has to leave everything behind. He will continue doing these humiliating gigs in order to earn some money, but with the encouragement of his internet friend Phoebe he has been writing his own songs with a view to recording an album. He does not know who will produce or distribute his music – in the past he never had to think about such tedious details, everything was done for him. But all this seems immaterial now, for as Phoebe keeps telling him, even if they have to sell self-made CDs off a pushcart on the corner of Nanjing Lu and Jiangning Lu, or from a stall in Qipu Lu, they will do so. She will personally see to it that his music is a success!

This is the kind of encouragement Phoebe gives Gary every time he is feeling down. She makes him feel that even without the support of a record company and studio mixing equipment, he is still capable of creating beautiful music. She believes in him even though she has never heard any of his songs; her optimism is unshakeable, and this in turn makes Gary feel invincible. He does not need backing singers and musicians; the songs on his new album will consist of just his voice over his own simple piano or guitar arrangements.

Of course Phoebe is unaware of the change in his fortunes. She thinks he is a young musician with no resources who is just starting out with his first album. The other day, in a moment of fatigue, he said:

It's never going to succeed. I can't do this on my own – other people have drummers, bassists, keyboardists, co-writers, great producers. I'm all on my own.

But Little Brother, one day you will have all that!

No, I will never have that.

Well, is that what you really want, anyway? To become like all those idiot pop stars who make fools of themselves?

No, I guess I don't.

Their careers just crash and disappear without a trace; no one really cares about them.

I know.

But you … when you are an old man, you will still be writing and singing great songs … and I will still be listening to them, ha ha!

Ha ha.

She really cheers him up when he is feeling depressed – which, these days, is far less often than before. She shares so much with him, gives so much of herself, that often he feels bad that he continues to hold back so much information. The other day they were talking about the kinds of music they liked, the singers who had inspired them during bad times. They discovered a mutual love of old Chinese love songs that reminded them of the tunes their mothers used to sing to them, which comforted them at times of nostalgia and homesickness. Gary said he was fascinated by jazz, but Phoebe said she didn't understand it. Later, she confessed that she liked pop music, even though she knew a lot of the singers were not very nice people in private. But it didn't matter, because some of their songs were really uplifting and pleasant to listen to in the office at work when things were not going smoothly. She listed the singers she liked: A-Mei, Chang Chen-Yue, Jolin Tsai. Not Jay Chou because he was too coarse, she preferred Wang Leehom, because he was a Quality Idol, and OK, even though they were just pretty boys, some of the songs of Fahrenheit were not bad. The same went for Top Combine, and actually, the last winner of the Super Voice Girl contest was not bad either. Finally, after a pause, Phoebe giggled and said,

I know it's not cool to say this, but … I have to confess …

What?

I used to loooove Gary.

A quick shooting sensation – of excitement, pain, danger, joy – ran through his temples.

Yes, Phoebe continued. When I was working in Guangzhou I used to have a picture of him stuck up next to my bed – you remember his milk powder advert? I tore it out of a magazine so I could look at him every evening. People say he's a pervert, but really I think he is a good person. You could say he kept me company all night, ha ha!

Ha ha.

Ever since that exchange, Gary has known that he will soon have to tell her who he really is. And that is one of the reasons he is so excited and optimistic about the future: he is looking forward not just to his new musical life, but also to revealing himself to Phoebe, to sharing everything with her. The idea of opening himself up to someone else is thrilling. Already he has begun to plan how and when he will do this. Soon, he thinks. He will send her a photo of himself to prove that he really is who he says – not some easy-to-get photo from a milk advert, but something deeply personal.

Imagining this delicious moment of revelation and intimacy makes him so excited that sometimes he can't sleep. He imagines how she will react – almost certainly she will be her customary effusive self (she always expresses her emotions easily), and be over-come with happiness that he has chosen to share such closeness with her. But then she will be practical and sensible as always, she will remind him that even though he has had an extraordinary life, he must concentrate on his new work, the songs he is writing. And his newly revealed identity will change nothing between them. It is he, not she, who will suggest a meeting in real life. She will resist, not because she is coy or intimidated, but because she does not want to appear too eager, or interested in what little celebrity he still has. She will not judge him, but she will not rush to meet him either. She is a person of great integrity. Finally, when they do meet, it will be as if they have known each other forever. They will end up selling his home-made CDs from a stand on a street corner somewhere. They will be happy.

Today's performance is at the Max-Mall in Meilong Town, just outside Amanda KTV, which offers karaoke services to women. Gary's agent thought it would be a good idea to connect with his core fan base, which has always been adolescent girls and young women. But Gary can sense the audience's boredom, and maybe if he looked at them closely he would see the pity they feel for him. Not so long ago – in the old days – it was he who pitied and despised them, but now it is the other way round. There are so many younger, cuter boys flooding the music scene now, like all those insect-thin kids with crazy hairstyles on the talent shows. Young women are no longer interested in Gary; they have moved on. This is the way things work in China, he knows that now: if you stop for one moment, you fall, you disappear. No one remembers you; people want to forget.

He sings the same tunes he always sings at shopping mall gigs – the catchy, sun-filled melodies he sang when he was first starting out. Last night he told Phoebe that he hated his present job, that it made him feel dirty and old. She replied,

We all have to do things that sully us while we wait for our real lives to happen.

This is what he keeps in mind as he goes through the dance routine that accompanies the chorus: two steps to the front, quick twirl, two steps back, forearms swivelling like a penguin's wings. Every time he performed this move at his old concerts, the entire audience would burst into song, and would dance along. Now, he is the only one doing it – a twenty-six-year-old man doing a child's dance routine, singing, *I want to hold your ha-a-and*. It embarrasses him to think that he has spent nearly ten years of his life performing this kind of song in public; he is ashamed that he has not moved on.

At least he will be able to go home and tell Phoebe about this humiliating experience. She will laugh and make jokes about it, and he will feel better. Although he still has not told her exactly what he does, he shares everything he feels with her. He loves sharing experiences with her; she makes it easy for him to talk about things that have happened in his life. Recently they have been exchanging stories of places they've visited, drawing up lists of all the countries they would like to see in the future. He has told her the truth – that he's been to many cities in China and Asia, but that he never gets to see anything because his work schedule is too heavy. Last night, just before signing off, she talked about going to Europe. 'I shall go to sleep dreaming of Paris,' she said. And he felt like telling her about the only time he had ever travelled anywhere on his own, and how exciting it had been. Yes, he will tell her later this evening about that experience – how he had been shooting a music video in London and polishing up some songs at a studio there. When it was over, the day he was due to fly back to Taipei, he bought a cheap ticket to Ibiza instead, because he had read an article about it in the in-flight magazine on the way over. He was only there for two days and a night – one long night, during which he went to a vast open-air club by the beach, surrounded by hundreds of beautiful young men and women from all over the world. The music was so loud that it erased everything inside him: the deep, rhythmic pounding of the bass line filled his head and ribcage, and the tinny notes of the keyboard were like a pulse in his brain, refusing to leave him. The notes and the melody repeated and repeated and repeated, mesmeric in their constancy, replacing his heartbeat, replacing every thought in his head; he did not have to think or feel anything. He danced without being aware of what his body was doing, without caring how he looked. He was just like everyone around him – he could feel the sticky warmth of their bodies, the brush of downy arms on his skin now and then. No one knew who he was, no one cared. At daybreak, when the shirtless boys and the girls wearing sunglasses and cowboy hats had finally gone to bed, Gary sat on the rocks by the water's edge, watching the waves wash delicately onto the sand. He had wondered if he would ever experience such freedom again; but even as he did so, he knew that as long as he continued with his career, he never would. He had held his phone at arm's length, slightly aloft, and taken a picture of himself, the sky behind him stained with the deep amber of dawn.

This is the photo he will show Phoebe tonight, when he finally reveals his true identity to her.

At home after the appearance at Amanda KTV, he takes a long shower – these days he feels dirty even after a short performance – and prepares for the evening's chat with Phoebe. He tidies up the empty instant noodle and takeaway cartons that lie scattered across the living room and wipes down the slightly grimy surfaces of the furniture. He has a quick glance at his laptop: 10 p.m. – she should be coming online sometime soon. He checks his appearance in the mirror, making sure his hair is combed neatly. And he thinks: This is crazy, she isn't even going to see me. But somehow it matters that everything is perfect for tonight's chat.

10.15; she is still not online. He begins to strum on his guitar, playing something he has written recently. He hums the tune – his mind can't settle; he is thinking too much about what he is going to tell Phoebe tonight, all the good news he has. He will need to work up to revealing his identity, he can't do it straight away. He has decided to start by telling her about a great musical opportunity that has come his way, which might change his life entirely. Remember that concert at Red Rooster Hotpot, when the speakers failed and he had to sing without accompaniment? There was a young man in the audience, a guy who owned an underground jazz and folk club who had just happened to be passing by (he was taking his grandmother on an outing); he had thought there was a moving quality to this Gary's voice, a certain sadness. He had spoken to Gary afterwards, and after a few phone conversations had offered him a chance to perform at his club, a tiny place in Hongkou that seated only thirty people – a low-key, acoustic performance to an audience mainly made up of students, artists and writers. Nothing fancy. Gary is very excited, as it will be a perfect opportunity for him to try out the new songs he has been writing with Phoebe's encouragement. Isn't that great?

10.40; she is still not online. Work has been really busy for her recently. She must have been held up at the spa.

He puts down the guitar, keeping the tune in his head, and looks at the lyrics he has written for the song. He changes the order of some of the words, deletes one or two here and there, trying to think of something more suitable. The song is based on a traditional Chinese melody that Phoebe said she liked; his mother also used to sing it to him, and although he himself never particularly loved it, he was moved by this coincidental link with his past, which he took as a sign of something important – a good omen that signalled a happy future for him, which was why he wanted to reinterpret the song. Soon, when he and Phoebe graduate to speaking on Skype or MSN video chat, he will strum her the tune without singing the words and see how long it takes her to recognise it – that will be fun! Because the opening is really unexpected, slower and more modern than the traditional version, and he's sure it will be a while before she realises what song he is playing, and then she will be amazed.

11.30; she is still not online. She's probably gone out with friends after work; perhaps she mentioned it to him, but he forgot.

He looks out of the window. Most of the apartments are dark now, but there are still a few rooms lit by stark overhead lights, and one or two illuminated only by the ghostly glow of the TV screen. There is no movement now; the children have long since gone to bed, and the adults have stopped their karaoke and their magazine reading, and are now dozing in front of the TV. Gary feels very tired all of a sudden, and has to fight the urge to fall asleep on his faux-leather sofa. Before, he would stay awake all night after a big concert, unable to sleep, still buzzing from the evening's performance. But nowadays all he wants to do is come home and chat to Phoebe; and because she is not there, he feels deflated and empty. There is nothing to do but sleep.

When he wakes up it is just before 6 a.m. The sky is lightening, and he can feel the city preparing to burst into life. He looks at his laptop and wonders if Phoebe came online during the night, while he was asleep on the sofa.

It is the same story that evening, and the evening after. He waits all night, but she does not come online.

20

居安思危

Anticipate Danger in Times of Peace

The meeting had not lasted as long as Yinghui had expected. The banker was Singaporean, a woman a couple of years younger than Yinghui who, it turned out, had been at university at the same time as she had (they vaguely remembered each other from the Malaysian and Singaporean Students' Association's monthly meeting). She had moved back to Singapore after graduation, and worked there for a few years for a local bank before being transferred to Shanghai about a year ago.

'That's a long time for Shanghai,' Yinghui remarked. 'Some people don't last more than a couple of months. How are you finding it?'

'Um, OK,' she replied. 'Not bad. A bit stressful.' The corners of her mouth and eyes were pinched, sleep-deprived, despite the veneer of a professional smile and discreet make-up. Yinghui recognised a restlessness in the banker's face, a mixture of excitement and apprehension that people exhibited when still new in Shanghai, in search of something, even though they could not articulate what that something was – maybe it was money, or status, or, God forbid, even love – but whatever it was, Shanghai was not about to give it to them. The city held its promises just out of reach, waiting to see how far you were willing to go to get what you wanted, how long you were prepared to wait. And until you adjusted your expectations to take account of that, you would always be on edge, for despite the restaurants and shops and art galleries and the feeling of unbridled potential, Shanghai would always seem to be accelerating a couple of steps ahead of you, no matter how hard you worked or played. The crowds, the traffic, the impenetrable dialect, the muddy rains that carried the remnants of the Gobi desert sandstorms and stained your clothes every March: the city was teasing you, testing your limits, using you. You arrived thinking you were going to use Shanghai to get what you wanted, and it would take time before you realised it was using you; that it had already moved on, and you were playing catch-up.

'Don't worry,' Yinghui said. 'You'll get used to it eventually.'

The banker had diligently gone through the file, and had double-checked some of the details with her colleagues. Yinghui delivered parts of the speech she had rehearsed, but the banker nodded absently as she spoke, turning the pages of the file as if everything Yinghui said merely confirmed what they both already knew: that hers was a tightly run business with crystal-clear accounts and no sloppy grey areas offering the potential for inefficiency.

'Could you explain a little more about the reasons for wanting a loan? We were all expecting an expansion of your existing business model, or something along similar lines, but the project you've detailed seems to be … quite different in flavour.' She leafed through the pages of the file that Walter had given Yinghui.

'It's a very exciting opportunity,' Yinghui began, 'a truly fascinating and ground-breaking project. Maybe even a first for China.' She proceeded to repeat the contents of the folder, describing the history of the impressive address right in the middle of the city, its potential, etc.

'Who are your business partners for this project?' the banker interrupted.

Yinghui stared at her – perhaps somewhat rudely, she thought, but she could not help herself. Of all the tricky questions she had expected to be asked, this was not one of them. 'It's all there, in that document you're holding.'

The banker continued to look at her, awaiting a response.

'Well, as you can see,' Yinghui said, trying her best not to sound patronising, 'it is an idea developed by the entrepreneur Walter Chao. He's … a friend of mine. There will be other parties, of course, but they will come on board later, once we have decided how we are going to proceed with the venture.'

'We? Oh, so you have a personal relationship with this Mr Chao, then.'

'Walter Chao?' Yinghui raised her eyebrows slightly. She was beginning to be annoyed by the lack of preparation the banker was displaying. 'Of course I do. I'm surprised you haven't heard of him.'

'No, I haven't,' the banker replied flatly, unapologetically. 'Do you have evidence of his track record?'

Yinghui tried not to sigh. She needed a loan from these people, she reminded herself, and until the deal was done, she had to be as charming as possible. 'I've included a sheet on him in the file. It's right there, yes, that page there.'

'But this is a Wikipedia page. From the internet.'

'I thought I'd just give you an introduction.'

The banker turned the pages of the file briskly but carefully, as if checking for something she might have missed. 'I'm sorry, but we're bankers, we like certainty. We like to see official company reports, annual accounts, that sort of thing. We can't base our opinions on Google searches. The internet is, well, not very reliable.'

Yinghui continued to smile. 'Of course. Reputation goes beyond the internet.' She hoped she did not come across as too superior.

'But that's the thing – none of my colleagues have ever come across Walter Chao personally. We are very experienced in the region, but we have no record of ever having dealt with him. We keep extensive files, and are very thorough in our research.'

Yinghui began to doubt whether she wanted a loan from these people. The banker suddenly seemed studious but amateurish, narrow-minded and unimaginative. Yes, she remembered her from university now: a dull, bespectacled girl who never had anything of note to say, who confined herself to her room where she read the books required for her studies (Economics? Management?) and nothing else. 'Maybe he's not yet well known in China.'

The banker closed the file. 'Anyway, it doesn't matter. We were just wondering about his track record when considering the totality of the deal. Your loan application is based on your existing business, not on future projects, so for us it was just a question of whether we believed in you as an entrepreneur, and what you have achieved thus far.'

The totality of the deal, Yinghui thought. What kind of human being spoke like that? She waited for the banker to continue; she didn't think she could keep smiling for much longer.

'Ms Leong, I have to say, I'm full of admiration for what you have accomplished since coming to China. For a sole proprietor to have built up a business as you have is really impressive. And, let's face it, things are still really tough for women. Even in a bank like this … let's just say I know how hard it must have been for you. You have an excellent reputation, and that must have taken a lot of sacrifice.'

Yinghui did not say anything; she found that she was holding her breath – actually holding her breath – while she waited for the banker to say what she was hoping to hear.

'The sum you have requested is a considerable one, but as you seem comfortable proceeding on the basis of a loan secured on the value of your business assets, and as we have the utmost confidence in your business, we are happy to advance you the money on these terms.'

Yinghui nodded. 'Great. Thank you.'

'I have a lot of respect for what you've done. And for you personally. Really.'

'Thank you.'

'I am sure you'll make a success of your new venture. However–' the banker paused. 'You are aware that there are a lot of crooks in China these days trying to make a fast buck.'

'I've been working here for nearly a decade,' Yinghui said coolly – perhaps too coolly. 'I'm well aware of the risks.'

'Of course. It's just that, from the bank's point of view, I would be a bit cautious about your business partners.'

'You mean Walter Chao.'

The banker smiled and arranged her papers into a neat pile. 'All I'm saying is, just be careful.'

Yinghui reciprocated with an equally professional smile, then stood to leave. After the two women had wished each other the best of luck for business and life in Shanghai, Yinghui got into the high-speed lift that carried her silently back down to street level. The banker's final words of advice continued to grate in her head. *Be careful.* It was just what her parents would have said.

That night, she met up with Walter in a restaurant they both knew well, a *faux*-Indonesian place in the middle of Jing'an, where the food was mediocre but the setting – favoured by couples on blind dates – was pleasant, fitting for a quiet celebration. It might remind them of home, Walter said.

'Is that a good thing?' Yinghui joked.

Just as they arrived, Yinghui's mobile phone rang; she could not hear it ringing over the noise of the traffic, but she felt it vibrate in her handbag. She let it ring through. She was about to celebrate a huge milestone in her career, and who knows, a turning point in her personal life; she did not feel like doing business tonight. But then it rang again, the insistent rumble sending shivers up her forearm. Someone wanted to get hold of her, and years of responding to the phone at any time of the day or night made it difficult for her to ignore calls. She had spent too long clutching at straws, grabbing each tiny opportunity, to be able to resist a ringing phone even now. She waved Walter ahead.

The voice on the other end of the line was crackly, as if the person was moving through a rainstorm, though she knew that was impossible: it was a local mobile number, and the weather was balmy and still. It was a man's voice that seemed at once familiar and foreign – someone she should have known but didn't. Every other word was swallowed up by static, making the man's voice sound robotic and dull, machine-like. She realised who it was just as his voice broke free of the fuzzy interference to say his name: Justin Lim.

She stood still for a few moments, listening to the monotone of his voice. It frightened her to think that it could still make her feel like this: alone, belittled and confused, even when he was just delivering pleasantries, making small talk about Shanghai life. She let him speak, interjecting blandly now and then; but the more he spoke the more it became clear to her that he had turned into what he had always been destined to become: a boring middle-aged man. Some people change, others don't, she thought; and suddenly she pitied him, for she had moved on, and he hadn't. He sounded tired and even a little nervous; nothing he said was of any interest to her. His voice belonged to a part of her life that was safely stored away now, an unimportant relic of the past, preserved in a glass box like a minor curiosity in her museum of memories, a place rarely, if ever, visited these days. Even as she spoke to him, she could feel herself striding forward in time, looking to the future as she always did. She had become a completely different person, but he was still the same.

She made her excuses politely, and promised to return his call. When she hung up they both knew, of course, that she would not.

She hurried into the restaurant, where a *kebaya*-clad Indonesian waitress had seated Walter at a table set apart from the others, on the edge of the little artificial lake, which was prettily decorated with lamps that cast a soft glow on the water lilies and rushes. The waitress was chatting to him with a certain degree of familiarity, sharing a joke while handing him the menu. She greeted Yinghui with perfunctory courtesy and unfolded the starched linen napkin on her lap for her.

'You seem to be a regular here too,' Yinghui said.

'Not at all — I just happened to have the same waitress when I came last week. She gave me this table then, too.'

Yinghui suddenly imagined someone else in her place, some-one younger, sitting opposite Walter. The image flashed into her mind without warning: the laughing, over-familiar waitress indulg-ing in a bit of banter with Walter as he waited for a new woman to take her place opposite him. It was ridiculous, she thought; yet she could not get rid of that sneaking suspicion.

'Sometimes I get the feeling you're auditioning me,' she said.

'If I am, you've passed the test with flying colours,' he said, unflustered and genial as usual. 'Important phone call? I hope you're starting to turn away all your suitors now that I've arrived on the scene.' He smiled as he poured her some San Pellegrino. 'Professionally speaking, of course.'

'Of course.'

They ordered their food quickly, and waited in silence for it to arrive. Yinghui felt curiously flat, the way she felt on getting out of a very hot bath – listless and a little sad; she had no appetite what-soever. She pretended to share Walter's nostalgic joy in recalling various meals he had had when he was a child in Malaysia. She was not interested in such recollections, which dragged her towards the past.

'So when were you last here?' she asked.

'Oh, I can't remember. Last week some time. With a client from Shandong. It was pretty dull.'

'I see.'

They ate in polite silence, punctuated by the occasional ques-tion from Walter. Yinghui felt increasingly frustrated by her inabil-ity to shrug off her feeling that a week ago, maybe less, another woman had been sitting in her place. How had he been with that other woman? Calm, solid, as he was now? Or flirtatious and seductive, as she had no doubt he could be. It was ludicrous that she should feel this way – Walter had never even hinted that he was in any way attracted to her other than as a business partner, and yet she felt curiously betrayed. It was her own fault: she had allowed her imagination to run riot. Why? It was unlike her to do so. She had to pull herself together, quickly, and start enjoying this evening, for it was a celebration of a momentous deal.

'You seem a bit tired,' Walter said. 'A bit down.'

Yinghui nodded. 'Yeah. Don't know why – sorry. Guess it's just the come-down after the adrenalin rush of this morning. Even though you know it's going to be horrible, going to see your banker always turns out to be more dispiriting than you expect. They're so anal. I hate the way they think they can control your life.'

'Agreed.' Walter laughed. 'You sure it was nothing to do with that phone call you took? It seemed to change your mood.'

'Of course not, don't be silly. I'm just tired, I told you. Listen – do you think we could skip dessert and go for a walk? It might do me good.'

He raised his hand and signalled for the bill. 'Sure. Shall we take a walk along the Bund? I know it's a cliché, but at this time of the night there won't be many people around, and we might just catch the last of the lights on the skyscrapers.'

'That sounds nice.' It was a lovely idea, a thoughtful suggestion which he clearly knew would make her feel better – often, on late spring evenings, a warm breeze would blow over the Huangpu, making the flags that stood tall on the noble buildings on the Bund flutter tensely; and young couples would stroll hand in hand eating ice cream and taking pictures of each other with their smart new camera phones. It was a perfect setting, and she should have been happy that her companion should be so considerate. But that was the problem: it had sounded casual, but the suggestion seemed too perfect, too calculated in its effect. A fun thing to do: nothing too heavy, a bit cheesy, but with definite romantic overtones – everything was carefully judged. It felt rehearsed, as if he had done it many times; as if he had done it only last week.

They got out of the taxi at Guangdong Lu, and at Yinghui's suggestion went to a bar for a drink before their stroll ('It might perk me up a bit,' she'd said). It was one of those famous Western bars full of glamorous young people, local and foreign, the sort of place where celebrities visiting Shanghai dropped in to enjoy a glass of champagne while enjoying the view of Pudong, and where last year a well-known Taiwanese singer had caused a scandal by getting into a drunken altercation.

In Mumbai or Singapore or Jakarta there would be equivalent places, where groups of young men and women bought magnums of champagne and the music was so loud it drowned out not just all conversation, but all sense of history too – but no other city went so far, so ruthlessly. It was as if the beautiful people who inhabited this world were trying to recreate time and space – and this new universe was the here and now of the shimmering bar, which directed the visitor's eye relentlessly towards a view of the brashest skyline in the world. When you were here you had no choice but to forget the past, and all that you might have been attached to, and for an hour or two believe in what the city wanted you to believe in.

And yet, Yinghui could not get rid of her lingering – and, in fact, now growing – feeling of jealousy. When they stepped into the bar it was crowded and noisy, with a predominantly Western after-dinner crowd; they were greeted by the female Australian manager, who kissed Walter on both cheeks, whispering a joke in his ear which made them both laugh. Walter placed a hand gently, very briefly, on Yinghui's waist, and then they both looked at her, simultaneously. *What do you think of this week's number? Better luck with the latest candidate. Not bad. Could do better.* What were they thinking as they sized her up? Yinghui couldn't help imagining that the secret joke Walter had shared with the manager had somehow involved her, a thought compounded by the manager's over-friendliness when she was introduced to Yinghui. 'So pleased to meet you!' she gushed slickly, emphasising nearly every word.

They were shown to a pair of low, comfortable chairs in a softly lit alcove where the plush furnishings made the music tolerable, and they could just about hear each other speak.

'Right, we need to talk business for a bit, I'm afraid,' Yinghui said. She had decided that this was the only way she was going to shake off her sudden and quite inexplicable feelings of insecurity. Talking about work made her feel as though she was on firm ground again, in control.

Walter frowned. 'I'm sure it can wait till tomorrow. Tonight's meant to be a bit of a celebration.'

'Sure. But maybe we should save the celebration for when the deal is actually done – I mean, contractually tied up, and all parties know exactly where they stand. At the moment there's a lot of vague goodwill, but no clear commitment yet.'

'Vague goodwill? I thought it was crystal clear. And without commitment we wouldn't be here. Why don't we order some drinks and leave work for tomorrow?' He handed her the cocktail menu, which she looked at without enthusiasm.

'Now that I know I have the loan money, I think we should push ahead, just as a tangible sign of partnership. I think it would be a smart move for us both to commit our respective shares into the joint venture company, so we can get things going.'

Walter was still frowning. 'There's no rush, really there isn't. I know how committed you are.'

'What if someone comes along with a better offer while we're still wavering instead of pushing on with our plans? Why hang back when you've got a good feeling about a joint project? How do you know I'm not going to take my new-found finances elsewhere?'

'If that did happen I would be very sad, because I think you are the perfect person for this ... partnership. Yes, I would be very sad.' He raised his hand and signalled to the waiter. 'But there would be nothing I could do about it. If you bail out, you bail out.'

'So you're willing to let me go just like that, huh? Or maybe you don't want me to commit my funds because you don't want to commit yours. Maybe you're actually not very serious. As I said, maybe you're just auditioning several candidates.'

His frown narrowed into a squint, an exaggerated sign of confusion. The waiter arrived and Walter said, 'The usual for me.'

'Same for me,' Yinghui added.

'You know what the position is,' Walter said. 'There will be other parties involved at a later stage – lots of them. But you and I are the ones closest to the project. We are the ones who are going to generate the idea. We are the heart and soul of the deal.'

Yinghui looked out of the window at the lights that flashed garishly across the faces of the skyscrapers across the river. 'Sorry, I'm a bit touchy this evening,' she said after a pause. 'That banker really got under my skin. She said she didn't know who you were, or about any of the projects you've completed. What kind of a banker is she? Such a loser.'

Walter laughed. 'Good to know that my policy of keeping a low profile works well. I try to organise everything through a series of companies, or I use my partners' names. I hate being known.' He looked her squarely in the eye, a hint of a smile still imprinted on his face. 'Those rich people who flaunt their wealth to the whole world … I *detest* them.'

Yinghui nodded. She sensed an earnestness in his regard, the force of his convictions; and suddenly she felt she needed to match his brutal forthrightness, needed to be close to this man who was so honest and direct. 'I agree. I hate publicity-seekers. All this vulgarity …' She gestured at the space around her, at the shiny, moneyed young faces and the silver-gilt décor.

Walter said, 'If it makes you feel better, we can arrange to draw up the paperwork for a proper, solid joint venture tomorrow. My lawyers have already set one up – there are bank accounts poised for action, all the admin is in place. I want you to feel totally secure.'

'I only feel secure,' Yinghui replied, 'when I have security.' She had hoped to appear self-mocking, but her voice sounded hard, over-determined. She paused for a moment before adding, more measuredly: 'I'll pay in my share next week, as soon as the bank deposits the loan money in my account.'

Walter shook his head. 'OK, you do whatever you wish, but as I say, there's really no rush. Of course, if you do so, I'll do the same. Contrary to what you think, I'm not hanging back at all.'

The drinks arrived – two simple flutes of champagne. Walter raised his glass. 'Are we done with business now?' he said.

She laughed. 'Yes. Sorry – you know me, work, work, work. I need to learn to lighten up. We should, um, do some fun things together.' They touched their glasses lightly in a toast. 'Mm, delicious,' she said.

'Krug, 1992,' Walter said. 'Hey, isn't that the actor who plays James Bond? In the grey suit over there.'

Yinghui turned around. 'Don't know – I don't really watch films that much nowadays.'

'We should put that right – go to the movies sometime. I know a wonderful cinema that shows old French films and new underground ones. Every banned film gets at least one screening there.'

'Excellent,' Yinghui replied. 'So many things we can look forward to.'

How to Hang on to Your Dreams – Property Management Case Study, Continued

We got the news about the housing development while I was still up in Kota Bharu. I had decided not to return to Johor just yet because I was worried about my father and wanted to be with him. He had just spent a whole week making rubber replicas of birds' nests – little boat-shaped cups – which he intended to glue to the ceilings of the hotel in order to encourage nesting birds to enter the building once again. I, meanwhile, had been trying to find a job in town, which was not easy. Nik K called round one afternoon.

'Good news for you, Boss,' he said. He was holding a couple of bags of *kacang putih* which he held out to us in an almost ceremonial fashion, as if they were a peace offering. 'Someone is going to buy this place, make all your troubles go away.'

'What troubles?' my father said.

Nik K looked up at the hotel, squinting into the sunlight. 'Everything is still top secret, OK? But it's going to be in the papers soon. This whole area is going to be transformed – big company from KL going to buy up all the land and build a new housing estate.'

We listened patiently as he told us of plans to redevelop nearly two thousand acres of countryside stretching south of town, as well as some of the run-down outskirts which included the old workshops and small godowns that formed the warren of streets around our property. Where the Tokyo Hotel now stood, there would soon be gardens and newly paved roads lined with ornamental bushes leading to long streets of single-storey link houses arranged in grids, hundreds and hundreds of them, each one identical, with a front garden behind a chain-link fence. There would be clusters of shop-houses dotted around the estate, where the residents would find sundry shops and laundries and hairdressers – all the modern conveniences people needed in this day and age.

'But,' my father said, interrupting Nik K's lengthy explanation, 'that means they are going to tear down this building also, ah?'

Nik K stared at him for a while, trying to figure out if he had understood anything at all. In the end, Nik K did not have to reply. My father turned away; he had indeed taken aboard everything Nik K had said. His question had not really been a question, but a distillation of Nik K's news. The hotel was going to be torn down: everything else – the development, the shops, the modern amenities – did not matter to my father.

'What about compensation?' I asked. 'How much are we going to be paid?'

Nik K shrugged. 'The land is being bought by the government – compulsory purchase scheme. You know what that means?'

I nodded.

'You will get fair money,' Nik K said.

'What is "fair"? What does that mean?' my father asked.

'It means enough-*lah*,' Nik K said, before getting into his Datsun and driving off.

Secretly, I was not displeased. I was even excited by this unexpected development. Someone was going to pay us for a building that was a wreck, a no-hope project that would surely ruin my father. I would no longer have to try to persuade him to sell it, for now we had no choice but to do so. The government wanted the land, and it would have it; there was no argument to be made.

We got the letter a few weeks later, stating the date by which we had to vacate the property and the amount of money we were to receive. I stood with the piece of paper in my hand, checking the number of zeros in the compensation sum by placing the tip of a pencil under each one, just to be sure I was not making a mistake. The price of the hotel was to be *less* than it had been when my father bought it over a year previously – in fact we were being paid just a third of its original value; nowhere near enough to cover the debt my father had taken on to buy it in the first place.

Still, I said to my father, we had no choice. The government had ordered the purchase of the land; there was nothing we could do to fight against it. It was true, we were being offered very little money, but at least it was something – we couldn't ask for any more. I knew it was not a good situation, but it would enable us to escape the Tokyo Hotel and make a fresh start somewhere else; a modest life that would suit us. We were not made for a life of wealth; we would never know how to be millionaires. We were made to be humble; it suited us. We could cut our losses and run. To our debtors we could plead bad luck: the government wanted the land, what could we do? Now that a return to a simple life had suddenly become a real possibility, I could not think of anything else. I urged my father to sign the papers as soon as possible: take the money, start anew, be content.

'But it's not fair,' my father repeated over and over again, as if that was all the reasoning he needed. Even as my desire to abandon the hotel grew, his obsession with completing his fledgling business became stronger, and I knew his will would prevail. For this is what I have always known about my father: his ambitions have a persuasive, almost transformative quality; he makes you believe in him, he absorbs you into his fantasies, even when all logic tells you that he will fail. I guess it is because we all want to live in hope rather than in despair, even when despair is all that we have – all that we are entitled to.

He began to bombard me with calculations of profits we could make in less than a year, persuading me that we would be comfortable in no time at all, and then all I wanted – a nice modern house, a small car, enough money to go on trips to Penang or Singapore – would be easily attainable. As long as we could keep the hotel, we would be fine. It was ours; we would make it work. He would go and speak to Nik K again, try to find a way of saving our property. If all else failed, we would organise a protest, show the entire world how unfair the whole business was. But Nik K seemed never to be around all of a sudden. His colleagues said he'd gone down to KL, that he had a lot of business there, that maybe he was getting a promotion – they didn't know.

Every week we would get a new letter reminding us of the deadline. We had to sign the documents soon, and then vacate the property, otherwise we would get nothing. Every day, my father cycled into town to find Nik K, but he was never there. Eventually he got hold of him by phone; he was in Terengganu on holiday with his kids. There was nothing he could do, he said: he was just a clerk. But sure, this was a free country – if my father wanted to complain or protest, he could do so.

'Who do I speak to?'

'I don't know,' Nik K replied. 'But the developer is a company called LKH Properties – there, you know, that Chinese company. Old man Cecil Lim Kee Huat and his sons and grandsons, rich *towkays* down in KL. The fat youngest son comes up here often. He's the big boss in charge. Anything else, don't ask me.'

21

拾人牙慧

Adopt Others' Thoughts as Though They Were Your Own

They had just finished dinner one Saturday evening, and were about to go and look for a jazz bar somewhere in Luwan that Phoebe had read about. It was already quite late, about 10.30. After they had got into the car Walter said, 'Oh, sorry, would you mind if we stopped by my apartment quickly? I've left my Hong Kong mobile phone there, and I just need to check it for messages. I'm in the middle of a business deal, you see.'

Phoebe thought at once, Aha, this is a seduction technique.

They had been going out for over two months now, so she had been expecting him to attempt something like this any time now. Even a man with sexual problems could surely not resist her attractions for this long. It was not that she herself desired more intimate relations – she still found Walter sexually blank, like a page with no words, impossible to read. It was just that all her books had told her that a healthy sexual relationship was the key to keeping your man, and recently she had started to worry that if she did not make him addicted to her feminine charms, he would begin to look elsewhere. All the girls at the spa agreed that this was not a good situation. They asked Phoebe whether he had proposed to her yet, whether she had moved in with him – and she realised that up to this point she had not succeeded in obtaining anything from him at all, apart from a few luxury fashion items and expensive meals in restaurants; and those would not support her in old age.

Even though he was not a soulmate, she knew she had to get closer to him, maybe get enough money to buy a car or an apartment, or a lease on a shop where she could start her own business. She would be happy being his mistress; she didn't care if he had someone else, as long as her future was secure. So she began to drop certain hints, such as leaving her hand on his arm for longer than usual whenever she greeted him, and pressing herself closer to his body when they hugged goodbye. Once she pretended to have a small tear in her tights just as she got into the car, so she could lift the hem of her skirt and expose her thigh. She was sure that before long he would find an excuse to get closer to her.

'It'll only take a few minutes – sorry.' He said it very casually, as if he really had forgotten his mobile phone. His brow was even wrinkled with a worried look, but she could not be fooled so easily.

'Sure,' she said. 'I'm not working tomorrow anyway – it's Sunday, my day off, remember?'

'Yes, otherwise I wouldn't suggest going out this late – I'd make sure you were home in bed early.'

Even though she was a little concerned about how she would respond to his sexual advances, she was excited because this would be the first time she had visited his apartment. They had driven past the building once, a discreet eight-storey condominium just south of Xintiandi Public Garden, which everyone knew was where rich foreigners lived, especially single men with large disposable incomes who wanted to be close to Western-style entertainment facilities. When he had pointed it out, she had wondered for a second if he was lying, if he was just a fantasist who made up stories about himself, or even worse, a fake like her, whose story was entirely believable yet entirely untrue.

But now, as they drove up to the building, she realised that her fears had been unfounded. They paused while the electronic gates opened very slowly. People who live here lead leisurely lives, Phoebe thought; even their gates open gracefully, unhurriedly. As the car passed through she caught the eye of one of the security guards, a young man barely past his teens. He looked at her with a wide-eyed expression of admiration, even fear, of something he would never be able to obtain. She saw herself through his eyes: the beautiful girlfriend of a millionaire, the kind of expensive, classy woman who strolled into hotels and restaurants as if blown in by a warm breeze, the kind of woman who would be rude to you without even knowing it, and you wouldn't mind her rudeness because she was pretty and rich, and you were nothing. As she caught his gaze and held it for a heartbeat, then two, she felt a great distance opening up between her and him. She felt as if she was perched on the top of a mountain and he was sliding away, down the rocky slope to the river valley below. And as he fell, he seemed to drag a part of her with him. She felt not just the great chasm between them, but also distanced from herself. She thought, Maybe this boy is my soulmate, maybe he is the one the fortune-teller spoke of, the romantic person I will spend my life with. She blinked, and cleared his image from her mind. No, he was not the soulmate she was searching for. He was nothing to her.

Walter drove down into the underground parking lot, the car's tyres squealing on the smooth polished concrete floor. As she walked with him to the lift she noticed that the air was fresh, and smelled of flowery perfume, unlike the stink of fumes and burnt rubber that filled most car parks. She pressed the 'up' button outside the first lift, but Walter beckoned her over to another, more discreet lift. When its doors opened she saw that it was lined with glossy wood. Walter inserted a card into a slot, tapped in a few numbers, and the doors closed. There were only three floors marked: 'B1', 'G', then, much higher up, 'P'.

Phoebe thought, I am going to a real-life *penthouse*.

When the lift doors opened, all she could see was the city arranged in front of her, sparkling, framed by darkness. As they walked into the apartment the lights came on automatically and she saw that there was a wall of glass that stretched from floor to ceiling. She walked up to it and looked down at the tops of the trees, so close that she felt she could reach out and touch them.

They looked soft and velvety in the warm early-summer breeze. Some people were taking their dogs for a late-night walk around the lake in the park. A tiny, delicate brown puppy with legs like matchsticks leapt up to a sausage-shaped dog with huge floppy ears and ran in excited circles around it. Phoebe could not hear it, but she could see that it was yapping as it played. An old couple strolled past the dogs, their arms linked at the elbows. The branches of the trees caught the wind, and as they fanned across the light from the street lamps their shadows cast pretty patterns on the pavements, flower shapes that danced and swirled then disappeared.

Phoebe could hear Walter somewhere behind her in the apartment, his voice sounding urgent as he spoke on the telephone in a businesslike tone she had not heard from him before. She turned and walked slowly around the huge space. There was barely any furniture in it, just two chairs placed at an angle to each other and, at the far end of the room, a dining table with no chairs. Halfway along, an aquarium was built into the wall, lit with a blue glow. There were no carpets anywhere, no rugs or cushions or anything soft. Phoebe's heels made a clacking noise on the floor that echoed so loudly she did not dare to walk quickly. When she reached the far end of the room she paused at the dining table. There was an empty Starbucks cup on it that filled the air with a stale coffee smell, and on the side of the cup was a mark where some coffee had spilled over, like a long brown tearstain. She peered through a door and saw a kitchen that was about three times the size of the room she shared with Yanyan, with a grey floor and cabinets made of smooth steel. There was no food to be seen, no stray plastic bags or washing-up liquid, just a coffee machine and a fridge made of the same cold steel as the cabinets. It reminded Phoebe of some of the factories she had worked in, only much cleaner.

She turned and walked back to the middle of the room, and looked out at the view. She thought, If I lived here I wouldn't know where to look. It frightened her to see the city like this, to be reminded of how big it was, and to know it would only get bigger and bigger. She wished there were curtains or blinds, but no, there was only the vast expanse of glass which did not hide anything. She could see Shanghai, Shanghai could see her.

She turned around. There was nowhere to sit except those chairs, like two small islands in the middle of a cold, cold ocean. It did not look as if anyone lived in this apartment. Phoebe suddenly thought, Maybe this is just a pretence. Maybe this place isn't really his. Maybe I've been duped.

She walked over to the aquarium. Inside, it looked like a painting, the rocks and coral arranged to look like mountains in an old watercolour landscape. When she was close to it she noticed two streams of fine bubbles rising from the gravel bed, the only movement she could see. There appeared to be no fish in the tank. She pressed her face close to the glass and peered in between the rocks – she saw the tip of a long, feathery tail, but could not make out a body.

'There used to be loads of fish, but they all died,' Walter said, startling her as he walked across the room towards her. He stood next to her and tapped the glass firmly with his knuckle. 'All except this one, who's still hanging on in there.'

A long, oval-shaped fish wriggled out of the rocks and drifted in the water for a few seconds, as if it was lost. It had markings on its side like ink spots, a large stain on its tail in the shape of a wide-open eye, and long tendrils trailed from its gills. Then it dived, darting to the bottom of the tank to hide behind a piece of coral.

'That's not a sea fish,' Phoebe said. 'That type lives in ponds and streams.'

'Are you an expert on fish?' Walter asked. 'You sound very knowledgeable.'

'No, I just know that kind of fish because it's really common in the ponds around where I grew up. The boys used to catch them and sell them to the aquarium shops in town.'

'In Guangzhou? I didn't know there were any ponds left there that were unpolluted enough to have fish in them.'

'Yes. In Guangzhou,' Phoebe said. She caught sight of her reflection in the glass, hovering against a background of coral and blue-tinged water. And she thought, It's so obvious I'm lying. I have the expression of a liar.

'Right, Guangzhou,' Walter said. Phoebe could tell he was smiling, even though his reflection was watery and dim. 'You know, you're unlike any Guangzhou girl I've ever met – you're funny.'

'Listen,' she said, 'it's getting a bit late. Do you mind if we just have a drink here?'

'Sure,' Walter said, shrugging his shoulders. She could see that he had a mobile phone in each hand. 'I don't mind either way, it's just that you seemed very keen on that jazz bar.'

Looking down at her feet, she smiled, then raised her eyes to meet his. It was a technique she had learnt from a book. It gave her a seductive look that men found irresistible. She had practised it in front of a mirror, and then with Yanyan until they agreed that she had fully mastered it. 'But you haven't given me a tour of your apartment yet. It's so, so … big and impressive.' She reached forward, and with one finger lightly touched the top button of his shirt, close to his collarbone. His face reddened, changing colour rapidly, like a chameleon. Phoebe thought, He's probably taken Viagra or something, that's why he's blushing so easily.

'Of course. What would you like?' said Walter as he walked to the kitchen. 'Tea? Coffee? I don't know if I have herbal tea.'

She followed him. 'Do you have cognac? I like Hennessy X.O. Or whisky. I'm in the mood for something *strong*.'

Walter opened a cabinet, but it was empty. 'Sorry, I don't spend much time here, so I don't know where everything is.'

Phoebe joined him in searching. She opened a cabinet filled with plates. None of them matched – they were all different kinds, cheap plastic ones mixed in with porcelain and china. Nearly all of them were marked with some brand or another – Nescafé, petrol, cornflakes, soya milk, Horlicks – the kind of thing you get for free if you cut out enough vouchers and send them off to the address on the back of the packet.

'Found the glasses,' Walter said. He produced two crystal tumblers, but Phoebe could see that the cabinet from which he took them was full of cheap plastic mugs. One of them had a picture of a cartoon movie character on it. She had been to see the film in Guangzhou more than a year ago, but she could not remember its name.

As he poured cognac into the glasses she said, 'Do you live here on your own?'

'Of course I do,' he said. 'No one would want to live with me.' He chuckled softly, but he was not smiling. Phoebe did not know whether it was meant as a joke; she did not know if she should laugh.

'Everything here is yours, then?'

'Yes. There isn't much though, just stuff I've picked up over the years.'

With their glasses in hand, they walked back to the living room. 'Are you going to give me a tour of the apartment, then?' Phoebe asked, giving him the head-down-eyes-up seductive look again. When she lowered her head she could smell the strong perfume of the cognac in the glass. She took a sip and felt the alcohol burn her throat, flowing down, down to the base of her stomach.

'There isn't much else to see, this is pretty much all of it. There's only one bedroom, believe it or not. I had it designed that way.'

Phoebe laughed. 'So I'm not allowed to see the bedroom?'

Walter shrugged. 'If you must. But I warn you, it's a real mess, because I haven't had time to clean up. My *ayi* doesn't come on weekends, so the place is quite dirty. I didn't think anyone would be seeing it.'

He opened a dark sliding door and stood to one side. Phoebe peered inside – a large room with an unmade bed facing the window. On the bedside table and on the floor next to the bed were piles of books. Some of them looked familiar. Phoebe walked across to look at them.

'I wouldn't go in if I were you,' Walter called out. 'It's really messy in there. The sheets haven't been changed all week.'

Phoebe picked up a few of the books. Some of them were in English, others in Chinese.

Get Rich in a Crisis
How to be Classy
How to be Successful: Tips from Billionaires
How to Meet Your Dream Partner
Broken Wings, Broken Dreams: How to Mend Your Inner Self

She pretended not to pay any particular attention to these books; instead she ran her hand over the rumpled bedsheet. 'Mm, you have very high-quality bed products.' She did not say that she had one or two of the books herself, did not say that she had spent many hours in bookshops reading such books, that she had seen some of these ones on the pavement stalls near Qipu Lu, that there was a time not so long ago when she couldn't afford even those pirated copies. At the bottom of one pile she saw a copy of the book she had discovered in Guangzhou a long time ago, the book written by that elegant older woman who had first inspired her to become the successful person she was today. It reminded her of why she had come to Shanghai. It was called *Secrets of a Five Star Billionaire*.

'Most of the books aren't mine,' Walter said. He was still standing by the door. 'I just borrowed them from friends.'

'There are a lot of them,' Phoebe said. She knelt down and tried to ease *Secrets of a Five Star Billionaire* from the bottom of the pile. 'Surely you haven't read every one?'

'Of course not. Actually, I'm just using them for reference. You see, I'm writing a book myself, a book about how to be successful. Based on my own life experiences. That's why I need so many books, to see what my competitors are doing.'

A few books toppled over as Phoebe extricated *Secrets of a Five Star Billionaire* from the pile. Its cover was worn, the spine creased. She sat on the bed and slowly turned its pages: many were dog-eared, the corners folded over in small, precise triangles. There were neatly written notes in the margins everywhere, and at least two sentences on every page had been carefully underlined with a pencil and ruler. 'I know this book,' she said. 'The woman who wrote it is really amazing.'

'Oh, but I wrote it,' Walter said. 'Under a pseudonym. I just hired an actor to make the video for me.'

'Liar!' Phoebe laughed. 'You think I can be fooled so easily? You're just telling stories to try to impress me.'

'It's true. Why else would I have a book like that?'

At first she thought he was lying to her, trying to trick her into believing he was the author of the book that had changed her life so she would have sex with him. But he looked so solemn, almost sad, that she was not so sure. Maybe he did write it – surely a rich man like him wouldn't need to buy a life manual. Whatever the truth was, the book seemed to have brought him no joy, she thought. She had gained so much from reading it, but none of these books had given him anything.

He sat next to her on the bed. He was looking red and flushed again. Phoebe could feel the alcohol beginning to pulse in her temples. Her face felt hot, and she wondered if her cheeks were turning pink too.

'Walter,' she said, 'why do you have so many shitty cheap plates and cups? Can't a man like you afford better stuff?'

He shrugged. 'Not sure. Just habit. We always used to do that at home, me and my dad. He loved collecting vouchers and exchanging them for plates, pens, anything. Everyone did that back then, where I come from. We couldn't afford nice things – those glass dishes, they were luxury items. You won't know what I mean; you're too young, a different generation. All you eighties kids, all you've known is this' – he gestured towards the glass wall, the view of Shanghai, its lights stretching infinitely. 'Look at you. You young Mainlanders are young and beautiful and affluent. You have the world at your feet. You haven't known any other life. You're so full of self-confidence. That's why you're so desirable, that's why all those rich men from Hong Kong and Singapore want a young Mainland concubine. It's not just that you're pretty, it's because you make the future seem limitless. That's why tired old men covet you. But I … I'm different. And so are you. You and I, we don't belong here.' He laughed a little and lay back on the bed, staring at the ceiling. He was still holding his glass, but Phoebe noticed it was empty.

'Yes,' she said. 'I know you're different.'

'These dreams that men seek – they are so easy, but so … harsh. I hate this harshness. Everything is so cruel. Everyone uses everyone else. Even me. I wish there could be a bit of tenderness. I think of the stupid small towns I grew up in. I remember the young women – they didn't know how to dress, they just wore cheap casual clothes all the time. Even when they made an effort to smarten themselves up for a wedding or something they looked bad. They didn't know how to behave like classy Shanghai girls, they didn't have any sophistication. But I liked that. No one pretended to be anything or anyone grand, unlike today. Sometimes I think: I hate China. I hate the whole world.'

Phoebe nodded. He placed his fingers over his brow, rubbing his forehead. He blinked once, twice, and his eyes became glassy and hollow. Then she felt his hand searching for hers, but she did not offer it, she kept it tucked under her thigh.

'Where I grew up,' he continued quietly, his voice becoming lower the way it did whenever he became emotional, 'it's a million miles from Shanghai. Rural Malaysia is really shit. It hardens you, warps you, but even so, you never really change. You understand what I mean. I know you do. That's why I feel close to you, because I don't have to explain myself to you.'

Phoebe wanted to say, Yes, I know exactly what you mean. I know exactly what you mean because I have lied to you for two months. There is not one aspect of myself that I haven't lied about. As the words ran through her head she was filled with a sudden feeling of joy – she saw her whole future open up ahead of her, a life in which she was always joking with him about how lousy their lousy villages were, about whose village was poorer and dirtier – a life in which they were living together, filling this empty apartment with nice furniture and memories of small towns in rural Malaysia. They would joke about the cheap clothes she used to wear, the fake handbags she had when she couldn't afford the real thing, the vulgar, slutty way she used to dress. The person she used to be, until recently. But maybe it was too late; she couldn't turn back now. The fake Phoebe had become too much a part of the real one; their histories were the same now, there was no difference between them. Walter would never be able to accept the lies and the cheating, the life of a low-class KTV hostess and migrant worker. He would always look down on her if he knew the truth. There was no way out for her – she had to continue being the Phoebe she had turned herself into.

'But you're a successful man now,' she said. 'The past doesn't matter.'

He sighed softly and closed his eyes. Creases formed around his mouth. He looked half smiling, half in pain, as usual. 'I know you understand me. We are very similar.'

She kissed him on the forehead and lay down next to him. His skin was warm and slightly greasy, and smelled faintly of wet leaves.

As she lay on the bed, the ceiling looked watery above her. She said, 'Brandy really gives me a headache.'

22

时过境迁

Boundaries Change
with the Passing of Time

W hy was it that he could not bring himself to get in touch with Yinghui, Justin wondered. Simple: it was because he was nothing now; he was no one. Yes, that was the brutal truth. It had nothing to do with the tangled way in which their pasts were enmeshed, like fishermen's nets washed up on shore after a storm – if anything, their recent meeting had offered him a chance to set things right, to explain if not to rectify past events. She and CS used to talk about 'closure' and how worthless it was – why is it that everyone these days needs resolution, why can't they just accept that life is messy, that it never works out neatly? American movies were to blame, they said. But Justin knew that he needed 'closure'; he needed things to be final.

What stopped him from ringing her now was his lack of achievement. He had done little with his life, and had now been reduced to absolute zero. On at least half a dozen occasions he had stood with his phone in his hand, her card on the table before him, the number already tapped out. All he had to do was press the green button and she would be there. What would he say then? How would he fill the spaces in the conversation, if not with tales of what he was doing in Shanghai, descriptions of success? He would have loved to be able to say, 'Didn't you hear? Well, yes, I've been running an art gallery for five years now, showing a few avant-garde Chinese artists.' Or, 'I moved into film production a few years back. Yes, I gave up the family business completely.'

'Why do you need to impress her?' Yanyan said one night as she and Justin sat on the front steps of the building, as they often did. She was wearing her Hello Kitty pyjamas and furry slippers with bunny heads on them, even though the night was warm and still, almost muggy. 'If she's the sort of woman who can be won over by money and status, is she really worth it?'

'It's not about that – she doesn't care about such things. It's about showing her the kind of person I really am. How I've changed.'

'Maybe she's changed too. People are like that.'

'No, I'm sure she's the same. With some people, you just know.'

'Are you sure you've changed? Because people always think they do, but really, they don't. Chinese people especially. Everyone talks about change, change, change. You open a newspaper or turn on the TV and all you see is CHANGE. Every village, every city, everything is changing. I get so bored with it. It's as if we're possessed by a spirit – like in a horror film. Sometimes I think we're all on drugs. I used to speak to foreigners on the phone at work; all they would say was, "I hear things are changing really fast over there." It's as if everyone here is addicted to change. But, really, how much have we changed? I'm still the same. I haven't changed since I was six years old. And I don't want to.'

He remained silent for a second or two, looking at the skyscrapers shimmering in the night. It was true what people said: the only thing that never changed in Shanghai was that it was always changing.

'But I have to do something about this … friend from my younger days,' he said. 'Whether or not I've changed.'

'Yes, I understand. You have unfinished business with her, that's clear. Go ahead, do it. Then you'll see that probably neither of you has changed. But first, could you buy me some red-bean ice cream?'

The next day Justin rang an old contact. He'd recently read about a former security guard at one of the condominium complexes his family had owned, a boy called Little Tang who had always been fiddling with a camera. In just two years he had built a reputation as a fashion photographer; now he was starting a venture turning disused factories into temporary studio spaces that young photographers and artists could rent for a week, a month, three months – however long it was before the site was demolished or converted to some other use. Justin had seen an article about him in one of those English-language listings magazines that lay in messy piles in all the Western cafés. The photographer went by the name David Tang now, a short, plumpish young man with an amiable smile, hair styled in a deliberately unkempt fashion, dressed in sleek, all-black clothes that the article called his 'signature style'. His name was still in Justin's phone. 'Boss, call me if ever you need me, day or night,' he'd once said. 'Need' was a changeable notion – back then he'd meant, if your lightbulbs need replacing or you need a new driver; now what Justin needed was a whole new career, a new life.

They went for a drink in a small hotel in the area real-estate agents nowadays called the Southern Bund, where the old docks used to be. It was being redeveloped: cranes dangled over the water, dust hung in the air, making the river seem blurry even in the spring sunshine; already there were hoardings for a Starbucks. Justin had difficulty finding the hotel – it looked unfinished, the cement rendering on the outside fallen away to reveal the brickwork underneath. Inside, in what must have been the foyer, were bare brick walls scarred by generations of water leaks and rust, exposed steel beams, staff wearing shapeless grey felt uniforms. He found Little Tang in the bar, sitting on a black-and-white cowhide sofa drinking a bottle of Qingdao.

It took them just a few minutes to discard the master–servant relationship of old. Little Tang – David – was warm, jocular and familiar. Any respect he showed Justin was due to the difference in age, not in status. No mention was made of David's past employment under Justin, apart from a quick reference to the smart new clothes he wore. Justin thought: only in China could people deal so swiftly with the past; only in China could they forget and move on without blinking. They talked instead about David's current projects: his forthcoming cover for *Vogue* China, his booming business, which he called 'guerrilla rentals', his new girlfriend, a razor-hipped model from Dongbei whose photos he showed Justin on his iPhone; she was six feet tall.

'So, Boss, what can I do for you?' He used the word 'Boss' differently now – playfully, almost ironically, as he might do every morning with the man who ran the fried-bread stall, or the janitor who cleaned the toilets.

'I'm not sure,' Justin replied. 'I just thought, maybe there was some way we could … work with each other. With my experience, I could be useful to you in some way – though I'm not sure how.'

David leant over and slapped Justin on the knee. 'Excellent idea, Boss!' He raised his hand and called to the waitress for two more beers. 'This is a good moment for both of us. I heard your family went bankrupt. That means you'll be free to take part in lots of new projects. Now, what could we do together? You don't want to run my rentals business for me, do you? No, too boring. We could start a publishing company – publish fashion magazines for Chinese people. Not just *Vogue* or *Elle* and all that rubbish, but arty ones. No, not serious enough for you. Let's think about this. So many possibilities!'

He had dealt with Justin's situation in one short, matter-of-fact sentence – *I heard your family went bankrupt.* And that was it. They had now moved on to the present, surging ever forward. No questions as to why, how come, how do you feel, etc. He wasn't interested in all that, only in what Justin could do for him now. History held no allure for him; all answers lay in the future.

'Well, for a start I could look after your rentals business, and we can think of new ventures for the future.'

'Really? But it's very boring. You'd be almost like … an office manager. That's too lowly and ordinary for you.'

'I'm not worried by that,' Justin said. 'I'd like to do it.'

'That's too crazy!' David Tang cried, laughing loudly in a series of hooting look-at-me bursts. Justin knew it was an affectation he had picked up recently, cultivated in the glamorous fashion circles in which he now moved; he had been a soft-spoken boy before. 'I'm going into business with Boss Lim – that's too crazy. We need to celebrate!'

They went to a Guizhou restaurant and ordered far too much food – at least five or six cold starters and eight or ten main dishes. Every time Justin urged restraint, David Tang said, 'This is completely my treat! We are going into business together, why should we hold back?' He ordered a bottle of Johnnie Walker Black Label; waitresses dressed in colourful ethnic costumes kept coming into the private room with buckets of ice and cold towels scented with chemical jasmine perfume. Justin had never had Guizhou food before; it was unexpectedly spicy. But when he reached for some water he realised that every glass on the table now had whisky in it. He looked at the bottle – it was two thirds empty. They had had a few bottles of beer before leaving the hotel, and a couple more on arrival at the restaurant. It felt like old times: all those long nights entertaining business partners and prospective clients. That was why Justin had been useful to the family in the role of fixer – he was sensible and he could hold his drink, just as Sixth Uncle could before him.

He looked at David Tang, whose jolly round face had turned scarlet from the drink. At this stage in the evening it was no longer important what either of them said; what would count was the impression of camaraderie, of beery bonding, which both men would remember the next day – a hazy memory of trust and openness. He smiled and muttered a pleasantry as Little Tang – David Tang – filled his glass again.

After the restaurant David insisted on joining some friends at a KTV place down the road. He loved karaoke, and was very good at it, he said. Justin had learnt to tolerate it – he had had to spend a fair bit of time at karaoke bars in his earlier days, when he was just starting out in the family business and had to entertain contractors, builders and low-level salesmen – the kind of working man who made the business tick at its most basic level. In the years since, he had left that kind of entertaining behind, but now, since he was back at that level again – perhaps even lower down, a mere employee – he said yes. Why not, he thought. It was entirely appropriate. But as soon as he walked into the dim, fabric-lined room, the muffled off-key singing from the other rooms and the rough-edged cries of drunk men made him remember why he had always hated the ambience of karaoke bars, why every evening he had ever spent in such establishments had been an evening of wasted life.

'Don't be such a damn snob,' Sixth Uncle had once told him as they were going into a karaoke bar. It was on one of their trips up north to visit their flagship project, a huge residential development on the outskirts of Kota Bharu, a two-thousand-acre piece of land – old shop-houses, paddy fields, scrubby forests and *kampung* houses cleared away to create neat lanes of identical single-storey link houses. Not cheap, not expensive – perfect for villagers wanting to live in a modern house, or young men who worked on the offshore oilrigs. It had been Justin's first big deal, a long and complicated affair that had dragged on for some years, but he had shown himself more than capable of handling the sticky matter of convincing local officials to grant permission for the felling of trees or the conversion of agricultural land to residential use. He had been affable – more innocent in his late twenties than he was now – and his charm made those officials believe that anything he asked was in good faith; that the gifts he gave them were out of the goodness of his heart and not an attempt at bribery; that all his plans were for the benefit of the local community. The project went ahead, and eventually flourished in spite of the numerous little hitches that continued long after the first residents moved in – protests by aggrieved former villagers, regional officials who had to be constantly flattered with gifts and dinners, maintenance problems arising from the marshy ground in some parts of the development. Every year, Sixth Uncle would insist on travelling up north to inspect the site and take the local contractors out for a night's entertainment.

'But that means … women,' Justin protested, shaking his head.

'Don't be such a fucking prude,' said Sixth Uncle. 'How many years have I been training you? *Aiya*, you're so frustrating! You do a great job, but you can't follow it through. I keep telling you, this side of the business is just as important as all the high-level finance stuff. You've got to keep the boys on our side.'

And so they had had a big meal at a Chinese restaurant where there'd been shark's-fin soup and only X.O.-and-Coke to drink, and afterwards they had stumbled into Ichiban Karaoke Bar – Justin remembered the name because he was struck by the sign on the door, written in a surprisingly elegant hand – which Sixth Uncle had hired in its entirety for the night ('Until daybreak, no problem,' Justin heard the manager say to Sixth Uncle). While the other men sloped into darkened corners accompanied by various women, Justin sat at the bar with Sixth Uncle.

'You've got to get off your ass with the New Cathay site,' Sixth Uncle said. 'Four months already, and nothing's happened. The longer you leave it, the harder it'll get. Look what's happened already with your brother's girlfriend and her bunch of heritage-building friends. All their stupid campaigns in the press, written by their tame journalists. Bunch of bloody faggots. They think they're in Europe or what? Saving old buildings, my foot. *Ei*, this is Malaysia, my friend! They're wasting their time, but still, we can do without it.'

Justin could barely hear what Sixth Uncle was saying; a man and woman were singing a duet – 'Don't Go Breaking My Heart' – but the man was drunk and couldn't keep up with the music, kept missing the beat and misreading words, and breaking into laughter instead. *I doe go breakin' my haaarrr, ha ha ha …*

'Come on, boy,' Sixth Uncle continued, pressing his forehead against Justin's. Justin could smell the sour stench of garlic and alcohol on his breath. 'I got faith in you. Is that a song title? I got faith in you. I've told your dad, give you more time. But you have to think of something to replace the New Cathay with – fast. Don't let those spoilt Bangsar kids screw things up for you. You remember, years ago, in Japan, I told you your brother is a good-for-nothing? I was right, wasn't I? Look at him, letting his girl-friend twist him round her little finger. Screw the both of them. You'll sort them out, *ya*? Promise? Good boy.'

As Sixth Uncle vanished into the shadows Justin wondered how much longer he would have to stay before he could slip away unnoticed. He thought of what Yinghui and CS would be doing at that precise moment, a quarter to midnight on a Saturday evening. They would be in the café Yinghui had just opened, spread out on comfortable sofas listening to Lou Reed or Cuban music, chatting about films and travel and love. She would be sitting with her legs on his lap, her bare feet tapping to the rhythm of the music as she talked; she would not even be aware that her feet were moving. If Justin had been there he would have been watching her, noticing again how her second toe was far longer than her big toe, how she had a habit of curling her feet into tight arcs every now and then, particularly when she laughed. Every so often she would get up and make herbal tea from plants that Justin had either never heard of before, or didn't think were even drinkable, like nettles; or Indian *chai*, which they served in the café, inspired by their jour-neys to the subcontinent.

I woe go breakin your haaarrr

Someone thumped Justin on the back – the man in charge of the sewerage system in the residential estate. 'Thanks for a fantastic evening, Boss!' he shouted over the music before walking away.

In two hours' time, Justin thought, he would still be in this karaoke bar, and Yinghui would be dozing on the sofa in her café. CS would be talking about a boring book he'd read; he would not notice how delicate Yinghui looked when she slept, how she had a habit of folding her arms loosely across her chest as if protecting herself from danger.

A woman sat next to Justin. 'You look lonely,' she said. She was maybe ten years older than him; not yet forty, but her eyes were bloodshot and heavy and made her seem older, her jaws were beginning to turn jowly, and she had drunk too much. Justin thought she must have had a hard life.

'I'm fine,' he said, retreating slightly into his personal space, away from the sudden warmth of her body. Her bare arm had pressed against his for a second – enough time to make him feel at once repulsed by and sorry for her. 'Listen, I don't really want company. Is that OK? Sorry.'

'Sure,' she said, but she did not leave. She stared at the aquarium behind the bar; its glass was hazy with moss and it was full of goldfish with tattered fins. Justin looked at her – the shiny spandex top she wore was too tight for her, and made her arms seem thicker than they actually were. Her skirt was too short and her high-heeled shoes too big for her; they kept slipping off her feet as she leant forward on the bar stool. It was as though she had dressed the way she imagined women dressed when they went to a karaoke bar. He was sure she didn't usually dress like this.

'Would you like a drink?' Justin asked.

She nodded, but did not make any effort to appear pleased. When she looked at Justin he could see how tired her eyes were. 'X.O.?' she said.

Justin signalled to the girl behind the bar. 'Two Coca-Colas, please.'

The woman laughed. '*Ya*, I've drunk too much tonight. Your friends, they're a crazy bunch. They bought me lots of drinks. I'm not used to it.'

'I can see.'

'So,' she said, reaching across to rest her hand on his thigh. 'You really look lonely, you know. You out-of-towners, you need company. I know you do. I've had experience of life.'

Justin felt the heat of her hand through his jeans. Between his legs, the beginnings of an erection. He moved away from her touch and felt her hand lift away.

'Are you from Kota Bharu?' he asked. Their Cokes arrived, and they raised their glasses to each other in a brief toast. The first bars of a sugary old love song started playing from a nearby room.

'Hey, I love this song,' she said. 'It's one of my favourites. You don't know it? It's called "Just Like Your Tenderness". I love classic old songs like this.' She started humming along, her voice surprisingly fine and perfectly tuned. '... *just like your tenderness* ...' she added with a little flourish at the end. She listened quietly until the song ended; all the time she kept staring at the fish tank. 'I live a few miles outside town,' she said eventually. 'Guys like you would call me a *kampung girl*.'

'Married? Kids? Family?'

She looked at Justin with watery eyes. He thought maybe he had gone too far, asked too intimate a question. But she smiled and shook her head. 'Divorced. You? A handsome young guy like you is sure to have someone.'

Justin shook his head. 'I'm a bachelor.'

'Bet you have a lot of girls everywhere you go.' She picked up her small handbag and fumbled with the clasp; on its flap it read *GUICCY.* She took out a pack of Winstons and reached for the book of matches perched on the edge of a plastic ashtray on the bar. It took her several strikes of the match before she managed to light it, the sudden amber glow of the flame illuminating her face. As she took a long drag on her cigarette Justin noticed the lines on her neck, the flesh pallid and waxy. He wondered how her skin would feel, whether it would be clammy and maybe a bit cold, or warm and smooth. 'What are you looking at?' she said, peering at him sideways as she exhaled a gentle stream of smoke in the opposite direction.

'Nothing.'

He felt her hand on his thigh again, and this time he did not move away. A song had just finished playing in the background – a long final off-key note accompanied by raucous men's laughter and hearty applause. 'Can we go into a private room?' she said. 'It's a bit noisy here.'

He ordered two more Cokes and arranged for a small room to be opened up specially for them. When they were inside, settled down in the velour sofa, he scrolled through the menu of songs, pretending to be looking for something they both liked. 'What do you want to sing?' he asked, even though he knew they had not come into the room to perform duets.

'Anything,' she said, sitting close to him. She eased her hand up his thigh until he felt it between his legs, warm and insistent. He placed his hand on her thigh, but hesitated. The heat of her body and the slight stickiness of her skin excited but also repulsed him; the purple glow of the TV set accentuated the blank look on her face, the absence of any intimacy. He was alarmed and a bit frightened by the thick knot of desire in his throat that made his breath heavy and coarse; he hated the fact that he could become aroused in a place like this, a small musty room that smelled of cheap air freshener and old tobacco – yet he did not leave or ask her to stop. She was just doing what she thought he expected of her, what all men like him expected – he knew she didn't really want to be there with him. He felt like saying, I don't want this either – but then again, he thought, Maybe I do. Maybe I'm just like all the other businessmen who pass through this small, sleepy town, guys who want a quickie and who might leave a couple of hundred *ringgit* for her at the end of the evening, so she can buy herself some clothes in the night market at the weekend. This is what his life had become, he thought: this was the kind of existence that awaited him, stretching infinitely into the future.

'Don't be nervous,' she said softly. 'It'll be nice, you'll see.'

After she had gone, Justin sat in the gloom with his head resting in his hands for a few moments. The Coke he had drunk had left a sickly taste in his mouth, like cough medicine, and made him feel like throwing up; his head was spinning from all the alcohol he had drunk throughout the evening, and he wanted to go back to the hotel. He thought of Yinghui and CS again, reclining on the sofa at Angie's, their ankles lazily interlaced as they leafed through magazines. They might be listening to the Velvet Underground at that very moment; once it got past midnight on a Saturday night Yinghui would put on 'Sunday Morning' and sing along. 'Yeah, yeah, I'm so predictable,' she would say, laughing, as she returned to the sofa. The previous Saturday, Justin had watched her mouthing the words to 'Pale Blue Eyes', her lips moving gently even though her eyelids were half closed with slumber. When she sang, *Sometimes I feel so happy*, she really did look completely contented. She and CS would never know what it was like to be in Justin's place, here in a karaoke bar in a small town up north – and Justin was glad, because he didn't want her to experience what men were capable of inflicting on others in this world he inhabited.

'You dirty rat,' Sixth Uncle said, patting him heavily on his back. 'Chatting up old women – I didn't know you liked the mature type. Naughty boy!'

'It wasn't anything. We were just talking. And singing.'

'Talking my foot! All the guys were taking bets on whether or not you were going to score with the old woman. I said, Man, he's going to score a hole-in-one. I had fifty bucks on you, Big Brother.'

'She wasn't old.'

'You should've invited her to the hotel, bit of takeaway – imagine, that poor woman, she'd still be talking about it in ten years' time if you'd taken her back to your room.'

Justin stood up and pushed past Sixth Uncle on his way to the exit. He wondered if, in the morning, Sixth Uncle and the rest of the men would remember the musty-sweet smell of Ichiban Karaoke Bar, its darkened corridors and worn-out carpets; whether they would recall the rising alcohol-induced nausea in their throats, their over-fed guts, the feeling of women's flesh through synthetic fabric; whether they would regret it.

The walk back to his hotel was not a long one, and as he strolled through the muggy night he thought the warm air would do him good. He inhaled deeply, trying to get some fresh air into his lungs, but after twenty paces or so he bent over and threw up violently in the drain beside the road. In the dark, against the oily-black tarmac, his vomit appeared pale, milky and copious. He remained bent double, his stomach heaving, trails of bitter spit dripping from his chin.

It was this that he remembered now, as he settled into the padded room with Little Tang and his friends late on this summer evening in Shanghai. Acrid sick, luminous, like a starburst against the night sky.

23

物极必反

Nothing Remains Good
or Bad Forever

The venue is dark and smoky and small enough for Gary to see the imperfections in the unpainted walls – the way some bricks are chipped and cracked, the way the mortar has fallen away in places, leaving a few bricks protruding precariously, as if they are about to fall. It is just before 10 p.m. and the room is full of men and women predominantly in their thirties, though he can make out some trendily dressed youngsters and a couple of people in their fifties who look like ageing hippies. He has never performed to such a mature audience before – at his concerts in the past he looked out at a sea of teenage girls, unwavering in their screeching devotion to him. In contrast, everyone before him now is seated and patient. There is a low buzz of conversation, and – maybe he is imagining it – a faint tremor of anticipation. They are scrutinising him as if he were a fascinating, little-known zoological species that has never before been on public display; they are impatient to see what he will deliver.

As he sits on the low, cramped stage, waiting patiently for the café owner and his friends to remove the superfluous drum kit to make a bit more room for him, he catches sight of the clock, its hands at exactly ten o'clock. Usually, at this precise moment he would be in his apartment, waiting for his internet friend Phoebe to come online so he can tell her about his day and catch up on all the crazy things she has been up to at work. This is the first time in three months that he has not been waiting patiently in front of the computer at the appointed hour, but he knows that in all probability he is not missing anything. She has not come online for over two weeks now. Even though he sometimes waits all night, constantly keeping an eye on the MSN chat window, he sees no trace of her.

Although he still keeps a vigil for her – more out of habit than hope – he knows it is unlikely he will ever be in touch with her again. He has seen enough of the world to know that there will be no fairytale ending to the friendship he had been enjoying with Phoebe Chen Aiping. He knows what life is really like – the moment you fall, you are left behind, especially in a place like China. People rush ahead of you; they have no time to look back. Unlike the songs he used to sing, the story he shared with Phoebe will not erupt in a sugary, joyous chorus. All those new, strange experiences he had hoped to enjoy with her – simple things like just going for bubble milk tea, as she once suggested – will remain unexplored.

Every night for the last two weeks, while waiting in vain for her to come online, he has assembled the story of his life in photos, putting together images and internet news articles that would prove to her who he really is. He has been doing this diligently, filling up the dead hours between 10 p.m. and daybreak, even though he knows it will ultimately be futile. The fragments that make up his history are pitiful, he realises, and anyone looking at them would think: What a sad, empty life this boy has had; he has hardly lived at all. But for Phoebe that paltry montage would have been enough – enough to show her that he has changed; that he has survived. Now that she will no longer see the evidence of his life, he looks at the carefully planned material and wonders why he bothered doing it. Maybe it was not so much to convince her that he was a wonderful person; maybe it was in fact to convince himself that he has had a life, that he has the right to exist in this world.

There is no explanation for her sudden disappearance, and he does not seek one. He is not stupid enough to want an answer, and even if he were, in all probability she would not be able to provide him with one. To her, abandoning their friendship probably involved no thought at all, hardly any feeling. That is what people are like today. Friendship, love, even family – all can be forgotten in an instant. Phoebe Chen Aiping. He wonders if that is even her real name.

He adjusts the microphone on the stand before him. The audience is settling down, hushed now as the room darkens and the spotlight falls harshly on Gary. He coughs to clear his throat, and hears the rawness of his breath in the microphone. The lights are trained at an angle that makes him squint. The audience are fascinated, tense – he can feel their anxiety, as if they are worried for him. They look at him with an air of concern and confusion, uncertain how they should respond to him. The poster on the door that evening, handwritten in heavy black marker pen, had announced simply: *Surprise Artiste – Gary Gao*. There had been no advance publicity for the event, no hype; the people who came to this café-bar were accustomed to hearing earnest young folk or jazz musicians performing at the end of the evening. But tonight they were confused – the name on the door sounded vaguely familiar, carrying echoes of not just celebrity but frothiness. Wasn't he a pop star? No, it must be a different person – someone like that would never perform in a place like this.

Now that Gary is on stage, the audience sees a young man dressed in a loose-fitting yellow T-shirt, black jeans and dirty Converse trainers. His head has been shaved and his skin looks sallow, as if he has not exercised recently. In fact, his entire body looks thin and unhealthy, just like many of the other young singers they have seen here before. But there is something in the way he leans in to the microphone that makes the audience feel that he is different – the way he reaches forward to grasp the microphone stand, the manner in which he occupies the stage, as if he is in charge of the space around him, unapproachable and distant – as if nothing apart from that stage exists in his consciousness at this moment.

He looks troubled. Maybe he is on drugs. But his voice is calm, almost subdued. He smiles and says, 'This song is not mine. I mean, it's not original. I took the original and counterfeited it.'

A warm tremble of laughter runs through the audience. Someone coughs.

'Like everything in life these days, I suppose you could say it's a copycat – a fake.'

When Gary speaks, his voice is deeper than his slight physique would suggest. But there is a delicate quality to it that hints at a softness which belies his dishevelled appearance. He begins to strum his guitar – the chords are simple, and there is a stillness to the song that is unsettling. The tune is familiar; it is an old-fashioned Chinese love song, the kind your mother might sing. Only it is slower than you remember it – much slower. Maybe it is not even the same song. Yes it is. It is called 'I Knew a Love'.

Gary begins to sing. His singing voice is lighter than his speaking voice, a clear, feathery tenor. There are no rough edges to it; every note is precise and clean and sustained, and carries the quality of refracted light. Suddenly you can see every colour clearly: the colour of joy, the colour of optimism, the colour of failed hope. The precision of his voice makes you feel sad; its clarity reminds you of a state of innocence, something you once had but have since lost; it reminds you how your life has, over the years, become complicated, muddy.

When he finishes – as quietly as he began – the audience remains silent for a few moments, as if they do not know quite how to react. It is as if they feel chastised, though they are not sure what they have done wrong. And somehow it feels wrong to break the stillness that Gary has cast over the room. But then the owner of the café cries out in encouragement – a strong, sharp 'Yeah' – and the room breaks into noisy applause. It *is* the same Gary who was a pop star, you know. My God, look how he's changed – I didn't even recognise him. I didn't know he could sing so well!

Gary's set consists of eight songs plus two encores – a mixture of traditional love songs which he has reinterpreted in his own fashion and new songs he has written himself. He performs them on either acoustic guitar or keyboard – the simplicity of the instrumentation shows off his musical sensitivity and his vocals, and the audience are completely won over by the unaffected charm of his music-making. By the end of the evening they feel moved and uplifted, as if they have been returned to a simpler, more innocent state of life.

The owner of the café is thrilled and gratified that his hunch has paid off. He knew, as soon as he heard Gary singing at the opening of Red Rooster Hotpot restaurant in that shopping mall in Jiangsu province, that he was a singer of genuine talent, and that all he had to do was to return to what he did best: singing. Forget all the glamour and showbiz, just sing!

This is what he is explaining once the café has closed and they are sitting down to a glass of brandy. There is a small group at the table – Gary, the café owner and a few of the owner's friends, including a Taiwanese film-maker whose work has been banned in China and a rich couple who are planning a charity concert in aid of the Sichuan earthquake victims. Everyone is amazed by Gary's talent. They are talking excitedly of new projects – the film-maker wants to shoot a film in Gary's native Malaysia, in which he would cast Gary in the role of an illegal immigrant who has an accident and cannot remember where he is from. It is a daring venture that will require Gary to appear fully nude and perhaps to simulate sex, which will almost certainly ensure that the film will be banned or at least heavily censored in most Asian countries, but artistically it will be ground-breaking and powerful. The film-maker is impressed by what he calls Gary's inherent transformative qualities – the ability to inspire optimism even while depicting tragedy.

The rich couple have invited Gary to perform at their charity concert, which will be a showcase of the biggest stars, both young and old. It will be a chance for him to relaunch himself as a singer, reintroduce himself to the public, though this time with a different image and a new range of songs. Once again, he will be performing in front of thirty thousand people.

Although Gary smiles and makes affirming, polite noises, he feels panicked by this sudden rush of enthusiasm. The thought of performing in front of a vast, clamouring audience makes him anxious – already he can feel the mounting weight of expectation and the attendant flash of nausea which he thought he would never experience again. This evening, his brief performance of ten quiet songs left him feeling quietly energised, as if he had just gone for a long, gentle run along the riverbank in the dark. At one point he had even thought that he would be happy performing like this every week for the rest of his life; but now all that calm energy seems about to dissipate.

'No pressure,' the man says. 'Just think about it.'

His companion nods in agreement. But she is less convinced, more restrained in her encouragement. She senses a fragility in Gary; she can tell that he is uncertain and stressed by the situation. When Gary looks at her he knows that she feels his confusion; he recognises a wariness in her eyes, just as she does in his. It is a look they both know well, a tightness of the brow and a slight emptiness of the regard designed to protect themselves against hurt. Although she is smiling and gently adding to the chorus of approval, she does not actively urge him on to greater, more complex projects as the others do. She appears to be lost herself, uncomfortable in her skin, distant in her thoughts.

'It's a chance to rebrand yourself,' her companion continues. He has no doubts as to who he is – clearly he is a man of action, certain of his ways, someone who is used to winning. 'You saw how much the people here loved you tonight. Your low-key approach is genius – the complete opposite to what you were before. Now people can appreciate your talent for what it is, and you can concentrate on what you want, which is to write songs and sing.'

'Absolutely,' the café owner adds. 'Don't you agree, Yinghui?'

'You guys mustn't push the poor boy,' the woman says. She turns to Gary and speaks to him in a soft, even voice. 'Just take your time and think about it. If you don't do this now, you can still do something else in the future. You're so young.'

When he gets into bed later that night after a long shower, for the first time in weeks Gary feels ready for sleep. He is not fidgety or anxious, as he has been lately. He has sung ten good songs to a small, appreciative audience, and has had a proper dinner for the first time in months. Just out of habit, he takes a quick look at his computer before turning out the light. In the MSN chat box, he sees Phoebe's name and photo. It is nearly 2 a.m. He hesitates for a moment before typing:

hi
Hi
Are you OK?
Yes, you?

Gary stops. There is something strange about her responses – they are delayed, much slower than they usually are. He suspects that she must be chatting to someone else at the same time, for she seems distracted. Even though he has tried to train himself to think of her in distant, emotionless terms, he finds that he cannot prevent his old enthusiasm from resurfacing. He tries to remain calm, but cannot help being anxious.

Where have you been? I was … worried
Work is very busy
But you surely don't work until after midnight? Why didn't you log on at all?
I went out
Every night?
En.
Who with?
Friends
Which friends?
People you don't know. Why all these strange questions?
They're not strange. I was just worried because I stayed up every

night looking for you and you did not come online
Don't u have a life? Why do u stay up all night waiting for me?
This is not a good situation
So you have a boyfriend now?
None of your business. Anyway, can we change the subject? You
are really giving me a bad mood
OK

She tells him about work, the same stories about the same girls with the same problems. But he is not in the mood to listen to them. After two weeks' absence he feels that she should not be recounting boring gossip about her colleagues. They should be talking about serious, life-changing subjects. He should be telling her about the gig he just did. Maybe it is because he has waited so long to tell her the important things about himself that he feels frustrated – he is not sure why, but something does not feel right tonight, he has never felt like this with Phoebe before. He thinks about all the pieces of his life he has assembled, ready to show her, but now they seem superfluous, for she is not interested in him. She talks and talks, and his only response is the occasional '*En*,' but still she does not sense that maybe he doesn't want to hear about these banal details. Usually she is quick to pick up on his moods, sensing when he is depressed or anxious or joyful, but today she does not seem to care. All that matters to her are these boring tales about her workplace, which he has heard many times before.

Sorry, he types suddenly, interrupting her. *I have something to tell you.*

There is a slight hesitation before she replies.

What is it? It sounds like bad news.

No, it's a good thing. Happy news.

But all at once he does not feel happy. All the optimism and excitement he felt previously has dissipated. Bottling up the news that he was so eager to tell her has enervated him, and now he is feeling deflated.

So … tell me, what is it?

It is as if she too is not very interested in what he has to tell her. But he knows that if he does not reveal himself to her now, his life will remain the same forever, unchanging in its loneliness. The timing does not feel right, but perhaps it never will. He decides that he has to be brave. He says:

I want to send you a photo of myself.

Ha ha ha. Ei, you scared me for a moment. I thought you were going to say you had a life-threatening disease like pancreatic cancer or AIDS.

No, I just want to send you some photos of myself, so that you know who I am.

I told you, I don't care who you really are in real life. If you are an African man hoping to bamboozle me of all my money, I don't care. If you are a Muslim man with four wives, I don't care. If you are a high-ranking party official, I don't care. Even if you are Wen Jiabao, I don't care. All that matters is that you are nice to me. The rest — I don't care.

I want you to know me. I know so much about you, and I want us to be equal.

You don't have to, really.

I want to. I need to. I want to share myself with someone. Please.

OK, sure.

He sends her a publicity shot from last year, in which he is dressed casually, posing in a lush tropical garden in Singapore. It is a high-quality professional photograph that takes a long time for her computer to download.

HA HA. That is funny!

Why?

Because I told you that I used to like Gary, so you sent me a photo of him! Ha ha. Wah, I am relieved! I was so nervous — for a moment, I thought you were actually going to send me a photo of yourself! You naughty devil! I should have known you were just going to play a practical joke on me as usual. This is why I like you so much … you really know how to make me laugh and cheer me up when I am depressed.

But that is me.

HA HA HA HA

No, seriously, I am Gary.

You are so funny! Really. I appreciate the joke a lot. It's been a hard few days for me and I need to laugh a bit.

I can send you another photo to prove it. Wait a second.

Ei … I just can't stop laughing.

He looks through the images he has prepared, trying to locate one of himself in an informal setting – an arty black-and-white shot of himself and Elva Hsiao in a recording studio, looking at the score of the duet they recorded together in 2008. He is wearing a woollen beanie and looks as if he has just tumbled out of bed, but in fact the photo was professionally styled, and was printed in an avant-garde magazine.

Wow, where did you find this cool photo? I thought the song Gary did with Elva was nice, but their voices didn't go together. What do you think?

He hesitates for a moment: instinct and habit make him want to refer to Gary in the third person, but he stops himself, remembering the task at hand.

It was a difficult record to make. We were under a lot of pressure. Our record companies forced us to do it because we looked good together. And also, because of the gossip going around at the time …

HA HA HA. Really, you are too good! Wah, you have hidden talents, you can even imitate Gary. What gossip – do you mean all the gay gossip? Everyone knows they did not go out together. She was just a front for him, a publicity stunt. All these celebrities – you never know who is benefiting from who. Everything is just about advertising. Their whole lives are a fake.

Yes, I know. That is why you need to know who I am, so I can stop pretending.

OK, OK, you have impressed me. It's a really great joke. Ha ha, really.

So you believe me?

Yes, yes, I believe you, Mr Gary.

Great.

Hang on, I have to get a tissue, I'm crying with laughter. OK now, tell me, what have you been up to today? How was work?

I had a performance a couple of weeks ago, really depressing. I wanted to tell you about it, but you didn't come online at all. That's why I've been down. Because I wanted to tell you what my work is — all the lousy little concerts I have to do these days. But now my luck is changing, I think. I've been offered the chance to sing my own songs, the ones you've been encouraging me to write ... some important guy asked me to sing at the big Sichuan earthquake charity concert that's coming up soon.

OK, you can stop the joke now, it's not funny any more.

But I AM Gary. I can prove it to you. What do you want as proof?

OK, OK, really that's too much now.

But I swear to you on my ancestors' graves, I am Gary. What more do you want? You want to go on Skype so you can see me on cam? Yes, let's do that!

No — what are you, some kind of pervert??

Please, give me a chance to prove to you who I am. I am really Gary.

Stop it now, please. Anyway, if you were Gary, you wouldn't be interested in me because everyone knows he's gay.

Don't go. I want you to stay and see me. I need you to know me.

You are frightening me.

Wait one second, I beg you. I can tell you something no one knows about me, not even my agent. On my left inner thigh I have a scar in the shape of a star. I got it because I fell onto a sharp spike while I was trying to climb a fence to pick some fruit in someone's garden. I had to walk home such a long way. I was only six or seven years old. When I got home I fainted, and when my mother came in she thought I was dead. No one knows this, only me, my mother ... and now you.

I think ... you are a weirdo. I am going to log off now.

WAIT!

Quickly, he sends her the photo he has saved as undeniable proof of his identity, the one he took of himself on his mobile phone, alone at the seaside on Ibiza, the blue-gold dawn in the background.

OK, this is really too scary now. How did you get this picture?

I took it myself, on my phone.

No, you must have stolen it. You are sick. I should report you to the police. You disgust me.

Really, I am telling you the truth.

Goodbye, you FREAK.

He tries to send her messages, but she has blocked him. He sends emails every day, begging her to forgive him, but after a week he knows she is not even reading them, and has probably changed her email and MSN accounts, making it impossible for him ever to contact her again.

24

后顾无忧

Embrace Your Bright Future

Later that week, Yinghui paid her share of the money into the bank account of the joint venture company she had set up with Walter. They were, so far, the only two signatories to the account and the company's only directors, a cosy intimacy she was beginning to enjoy. There was a compactness and solidity to the pairing which felt safe to her, and she began to wish it could have been possible for them to complete the project without anyone else, just the two of them. Although she knew that as it grew, a project this size would very soon require additional directors, she felt that if she could at least push ahead with some key aspects of the development, such as the future financing and the precise use of the building (what percentage of it would be community-based, artistic, charitable, commercial, etc.?), she would cement her position at the head of the deal. Whoever else came on board subsequently would have to assume positions secondary to hers, even though on paper they might be co-directors. By then she would be more than just the right-hand woman of the tycoon Walter Chao himself; she would be his equal, the two of them acknowledged as the pioneering visionaries of the project.

After she had paid in the money she stayed up late into the night writing a report entitled 'Next Steps' – best to be direct, she thought – outlining what she thought should be done in the coming weeks in order to drive the project forward. She emailed it to Walter early the following morning, together with a note informing him that she had paid in her share of the capital as a sign of her commitment to their joint venture, and that she believed they ought to make use of the momentum they had built up thus far, and speed up proceedings.

After she had sent them, it occurred to her that the tone of both her paper and her email was a touch too businesslike, ignoring the personal rapport they had established, a connection that seemed to have been strengthening more quickly than their actual working relationship. This troubled Yinghui, making her realise that she was less skilled at navigating the murky waters of courtship than she had thought – it had been so long since her last romantic voyage, after all, and contrary to what her girlfriends said, it was not like riding a bicycle: one *did* forget. She did not enjoy the sensation of not being in control; the symptoms of her lack of authority over the situation were irrational flashes of jealousy and suspicion – the feeling that she was walking on a slope of loose rocks that might give way at any moment. So she decided to fall back onto more familiar territory – the dealings of business, where she was in total command, like a skipper at the helm, riding choppy seas with ease.

Walter did not reply to her email all day; it was only after lunch the following day – a whole thirty hours after she'd sent him her thoughts on the way forward – that he replied with an email that read simply: 'Noted. Thanks.' She tried to read between the lines, attempting to get a sense of the message he was trying to convey to her, for surely it must mean more than the two scant words, which in themselves signified little. It read like a snub, a rapid shrinking of interest or a sharp change in direction. She read her paper again, looking out for anything that might have offended him, but could find nothing. She picked up the phone and rang him: it was better to clear the air than to harbour minor grievances, she thought. That was something she had learnt after many years in business – if something bothers you, challenge it straight away, and you will usually find that the solution is much simpler than you might have thought. But his phone was switched off, and even though she left a message, it was not until late that evening that he rang back. He was calling from Beijing, he said, from a cab; she was relieved to find that his silence had been due to nothing more than the fact that he had been on board an aeroplane for several hours.

'So, have you read my report?' she asked.

'Not yet,' he said. She could hear him issuing directions to the driver; excited voices on the taxi's radio; a cheery advertisement jingle. 'I haven't had a chance.'

'Sure. I just thought maybe there were things we could be getting on with in the coming days.'

'I'm very busy at the moment. I thought I told you I had to attend a conference here, then I have some business to look after in Indonesia.'

'Perhaps I could take the initiative on a couple of things, if you're busy at the moment.'

A pause at the other end. 'Yes,' he said eventually.

'Can I ask you something?' Yinghui said in a strong, business-like voice, making sure there were no emotive inflections in the way she spoke. 'Has your interest in the project cooled in the last couple of days? You don't seem as responsive or as committed as you were previously. I'm just wondering, because it sometimes happens that when a deal is completed, people lose interest for a while and the momentum of the project slows down, and before they know it, everything grinds to a halt. I want to make sure that we capitalise on –'

'Of course I'm still committed,' Walter interrupted. 'It's just that … I'm wondering why you want to push on so quickly. There's really no hurry.'

'Agreed, but the sooner we put things in place, the better, and there are so many details yet to be finalised. We need to sharpen up our concept, start thinking of more detailed financial models … we need to nail things down.'

She heard his voice muffle as he cupped his hand over the phone. When he came back on, she had the impression that he was laughing, but she couldn't be certain; the line was momentarily interrupted by static, which made his voice sound distant and hollow. There was the final note of a soft, melodic chuckle – a woman's laugh. Maybe it was on the radio, maybe a distortion of the phone line – Yinghui couldn't tell.

'I don't want to rush things,' he said. 'We have plenty of time. I mean, really loads of time. The purchase of the site hasn't even been formally approved by the municipal council yet.'

'Would you like me to chase that up while you're away?'

'No, no, I'll handle it. My contacts there are used to dealing with me. I've got that under control. Listen, just relax, OK? I think you're still on an adrenalin rush after securing that big loan. Just take a few days away from the deal and wait for me to come back to Shanghai. I'd really appreciate more time just to chat things through with you. I mean, the philosophy of what we're doing is of the utmost importance. We need to take time to think fully about what we're doing, and not just rush it through as if it were some ordinary development. This project needs someone with *soul* – that's why I got you on board before anyone else.'

'I see. Yes, I understand.'

'I'd really like to have a bit more of what we had in Hangzhou. You know, when we went away for the weekend.'

'Really?'

'Yes. Just, you know, to chat about everything and nothing. I find it so stimulating. Beneficial for work, I mean.'

Over the next few days Yinghui tried to concentrate on her existing businesses. She had been receiving daily reports on the state of each enterprise from her managers – the lingerie art galleries were continuing to progress without problems; the FILGirl clothes brand was just beginning its operations, and trading figures in its first few days were encouraging; the Thai spa had had a magnificent start, and Yinghui had received breathlessly upbeat reports from the diligent girl she had recently promoted to manager. These ventures felt to her like long-conquered lands, even though most of them were only in their infancy – it was difficult for her to muster much enthusiasm for them, for they offered her no new possibilities. Returning to them even for a few days felt like a return to a former, more restricted life. She had already moved on, pushing forward relentlessly as she had always promised herself she would.

Still, she forced herself to take time away from the project with Walter in order to visit her old businesses (yes, it was strange, but she was already beginning to think of them as 'old'). The lingerie boutiques were coolly elegant, filled with professional women sipping coffee while typing into their BlackBerrys; the small warehouse that held the stock of clothing for the internet business hummed with quiet efficiency. She had always prided herself on being a hands-on leader, and had enjoyed the feeling of being personally involved in the daily workings of her ventures; but now, standing in the warehouse chatting to the young man who organised the stock in neat categories according to clothing type, colour and age range, she felt unmistakably, crushingly bored. Her mind was already beginning to generate ideas and calculations for her project with Walter, preparing an invisible dossier so that when he returned to Shanghai in a few days she would be ready to impress him.

In fact, her old businesses scarcely felt as if they still belonged to her. When she thought of them, she felt the overwhelming solitude of her position – they reminded her that she had accomplished everything on her own, built a modest empire by her own skill and determination. A single woman in the biggest city in the world. It was something for which she had hitherto been lauded, and even she had believed in the myth of her success; but now, surveying the warehouse with its stark fluorescent lighting, surrounded by piles of cheap multicoloured cloth, she wondered whether there was truly anything to celebrate in her life so far. Could she really cheer her own loneliness?

She thought of all the things Walter had told her – how he wanted them to take their time, get to know and understand each other, not rush into anything – and the more these phrases repeated in her head, the more she realised that they were a timid, awkwardly veiled invitation to a romance; that, being a gentleman, Walter had simply left open a suggestion of intimacy, waiting for her to respond. But she, blinded and scarred by the past, had clumsily declined to accept. As the warehouse manager pointed out all the stock that had recently arrived, Yinghui decided that her boldness in her professional life should now be matched by a similar courage in *romance*. The very sound of the word seemed thrilling and dangerous to her.

She made her excuses, and got into her car to head for the Thai spa. She had decided to call it *Apsara* – those celestial nymphs whose name evoked grace and beauty – but she had in fact been thinking of another of their attributes: their shape-shifting powers, constantly evolving at will, gambling with fate's fortune. She had thought it fitting given her own circumstances, even if she was someone with 'style issues'. In any event, the name seemed to have brought with it the blessing of the deities, for the spa had been fully booked virtually from the day it opened its doors.

It was early in the afternoon when she arrived, and she did not expect the spa to be busy. But she was shocked, nonetheless, to find the reception area in a state of obvious neglect – the flowers in the large vase on the counter were nearly dead, the water turning honey-coloured and slimy; there was no one at reception, but two of the beauticians were sitting in the silk-upholstered armchairs reserved for clients, reading magazines and listening to music being played on one of their mobile phones. A third was sitting on the floor painting her toenails. Only one of them was wearing her uniform.

'Where is Miss Xu?' Yinghui demanded.

The girls stood up quickly, tidying the magazines into a neat stack and plumping the cushions. 'We don't know where Phoebe is,' one of them said. 'She hasn't really been coming in very much.'

'I think she must be sick,' another added.

'How long has this been going on?' Yinghui said, walking towards the office.

The girls shrugged. A few days, a week – they weren't really sure.

The office was in similar disarray, with boxes of beauty products heaped in random piles, nail files and unopened envelopes lying on the desk. When she sat in front of the computer, Yinghui found that someone was in the process of downloading a Hollywood film on it. There were empty noodle cartons piled in the sink, and half-empty mugs of tea everywhere. The computer booking system still showed some clients with appointments, although their number had halved since the previous month. Yinghui rang Phoebe Xu Chunyan's mobile number. The phone was turned off, so she left a message instructing her to return the call as soon as possible.

She left the spa and headed home. It frustrated her to think that she would have to spend at least a whole day or two sorting out this mess, which detracted from the delicious possibilities of her situation with Walter. She had thought that she was above such banal, everyday troubles as disciplining negligent staff. But that was the problem with hiring girls from the provinces. She was sorry to say it, but they always required far more supervision than you expected. It was proof, if she had needed it, that she had outgrown such small-scale businesses, that she was ready for something more befitting her swelling ambitions. As soon as she could, she would find a buyer for the spa – and, who knows, perhaps for the other businesses too. She would invest herself entirely in Walter's project; in *their* project.

She had barely settled down to a cup of Anhui white tea and a spreadsheet of figures when her phone rang. She knew who it would be even before she answered; it was as if fortune had decided to bestow itself entirely upon her, as if all her stars were organising themselves in perfect alignment. Sometimes, she thought, life seemed so easy.

'Hey, I was just thinking,' Walter said without introducing himself, 'I'm pretty much alone in Beijing this weekend, and I don't have all that much to do, so I was wondering if you might like to join me. Just a spur-of-the-moment thing. I completely understand if you need to look after your businesses. I'm sure you must be very busy.'

'Actually, funny you should say that, but I'm feeling sort of ... fatigued by work at the moment. I could do with a break.'

'Really? I don't want to drag you away from your obligations. But if you really can come just for a night or two, I'll get my PA to organise flights and a hotel room. When would you like to come?'

Once she was in Beijing, Yinghui felt charged with an easy energy. She enjoyed the scale of the long, wide avenues, unerring in their straightness – their grandeur suited her current state of mind: full of light and life and possibility, and she found herself thinking about the development project in a similarly grandiose manner. Already, she imagined her name and Walter's attached discreetly to the project, so that for years to come, every time the building was mentioned, her name would be whispered reverently too. While Walter attended meetings on the Saturday morning, she spent a few hours watching TV in her room, a luxury she rarely allowed herself, before going downstairs to sit in the café, a light-filled space on the ground floor of the avant-garde hotel built by the architect Walter was hoping to engage for their project – their project – in Shanghai. There, sipping lemongrass tea, she read Camus' *The Plague*, which she had found incongruously sitting on the racks of the used section of a bookstand in Sanlitun during her morning walk. A young Chinese-American man at the next table leant over and said, 'I read that at college – it sucks.'

'Really? Why?'

'I don't know,' he shrugged, smiling charmingly. 'I just never got into all that existentialist stuff. It just didn't seem ... relevant to the world.'

They chatted for a while about which authors they liked and hated; and as he ordered another coffee for himself and a herbal infusion for her, she tried to remember when she had last had a conversation with a complete stranger about books; or in fact any exchange that did not involve business or money or marriage. It was a way of being that came back so easily to her – now this *was* like riding a bike – and she remembered something else: that she could be good company, lively and receptive and provocative.

After they had bade each other goodbye she went downstairs to the swimming pool, a silent, shadowy rectangle lined in steel the texture of shark skin, lit by a rich amber glow. She was the only one there, splashing languidly on her back, allowing herself to drift into an arc of light that fell through a glass panel over one end of the pool. Staring at the filtered light above, she floated calmly for a while. With her ears in the water, she could hear only a vast hollowness punctuated by an occasional clicking; she felt a lightness to her body that was entirely new, at once exciting and soothing – it was cosseting to be borne by the water and have it turn her body gently in directions she could not control. It seemed pointless to plough up and down the pool as she had recently taken to doing, squeezing in her forty laps each lunchtime, so when she was bored with floating on her back she frog-kicked her way underwater, watching how the thin strips of light at the bottom of the pool reflected on the surface of the water.

Walter collected her early that evening and they went to dinner at a restaurant with views over the Forbidden City.

'I was thinking about what you said about formalising our partnership,' he said as they sat down. 'Although I still think it's early in the day, I agree that we should have some paperwork drawn up. I've instructed my lawyers to get moving, so you should have something to look at later this week.'

'Great.'

'I wanted to address your concerns,' he said, as he gestured to the waiter. 'About security.'

'Thank you,' Yinghui said, suddenly feeling embarrassed at having ever mentioned her need for security.

'Now that we've got business out of the way, can we start enjoying each other's company?'

Yinghui smiled. 'We always do, even when we're conducting business – don't we?'

The lightness and ease she had felt in the swimming pool earlier that day had stayed with her, and she found conversation with Walter similarly smooth and energised, the sentences slipping out of her mouth with a litheness she had forgotten she was capable of. He too seemed lifted by her vivacity, and there were points at which it felt as though they were stumbling over each other to ask questions, to venture an opinion on what the other had just said, to come up with a wisecrack that would make the other laugh. He had ordered a bottle of vintage Ruinart, which made Yinghui's cheeks feel warm and rosy; at one point she had the impression that she was drinking much more than he. They were talking and laughing more than they were eating, and by the time they had finished their main courses the restaurant was nearly empty.

'You see, we managed to get through an entire dinner without even once talking about our project,' Walter said.

'Yes,' Yinghui laughed. *Our* project. That's what he had said; she liked the sound of it.

'You didn't always want to be a businesswoman, did you?' Walter asked, pouring himself some water. 'I mean, when you were a child.'

'Is it that obvious?' Yinghui smiled. 'I wanted to be a doctor working in Africa, or an anthropologist. I really, *really* wanted to be a vet at one point. And then when I was a bit older, in my late teens, I thought I would be a charity worker in India.' It was the truth, but it seemed comical to admit this now – which was why she was confessing it. 'What about you? Let me guess. Carpenter?'

'Wrong,' he said, smiling. 'Actually, it was pretty obvious to me from quite a young age what my life would involve.'

'Ooo, that sounds soooo deep.' Yinghui's laughter rang out more loudly than she had expected; the restaurant was empty now, apart from the waiters hanging around by the bar pretending to wipe down the wine glasses. Out the window, they could see the roofs of the pavilions in the Forbidden City lit against the powder-black sky, the eaves curling gently towards the heavens.

'And your parents,' he continued. 'Were they encouraging in your quest to become Mother Teresa?'

Yinghui sensed a sudden change in the tone of his voice, a sharp, probing edge that caught her off guard. She looked into her empty glass. 'I guess.'

'Meaning?' he asked.

'Meaning, sort of.'

She should have expected that the conversation would take a turn this way – after all, they were talking about themselves, so it was entirely natural for him to ask her about her family; if she felt a sudden deflating of her energies it was because she was disappointed in herself – annoyed that she should still feel closed and defensive about the past.

'What about *your* parents?' she asked as brightly as she could manage. 'Were they encouraging of your business ventures?'

'They died before I accomplished anything,' Walter replied matter-of-factly. 'I lost my mother when I was an infant. My father died when I was quite young – about nineteen.'

'I'm sorry,' she said.

He looked at her for a while, holding her gaze until she felt uncomfortable and looked away. 'Don't be,' he said. 'Life doesn't treat all of us equally, does it?'

At Yinghui's suggestion, they decided to have another glass of champagne instead of dessert – she needed a way to cheer up for the remainder of the night. When they had finished they went for a stroll, skirting the vast perimeter of Tiananmen Square and aiming vaguely for the outer waterways of the Forbidden City. The air was much drier here than in Shanghai, and Yinghui's skin began to feel parched and brittle. The pavement was crunchy underfoot with a layer of gritty dust, and when, occasionally, a breath of wind swept along the avenues, it carried an imprint of warmth, even though it was late at night. The cheery banter they had fabricated over dinner had crumbled away now, and it felt once more as if they were trying to bridge a void between them.

As they walked along a silent stretch of water under the feathery reaches of the overhanging willow trees, Yinghui moved close to Walter, hoping that it would make it easier for him to reach out and take her hand – it was a gesture of desperation, she knew, trying to establish physical closeness in order to replace a widening emotional gap; but she thought it would reassure them nonetheless. The water appeared black and utterly still in the dark, but flecks of dust and froth glimmered on its surface. Even though it was nearly midnight, old men were still sitting passively with their fishing rods poised over the water, motionless as statues. Small groups of people were playing *xiangqi*, sliding the chess pieces across grid-patterned paper laid out on the paving stones. Young lovers wandered slowly in the dusky moonlight, pausing now and then to peer into the water – just as Yinghui and Walter were doing.

Yinghui felt Walter's hand brush hers as they walked; his pace had slowed, as if he wanted to speak but did not wish to be hurried. They came to a small stone bench and paused to sit down. He looked her in the eye. She thought that maybe he was going to kiss her now, but instead he said, 'Is it true that your father was murdered?' His voice was clear and insistent; the question seemed to hang in the air, refusing to budge until it was met with an answer.

'I guess it's not the sort of thing one can keep secret forever.'

'Yes, someone told me,' he said calmly – too calmly, she thought, as if he had been waiting for an opportunity to bring up the topic. 'There was a scandal. I remembered the incident – it was all over the papers at the time. There were photos of you and your mother, too. I just hadn't made the connection.'

'Yes, that was my dad. That was us.' She felt a numbness settling over her, an urge to answer only in grunted monosyllables until he changed the subject. 'I hate the way people say it was a scandal, as if he had anything to do with it.'

'Mm,' Walter said, waiting for her to go on.

She felt the weight of his expectation for answers growing with each second, a sense of shame replacing the numbness. But what was she ashamed of? She had done nothing wrong. Yet she could not shake the rising humiliation she felt.

'I suppose you don't want to do business with me now – and I guess that's why you were hesitant about taking the plunge. You thought there might be something *wrong* with me. Don't worry, you won't be the first to do so. Funny how people don't like trouble, even when it's long gone. You get into trouble and everyone avoids you forever, even though you've done nothing wrong. It must be an Asian thing. Shame, loss of face, that sort of shit. Someone fucks your life up, and somehow the shame becomes yours.'

Walter put his arm briefly around her shoulders before withdrawing it. 'The business side of things is fine, don't worry. I'm just interested to hear about your past, that's all.'

The sudden closeness of his body – the unexpected weight of his arm, the slight sour notes in his breath – made her breath quicken; the warm, witty responses she might have come up with in a similar situation died in her throat. She closed her eyes, and the first image that came into her mind was of Shanghai, of driving home at night along the Bund section of Zhongshan Lu after a long day's work, sweeping over Suzhou Creek, tired but glowing with satisfaction. The lights of the skyscrapers in Pudong would be off now, but there would still be light coming off the river, and a breeze that ruffled the surface of the water and made it choppy; and in the summer months, when she drove with the windows down, the wind that eddied and swirled in the car would be soft and reassuring, with whispers of the tropics. She wished she were back in Shanghai, back in her comforting routine; she did not want to be in this arid northern city any more.

'I just want you to feel comfortable with me,' he continued. 'You do trust me, don't you?'

She nodded, allowing herself to rest more heavily against him. They remained that way for a while, awkwardly poised against each other, their elbows, shoulders and hands seeming to get in the way, their bodies never able to gain greater proximity, no matter how she tried to manoeuvre herself.

'What happened?' he said after a while. 'You don't have to tell me if you don't want to.'

What happened. Yinghui thought for a moment. It was so long ago, maybe she had forgotten. It was so long ago, she had travelled so far, changed so much, changed completely; maybe she no longer remembered what had happened. But no – it was all still there, playing in a long, never-ending loop in the background of her life every day, like an insidious TV ad that got into your head and refused to go away. It had accompanied her every second of every day and night, she realised now, and though in the bright light of her office she had been able to banish it to the shadows, it had remained there, ready to announce itself at any moment.

Of course she could remember what happened. Of course she could remember arriving at her parents' that Sunday evening, after a day tidying up and stocktaking at Angie's. It had been a quiet day at the café – Sundays always were, but that day even more so because her friends had begun to distance themselves from her following her father's court case, as if the suspicion that continued to hover over her family might somehow infect them if they continued to hang out with her. She had had an argument with CS; they'd been having quite a few of those of late, disputes that seemed more profound and troubling than their usual squabbles. They'd always been a tempestuous couple, and fierce debates were part of the way they expressed their passion for each other; it was their way of showing commitment to their relationship.

They had not argued this time about Miłosz or the illusion of free democracy – that kind of argument seemed to belong to a distant past – but about something much more bourgeois. It was so petty, Yinghui had thought at the time, but she couldn't help herself; it had seemed so important. They had become engaged on a trip to India the previous month – bought each other rings in Udaipur and exchanged them on the banks of Lake Pichola. They had treated themselves and spent an extravagant night at the Lake Palace Hotel, marooned on an island in the midst of a teeming city – it was as if they would always be alone in their coupledom, and they had loved that feeling. But now he was refusing to tell anyone about the engagement – hiding it, in fact, by making jokes to their friends. '*Ya*, look at me, I never notice other girls now because I'm pretty much engaged, aren't I? Ha ha.' She couldn't say, in front of everyone, Yes, you are engaged. And then, just that day, he'd said to his brother and some friends, 'Marriage is a disgraceful institution. It forces people into an unthinking and unquestioning social arrangement. I'd never do it.' She'd laughed along at the time, made it seem as though it was just another joke. But afterwards, when they were on their own, she'd asked him if he'd meant what he'd said. To which he'd replied,

'Don't ask me such dumb questions.'

'What do you mean by that?'

'I mean, don't be so damn boring. Marriage, marriage, marriage, that's all you talk about these days. You're turning into one of those boring women you've always hated.'

It got worse from then on. She accused him of a lack of commitment, of being ashamed of her. He accused her of being a pre-feminist woman, which enraged her. He left her in the stock room, holding her clipboard in front of a stack of organic kidney beans. For a while she had listened out for the front door in case he came back, but all she heard was the low murmuring of the chiller cabinets.

When she arrived back at her parents' house she was almost grateful for the routine that lay ahead of her – the disjointed conversation around the dinner table, with her mother fussing over the price of food or the lack of time she'd had to prepare dinner that day, and her father nodding in agreement like an automaton. Sometimes he would refer to his life in the past tense, as if resigning from his job had meant the end of time for him. *I was quite a sporty fellow. I liked Penang a lot, nice atmosphere*. But Yinghui did not mind; it would allow her to rest in her own thoughts, and be present without actually participating. Her parents wouldn't notice the absent look on her face, or the obvious signs of fatigue – the dark puffy circles under her eyes, the pinched smile, the fingernails at which she had been nibbling constantly.

Her mother was just dishing out some lotus-stem soup ('The stems are so small nowadays – remember when they were so fat and cheap?') when the doorbell rang. The neighbours' dog started barking, a monotonous oof-oof-oof that betrayed little interest, no danger – the same call it made when the postman came round on his scooter every morning. It was a fat, pampered German shepherd that ate boiled chicken and long beans for lunch – it wasn't there to guard against anything. It barked for a few more seconds when the doorbell rang again, but then fell silent. Yinghui didn't stir from her thoughts – she'd grown so accustomed over the years to her father having late-night meetings on governmental matters, men calling round for a drink to discuss the week's developments. At that precise moment, she was thinking: What if I broke off my engagement with CS? What if I broke up with him altogether? That would take him by surprise.

'Who's that so late on a Sunday night?' her mother said, looking at her father. She'd dipped the ladle into the soup; Yinghui watched the thin circles of oil separate into little greasy pearls on its cloudy surface.

Her father looked in the direction of the door. He did not seem surprised. 'I don't know.'

Yes, Yinghui thought, she would break up with CS. He would not be expecting that at all.

'Darling, don't go,' her mother said.

'*Aiya*, don't worry,' her father said, laughing as he rose to go and see who it was.

'Darling, be careful.'

Yinghui thought: What if I just suddenly announced, here and now, that I'm going to break up with CS? Would my parents be pleased? They've never been very keen on him. But how would they feel about a daughter of marriageable age who split up with a boy she'd practically lived with for nearly six years?

Her mother was looking out of the window, soup ladle still in her hand. 'So dark outside,' she said. 'Can't see anything.' She returned to the table and continued to dish out the soup.

The thought of breaking up with CS had given Yinghui a few moments' exhilaration, but it evaporated as soon as it had appeared, and suddenly she was alone with her doubts again. She could not break up with him, could not imagine a life in KL without him. If ever it happened, she would have to move a million miles away, retrain as an astronaut so she'd never have to inhabit the same planet as him. Tomorrow, she would patch things up with him. She would go to the café as usual, and he would appear, just before opening time, with a bouquet of flowers, which is what he always did after a fight. Once he'd appeared bearing a bunch of roses and a first edition of *Lolita* with a note saying, '*If I had a nymphet, it would be you.*'

The first noise they heard was strange and unrecognisable, as if disconnected from time and space: firecrackers at this time of the year? No: not the usual rapid chatter, but a single sound that punctured the silence of the night with the violence of a whip on flesh, the shattering of the sound barrier by a jet in the sky. The neighbours' dog barking. And then – one, two, three seconds later? – the same noise again, and this time they knew. She had never heard a gunshot before, but somehow Yinghui recognised it. The dog was barking furiously now – not its low, lazy calls but a hysterical high-pitched yelp, as if it were choking, over and over, as if it would never stop. Yinghui ran out of the door into the front yard, across the small stretch of lawn – the last bit of the garden that hadn't been built over – and onto the driveway. Behind her she could hear her mother screaming, '*Be careful! Come back, be careful!*' Her father lay on the concrete, face down, hands bunched together near his face, as if searching for some microscopic object in the earth. In the darkness the pool of blood that was seeping out from under him appeared black and inky against the paleness of the concrete. She looked around, but she knew she would see no one, knew she was not in danger, knew this was the full stop to the messy story that had spanned the whole of the last year, the one everyone referred to as *the scandal*. She crouched down next to her father, thinking that maybe she might hear gurgled, frothy breaths. She could feel the blood – tepid and moist on her hands and ear. She could feel the warm presence of her father's body, as if he was still alive. But she could hear nothing. Just the dog barking, crazed and strangulated; her mother standing at the door shouting, '*Come back! Be careful!*' over and over again. The word 'careful' was stretched by her low cries; it rang out in the night, caref*uuuuul*, caref*uuuuuuuuul*. And then she broke down into deep, moaning sobs.

Yinghui thought: It's better this way. It felt like a relief. She remained crouched by her father's side for a long time, knowing he was dead, comforted by the certainty of it. She did not shout, 'Call for an ambulance!' the way people did in films; she just stayed there, listening to her mother's animal wail settling into a rhythm. Moan-cough-moan. And the fat German shepherd barking its hysterical bark, its owners unable to calm it.

'Why did they do it?' her mother would ask over and over again in the days that followed. 'He was already ruined, his life was over. They didn't have to kill him twice. What did he do that was so wrong? He never hurt anyone, he never hurt anyone in his whole life.'

The newspapers adopted the same tone: he was a good, hard-working man who left behind a grieving wife and daughter. There were photos of Yinghui holding her mother's arm after the funeral, her mother's face collapsed in anguish; in her pain she was oblivious to the cameras. It was always like this with Asian people, thought Yinghui: when a man is alive, he is vilified; when he is dead he is honoured. And yet, in every article about his death there was a line right at the end, almost a footnote: '*In the last year of his life he was involved in a lengthy court case arising from accusations of corruption, but was acquitted of all the main charges.*' It was a case of the footnote being more important than the rest of the book, and Yinghui could not ignore the barb in these throwaway comments, as if every article about her father was intended to rob him of all the respect he had wanted, all the respect he had accumulated throughout his life.

'I honestly can't remember all the details,' Yinghui said now, feeling the warmth of Walter's body; his shirt was slightly damp with sweat, for even though it was late, the night was still warm. 'It was so long ago.'

Further Notes:
How to be Charitable

Some months ago I had a very interesting meeting with a highly principled woman who works in the planning department of Shanghai Municipal Council. She is a bright, educated person in her early forties who in a few years' time might easily be the mayor of this great metropolis. But for now she is not yet even the head of department; she is only one of the deputy heads, with a particular responsibility for preservation and heritage – a thankless task if ever there was one: look at all the relentless development going on across the city! Nonetheless, she does her job admirably, for she is good with detail and vigorous in her approach. She is a *touch* unimaginative, I might add, unwilling to take risks beyond the strict confines of her job. But still, those are qualities that make her admired in her post, and I dare say she will be head of her division within the next year.

I obtained her name from local contacts of mine who thought I would find her interesting, given my record of involvement with conservation and my present interest in sustainable development. So I invited her for a business lunch at a quiet restaurant, and I must say, I left the meeting feeling more than satisfied.

She has a daughter who is seventeen and is brilliant at her studies, she told me over lunch. This young girl has been top of her class every year since the age of ten, and dreams of going to

Stanford, where she has already won a place. 'Congratulations!' I said. 'You must be very happy. But why do you seem sad and worried?'

'Well,' the woman replied, 'it's because I can't afford to send her there; tuition fees in the US are just too expensive.'

It turns out that this noble woman is married to a rather feckless petty businessman, who was pampered by his parents and has been weakened by a tendency to gamble away his earnings in Macau. He recently went to the newly opened casino in Singapore and lost RMB 40,000 of their savings. Even with her respectable salary, there is no way they can afford to send their daughter to the States.

I sighed. This sort of situation is so common in China these days – a woman battling the odds while accommodating a dead-weight of a husband.

'Maybe I could help,' I said.

She looked at me, at once confused and hopeful.

I was touched by the plight of this poor girl, I explained. I am moved by people with extraordinary dreams in a country where most people yearn only to be bankers or successful in business. I would pay her tuition fees, I said.

'But how?' the woman asked, startled and almost at a loss for words. 'I … you don't even know me. What could I possibly do to repay you?'

'Nothing,' I said. 'This is an act of charity. I too was in your daughter's position, full of dreams, but no one came to help me. Now that I am in a position to change someone's life for the better, I will.'

'I feel so humbled, I feel at your service,' she said. If we had not been sitting down she would have been bowing and scraping. I began to feel quite embarrassed by her over-effusive display of gratitude.

'Please, you're making me feel uncomfortable. What I am doing is not extraordinary – it should be normal in our world, it should happen more often. Think of it as a just reward for all your hard work. I am …' I paused to find the right words, 'I am so impressed by the way you perform your job.'

'You will really do this for a complete stranger?' she continued. 'You really are an outstanding man. My colleagues and family will be astonished. How will I explain it to them? Is it possible? Oh my heavens, I don't believe it, I don't believe it. But …' She suddenly looked anxious. 'What if they think I'm corrupt? China is so ridden with that sort of thing these days.'

I explained calmly that it would be easy for me to facilitate the transaction. I could have the money paid directly from an account in Geneva, and no one would ever know anything. She could simply say her daughter had received a scholarship.

'I don't know how to thank you, Mr Chao.' She was beginning to cry, dabbing her eyes with a tissue without making any attempt to hide the fact that she was overcome with emotion. 'My family and I will forever be indebted to you.'

'Think nothing more of it – say no more, or you will embarrass me.'

'I will forever be indebted to you,' she repeated, ignoring what I had just said.

'Let's change the subject,' I said, pouring her some tea. 'As I said at the start of our conversation, I am really interested in developing an old landmark building – a project that will help preserve a famous heritage site.'

'Yes, you are really a generous person, you are so admirable.'

'I've heard about a place called 969 Weihai Lu that sounds suitable for my purposes.'

She looked alarmed. '969 Weihai Lu is not possible, Mr Chao – it has already been sold. Well, I mean, an agreement in principle has been signed with an overseas developer. Anyway, you don't want that building. It's too shabby. I'll search the records and find you a much better site.'

'Who is going to buy 969, then?'

'I'm not sure. I can't remember.'

'I've heard that it's LKH Properties from Malaysia.'

She looked at me with red eyes, and bowed her head. 'Yes,' she replied. 'It's supposed to be confidential, but I can confirm that fact to you.'

'Well, that's a shame, because I really want that site.'

'But Mr Chao, there are many other buildings in Shanghai – much better ones.'

I shrugged. 'This one has a sort of emotional appeal to me. And anyway, I hear that company is in trouble. Are you sure they can complete the deal?'

She looked at me for a few moments. 'I'll check the situation as soon as I get back to the office.'

I signalled for the bill and smiled. 'I'm full of admiration for your work. And I'm so excited that your daughter's future is secured, and that she will be able to fulfil all her dreams. It would be such a shame if that didn't turn out. I would be very sad.'

'If you need any information, or any help at all, please call me, Mr Chao,' she said, handing me her card.

'Please send me your daughter's details as soon as possible,' I said as I was leaving.

She nodded. 'You really are an outstanding, charitable man, Mr Chao.'

25

得大於失

Know When to
Cut Your Losses

Phoebe did not dare to look at her phone. She put it on silent mode, but every time she felt it vibrate in her handbag, her stomach would begin to clench, small knots forming in her gut. Walter had left eight voicemail messages and countless texts, which she had deleted without reading. Luckily, she had not told him exactly where she worked, otherwise she was sure he would have come looking for her. It was ten days since their last contact, and he would be very anxious by now.

In the first of the messages she'd listened to, he sounded happy and calm, wanting to know when they were next going to meet. For him, it was as if nothing had happened. In fact, she thought his voice carried more intimacy than before, as if he assumed that their relationship had passed to another level. In the second message, still sounding happy, he signed off by saying, 'OK, well, see you on Sunday as usual. I think you'll like the restaurant … *sweetheart.*' There had been a moment's pause before he said the word, as if he was searching for the right expression or summoning up the courage to say it. His voice quietened slightly as he said it, hurrying the syllables the way teenage boys do when they are afraid or nervous. She felt a darkness rising from her belly and spreading into her chest. She deleted the message at once, but Walter's low voice remained in her head. *Sweetheart. Sweetheart.*

She had been avoiding him ever since that night at his apartment. She did not even want to think about what had happened, she was so embarrassed. She had got drunk on Hennessy X.O., she had not felt good, she had even been a bit teary, though luckily he had not noticed. She had refilled her glass several times, and on one occasion she had heard Walter say, 'It's brandy, not wine; you shouldn't pour so much.' He said it faintly, his voice surprising her because she thought he had fallen asleep. He had been stretched out on the bed, his feet dangling over the side, his shoes so smooth and clean that they shone in the light of the crystal bedside lamp. She had been lying next to him, talking, telling him stuff that made no sense, all sorts of secrets about herself – things she liked, things she disliked, things that made her sad. She had spoken in long breathless sentences that ran on and on, tumbling from one subject to another. Once or twice she knew she had become agitated, lost her temper and lashed out at all the injustices in the world.

She could not remember most of what she'd said, but one or two sentences would come back to her now and then, making her freeze with terror and shame at the things she might have revealed about herself. She recalled saying at one point, '... and my most hated thing of all is when men lie about being married or having a steady girlfriend. If you're already attached, who cares? I can just use you for sexual relations, so why hide it? You think I've never experienced casual sex acts with men? Huh! Men always think women only want love, but do you really think I want love? You truly think I need a man to love me? Hey Big Brother, I'm OK just by myself, you know.'

She had felt his immobile body next to her, his breathing steady, deep and heavy. By then she had lost her composure, she knew she had. All she had learnt from her books and practised over the last nine months had vanished into the hot summer air. She could hear her voice becoming rough, her coarse pronunciation creeping through. When she sat up she felt her shoulders hunch and her back slump, the way lazy girls in rural coffee shops sat while waiting for customers who would never come. She did not have the strength to adopt a perfect posture, so she lay down again. That way at least he would not see the silhouette of a rough village girl. And she had said, 'I only came to this city to find love. I don't care about the rest. I don't care about money or handbags or an apartment, all I want is to find someone who will love me and look after me.' She had waited in silence for his response. There was a problem with the automatic dimmer on one of the bedside lamps – it would light up brightly, casting the room into blinding light before fading to near-darkness. It gave Phoebe a sick feeling. Then she realised that his breathing had become sharper, noisier. His nose was blocked, he was snoring softly. She got up and turned off all the lights before coming back to bed.

She edged up next to him and put her head on his chest. She could hear his heartbeat, which was quick and strong. But then she thought that maybe it wasn't his heartbeat but the pounding in her own head, the blood coursing through her temples. She could feel the warmth of his body through his shirt; it was burning, sticky. She felt herself falling into a heavy sleep, as if she were stepping off a cliff, dropping like a stone into warm, dark water.

When she woke up, daylight was flooding the room – the pale golden light in the minutes just after dawn. She had somehow become wrapped up like a steamed dumpling in a blanket, which was gathered around her neck. Walter was asleep on the far side of the bed. His back was turned to her and he was wearing the same clothes as last night. She too was fully clothed. She found her shoes on the floor and gathered her handbag before leaving the apartment. She walked for a while before she was able to find a taxi. As it sped through the empty streets she sent Walter a text message saying, *Unexpected work call – new business proposal, sorry.* Even though it was very early in the morning the day was already warm, and she could feel the humidity gathering in the air. She wound down the window of the taxi and thought, Alcohol really gives me a bad feeling.

Not only was she ashamed at her non-classy behaviour (all her books were clear that excessive consumption of alcohol was a huge barrier to attaining feminine elegance), she was worried about what she might have revealed about herself. She had not only lost face, she had lost control. That was the most worrying aspect of the evening – maybe she had exposed herself as a liar and a fake, an illegal immigrant from a poor background, and not the sophisticated girl he thought she was. It was so embarrassing to think that she might have divulged her secrets by accident – she could not be sure of what she had said, or how much he had heard. Therefore she no longer knew how she should behave with him, whether she should be shy or forthright, seductive and sexually wanton, or cool and educated. She spent all her time thinking about it, trying to devise a strategy to cover her lies, but the shame of being revealed for who she really was was too crushing; it blackened her days completely. Her head felt as if it would explode with all the conflicting thoughts spinning around in her brain.

Of course, her distracted and unstable mood affected her work. She tried to hide it, but the other girls noticed her lack of concentration, her fatigue, the way she started nervously every time her mobile phone rang, the way she remained slumped in the office in front of the computer, no longer sitting proudly at the reception desk or making half-hourly rounds of the spa to check every smallest detail, such as whether the towels had been folded and stacked with the beautiful precision for which their establishment had already become noted.

'Phoebe, you seem very tired these days. Are you sleeping well?' the girls said. They could not conceal their sly pleasure at her shabby and unprofessional appearance. Once, when she unexpectedly came out into the reception area from the office, she interrupted a whispered conversation between the receptionists. '… and her unwashed hair …' she heard one of them say. When they saw her they pulled apart abruptly and pretended to look through some papers, but they could not conceal their smirks, even though their heads were bowed.

Phoebe went straight to the bathroom and locked the door. It was true, her immaculate styling had evaporated in the heat of the

Shanghai summer. Under the unforgiving fluorescent lights, her complexion looked dry and powdery, her make-up uneven. Her eyes were bloodshot, and when she tried to smile she saw none of her usual radiance, only the beginnings of fine lines along her temples like the skeletons of frail paper fans. Usually she went to the salon twice a week to make sure her hair was set and blow-dried exactly as she wanted it, but it was now nearly two weeks since she had been, and the constant heat and humidity that hung in the air had made it flat and damp. Her eyeliner and eyeshadow had been applied too thickly. The worst thing was, she didn't really care.

She tried to reassert her control over the spa, sitting at the reception desk to make sure all the girls knew she was still the manager, but somehow it did not work. The girls lounged on the silk-covered sofas normally reserved for clients, drinking tea and gossiping. Once, even though there was a client waiting for her treatment, one of the beauticians sat on the sofa chatting loudly to her boyfriend on her mobile phone. Two masseuses walked in with their takeaway lunches, the smell of the noodles overpowering the delicate fragrance of the waiting room. Phoebe watched them as they sat down in the guest waiting area, snapped apart their chopsticks and slurped on their iced bubble tea. She could not find the words to reprimand them or tell them to move. The huge bouquet of flowers on the granite reception counter was beginning to wilt. The water in the vase was turning murky and a bit slimy. It smelled of blocked drains. It should have been changed days ago, but Phoebe could not be bothered.

The girls said, 'Poor Phoebe, she got dumped by her boyfriend.' But they were not sad for her, they were happy that she no longer had a rich boyfriend, because she was now just like them. When she was arranging the bathrobes in the laundry room one afternoon, she heard someone say, 'That's what happens when you go after rich men.'

She began to stretch her lunch breaks, staying out longer and longer until she was spending almost two hours away from the spa.

The pavements were sticky with heat now, and even in the shade of her special reflective umbrella she could feel the strength of the sun, burning her everywhere she went. She walked aimlessly, the buildings she had only recently found fascinating and impressive now looking identical in their silvery blandness. Every road, every alley seemed the same to her now, empty and oppressive. Around her, everyone was complaining about the heat. There was no air, they said. Shanghai in the summer is suffocating, it gives us heat stroke. One afternoon she went into a shaved-ice drinks store she liked – it gave her a nice cooling sensation as she entered it, and it was far enough from the spa that none of the girls would want to walk there in this weather. While she was sitting there her phone rang, startling her. When she checked, there was no voicemail message, just a text from Boss Leong Yinghui, who had just visited the spa on a whim and been shocked to find it in such a sorry condition, obviously due to Phoebe's neglect and unprofessionalism. Unless there was a good explanation, Phoebe should not expect to be employed there much longer. Boss Leong was leaving for Beijing, but she demanded a meeting with Phoebe *upon her return*.

Phoebe stared at the message … *should not expect to be employed* … But still all she could think of was the feeling of dread and sickness she had experienced when she woke up that morning in Walter's apartment – the feeling that she had shamed herself and thrown away a golden chance to improve her life status. She could not stop worrying that he now looked down on her.

'You should ring him back,' Yanyan said that night. She was sitting on the bed eating pumpkin seeds, pausing every few seconds to split one with her front teeth. 'That is the only solution. He obviously loves you a lot, he is a really romantic guy.'

'Huh? Romantic? He doesn't even want to kiss me – holding my hand is the highest form of his romantic expression. I want a soulmate, Yanyan, not just some boring … *practical guy*.'

'In this world, everyone is always looking for something better. Nothing they have is good enough. As soon as they achieve their goals they want something more. Always more and more and more.'

'Hmph, what would you know?' Phoebe said. Yanyan's last job had been as an office girl in a baby food company that went bust because its products were full of silicon, and even that was more than a year and a half ago now – she was hardly qualified to lecture Phoebe on ambition.

'That's the problem with China these days, everyone is so arrogant,' Yanyan continued. 'No one can take any criticism any more. Look at you, willing to sacrifice love just because you think you've lost face. He doesn't judge you, he knows you're a decent person. You behaved like a slut with him, and he didn't even take advantage of you. I don't know why you think that's a loss of face. Just ring him.'

Phoebe turned over and closed her eyes, listening to the sharp, splintering noise as Yanyan split open the pumpkin seeds before dropping them into a tin. She had not told Yanyan that she was probably going to be fired, and that soon they would not be able to eat crabmeat dumplings and Australian grapes, that they would be back to where they were before, unable to pay the rent. 'You just want me to get back with him so he can give you concert tickets,' she said.

Yanyan laughed. 'Who doesn't want to hear Gary and Chang Chen-Yue live? You're really crazy. It's a once-in-a-lifetime opportunity for me. Anyway, I think my time in Shanghai is over.'

Phoebe sat up and looked at Yanyan. She was still eating her pumpkin seeds, one after another, like a machine, each movement identical to the last.

'You're not joking,' Phoebe said quietly.

Yanyan shook her head.

'But where will you go? To … your village?'

Yanyan nodded.

'But you can't do that. You said there's nothing there.'

'What else can I do?'

Phoebe got up and sat on the bed next to Yanyan. 'When you first left your village, when you first went out, didn't you dream of seeing the world? Didn't you want to make lots of money and achieve great things?'

Yanyan bit into another seed without answering.

'If you give up now and go back to your village, there will be no dreams there, nothing.'

Yanyan picked at some bits of shell that had fallen on the bed. She stood up and dusted off her trousers. 'Where else am I supposed to go?'

By the time Phoebe reached work the following day she had decided what to do. She had not slept; all night she had listened to Yanyan's slow, even breathing. Yanyan did not move at all during the entire night – she lay curled up with one hand resting against her cheek, the other flung out wide as if reaching for an invisible object. Her eyelids did not tremble, her brow was not troubled by nightmares. She didn't have dreams, Phoebe thought; her life was sheltered from ambition. It was better that way.

As Phoebe walked along the streets of Jing'an, the early-morning sunlight glinted off the mirrored-glass windows of the office blocks like daytime stars, and the branches of the plane trees were already hanging heavy with heat. The people who ran the small food shops that lined the back alleys were setting out the plastic stools outside their stalls, the smell of pancakes and griddled bread filling the air. Already the streets were busy with crisscrossing lines of traffic.

She thought, There is no real decision to be made, for a true decision requires true choice, and I have no choice.

She arrived at the spa a whole two hours before it was due to open, surprising the cleaning staff, who were half-heartedly sweeping the floor of the reception. One of them was even digging through the bowl of sweets on the counter trying to find her favourite flavour. Phoebe gave them firm instructions, and stood by as they carried out their tasks. She needed the place to return to its former state of perfection. Once they had gone she checked her watch – there was still half an hour before the first of the girls would arrive, and since they were always late these days, she had plenty of time to organise herself.

She locked the front door and retreated to the office. The fluorescent strip lights flickered into life row by row, and she settled down in front of the computer. First she checked the accounts – it was true, the last two weeks had not been healthy; there had been too many cancellations and too few new bookings while she had been neglecting her duties. But the important thing was that there was still plenty of money in the bank – Boss Leong left it there as a sign of confidence. 'Good businesses run themselves,' she would say in her robotic manner. Phoebe wondered what book she'd read that in – it didn't sound very convincing. Maybe Boss Leong should have bought a book to advise her on personal style and elegance too. If Phoebe had been in charge of the business she would not have left so much money sitting in the bank like that, she would not have trusted the people who worked for her. Phoebe had learnt not to place confidence in anyone but herself, and maybe that was the difference between her and Boss Leong. Boss Leong had never been hurt or cheated the way she had. Rich people are always more trusting, because they can afford to protect themselves against life. That is why rich people do not suffer.

She took out a piece of paper and held a pen above it. She had chosen a special black ink rollerball for this purpose. She lowered it onto the paper, her hand moving fluently without her even thinking what to do. She had practised this so many times, but had never thought she would actually do it – she had just done it out of boredom, just for fun. She hadn't even known why she was doing it. Now she saw the result of her unthinking scrawls – Boss Leong's signature, the fat bubbly letters seeming to bounce into each other. She compared it to a letter that Boss Leong had signed herself. No difference at all. Then she opened the safe and took out the chequebook. She signed her own name on the first cheque, took a deep breath, and added Boss Leong's signature. They matched well, her own narrow signature, full of tight unreadable symbols, next to Boss Leong's big messy one. A good balance – you could even consider it beautiful, she thought. No one would ever suspect that anything was wrong.

The sum she wrote on the cheque was not huge, even though it needed Boss Leong's counter-signature. It would raise no alarm bells, no one would even think of ringing Boss Leong for confirmation. It was just enough to buy Phoebe a plane ticket, plus a little bit more to cover a few months' rent. The ticket would be one-way – it would not cost that much. And although she'd heard that the cost of living in Malaysia was higher these days than before, it could not be anywhere near as expensive as Shanghai. With the money she was taking, she'd be surprised if she couldn't get somewhere for at least six months.

She wrote a long email to Boss Leong, apologising for her unsatisfactory recent performance. Her mother had been very unwell, and it was weighing on her mind. She'd been very sad, she thought maybe it was depression. She wasn't sure why, but she was questioning everything in her life. She hoped Boss Leong would understand. But it was all fine now, and she would make sure that everything at the spa ran smoothly again. There was nothing for Boss Leong to worry about.

Within minutes a reply appeared. *Sorry to hear about mother. Pleased all sorted. Suggest you move back to reception for time being pending further assessment/discussion. Will call in to see you on my return tomorrow. Best, LYH.*

Phoebe went to the store room, did a quick check on the supplies, and folded the towels. She checked the rota for the coming month – she would call each girl in and give her a lecture reminding her about her duties. They would be surprised by her return to form. When she left in a few days' time, the spa would be running like clockwork again, she would be on good terms with Boss

Leong, her conscience would be clear. She would slip away, vanish mysteriously, and for a few days Boss Leong would be perplexed, even angry at the inconvenience. But in Shanghai everyone is replaceable, and before the week was up another girl would have taken her place. By the end of the month, most of the girls at the spa would not even know that Phoebe had once worked there.

That is what happens in Shanghai. People say it is the size of a small country, but it is not, it is bigger, like a whole continent, with a heart as deep and unknown as the forests of the Amazon and as vast and wild as the deserts of Africa. People come here like explorers, but soon they disappear; no one even hears them as they fade away, and no one remembers them.

She looked at the clock – just a few minutes before the first of the girls arrived. She dialled Walter's number on her mobile. It rang and rang until his voicemail kicked in.

They met two days later underneath a giant flyover on the edge of Xizang Lu. He arrived on time, emerging suddenly through the early-evening crowd on the pavement, walking briskly, his head held high, looking out for her. His face was troubled by a frown – he had come directly from the airport, as he'd spent the weekend in Beijing – but as soon as he saw her his expression relaxed, leaving only the deep lines by his eyes that would never go away. She had already been there for some time.

'Are you sure that's safe?' he said, looking at the electric scooter she had with her. 'I didn't even know you had one.'

'It's Yanyan's,' she replied, starting to wheel it along the road. 'I've just borrowed it for this evening.'

'You're taking me for a ride?'

'Actually, I haven't decided what we're going to do. As I said on the phone, the only rule this evening is that everything is my treat. You've invited me to so many places, now it's my turn. You have to come to my favourite hangouts.'

'Sounds good.'

'You haven't seen them yet.' She looked at his blue shirt and smart trousers made of a shiny grey material, as if he had only just walked out of a business meeting and had left his jacket on the back of his chair. Patches of sweat darkened his shirt. Summer in Shanghai was so airless. It was as if everyone was competing for oxygen, and there was not enough to go round. Phoebe felt the sweat on the back of her own neck, but she didn't care. She hadn't even worn any make-up.

They crossed the road to a narrow alley lined with small food stalls, their fronts lit by bright yellow signs. Kitchen hands were hauling large plastic basins full of dirty plastic dishes into the street to be washed by teenage boys and girls who squatted on the uneven tarmac, going about their task wordlessly. Outside every shop young couples queued for tables, holding hands or playing games on their mobile phones. The girls were glossy-haired and dressed in sleeveless blouses, the boys slim-jawed and serious. The light from the neon signs bleached their skins of colour and made them look pale-skinned and delicate. They had the whole night ahead of them, warm and dark and unending.

Walter said, 'These are what Westerners call *hole in the wall* restaurants.'

'Where I grew up,' Phoebe said, 'every restaurant was like this. I'm used to eating in such places. I thought maybe you would find it interesting to go to this kind of place for a change. You can't always eat in expensive restaurants.'

Phoebe and Walter joined the queue for the Changsha Noodle Stall, outside which a cook was throwing basketfuls of crayfish into a huge cauldron full of boiling red-tinged oil. Phoebe and Walter waited in silence. She knew he was looking at her, but averted her gaze to watch the stall-holders preparing their dishes.

'The stinky tofu looks delicious,' she said.

She had prepared a speech, a full explanation of why she had not returned his calls, why she had disappeared for two weeks, why she was going to disappear forever, but she wanted to wait until they were seated, when they had something to distract them from the conversation. She could pretend to be concentrating on her food. That way she would not have to look him in the eye. It was always easier to tell untruths when the other person was occupied with a task – she was not sure if this was something she had once read in a book, or if she had invented it herself. It didn't matter now. After this evening, she thought, she would never lie to anyone about herself again.

They ordered two big baskets of crayfish with exploding-spicy flavour. Almost as soon as he began eating, Walter's eyes were watering. He bit through the hard shells impatiently, discarding half of each crayfish uneaten. His nose began to drip, and beads of sweat collected on his forehead. His fine shirt was flecked with amber-coloured oil spots, but he did not complain, just sat with his head bowed in concentration.

'I'm really sorry about my silence these last weeks,' Phoebe said. 'But I think I mentioned I had an urgent work development. A really big, exciting project. A billionaire investor wants to help me expand my spa business, set up branches all over South-East Asia. *Aiya*, he's so demanding – I've been working all hours of the day and through the night. I'm so exhausted.'

'That sounds promising. Would you like me to help you with anything? Look over the business plan or the financial proposals?'

'Oh no, ha ha. Thanks – it's all under control. The thing is' – Phoebe paused and placed two more crayfish on Walter's plate – 'I'm going to have to go abroad a lot. It's really a wonderful opportunity for me.'

'Who is this investor? You need to be careful. There are lots of unscrupulous crooks around these days.'

'*Ei*, don't be so negative. It's a great chance for me to do a lot of travelling. I'll have to go to Hong Kong, Japan, Korea …'

'Yes,' Walter nodded, wiping his eyes with the back of his wrist and sniffing loudly. 'Sounds excellent. When do you have to leave?'

'I'm not sure, but probably in the next week or so. I'll be back and forth a lot, but my life will no longer be the same – I won't be around much.'

With his index finger, Walter prodded the sole crayfish that remained on his plate. It was bright red, a colour that seemed electric, artificial, like a little plastic toy you would find at the bottom of a packet of noodles or Sellotaped to a box of biscuits. He picked it up and held it close to Phoebe's face, its belly facing her, then wiggled it around and said, '*Bon voyage*, Phoebe. I hope you're successful. May the wind carry you safely and smoothly.' He looked at the crayfish for a moment before snapping off its head and claws. 'Maybe we can meet sometime on your travels? I'm on the road a lot too, as you know – perhaps our paths will cross.'

Phoebe reached for the toothpicks. 'I think that might be difficult. I just don't know what my schedule is going to be.'

Walter gulped his drink in one go. His face was red and sweaty.

Phoebe said, 'You can't take spicy.'

'My stomach is burning.'

They went to a Taiwanese ice-sand restaurant for dessert. 'Some mango ice will put out the fire in your stomach,' she said. The floors were of a shiny black terrazzo inlaid with fine gold and silver glitter, and there were mirrors on the walls and flowers overflowing from huge vases on the reception desk. When she was a child in small-town Malaysia, this was the kind of restaurant she had dreamt of eating in – how sophisticated, how lucky the people were who had the chance to do so. In those days when she closed her eyes she imagined walking into somewhere like this as if it were no big deal, as if she did it all the time. It was not luxury alone that excited her, it was the habit of luxury, a life in which even the finest things became ordinary. In those childhood imaginings she would be with a man, a rich man of course, who drove a nice car and had a fantastic job she didn't really understand, would never understand, would be happy not to understand.

And she thought, Now I have that life, but I'm about to throw it away.

The bowls of ice-sand they ordered were too big – they should have shared one between them, but instead they'd ordered one each, mango and peanut, and they couldn't finish them. The fluffy pyramids of shaved ice melted over the sides of the bowls, dissolving into a pool of slush. At the table next to theirs, an old couple were taking turns feeding each other a tapioca dessert. Phoebe thought, They're not even having an illicit affair, yet they're behaving like lovers. She looked at Walter, but now it was he who was avoiding her gaze as he stirred the mud-coloured sludge with his spoon. The noises of the restaurant – the people laughing, calling out to the waitresses, the clink of spoons on bowls – filled the air, but Walter's silence was louder than all of them. It crushed Phoebe with the weight of a boulder. She thought she was going to die. Yanyan was right, Phoebe thought – she would have to tell him the truth about herself. She would not be able to leave Shanghai with a clear conscience otherwise. It was the only way.

'Let's go for a ride on Yanyan's scooter,' she said. 'It's good to take some air after a big meal.'

They rode slowly along the wide avenues, the scooter too small and unsteady to go any faster. Behind her, Phoebe felt the weight of Walter's body, immobile and solid, as if he was afraid to move a muscle for fear of upsetting the scooter. He did not ask where they were going, and his silence added to her anxiety. She tried to think of somewhere quiet where she would be able to talk openly about herself, but there were people everywhere, there was no chance of being alone in Shanghai. She should have planned things properly, should not have left the evening to chance like this. They rode further and further, trapped by the flow of the traffic, which bore them along like a piece of debris on the surface of a swirling river whose current she could not resist. She saw that they were approaching the intersection near Zhongshan Park – they had just passed the gates of East China Normal University, the handsome pillars framing the lawns and the lines of trees.

She parked the scooter, and they dismounted and began to stroll amongst the students who were drifting back from late dinners in the nearby shopping malls and little street stalls. They passed a basketball court where three students were playing in the half-darkness, illuminated only by the light from the adjacent dormitory block. One of them was a girl, her hair cut very short, just like a boy's. When one of the boys came over and kissed her, Phoebe did not know why, but it made her turn away in embarrassment.

They came to the bank of what looked like a small, sluggish river or canal, willow trees overhanging the still water, and followed the path that ran along the water's edge, hoping that it would eventually lead them to the openness of Suzhou Creek; but in truth they had no idea, they were simply wandering in the dark. Couples embraced in silence on the benches they passed. The noise of the traffic seemed far away.

'There's a really romantic atmosphere here,' Phoebe said. 'You could imagine you weren't in the middle of a big city.'

'Well, apart from the high-rise buildings and the pollution,' Walter replied.

From somewhere in the dark they heard music – old love songs played on classical instruments. In the night air Phoebe could make out the fine swaying notes of the *erhu* and the featherlight plucking of the *guqin*. A woman started singing, her voice measured and sad.

'I hate these old songs,' Walter said. 'Why are they always so tragic? Why aren't any of them happy?'

'They're about love,' said Phoebe.

They found themselves on a bridge over a pond. The music was drifting over the water, but they could not see where it came from. They stopped and leant on the wooden handrail. 'When I was young, my mother used to sing these songs. I guess that's why I feel nostalgic about them. To tell the truth, you're right, they're too sad. But I like them, because they remind me of when I was small.'

'But we live in modern times,' Walter said. He perched his elbows on the handrail and folded his arms, stretching his back. 'Anyway, didn't you once tell me that the past isn't important, and that all that matters is what we're going to do in the future?'

'Yes, sure, but,' Phoebe could sense herself becoming flustered – men always tried to defeat her by twisting her logic – 'but how can you just forget your childhood and upbringing?'

'Quite easily.'

'I can't. That's why, in spite of my achievements, sometimes my heart feels heavy. Hearing this music – it really gives me a nostalgic feeling. I can't help thinking of my mother and my childhood.'

'All those years growing up in Guangzhou?'

Phoebe paused. This was the moment. She could say, No, not Guangzhou, I didn't grow up in that huge ugly polluted city, I grew up in a place surrounded by forests and lakes and warm winds, not far from the sea, where you could walk in the heavy rain and not fall sick with cold, where the tallest building was four storeys high – a place many thousands of miles from here. I am not what you think I am, I am just an idea in your head. I don't really exist at all.

Yes, he would be confused at first, maybe he would even be angry, because no one likes being tricked. But soon he would see that he had been fortunate to be rid of her. He would say to himself, Thank God I didn't end up with an unsophisticated, lying village girl, a gold-digger. What a lucky escape that was. He'd been in love with an idea of someone, an illusion, and like all ideas, she would be forgotten quickly. It would take no more than a few days, a week maybe, and then the memory of her would vanish from his mind. The pain of being tricked, that might linger a bit longer, but the affection would have long since disappeared. Sweetheart. Cutie. He would forget he'd ever called her those things. The past doesn't matter – he'd said it himself, not half a minute ago. Just a few days from now, the slate would be wiped clean. It would be so easy.

She looked at him, the outline of his face barely visible in the dark – his wide, flat nose, the sticky-out ears. He was looking out across the water, trying to spot where the music was coming from.

'You know you once told me you were different?' Phoebe said. 'I'm different too.'

He nodded. 'That's why … that's why I like you.'

Phoebe looked away. She wanted to tell him everything that was on her mind, everything about herself, but all she could feel was shame. Crushing, sickening shame. 'I have to leave China,' she said. The words choked her, she could hardly speak, she felt she was suffocating with nausea. 'I can't stand it here any more.'

A song floated over the park, a thin voice singing 'The Wandering Songstress'.

'Are you OK?' he asked, turning to face her. He leant close and looked intently at her. 'You seem unwell.'

'I feel a bit sick. My liver has an imbalanced feeling. Must be the food, I think. I ate too much.'

'Who can't take spicy now? Give me the keys to the scooter. I'll take you home. You should get some rest. If you don't feel better tomorrow we should forget about going to the concert at the weekend. You can give the tickets to Yanyan. You really don't look well.'

The wide avenues that cut through the city were quieter now, and Walter rode fast and sharp over the elevated sections. The apartment blocks lined the highways like ranks of sentries, and the undersides of the giant flyovers were lit with soft blue light, the colour of exotic birds. The warm air that rushed against Phoebe's face made it hard for her to breathe – it stole the air from her lungs and made her feel giddy. She turned her face to shelter it from the wind, and placed her cheek on Walter's back, between his shoulderblades. She tried to listen for his heartbeat, but the noise of the scooter and the wind was too great, and she heard nothing.

26

豁然贯通

Strive to Understand
the Big Picture

Justin dialled Yinghui's number. He had saved it in his phone, as if she were a regular contact – a friend.

He had been working with Little Tang for a while now, long enough to feel part of the business leasing short-term studio spaces to young artists and photographers. It was undemanding, slightly dull work, but it suited Justin's current frame of mind; best of all, though, it sounded interesting when he described it to strangers: 'a new concept that we call "guerrilla" rentals to young artists'. It had an edgy feel to it that would appeal to Yinghui, he thought; she wouldn't know how banal it was in reality. Little Tang had been pushing Justin to get involved in some new, bigger projects – a photography gallery, an arts centre. But his enthusiastic insistence made Justin anxious, reminded him of the life he had had. Little Tang wanted more, more, more, wanted to absorb Justin into his ambition; but Justin wanted to stay as he was. He did not want anything big now. Being an employee was enough for the moment.

Before ringing Yinghui, Justin rehearsed what he would say to her. He practised the tone – breezy, friendly, not too familiar, not too keen to re-establish contact; he would tell her about his modest new life, but would not be too obvious about how he was a different person now, would not speak about his family's downfall – all things that would have pleased her. He would let her join the dots and form her own conclusion.

In the morning her phone was diverting all calls directly to voicemail. In the afternoon it rang and rang – then voicemail. Unsure of what to say (he had only rehearsed a proper conversation, not leaving a message), Justin hung up each time he heard her recorded voice. But as he was waiting for the lift up to his apartment that evening, his phone rang. He checked the caller's name: LEONG Yinghui. Jostled by bodies as he squeezed into the tiny lift, he hesitated for a second, not wanting to take such an important call while crammed in among a dozen other people. But what if she didn't ring back?

'I got a few calls from this number,' she said as soon as he answered. Her voice was brisk, challenging, as if she was in the middle of something else.

'Oh, hi, yeah. It's me, Justin.'

'Who? Can you speak up? I can't hear.'

'Justin. Justin Lim,' he repeated, whispering. This wasn't the way he had planned his reintroduction into her life.

'Who is it? You're breaking up.'

'Yinghui, it's me, Justin Lim.'

Silence; the noise of traffic – a scooter beeping; radio announcements.

'Yinghui?'

'Yes. Hello.'

The lift doors opened at Justin's floor, and as he pushed his way out of the lift he realised he was strangely out of breath. 'Sorry, I was in a crowded place. Can you hear me now?'

'Yes. How can I help you?' She sounded like a disgruntled hotel receptionist, polite only because she was obliged to be.

'Sorry I didn't ring earlier. It's been ages since I saw you at that awards ceremony. Congratulations, by the way.'

'I didn't win.'

'I don't know how, but I lost your card, and I just found it the other day by chance and thought, hey, why don't I just call her and catch up properly? It's been years and years – no doubt plenty has happened in both our lives. It would be interesting to catch up over a drink or lunch or dinner, don't you think?'

A moment's pause; a car door closing.

'That would be nice, but you know, I'm really busy right now. Lots of projects on at the moment, and I've just taken on the mother of all deals.'

'Right, sure. That sounds interesting. What kind of deals?'

'Oh – really complicated stuff. I think I'm out of my depth! Anyway, look, I'm in a rush. Can I call you back sometime? When things are a bit calmer?'

He paused, imagining her in the middle of complicated financial arrangements she couldn't handle. His first instinct was to offer to help her – he remembered how hopeless she had been at running her little café back in Malaysia, how she couldn't even get the accounts straight or pay the bills on time – but now he sensed a hard edge to her voice, an efficiency he recognised from having worked for so long with similar people. When she said she was out of her depth, she didn't mean it at all.

'Sure, yes, do call me.'

More rustling on the other end of the phone. He heard a man's voice saying something – muffled, as if Yinghui had tried to cover the phone but hadn't done so completely … *I'll go in first and grab a table.*

'Yinghui? You there?'

She said, '… *sorry, give me a sec, I won't be long.* Hello? Yes, Justin, well, nice of you to call. Let's be in touch soon. All OK with you?'

'Yes. All fine.'

She laughed – a soft, gentle laugh. 'Everything's always been fine with you. OK, great, I'll call you. Bye.'

And he knew, of course, that she would not call.

He had barely stepped into his apartment when the call ended. He had imagined it lasting longer, imagined himself on the sofa with a glass of wine, listening to her telling him how she had moved to Shanghai, how she was looking forward to meeting up later that week for lunch. Now he found himself standing on the doormat, phone in one hand, *Shanghai Daily* in the other, not knowing what to do next. He went to the kitchen and poured himself a glass of wine anyway. He could not be bothered to turn on any of the lamps. The summer night sky and the lights from the buildings beyond lit the living room – a coloured twilight. He sat down on the sofa and stared at the skyscrapers, their lights so familiar to him now. Nothing he planned ever came to fruition.

He wondered if that was the last conversation he would ever have with Yinghui – very probably, he thought. He wished it had turned out differently, or at least that he had anticipated its finality, and planned a more polite, gentler ending. Still, when viewed in the context of their past relationship, that minute and a half had been an unexpected bonus, a civil, mature coda to a ragged symphony. Maybe it was enough to count as 'closure', and he should be content with that. After all, the last time he saw her in Malaysia, when they were both still young, she had said, 'Please don't ever speak to me again.'

He had planned, nearly fifteen years ago, to tell her that he was in love with her – or words to that effect. It would have been a young man's act of bravado, he recognised that now – an out-of-the-blue, unilateral declaration. It wouldn't have been welcome, but he would have done it anyway. Just as well, like most of his plans, that that one had been thwarted.

There had been a campaign in the press to save the New Cathay cinema, led by Yinghui and her Friends of Old KL – unprecedented in the amount of coverage it attracted. On the cover of the *Sunday Star* magazine there was a portrait of the old Indian *jaga* who had sat in his little booth in the car park of the New Cathay for fifty years, making sure the cinema didn't get broken into at night. The photo was taken by a friend of Yinghui's, a professional photographer who had used a large old-fashioned camera that captured every line on the old man's face, the whites of his eyes glowing milk-like as he stared at the lens. What would his fate be if the cinema closed down? Every day there was a famous person in the newspapers reminiscing about childhood outings to the New Cathay – local celebrities and film-makers, actors who had been inspired to perform by early experiences at the New Cathay.

'It's all these stupid rich kids coming back from university overseas,' Sixth Uncle complained on the telephone to Justin. 'No one gives a shit about that old dump, it's just a bunch of idiots who've taken over the newspapers. Why are your friends so stupid?'

Justin wanted to point out that they were not his friends, they were his brother's. But CS, with his customary ease, managed to avoid being implicated; he spent all his time with the very people who were campaigning against his family's plans to redevelop the cinema, but in his family's eyes, his 'artistic temperament' absolved him from any responsibility. No one ever told him to have a discreet word with his girlfriend, or to stand up for his family's interests. Yinghui continued to visit the family home. By virtue of being CS's future fiancée, she was exempt from criticism. She too played her part in the transaction, becoming strangely docile and uncombative whenever she was with his parents. It was as if CS's presence smoothed away all conflict: everyone was willing to forget their disputes to make him happy. It was Justin who bore the brunt of his family's frustrations at not being able to advance their plans.

'There's nothing I can do right now,' Justin protested at yet another meeting with his father and Sixth Uncle. 'There's too much bad publicity. No investor wants to touch the place. We just need to let the fuss die down, then we'll see.'

'You shouldn't have let it get to this stage,' his father said. 'A sleeping site like that is costing us millions in lost revenue.'

'You're too soft,' said Sixth Uncle. 'You need to harden up.'

'And do what?' Justin retorted. He thought of Yinghui, of how she would react if he could find some way of saving the cinema. What would she say when, one evening, he casually announced that he had convinced the family to restore it to its former glory? If he could delay their plans for development as long as possible, surely his family would lose interest.

One evening he called in at Angie's, where he knew he would find Yinghui and CS, along with the general air of hostility that seemed to greet him there these days. It was late, and the 'CLOSED' sign had long since been hung on the door, but they were still sipping green tea inside and listening to Tom Waits. On the noticeboard, the front page of that day's *New Straits Times* had been triumphantly pinned up like a trophy: TOWN HALL DELAYS DECISION ON NEW CATHAY CINEMA – a stay of execution, following a huge petition organised by Yinghui and her friends.

'Here comes your property magnate brother,' Yinghui said to CS as Justin sat down with them. 'How's the heritage-destruction business these days?'

'Sweetie, just drop it for tonight, OK?' CS said. 'We're drinking oolong – want some, bro?'

'Sure,' Justin said. 'I've just been at a meeting with Dad and Sixth Uncle. I'm so tired.'

'Vandalism is tiring business,' Yinghui said, turning the pages of her magazine without looking up.

'Actually, they're pissed off with me for not doing anything with the New Cathay. I had to tell them the whole business isn't really my sort of thing.'

'Yeah?' Yinghui poured Justin a cup of tea from the small earthenware teapot CS had just placed on the table. It was decorated with a fine drawing of a blade of wheat – a ghost of a shadow, barely noticeable. 'Then just tell them that there's no deal to be made.'

CS pretended to read his magazine – the *London Review of Books*, Justin noticed; every time he felt uncomfortable, he would engage in earnest reading to extract himself from the conversation. It was his default setting.

Justin sipped from the tiny porcelain cup. 'You know, it's not that easy with my family, but to tell you the truth' – he lowered his voice – 'I'm pretty sure I'll manage to find a way to save the cinema. Please don't go telling this to your friends and publishing stuff in the papers. I'm telling you this in confidence, as my brother's soon-to-be fiancée, not as a random journalist, or campaigner, or whatever you are these days.'

Yinghui looked at him and nodded. She refilled his cup. 'Sure. Are you serious?'

Justin nodded.

'Listen, did CS tell you we're going to the seaside this weekend? We're going to fill the family house down there with a bunch of friends. Talk about abandoned old buildings – that place hardly gets used. Why don't you come along too?'

CS stood up and ran his hand through Yinghui's hair. He stretched, yawned, and said, 'Yeah, come.' She reached back and gently touched his hands as he stood behind her massaging her shoulders. She closed her eyes and let her chin fall to her chest, a faint smile on her face.

CS said, 'I gotta take a piss – too much tea.'

That weekend Justin drove down to Port Dickson on his own. Yinghui and CS had already gone down with another couple to set the house up – open the shutters, sweep the veranda, raise the bamboo chicks, make up the beds. When he arrived he found them on the sandy lawn that ran down to the beach; they had brought out the old rattan chairs and were sitting in the scant shade of the coconut trees, sipping cold drinks and listening to P. Ramlee songs playing on a small portable stereo. The day was overcast, the sun warm but barely visible behind the clouds. Yinghui was lying in a hammock strung up between two trees, fanning herself with a broad-rimmed straw hat.

'Look, it's Eldest Brother himself,' she said when she saw him. She struggled to get out of the hammock, then came over and greeted him with a touch of her hand on his elbow. In his chinos and long-sleeved shirt he felt overdressed and stiff – the others were in shorts and T-shirts; CS was shirtless, the razor-sharp lines of his ribs and haunches giving him the look of a sixties hippie after a month in an ashram, an impression accentuated by his long hair, which made his head seem out of proportion with his body – all he needed was a beard, Justin thought.

'Sorry, I've just come from the office,' Justin said, undoing the top button of his shirt as he sat down.

'But it's Saturday afternoon. You must be very busy,' someone said – a Malay girl Justin did not recognise. She had a small, oval-shaped face and was wearing a T-shirt that said LOVE HATE and bright-pink shorts.

'Didn't you know?' Yinghui said, pouring Justin some iced lemon tea. 'Justin's working to save the New Cathay.'

'Really?' There was a murmur of excitement; soft exclamations of approval.

'No, well, yes,' Justin began. 'I'm working on it. There's still a long way to go – you know what things are like in Malaysia. Bureaucracy, the whole system, you know …'

'Bureaucracy? You mean corruption! But well done, man.'

'*Ya* man, we're proud of you,' the Malay girl's boyfriend said. Justin recognised him, a contemporary of CS's at St John's called Tony Ramakrishnan. When he was younger, he used to wet the bed every time he stayed over, even when he was ten or eleven – anxiety, Justin's mother had said. Now he was six foot one, Oxford-educated, and recently qualified as a criminal lawyer. 'People like us, we have to take a stand. Funny, I always thought of you as a real establishment figure, but actually you're a pretty cool guy – you're one of us.'

Yinghui laughed. 'You know these Lim boys – full of hidden depths.' She looked at Justin as she climbed back into the hammock, her legs scrabbling awkwardly.

Time – how it expands to fill the spaces you create; how it makes meagre experiences seem never-ending. Whenever he heard people talk about the ravages of time, about how it robbed and deprived, Justin always smiled; because for him, time was an accomplice, plugging the gaps and fleshing out morsels of memory so he would have something substantial to hang on to. That way, however little he had seen or felt, he would always feel as if he had more: a life far richer than the truth.

Later that afternoon, they went swimming. The sea was warm and grey, and there was flotsam in the water – small pieces of driftwood, rafts of casuarina needles, plastic bottles. There must have been a storm out at sea, someone said: everything was churned up. The boys had had a few beers; Yinghui was the only girl who'd joined them in drinking, but the alcohol had made her silent, not raucous. She swam on her own, breast-stroking placidly with her head above the low waves. They swam for an hour, perhaps, until dusk began to settle, an unshifting cloud dampening the colours of the sunset. But in Justin's mind, that relatively brief time spent floating in a warm sea swelled and expanded over the years, and now seemed like hours and hours, stretching into eternity. Any remark she made – a compliment on his powerful swimming stroke, his unexpected grace in the water, the fact that his skin seemed to tan easily, that the turtles on his shorts were kind of cute – offhand comments, blithely delivered over the foamy wash of the waves, seemed rich with significance, even though she meant nothing by them, he knew that. She might have said the same things to anyone present, but time made those compliments belong entirely to him.

They stayed up late that night, chatting about how they were going to save their country. They had a vision of how the future should be. But in planning so assiduously, they failed to take into account that they themselves would change. Tony Ramakrishnan would eventually abandon the criminal bar to set up a telecommunications company with a former client of his, supplying satellite TV and mobile phone services to 80 per cent of the country; his pretty Malay girlfriend would be discovered by a new TV channel and become a celebrity, famous for being famous. CS would end up running the family firm when it was on its last legs, trying in vain to save it from total collapse, spending his days looking over accounts and spreadsheets he did not understand, married to a woman who had fallen in love with him because of the lifestyle he had once represented, but now didn't, their marriage permanently alternating between boredom and semi-separation; they would stay together only for the sake of their two young children, and because they lacked the youth and the courage to start afresh with someone else. Yinghui would go to Shanghai, where she would, against all odds and contrary to everyone's expectations, become a businesswoman – a job description she had once described as worse than a death sentence. And Justin – he would meet a sad fate, 'gone a bit loco', people would say. Or, as the more polite put it, 'He opted out of the system.'

At around 1 a.m. they began to tire. They had promised to stay up to witness the dawn, but the beer had taken its toll and, slumped in their deep rattan armchairs, they began to doze. Yinghui was snoring gently with her mouth open, her head thrown back, face to the night sky. CS was fidgeting as he tried to find a comfortable position, pulling his knees up to rest his feet on the chair. Justin fought against the weight of slumber, but eventually he too fell asleep, and when he opened his eyes no one else was there. The chairs were empty, the kerosene lamps that had lit their little circle were gone. The lawn was dark, bounded by the silhouettes of the coconut trees that ran parallel to the beach.

The house too was dark, and Justin had no clue who was sleeping in which room. He stood up and walked down to the beach. He was tired, but he did not want to go into the house and stumble around trying to locate his room, waking everyone up in the process. He walked along the beach, following the line where the waves washed onto the shore. Even in the dark, this stretch of the coast seemed familiar to him, as if illuminated in permanent daylight. He had known it ever since he was a small child, and even with his eyes shut he knew where the fine sand became studded with seashells before turning briefly to gravel; he knew where the lines of fishing boats were tethered to a row of coconut trees; knew where the rocky barriers jutted out into the water, knew the best places to clamber over them. He walked for a long time, until he was far from the house and could see it from the other end of the bay. Framed by low hills, it looked the same as it always had. He had spent the whole evening talking about change, yet it was familiarity that moved him, he thought.

He decided to walk back along the road. He would have to cut through a small coconut plantation to reach it – a place he had been forbidden to enter when he was a child because it had, for a while, been a gathering place for drug users. It was overgrown with low shrubs, but its paths were still clear enough, even at night, and he had no trouble easing his way through the vegetation. He was just approaching the run-down *attap* hut that lay in the middle of the grove when he saw two people standing in its shadows, their T-shirts gleaming ghostly white in the gloom. One of them stood close to the shack, the other kept pulling away before drifting slowly back. Justin crouched down behind some bushes. Even in the darkness he could tell that the person leaning against the hut was his brother – the movement of his arms, the way he inclined his head to kiss the other person: CS was unmistakable. Gradually the other person ceased to move away from CS, and remained close to him, their forms becoming indistinct. Justin looked at the ground, at the black earth under his feet. He was trapped now – any movement would have alerted the amorous couple. Eventually the other person walked swiftly away, down a path that led to the beach. As she passed, not ten paces from Justin, he saw it was the pretty Malay girl, Tony Ramakrishnan's girlfriend, picking her way doe-like through the shrubs. Ten long minutes later, CS walked off in the opposite direction, towards the road, where Justin had been heading.

Justin waited, crouching motionless in the dark, long after CS had gone – as if it was he who had done something wrong, which was ridiculous, he thought; yet he was incapable of moving. Eventually he stood and headed back to the beach, walking as slowly as he could. By the time he arrived back at the house the sky was beginning to lighten, the first hints of dawn appearing in the inky sky.

He sat on the sand in front of the lawn. The waves seemed stronger now, as if enthused by the prospect of dawn; a westerly wind blew across them, rippling their crests. He heard footsteps approaching, the creaking of the low gate that led from the lawn to the beach. He turned and saw Yinghui walking towards him.

'I didn't think anyone else would be awake,' she said. 'Everyone said they'd be up to watch the sunrise, but I think it's just going to be you and me. I don't think CS is going to make it. He's only just stumbled into bed. I guess you guys have been chatting all night long.'

Justin nodded. 'Yes. You know, brotherly stuff.'

'That's what he said – shooting the breeze and all that. It's good for him to chat with you. Sometimes I think you guys are so different that you have nothing in common, but I guess brothers always have a lot to talk about – especially now.'

Justin shrugged.

'Will you get into huge trouble with your family for saving the New Cathay?' she asked after a while. She had been rubbing her eyes with the backs of her hands, but when she looked at him she seemed alert, her gaze steady, patiently awaiting his response as usual.

'I'm going to try to find a way to please everyone,' said Justin. 'There's got to be a solution that will appease them as well as saving the cinema.'

'You think so? I don't see how that's possible. That's why I think you're incredibly courageous.' Her gaze did not waver. 'It means a lot to me that you're doing this.'

'Um,' he said.

'I was really surprised, to tell the truth. But now I think of it, you've never actually done anything bad. I don't know why I've thought of you as one of them. I'm not even sure who *they* are. Just not us.'

'There's lots of stuff about me you don't know.'

She smiled. 'Yes, I'm sure there is. Thanks anyway for all you're doing. It feels like … something personal. I know this sounds silly, but it makes me feel as if you're doing it to make me and CS happy.'

Justin remained silent for a while. The clouds were beginning to lighten, their velvety texture and soft folds becoming apparent. 'It's going to be dawn soon.'

'Yeah. I'm really sleepy.' She laid her head on his shoulder; it felt comfortingly heavy. 'By the way, if you need any help, just let me know.'

The sky lightened, but there was no amber dawn, no dazzling colour, just cloud on cloud, a marbling of cobalt and grey.

'Rain today,' he said, but her breathing was already sleep-heavy.

Early that afternoon, when they had just about slept off their late night, Justin drove CS and Yinghui back to KL. The roads were busy with people driving back to the city. It had started to rain, not heavily, but enough to make the streets slippery and slow, and even the highways were stop-start with traffic. He dropped Yinghui off at her parents' house, stopping for a moment with the engine running as she collected her things from the boot.

'Time for the usual Sunday-evening dinner ritual,' she said as she leant in through the window to give CS a quick kiss on the cheek. She reached across and squeezed Justin's forearm. 'Thanks for the lift, Elder Brother.' He watched as she walked through the electric gates, flanked on either side by a pair of scarlet-stemmed rajah palms; he waited until the gates had closed and she was safely inside.

'Can you step on it, please?' CS said, stretching and yawning. 'There's a TV show I want to watch. Oh God, I drank too much last night.'

'She's great, Yinghui,' said Justin.

'Yeah. But.'

'Things not going so well?'

'Yeah, it's all fine,' CS said, yawning again. 'It's just I'm feeling a bit … stale. You know?'

Justin shrugged and drove on in silence until they reached home. He had been planning to spend the evening going over the papers concerning the New Cathay: on the drive back from the seaside it had occurred to him that he might be able to make a viable financial case for turning it into a mixed-use development, the kind he'd heard of in cities like London or New York, where old buildings had been converted into five-star hotels and high-end apartments, alongside shops selling luxury brands. Why not the New Cathay? It would make a splendidly situated boutique hotel right in the middle of town, where there was nothing of the kind, and would revitalise the area. Yinghui and her friends would complain that its original use hadn't been preserved, but it wouldn't take them long to realise that what he had done was better than nothing; at least the building was still there. It was true what people would soon begin to say of him in his professional life: compromise was his forte; he always found a way to sort things out.

He had just started to look at some accounts when the phone rang – Sixth Uncle inviting him out to dinner, sounding bright and over-cheerful. In their family's unspoken code, Justin knew something was wrong, and this was not the casual invitation it purported to be.

'I can't,' he said. 'I'm busy preparing for Monday. In fact I'm looking at figures for the Cathay.'

'The Cathay, huh? Forget that for now, let your uncle buy you a chicken chop at Coliseum. You used to love it there when you were a boy, all the old Hainanese guys fussing over you. See you there in an hour, OK? Take a taxi – big traffic jam here. It's the rain, isn't it?'

Sixth Uncle was right, the roads were terrible. Tired of waiting in the unmoving taxi, Justin got out and walked the last half-mile in the rain, his sneakers growing damp even though he had a big golf umbrella with him. The sky was darkening swiftly; what little light remained of the afternoon was giving way to night, a deepening gloom urged on by the rainclouds. Scooters streaked through puddles, splashing muddy water onto his ankles as he walked along the broken pavements. Everywhere, people were wearing plastic ponchos that hid the shapes of their bodies. Jostled by the crowds, Justin stepped into the road, his foot sinking into a rivulet of water, the grit soon working its way between his toes.

Sixth Uncle was waiting for him outside the restaurant, taking a final drag from the stub of his Benson & Hedges.

'It's packed in there. I said we'd come back in a few minutes – they're going to keep a table for us,' he said. 'Why don't we take a walk round the block?'

'But Sixth Uncle, it's raining.'

'Fuck the rain,' Sixth Uncle said as he lit another cigarette and began walking away from the restaurant. 'Stop being such a pussy.'

The traffic was still tightly packed, but the honking and jostling had calmed down as drivers resigned themselves to the situation. Some roads had been cordoned off, and a fire engine was blocking one of the main intersections.

'What a mess,' said Justin. 'Something must be going on.'

'Um,' Sixth Uncle grunted. 'So, how was the weekend? The old house still standing? I haven't been down to Port Dickson in so long – I keep thinking maybe the old caretaker down there is dead.'

'No, all is fine. Yeah, it was cool.'

'Good.'

They rounded a corner and saw a small group of fire engines in the distance. Here too, a calm had settled over the proceedings: firemen were standing around drinking *teh-tarik* from plastic bags, the lights of the engines still flashing but the sirens silent; shop-keepers were standing or sitting on rattan stools outside their shops, looking vaguely in the direction of the fire engines. Everywhere there was the sort of lassitude one feels when a moment of danger has passed and one realises that life will continue as it always has. Beyond the fire engines, a thin spire of smoke rose into the sky, barely discernible in the damp gloom.

'Lucky thing it was raining,' Justin heard a shopkeeper say to a passer-by, 'otherwise I think all these shops around here also *kena* burn to the ground.'

'*Ya-lah, nasib.*'

Justin slowed his pace as they neared the fire engines, allowing Sixth Uncle to walk ahead. He paused by a group of shopkeepers who were standing at the entrance to a Chinese medicine shop, the shutters pulled halfway down. 'Morning already it started, what time I don't know – ten, eleven? After lunch only the firemen can put it out. Thirty over firemen, you know. You see? Now also still got smoke and all that. *Wah*, it was really big, man. Old buildings like that, not surprising, what. The electric wires all *rosak* already, isn't it?'

Partly obscured by the fire engines, Justin could now see a charred mass of timber that jutted at odd angles, rising half a storey into the air – it looked like one of those ghostly pictures of a forest after a fire, silent and still. It took him a few moments to recognise this as the site of the New Cathay cinema; above the quietening hush of the rain and the low rumble of the traffic, he thought he could hear the sizzle and fizz of the ashes.

'What?' Sixth Uncle said. 'What are you giving me that look for? You spend all your time relaxing with your friends, *lepak*-ing down by the beach, and I have to sort out your shit.'

'I said I was going to figure things out.'

'Figure things out, figure things out. How damn long was it going to take you? You're still such a mummy's boy. You need to grow up, stop being a sissy.' He put his arm around Justin's shoulder. 'Sometimes we have to do stuff we don't like. I've tidied things up for you this time, but next time you'll have to do it yourself. Come on, the table will be ready now. I'm hungry. What are you going to have – chicken chop as usual?'

They turned and began to walk slowly back to the restaurant. Sixth Uncle took out his pack of cigarettes but found it was empty; he scrunched it up and threw it into the drain. 'Dammit, I'm getting too old for this,' he said as he entered the restaurant.

Justin stood outside for a moment, looking into the sky to try to find the spire of smoke again. The rain was clearing; the twilight was tinged an otherworldly ash-brown; the traffic was still solid, people were still walking about wearing plastic ponchos, there were still scooters weaving their way between the stationary cars. Time, Justin thought again: how it expands to fill the spaces that life creates, how it stretches brief moments and makes them last forever.

27

风雨飘摇

Nothing in Life
Lasts Forever

On their return from Beijing, both Yinghui and Walter were swept up by other business and could not concentrate on their joint venture, as they had promised each other they would. Yinghui tried to think of their collaboration solely as a business enterprise, but it was not easy now; things had changed.

In Beijing, she had made a fool of herself. Sitting with Walter on a bench on the edge of a canal with the walls of the Forbidden City as a backdrop, she had become tired and teary, alarmed at how rapidly she had lost her composure. She had thought that she had mastered her emotions, that she had dealt with everything that had happened with her father a long time ago. Her frantic work routine, her multiple-award-winning businesses, her yoga – all these things had helped her pack away the messiness of the past in neat little trunks; but suddenly it had been strewn across her memory, swirling around as if carried by swift-flowing floodwater. She had leant over and rested her head on Walter's chest, expecting him – needing him – to wrap his arms protectively around her; when he did not, she clutched at his shirt, sobbing silently. His body felt hot and damp and unmoving, as if petrified by terror and revulsion. After a while – she wasn't sure how long exactly – when it was clear that he was not going to embrace her, she pulled away from him, still panting in short heavy breaths, her nose running.

It took her a few moments to gather herself; her cheeks and eyes felt puffy, and her carefully styled hair stuck to her face in wisps. She remembered the breathing techniques she had learnt in her various forms of exercise, from Tai Chi to Vinyasa to half-marathon running, and after a few minutes she was able to calm down. But what she could not shake was the embarrassment, the feeling of having exposed herself as lacking in grace and strength – and above all, needy. Need equalled shame, she had always thought; to need someone was shameful, the opposite of respect. Even the word itself sounded weak, wheedling: *need*. The thin, elongated vowel signalled an emptiness of the imagination – the cry of a damsel in distress or a hapless child who needed protecting. He could never respect her now.

Love, of course, was out of the question.

By the time they got back to the hotel, after a taxi ride that seemed extraordinarily complicated – the driver had lost his way – she was sufficiently in command of her emotions to be able to make a joke or two. Lucky they made it back, she said. She had been worried that the cab driver was going to abduct them and take them to Tianjin to sell their kidneys to underworld gangs. Walter laughed politely, and they took the lift up to their rooms in silence, staring at the ascending numbers, feeling that the count from one to five had never seemed so long. He got out at his floor and stood looking at her as the glass doors of the lift closed. As the lift carried her up and away, she wondered if that would be the last time she saw him.

Back in Shanghai, she was glad of his text message saying he would be very busy in the coming days organising his charity concert for the Sichuan earthquake orphans, and would not be able to see much of her. It suited her that he was otherwise occupied, for it would give her time to reassert her boundaries and restore her independence. Whereas just a short time ago she had found her businesses limiting and suffocating, she now found them reassuring in their familiarity. When she saw the new advertisements her team had produced for the FILGirl clothes range, she smiled at the images of small children playing in sunlit fields. The posters shone with garish primary colours, the sun wore a smiley face, the grass was plasticky-green, and the robin that perched on one of the children's fingers looked stiff and flightless. It was almost tacky in its effect, but its simplicity made Yinghui feel happy. The girl in the middle of the picture wore a colourful pinafore printed with red flowers as she smiled open-mouthed with wonder and delight, reaching out to touch the unmoving bird. Yinghui and her team spent a whole afternoon drinking tea and eating egg tarts she had bought as they discussed which pictures should be used for their next online campaign.

Elsewhere, even the niggly problems that had been plaguing the Thai spa seemed no longer to be a source of worry, but a chance for Yinghui to apply herself to what she did best – the resolution of tricky situations. It turned out that the former manageress had left for good, as girls often did nowadays, without a satisfactory explanation. Yinghui was obliged to spend several days in the spa, personally reorganising the rota, calling each employee into the office for an interview during which she reminded them of the terms of their employment; she was obliged to fire one girl who admitted to stealing nail varnish and body cream from company stocks. She spent a few long hours in the stock room, counting each carton of shampoo as if she were a small-town shopkeeper, and on a few evenings she stayed until closing time to verify the smooth running of the spa up to the very last minute.

She found the ritual of such mundane tasks comforting; the act of ticking off each tiny item from her 'to do' list felt richly satisfying, even empowering. She went to yoga twice a day that week, at lunchtime and in the evening, feeling a measured calm at the end of each class as she lay on the mat in the dimmed, silent space, a sensation of solidity and strength rising from her stomach and spreading into her chest and shoulders. She liked the intensity of these sessions, and even the yogic rituals and chanting that she had never really believed in now felt important, grounding. She slept well at night, and when she finally received a call from Walter inviting her to go to a bar to listen to folk music, she tried to keep calm. He wanted to smooth over the awkwardness between them, she told herself, to confirm that their relationship was a friendly yet thoroughly professional arrangement; yet she could not quite ignore the passing thought that he wanted to make up for his over-intrusive questions in Beijing, and that he still wished for a more intimate relationship with her. It was silly to expect anything more of him than just business, she told herself, but a tiny grain of possibility had lodged in her head once more, and she found it impossible to dig it out.

They went to a bar-café called *État d'âme*, which occupied a cramped space on the ground floor of a small warehouse in Hongkou, not far from the artist colonies and galleries by Suzhou Creek. The room was full of young men and women who looked like hippies who had arrived too late on the scene. Had Yinghui seen any of them out on the street they would have seemed anomalous in the fast-forward glitter of Shanghai, but here, in their midst, it was she who felt incongruous, dressed in her sleek black work clothes – a trouser suit and high heels. She made polite conversation with Walter and the café owner, a man in his twenties with long hair and small round glasses. She had become good at this sort of professional relating, striking the right note between cordiality and distance.

They listened to a boy singing simple love songs while he strummed a guitar or played a keyboard. He was not a great musician, but his voice was delicate and haunting; he held each note perfectly, not seeming even to breathe, the sound simply emerging from his mouth like birdsong. The low, slow melodies he sang unnerved her; they spoke of naïveté and innocence, yet he sang them as if all that youthful joy was now dead. It was as though he wanted to share his pain with her, was deliberately trying to wound her with his loss. She recognised a hollowness in his eyes, and felt a shivering note of panic rise in her throat – the same sensation she had experienced in Beijing with Walter. She breathed deeply, as she did during her meditation classes, and eventually she was able to calm herself.

'How old is he?' she whispered to the café owner.

'I guess about my age – twenty-five, twenty-six? He used to be a pop star.'

He looked about fourteen, but seemed ageless in his sadness.

Walter leant over and said, 'I want him for my concert. He'll really help boost publicity.'

After the performance, she wanted to take a cab home, but Walter insisted on giving her a lift. She decided it would be better to go along with his proposal, in order to show that she did not find their situation awkward – that they had re-established their boundaries and were comfortable with one another.

'I need to stop by the spa,' she said, suddenly remembering that she had left a stack of CVs from girls applying for the now vacant post of manager on her desk. It was no bad thing, she thought, for it would add a businesslike note to the end of the evening, remind-ing him – in case he was in any doubt – that she had work on her mind, and that she intended to go home to continue working. She wanted him to know that she was not holding out for an intimate late-night drink with him. She did not need him to keep her company throughout the night. She was not lonely.

The streets were quiet, and they glided along without fuss.

'Wow, very stylish,' he said as they drew up in front of the spa.

'Yes, I had that carving specially brought over from Chatuchak market in Bangkok – cost a fortune in freight.'

'Worth it, though,' he said. 'Shall I come in with you?'

'No, don't worry, I'm just going to pick something up. I'll be literally one minute.'

The spa was dark, apart from a thin sliver of light coming from the office in the back. As she approached, the light went out. She pushed the door, and found it unlocked. As she entered the spa she saw the former manageress hurrying towards her. She stopped when she saw Yinghui.

'Phoebe?' Yinghui said. 'What are you doing here?'

Phoebe shook her head. 'Nothing.'

'The girls said you had left for good. You should have returned your keys if that was the case. Do you know that your being here constitutes trespass?'

'I left something behind. I just came to collect it.'

'If you've stolen anything, I won't hesitate to contact the police. I have your ID and all your details on file.'

Phoebe shrugged and said, 'I don't care.' She was clutching something in her hand, but in the half-darkness Yinghui could not make out what it was.

'What's that you're holding?' Yinghui demanded.

'It's the thing I came to collect. It belongs to me, not you.' She opened her hand. On her palm there lay a keyring – a small cartoon cat with a blue face, lifting some noodles to its whiskery mouth with chopsticks. She closed her fist again and made to push past Yinghui, but then hesitated. The car was standing outside with its engine running. The pale yellow glow of a street lamp lit Walter's face in profile, casting a shadow across his cheek. Phoebe stood and stared at the car – apprehensively, Yinghui thought, as if it were a police car. The thought suddenly crossed Yinghui's mind that Phoebe was an illegal, a girl from the provinces who had faked her papers.

'Really,' Yinghui said, 'it was very irresponsible of you to leave without giving any notice. And making up all those stupid lies about your mother or grandmother being ill or whatever. I had faith in you, but you've shown me that you're just the same as everyone else here. I can't trust anyone.'

Phoebe remained motionless, as if oblivious to what Yinghui was saying. 'What's the matter with you?' Yinghui said.

'Nothing,' Phoebe mumbled, her voice barely a whisper.

Yinghui thought, This girl has no emotion at all. It frustrated her to think that she had misjudged Phoebe so badly; she rarely suffered from errors of judgement. Whenever Phoebe had spoken to her in the past she had sensed a mutual understanding between them, as if they were both tuned in to an obscure wavelength. Yet now she realised she had been mistaken. 'Do you think you were right to just abandon your job? You were doing so well. Everyone liked you. I thought you were different, better than the others. You let me down.'

Phoebe continued to gaze out into the night, ignoring what Yinghui was saying. '*En*,' she grunted after a while.

'*En* what?'

Phoebe said, 'This is not a good situation.'

'I agree. Give me the keys and leave at once.'

Phoebe handed her the keys, smiled and said, 'Boss Leong, thanks for everything.' Then she went out of the door, turned left sharply and walked briskly along the pavement, close to the row of buildings, like a mouse scuttling in the shadows, until she reached the corner, where she disappeared from sight.

Yinghui went into the office and retrieved the papers she wanted, then locked the door behind her as she left. Walter was typing on his BlackBerry when she got back to the car, his head bowed, frowning in concentration.

'Sorry about that,' Yinghui said. 'I ran into the errant ex-manageress, who'd snuck in unannounced – probably to steal things, though she denies it.'

'Oh, really?' Walter said, looking up.

'Well, anyway, she's gone now. For good, hopefully. These people are all the same. Hey, you look tired. I can easily catch a cab home, you know. You don't have to drive me all the way back.'

'No, really, it's fine. I just got a bit stressed by an email I was typing.'

They drove in silence, but Yinghui did not feel awkward. It was good that she had re-established her personal and professional boundaries with Walter, she thought; the evening had proved that she could master her emotions in the face of upheaval.

As she got out of the car, Walter promised that he would be in touch very soon to arrange a meeting about their future project, which he was looking forward to greatly. He said he would call within a few days, a week at the most, because he could feel that this was going to be an amazing project, and they should start work in earnest.

How Not to Forget –
Property Case Study, Concluded

We took the bus down to Kuala Lumpur. The rains had started early that year, and the stretch of road down to Kuantan was flooded, forcing the bus to take a detour. We rode for long hours through the night. When we stopped at Kuala Lipis we bought some curry puffs and *Mee Siam* that later made my stomach churn, knotting my insides until I was bent over in pain. My father, however, was in high spirits, and kept talking about what he would do with his business once we got approval to keep the building. He would take out another loan and invest in a mechanised cleaning system to process the birds' nests – that would be cheaper than hiring Indonesian migrant workers the way other people did. The birds' nests would be more hygienic and aesthetically pleasing, and would therefore command a higher price; and the quality of his product would be such that he would even be able to get an ISO 9000 certification for it. He would start a chain of shops bearing my name – his legacy to me. He spoke about these ventures as if they were a real possibility, as if the hotel belonged entirely to us, and was bursting with nesting birds – not empty and boarded up and about to be torn down.

'What's the matter with you?' he asked, noticing my silence.

'Nothing.' My stomach felt twisted on the right side, and occasionally there was a shooting pain in my kidneys.

'Serves you right for eating so many curry puffs,' he said.

He continued to talk through the night, detailing his plans as we bumped slowly over the potholes and the pools of floodwater that had collected in the road. The rain lightened to a steady drizzle, and as the road cut through the unending plantations of rubber and palm trees, the headlamps of the bus cast a stark pool of light that would illuminate the military-straight rows of trees before leaving them in darkness once more. As dawn began to break, my father finally fell asleep. We were just entering the outskirts of Kuala Lumpur, with its vast estates of small single-storey houses separated by chain-link fences, each one indistinguishable from the next; the factories that made tyres and refrigerators and VCR sets; the cheap Chinese groceries starting to open their heavy metal shutters, the shopkeepers hanging combs of ripening bananas along the tops of the doorways as if they were decorations. I had not slept all night, and was beginning to feel drowsy, the cityscape appearing misty and dream-shrouded in my fatigue. The twisting, stabbing pain in my gut continued, and when we finally reached the bus station I had to rush to the toilet, simultaneously nauseous and diarrhoetic.

My father had an address written down on a piece of paper in his shirt pocket, a page torn from a school exercise book, folded and refolded many times and now soft and rumpled from his sweat. We walked for a long time – the city was full of hot concrete, the air unmoving – before finding the address, a modern high-rise block, twenty-eight storeys all told, dressed in steel and shiny blue-green windows that reflected the clouds and the sky and hid the people who worked within. In the smooth paved forecourt and at the very top of the building were big red letters announcing its name, the kind of signs that would remain lit throughout the night: Wisma LKH.

I thought the security guard was going to stop us at the door, but he allowed us to walk through to the reception desk, from behind which two old Chinese men studied us as we approached, their faces betraying no emotion at all. One of them had been reading the *Nanyang Siang Pau* – I can still remember its headline:

'USSR Shoots Down Korean Air Lines 747'. The thin rubber soles of my Fung Keong sneakers squeaked on the polished terrazzo floor as we walked across the lobby; it seemed to be the only sound in that vast, echoing space.

My father introduced us and our purpose in visiting Mr Lim … (here he had to take out the piece of paper from his pocket) Mr Lim Chee Huat, the man in charge of the Property Division.

'Do you have an appointment?' one of the Chinese men asked.

My father shook his head. He was still smiling, as if he did not understand why we would need an appointment. I was embarrassed, because I knew this was how the sophisticated world of business worked. Appointments, dates, times, names. That was how rich, successful people lived.

'Then it's not possible. He's a busy man.'

'But,' my father continued, still unhesitating, still uncomprehending, 'it is very important. It's about our home.'

The two men looked at us with unchanging expressions. I thought they were going to lose patience and call for the security guard. I stared down at my shoes, noticing how worn and soiled the canvas looked against the shiny floor. My hands and fingernails were dirty. I wanted to leave.

One of the men looked at me. 'Where are you from?' he asked.

'Kelantan,' my father replied on my behalf. 'We just arrived.'

'Kelantan,' the man repeated. 'My mother was from Kelantan. How old is your son?'

'Nineteen.'

'Nearly a man.' He looked at me, and in his face I saw what I then took to be kindness; but now, looking back, I realise that it was pity.

He picked up a phone and muttered a few words I couldn't hear. After putting the phone down he said, 'This is your lucky day. The boss is supposed to be on leave today, but he just came in for a few minutes and his secretary says he's free. I'll take you up.'

We took the lift to the eighth floor, where we sat on a soft brown sofa in the waiting room. My father was humming a happy repetitive tune I didn't recognise. His optimism made him oblivious to the dangers that lay ahead.

'This man, Mr Lim – he's not your friend at all, is he?' I said.

'Of course he is, you'll see. When he sees me he'll greet me just like a brother, because I'm a friend of Nik's. It's how old-style friendships work. You young guys don't understand how we old men work – everyone helps each other. We're all simple village people, we don't make enemies and squabble the way you youngsters do.'

Eventually a young woman came and led us down a corridor lined with old black-and-white photographs of rubber plantations and tin mines and the occasional portrait of an aged Chinese *towkay*, stiff and formal, almost petrified before the camera. My father was still humming his little tune, walking with a spring in his step, as if impatient to see a long-lost friend.

We came to an office that occupied the corner of the building. A man was sitting behind a desk, talking loudly on the phone, laughing heartily. He glanced at us and then began drawing something on a piece of paper in front of him.

'*Ya ya ya*, ha ha ha.' He wore spectacles, and his hair was styled with brilliantine, slicked back in the manner of a fifties rock 'n' roller. He was plump and jolly-looking, not at all what I expected of the Big Boss of a huge company. As he laughed, I almost believed he was a long-forgotten comrade from my father's village, and that he would leap up and embrace my father with the warmth of a brother.

There was a teenager sitting in an armchair in the corner of the room, playing on a hand-held video game. He did not look up at us at all. He was maybe a year or two younger than me, but his height and broad shoulders made him seem much older, more powerful. Even seated, he looked tall and athletic. He wore colourful ankle-high basketball shoes and blue jeans; his skin and hair had a lustre of health, a protective sheen that looked as if it could ward off all illness and bad fortune. But in spite of his large frame there was something childlike in the way he slumped in his chair and sometimes grimaced as he pressed the buttons of his game. I noticed his hands, his long fingers that manipulated his electronic toy with a deftness mine would never have. My own hands suddenly felt thick and rough with calluses, disfigured by the scars of the many cuts I had suffered during those years working on my great-aunt's pineapple farm as a child. I kept them in my pockets, where the shame of their ugliness would not be seen.

The man ended his telephone conversation and said, 'So you are the guy Nik was talking about.'

My father nodded. But he was looking down at his feet, as if incapable of holding the man's gaze.

'*Ya*,' the man continued. 'Nik told me there might be someone coming to make trouble.'

'No, sir, I don't want to make trouble at all.'

'Then what is it you want?'

My feet had begun to ache, and I wondered if the man was going to ask us to sit down in the two empty chairs in front of his desk. We had come a long way to find this place, and a cramp was starting to seize the little toe of my right foot. I tried to keep still, but was aware that I was fidgeting.

'We just want to keep our house,' my father said.

'We just want to keep our house,' the man repeated, mocking my father's heavy rural Chinese accent. 'This guy is really something.' He laughed, shaking his head. 'Do you understand what is happening to the whole damn area around your house? It is being redeveloped.'

'Yes,' my father replied, 'that's why I came to talk to you. To ask you to make an exception for us.'

'You're going to be paid for your property, you know. It's not some illegal land grab. You're being compensated, so what more do you want?'

'The money is too little,' my father said, a sudden note of anger creeping into his voice. 'Everyone is unhappy.'

'Oh, I see. Like *that*, ah?' the man said, leaning back in his chair and casually tossing the pen he was holding onto the desk. 'First it's

"Please let me keep my house," but now we see the truth. It's all about money. OK, so how much do you want?'

My father shook his head. 'I want to keep my house, I don't want money. Many people are angry. If you don't change your plans, I can organise a protest.'

'*Wa-seh!*' the man exclaimed, laughing. 'Justin, did you hear that? *Ey*, Justin, turn that stupid game off and come and sit here.' He beckoned the boy over to an empty chair next to the desk.

'Yes, Sixth Uncle.' The teenager sat down, staring at us with a mixture of boredom and irritation.

'Justin, these guys have come here to threaten us over a normal, legitimate job we are doing. What should we do under these circumstances?'

Justin stared at us without answering.

'You think we should give in to their demands, or tell them to fuck off?'

'We should not be intimidated by anyone, under any circumstances,' the boy answered robotically.

'Good, you've remembered what I told you.'

All this time my father remained motionless, his back stiff and unyielding. I could tell, even at this point, that he was still expecting a favourable outcome. He turned briefly to look at me and I could discern a glint of optimism in his eye, the look of a man on the brink of a great triumph. I wanted to say, No, stop – we should just go now, Father. We're being kept here for this man's amusement; we'll never get what we came for. But I said nothing.

'We're just the damn developers, you know,' the man said, still leaning back in his chair. It rocked gently, giving him the appearance of someone relaxing in a hammock. 'That whole shitty area has been earmarked for development, so if you want to protest, go and talk to the Minister for Housing. Ha, *ya*, see what Minister Leong will say.'

'You can't expect us to move out of our homes. The money is … so little. I can tell the newspapers.'

The man looked at his nephew and then pulled his chair closer to the desk, and rested his forearms on its green leather surface. 'Listen, old man,' he said calmly. 'You are being paid peanuts because your house is worth peanuts. I would explain to you how much the development project is worth, but the figure would be too great for your simple little head. You can try and organise your stupid protests – go on, be my guest – but if you do, I will make your life hell. You think the newspapers care about people like you? Friend, no one cares. I make one call to Minister Leong right now, and no paper will ever print what you say. You really make me laugh.'

'I can pay you,' my father said. He was breathing quickly now. 'I can borrow money and pay you the right price, maybe you can let my house remain.'

'Borrow money, huh. Check that out, Justin. He wants to borrow money to pay us off. He's going to have to borrow fucking Fort Knox.'

The boy was looking out of the window – our plight was too minor for him; he barely noticed that we were present. He only smiled when his uncle repeated the joke.

The door behind us opened. 'Minister Leong on the phone,' the secretary said.

'Speak of the devil,' the man said, picking up the phone. He scribbled a few notes on a piece of paper without looking at us. It was clear that we had already disappeared from his world. We had scarcely existed for him, and I knew that in a couple of days he would not even be able to recall our faces – our bland, rustic features. In a couple of weeks he would not even remember that we had ever come to his office.

As we left the office I could hear his voice, jovial once again as he spoke on the telephone. I heard the electronic beeping of the boy's game, and caught one last glimpse of his bored face and his colourful shoes. We took the bus back up north that same day.

Back in Kota Bharu, it was my turn to be optimistic. I remembered those surprising things my father had said about organising demonstrations and journalists, and kept expecting him to spring into action. I even said, 'Let's get some people together and protest outside the land office.' But it was one of those thoughts that, as soon as they are articulated, dissolve into thin air, like night-time dreams vanishing into the clarity of day. Neither he nor I ever organised anything, of course. He began gambling to pay off his debts – first on four-digit numbers, then at mahjong, then cards. I went back down south to continue my studies. Occasionally I would get a letter, optimistic as ever, about his plans to develop the birds'-nest business. It was as if he was deliberately ignoring the fact that the building would soon be destroyed and he would be left with nothing but a small amount of cash that would pay off only a fraction of his debts. The more cheerful and optimistic his letters were, the worse I knew the gambling had become, and after a while I stopped opening them.

People talk about what parents leave their children: a legacy of money or education, or even the unquantifiable qualities of life, such as good genes or happy memories. Mine would leave me only debts; I knew this in advance. And so I changed my name by deed poll, abandoned my studies, and got a job in Singapore, working my way up the glittering skyscraper of life until I reached its summit.

There were times when I remembered that fateful journey to KL. And curiously, what I remember most is not my father begging a complete stranger for one last chance before descending into total ruin. I remember, instead, that tall teenager and his good hair and colourful shoes, playing on his computer game.

He would never, I'm sure, be able to recall me.

But I remember him, always.

28

四海为家
Travel Far, Keep Searching

'No, *you* go,' Yanyan insisted. She sat on the bed holding the pair of concert tickets out to Phoebe.

Phoebe remained sitting on the mattress on the floor. She sucked at her bubble tea, but a gummy black pearl had got stuck in the straw and she found she wasn't drinking anything, just making a loud foamy noise. '*Ai*, Yanyan, you are really giving me a headache. How many times do I have to tell you, I don't want to go. I told him I still had stomach problems from the spicy crayfish the other night, and he said no problem, just give the tickets to Yanyan. Take your new boyfriend.'

'He's not my boyfriend, he's just a neighbour I talk to sometimes.'

Phoebe snorted. 'You think I'm a stupid, innocent girl, but hey, Little Miss, I know what you're up to!'

'You don't know anything at all. It's not like you and your rich man. I'm telling you, you must not let go of him. At least go and ask him for an explanation.'

Phoebe shook her head. She did not need an explanation – everything was clear, in fact it had been clear right from the start, only she hadn't seen it. Of course no man like him would be interested in a girl like her, he would only be interested in women like Boss Leong, even though to the rest of the world women like her seemed unstylish and unsophisticated. Because, even if you wear fashionable dresses that show your beauty to the whole world, you will never have what Boss Leong has, which is an education. All those people who look at you – they know. They know that you are nothing, they know that when the man you are with is tired of you, you will fade back into obscurity. So when they look at you, it is not just with jealousy, but also with mockery. They want what you have now, but they know they will never end up like you. And while they will never be jealous of Boss Leong, they will never mock her either, because all the things that she has, she can never lose.

'Hey,' Yanyan continued, 'this isn't a matter of snaring a husband or a rich man to become his concubine. It's a matter of love.'

'You really have mental problems,' Phoebe said. 'I don't love him.'

'Yes you do,' Yanyan said, throwing the tickets at Phoebe. 'I know you do because I stole a look at your journal. You wrote, "This man is so sweet, he is so kind and nice to me, he –"'

'You looked at my journal?' Phoebe cried. 'You are really too outrageous.'

Yanyan shrugged and reached for her bubble tea. She was smiling – she didn't care if she had invaded Phoebe's privacy. Sometimes, Phoebe thought, Yanyan really knew how to give her a bad mood.

'Go on,' Yanyan said, 'ring him and tell him you'll meet him there after all. You should take control of the situation and not let him just disappear from your life. If he wants to leave you, at least make him justify himself. He shouldn't just vanish like smoke. He owes you something. And if he doesn't turn up, at least you can still go to the concert. Chang Chen-Yue is confirmed, and I hear rumours that Gary is singing too.'

Phoebe shook her head. She looked at the tickets lying by her feet. They were marked: EXCLUSIVE PRIVATE SEATS. She imagined what those seats would be like – big and velvet-covered, soft and bouncy.

The road leading up to the stadium was crowded with people. Phoebe stood by the west door, the entrance marked on the ticket, at the exact place she had agreed with Walter the previous week. There was a sign saying 'VIP and Artistes Only', and men in security uniforms were checking the handbags of the women going into the stadium – women dressed the way Phoebe used to dress, stylishly and elegantly. But today she had come in her everyday clothes, her three-quarter-length jeans which she knew were not fashionable, but which were comfortable in the heat of the summer night. She had sold all her expensive clothes and handbags and shoes on the internet and used the money to buy a plane ticket back to Malaysia. She knew she no longer looked as attractive as she did a few weeks ago, but she did not care. She had not told Yanyan that she did not intend to go to the concert, but would merely wait for Walter and return the tickets to him. She wanted their story to be closed, for everything to be in its place when she left China. She was not hoping for him to say he was sorry and take her back. She knew that would not happen. She did not even want an explanation.

She could hear cheers and applause from inside the stadium, rising like a swelling wave. Phoebe checked her watch – there were still ten minutes to go before the start of the concert. There was a constant stream of people going in through the VIP entrance, though fewer now than before. Around her, hawkers were pushing their carts, selling grilled meat skewers and dumplings and fruit and ice drinks. A young couple, teenagers, ran past, arm in arm, dashing towards the main entrance around the corner.

'Hey,' one of the hawkers called out to Phoebe. 'You've been waiting a long time. You sure your friends aren't round at the other entrance?'

She held up the special green-coloured VIP tickets for him to see.

'Lucky you!' he said.

There was a deep rumble, like thunder, as music started inside the stadium. The first notes were accompanied by a huge cheer, and when Phoebe looked up into the sky she saw multicoloured lasers crisscrossing, pulsing to match the excitement of the crowd. She heard the heavy, rhythmic beats of a drum, and more loud cheers. A few last people were walking briskly up to the stadium, the road lined with trees laced with twinkly white fairy lights, and the smoke from the street stalls silvery as it rose into the night air.

The music ebbed and flowed, and then suddenly there was a burst of bright sound – drums, guitars and voices singing in chorus. The audience cheered and began singing along. Phoebe recognised the song, but couldn't place the singer. It was a breezy, rhythmic tune that made her want to dance, and she could imagine the audience bouncing on their toes, swaying to the music. Three more songs like that one followed, and then someone speaking, but Phoebe couldn't make out what was being said. The next songs were slow and sentimental, though Phoebe couldn't tell what language they were being sung in. The voice was low and muffled and sad, and made her want to leave. She had to say she didn't like this music. It was not very cheerful.

'Hey, Little Miss,' the man selling skewers called out again. 'I think your friend isn't coming. You should go in and enjoy the concert. Give me the other ticket – I'll be your date for tonight!'

Phoebe smiled. 'He might still come,' she said. 'I'll wait a while longer.'

'Have a snack,' the man said, holding out a chicken-wing skewer.

'Thanks,' Phoebe said.

More cheers erupted in the stadium – a chorus of happy people. The tune was a fast modern version of 'Sweet Little Rose'. She thought about that evening when she had taken Walter to eat crayfish in the Changsha Noodle Stall, and they had ridden Yanyan's scooter through the city. When they rode over the giant flyovers, the headlamps of the streams of cars flowing under them, over them, around them, had made Phoebe feel as if she were in an amusement park, on a rollercoaster that made her giddy and dreamy and forgetful. In any other place, at any other time, that would have been a proper date, and she would have been happy. It made her sad that she had not been able to be happy in a situation that was perfect for being happy.

Hearing some music she recognised, she turned to the skewer-seller and said, 'Here, take these. If you hurry, you might be able to catch Chang Chen-Yue.'

'Huh?' he said, staring at the tickets.

'What? You don't like Chang Chen-Yue?' she joked. 'Take them.'

She walked away down the road, the sound of the music from inside the stadium becoming fainter every minute. The night seemed less muggy now. She took the metro, which was not busy at this time of the evening. The coolness of the air conditioning gave her goosepimples, and she realised her skin had become sticky from standing out in the heat for so long. She got off a few stops early and walked along Nanjing Xi Lu, past the boutiques that were now shut for the night. She wanted to see the lights, the gilding and the clean wide pavements one last time. As she walked past the glittering windows of the shops, she remembered that she had the Journal of Her Secret Self in her bag. It did not seem so secret now that Yanyan had read it. She had always planned that one day she would throw it ceremoniously into the Huangpu River. In her dreams she was rich and successful when she cast adrift the journal that contained her darkest fears and ambitions. But now that she was leaving – now that she was a failure – it seemed meaningless and empty to perform such a grand ritual. She took it from her bag and dropped it into a rubbish bin.

The same street vendor she remembered from several months earlier was still standing before his pushcart, selling his home-made CDs of what she now knew was Cuban music, which he played through a loudspeaker strapped to his motorbike. It was the same music he had been playing the night Phoebe first met Walter – soft and gentle as a spring wind, drifting in the night, even though there were only a few people around to hear it. She had learnt from Walter that Cuba was not near Spain, as she had once thought.

He had played her different kinds of music in his car as they drove round the city, telling her which country each was from. Once she had twirled her torso in the way she imagined Cuban dancers might, to which he had said, 'You are really *too* funny.'

29

浮云朝露

Life is a Floating Dream

'You were going to buy that building?' Yanyan said. '*You*?' The newspaper was spread out on the floor, and she pulled it towards her to take a better look at the small photo.

'Not me, exactly,' Justin replied. 'My family.'

'Lucky thing you didn't – it looks cheap and horrible. It's just … a *factory*.'

Justin laughed. It was true that the photo did not show the building in its best light. Taken from afar, all one could see was a structure of irregular grey concrete blocks covered in wires and broken antennas. The article was a short one, at the bottom corner of the page, a mere whisper about the collapse of the deal to redevelop the building. No reason was given for the collapse of the project.

It was late at night, and they were sitting on the front steps of the apartment block eating red-bean ice cream and groundnut *mochi*, a habit that had grown increasingly frequent over the summer. The nights were still warm but no longer muggy, touched by the freshness of the first winds of autumn. Before them Suzhou Creek lay still and flat, reflecting the lights of the buildings as if in a black mirror. The days were now clear and bright, the sun high and unfiltered as it was in the Mediterranean, Justin thought, warm and unscorching. He wondered if autumn in Shanghai was always like this, or whether this was exceptional; maybe he had simply never noticed it.

In his jeans pocket he could feel his phone pressing against his thigh. He had become unusually aware of its physical presence ever since he had received a message from Leong Yinghui two days earlier. It was as if the unanswered message added to the weight of the phone, at the same time rendering it more valuable, more fragile and precious. He carried it with him all the time now, tucking it into his pocket so he could feel its hard edges insisting themselves against his flesh, comforting in their solidity. Even when he was in the shower he made sure he did not lose sight of it.

And yet he did not reply to the message. He had found it on his phone when he woke up one morning. It had been left at 1.52 a.m., long after he had gone to bed and turned the phone off. Her voice had been calm and matter-of-fact, without any trace of hesitation — in fact, it began so smoothly he had the impression that she had rehearsed the entire message before ringing him. She said she had been involved in a large deal to purchase a landmark site he might have heard of — a building called simply 969 — and had taken out considerable loans secured on her existing businesses. It turned out — ha ha — that her business partner had siphoned all the money from their joint business account. She'd woken up one day and he had vanished, and the money too. Well, it was her fault; she hadn't taken the requisite precautions. She had let her guard down, and you know what happens in Shanghai if you let your guard down. Maybe she was never destined to be a good businesswoman after all. She was sure that Justin wouldn't recall it, but years ago CS had once said that when it was deconstructed, business was philosophically unchallenging — remember that? What a joke. (Here, she half laughed.) The mess she'd made of the deal had made her remember what Justin and everyone else had said many years ago, that she would never understand business. He'd known her better than she thought, she now realised. She'd spent days thinking about what kind of person she'd been back then, and what she'd become. She wondered what Justin would make of her today — compared to before, she meant. (A noise — maybe a sniff, a runny nose? Her voice had begun to waver, softening.) Losing the money was painful, but what was worse was that she had been stupid, really stupid. (Here, a short pause; a muffled noise as if she had cupped her hand over the phone.) Anyway, she really didn't mean to bore him with details of her misery. No, in fact she was going to go back to the drawing board, to try to salvage what she could from her other businesses. She knew she really wasn't *that* bad at business. Maybe not great, but definitely not terrible. She was going to stick it out in China and rise from the ashes – again. (There, another pause, so long that the first time Justin listened to it he wondered if she had hung up.) It would be hard, but that's life. She'd experienced worse in the past. So, if he wanted to meet for a drink sometime, just to catch up on old times, give her a call. Or, maybe (laugh) it would be better if they didn't catch up on old times and simply chatted about the weather, restaurants, that kind of thing. All the best.

All the best – as if she were signing off a letter to a casual acquaintance.

He had listened to the whole message at least ten times, tracking every nuance of emotion – sadness, nostalgia, friendliness, forgiveness – and for the first time he felt an intimacy with her. In a single phone message she had opened herself up to him far more than she ever had during those years they had spent together. The sudden closeness he felt for her frightened him, and now it was his turn to be reticent about returning her call. Half of him wanted to savour the message; the other half was terrified by it. It was thrilling to hear her say, 'You knew me better than I thought.' But then he felt a raw grating in the pit of his stomach when she said, 'I've experienced worse in the past.' The deliberate flatness of her voice seemed to contain an accusation of hurt that neither of them could ever forget, and it made him feel ashamed to think that he had simply rung her out of the blue, imagining that they would both have moved on sufficiently to realise that neither of them had been in control of their past; that they had been mere actors playing out their roles, while others directed from behind the scenes.

He remembered how CS had played his role too, that of the weak younger brother, so sensitive that his break-up with Yinghui caused him to fall ill for three whole weeks. He had ignored his family's disapproval of the relationship – the nature of Yinghui's father's death and the rumours of his involvement with the Lim family's property business made for unwanted publicity – but when his parents suggested that CS place some distance between himself and Yinghui, he made little attempt to argue against them. He'd moved on, he shrugged to Justin; he and Yinghui had got stuck in a rut, he wasn't excited by the relationship any more, he was too young to settle down. And yet, after he rang her to tell her he was breaking up with her (she wasn't in, so he left a message on her answering machine), he began to feel sick. A fever set in, and his joints were so painful he could not make it downstairs for meals. He stayed in his room, shivering between damp sheets, trembling every time she rang to ask for him (the maids politely told her that he wasn't around). He felt like a real bastard, he said to Justin; he felt so bad for her; he guessed he must really have loved her after all. Yet he could not face her to explain why he had broken up with her.

'Please, Justin, you go,' he'd mumbled into his pillow. 'Just tell her anything you want. Blame it on the family – anything.'

And so Justin had driven over to Angie's, knowing he would find Yinghui there, even though the café had ceased operating some weeks before. The shelves, chiller cabinets and refrigerators had been stripped bare, and the light fittings removed. There were a couple of plastic stacking crates with pots and pans in them in the middle of the floor. What remained of the furniture had been pushed against one wall, but the space that created made the café look smaller rather than bigger. The only decorations that remained were the meaningless signs she and CS had had lovingly painted and hung up: *All Great Novels are Bisexual*. In the middle of the damp, airless space lay the long grey sofa that CS had occupied virtually every night since the café had opened. It was the only thing that had not been moved.

When Justin arrived, Yinghui was sitting cross-legged on the sofa peering at some papers containing lists of numbers. She leafed through them, occasionally going back to one she'd just looked at. It was obvious to Justin that she did not understand what she was reading. There was music playing from a portable stereo on the floor – the Tom Waits CD she and CS had liked so much.

'Need some help with those figures?'

She looked at him and shook her head. She held his gaze, as she always did – that calm, expectant seizing of his attention, waiting for him to say something. But it was she who spoke first. 'Don't bother,' she said, smiling. 'Nothing you say will make sense to me. I will never understand anything you tell me.'

He stood there for a few moments while she continued to go through the papers. She did not look up at him all the time he delivered the speech he had prepared – about how he was genuinely sorry about what had happened, that it was difficult for CS too, that their family was not an easy one to grow up in, that they lived with certain pressures. He had planned a light-hearted joke or two to show his human side, make it less painful for her. But the timing felt wrong, so he left them out, merely delivering the salient points as quickly as possible: the apology, the finality of CS's decision, the lack of any malice or ill feeling at all towards her.

As he stood looking at her on the sofa, the music on the stereo seemed the only thing alive in the concrete space. The late-night bluesy tinkling of the piano made him wish he were somewhere else, in a smoky bar in a cold country, where he would step out into the street and find it snowy and calm, the sky indigo-coloured with the promise of dawn.

She sat with her feet up on the sofa, one knee raised, the other stretched out. Her head was bowed over the papers on her lap, but he noticed as he was leaving that she had closed her eyes.

Those expansive qualities of time again: he knew, even then, that those moments would fill the canvas of his memory and seem longer, more important than they really were. He had once heard Yinghui and CS arguing about memory. What we retain in our minds is not necessarily what matters the most, CS had said. We are conditioned by our times and the petty pressures of the world we live in to hang on to certain images and feelings, things that are ultimately trivial. The passage of time exaggerates these fragments of memory, he said, accusing her of being juvenile and schoolgirl-ish. If you pine for a long-lost love years later, it is just sentimental puff, not really love at all. But Yinghui had disagreed. If someone really matters to you, if you really, *really* love them (she'd clenched her fists as she said this, holding them tightly under her chin as if grasping something precious), the memory of that person would always be true and clear; she didn't care if people thought she was soppy.

'Hello, sir. What are you thinking about? Your eyes have gone blank,' Yanyan said as she finished the last of the red-bean ice cream, the spoon scraping against the cardboard tub. 'I hope you're not dreaming of that stupid building. If you ask me, it's a wreck, and you were lucky you didn't buy it. Fate was kind to you.'

Justin eased the phone from his pocket, and looked at it as it lay cradled in the palm of his hand.

'Oh, I see. It's that woman you were telling me about. Are you going to call her back?'

'I don't know.'

Yanyan stood up and yawned. 'Just remember, women don't hang around waiting forever, you know.'

Long after she had left, Justin remained sitting on the steps star-ing at the empty street and the recently planted sycamore saplings, each one supported by a low wooden tripod. In the distance he could just make out the tops of the towers of Pudong. There were faint trails of summer clouds around the peaks of the buildings, visible only because the light from the towers made them glow white against the night sky. The view had not changed since he'd arrived in Shanghai, Justin thought: it was comforting in its predictability. He liked it that there were things in the world that never altered their form or habit; that way he could measure himself against them and would always know where he stood, would always know if he was moving or rooted, like those silent, immutable buildings.

He looked at his phone again. He had already added Yinghui's number as a contact, ready to be dialled whenever he wished. He had not known when that would be – a couple of weeks, a few months, a year? Perhaps never. He wondered if she had changed; wondered if he would be as tongue-tied with her as he had been nearly twenty years ago.

He stood up, and waited patiently for the slow, cigarette-smoke-filled lift to arrive. When he was back in his apartment he made himself some green tea, which he drank with the last of the *mochi* snacks he had bought for Yanyan. He gazed at the view of the skyscrapers that had kept him company throughout the last nine months. It was true, he thought: each one of them had its own personality, its own imprint of life. They were not at all alike, not what their perfunctory daytime selves suggested. When he had finished his tea, he picked up the phone and pressed Yinghui's number, even though it was very late at night.

30

跋山涉水
The Journey is Long

As Gary takes the stage for his solo set he feels calm, knowing that the four songs ahead of him will go well. Sometimes he just knows that a performance will go smoothly – that he will find his range and pitch from the first note, and his voice will be strong and clear, rising from his belly to his throat, velvety in texture. His nerves have been helped by the fact that he has already been on stage this evening, to perform a duet with Tsai Chin – they sang 'Neverending Love', one of the songs his mother used to sing to him, sometimes pretending that *she* was Tsai Chin. So for Gary it felt at once strange and touching that he should not only be singing with Tsai Chin, but that she should be so maternal and protective towards him. She had helped him get over the shock of being in front of a large audience once again, holding out her hand to him so he would have something to hang on to. There had been an audible gasp when she beckoned to the wings and Gary appeared, walking unsteadily to join her in the middle of the stage. The audience was astounded to see him again after his months of seclusion, and he knew that there was an element of shock at seeing him so pale and thin, his hair shaved like a soldier's. His voice, too, seemed richer and sadder than before; but it was indeed him, just as the hastily amended posters had announced.

Now, as he stands alone on the vast stage, staring out into the darkness, he finds that he is still perfectly at home appearing in public. If he is calm, it is because he has no fear of his audience. He realises now that he was always intimidated by them – not the people themselves, but what they expected of him. Every time he took the stage he felt the crushing weight of their demands – that he be beautiful, romantic, energetic, outstanding. But now he has no need to pretend; everyone has seen who he really is.

The darkened stadium is filled with people waving colourful fluorescent batons slowly above their heads as the music begins – the first strains of a song Gary has written himself. He sings in *Minnan hua*, the dialect of his mother, of his youth – an earthy, rustic language that some would call coarse. Maybe that is why it suits the song so well; maybe that is why it suits him so well, Gary thinks, for after all, he is just a rough country boy. Maybe everything the papers said about him all those months ago is true. No one in the audience can follow the words, no one sings along. Singing in his mother tongue reminds him of the quiet loneliness of his childhood – of the long hours sitting on the porch of his village house watching the rain falling, hoping it would end, though often it would last until nightfall, hastening the arrival of darkness. He feels, for the first time at a big concert, that he is completely alone, but it is a solitude that feels calm, as it did many years before, when he was small. Only he can appreciate the quality of the voice filling his lungs, filling the vast space above him.

Acknowledgements

I am indebted to the following people and organisations, whose extraordinary kindness and generosity allowed me to live in Shanghai at various times during the writing of this novel: the Shanghai Writers' Association, with special thanks to Wang Anyi and Hu Pei; everyone at the M Literary Residency, especially Michelle Garnaut, Tina Kanagaratnam, Bruno Van Der Burg and Jane Chen; the Society of Authors for the award of an Authors' Foundation grant.

Of the many books I consulted while researching this novel, Leslie Chang's ground-breaking study of migrant workers, *Factory Girls*, proved the most inspirational.

I am also deeply grateful to friends and family who fed and supported me whilst I wrote this novel: Clare Allan, Liling and James Arnold, David Godwin, Philip Goff, Sue-Ling and Alistair Griffin, Charlie Gurdon, Tony Hardy, Francis Hétroy, Huang Bei, DD Johnson, Michelle Kane, Marianna Kennedy and Charles Gledhill, Mimi and Aaron Kuo-Deemer, Alison MacDonald and Adam Thirlwell, Andrew Mills, Beatrice Monti Von Rezzori, Siddharth Shanghvi, Joo Teoh, Anna Watkins, You Sha and Jeff Weil, Adele You Yun.

Thanks also to: Nicholas Pearson and Robert Lacey in London; Cindy Spiegel in New York; Maggie Doyle in Paris; Kamloon Woo in Taipei.